Marry Me... Again!

There are *some* men you never forget!

They're handsome and sexy.
They're demanding—unreasonable.
You know the type...

But while they're hard to live *with*,
they're *impossible* to live without.

So when a man like that says

Marry Me...
Again!

there's only one answer.
Yes!

Two complete novels by your favourite authors!

Michelle Reid grew up on the southern edges of Manchester the youngest in a family of five lively children. But now she lives in the beautiful county of Cheshire with her busy executive husband and two grown-up daughters. She loves reading, the ballet, and playing tennis when she gets the chance. She hates cooking, cleaning, and despises ironing! Sleep she can do without and produces some of her best written work during the early hours of the morning.

Rebecca Winters, an American writer and mother of four, is a graduate of the University of Utah, who has also studied at schools in Switzerland and France, including the Sorbonne. She is currently teaching French and Spanish to junior high school students. Despite her busy schedule Rebecca always finds time to write.

Marry Me... Again!

LOST IN LOVE
by
Michelle Reid

FULLY INVOLVED
by
Rebecca Winters

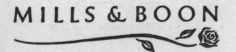

MILLS & BOON

*MILLS & BOON, the Rose Device and By Request
are trademarks of the publisher.
Harlequin Mills & Boon Limited,
Eton House, 18-24 Paradise Road, Richmond, Surrey, TW9 1SR*

Lost in Love was first published in Great Britain by Mills & Boon
Limited in a single volume in 1993.
Fully Involved was first published in Great Britain by Mills & Boon
Limited in a single hardback volume in 1991.

Lost in Love © Michelle Reid 1993
Fully Involved © Rebecca Winters 1991

ISBN 0 263 79217 X

*Set in Times Roman 10 on 12 pt
05-9602-98560 C*

*Printed in Great Britain by
BPC Paperbacks Ltd*

LOST IN LOVE

CHAPTER ONE

'No.' MARNIE threw down her paintbrush and turned to find a rag to wipe the paint from her fingers. 'I won't do it,' she refused. 'And I don't know how you have the gall to ask me!'

Her brother's face was surly to say the least. 'I've got to have it by tomorrow or I've had it!' he cried. 'There isn't anyone else I know I can turn to. And if you asked him, he'd...'

'I said no.'

They glared at each other across the width of her studio, Marnie with her arms folded across her chest in that stubborn, immovable way her brother knew only too well, her cool gaze refusing to so much as glance at the arm he had wrapped in a white linen sling or the vivid bruise he was wearing down one side of his face.

She made an impatient flick with her hand. 'The last time you talked me into going begging to Guy, I had to stand there and endure a thirty-minute lecture on your weak character—and my own stupidity for pandering to it!' she reminded Jamie. 'I will not give him another chance to repeat that little scene—even if it does mean you having to face the music for a change!'

'I can't believe you're going to let me down like this!' Jamie cried. 'We both know Guy is still crazy about you! He can't refuse you a damned——'

5

'*Jamie*——!' she warned. Her relationship, hostile or otherwise, with Guy Frabosa was always a risky subject to get on to at the best of times, and her warning had her brother shifting uncomfortably where he stood.

'Well, it's true,' he mumbled, unable to hold her gaze. 'The last time it happened,' he persisted none the less, 'I admit it was my own stupid fault, and Guy was probably right to send me packing—but . . .'

'It wasn't *you* he sent packing,' his sister angrily pointed out. 'It was me! It wasn't *you* who had to listen to him verbally annihilate your family, it was me! And it certainly was not you who had to stand there taking it all firmly in the face without a word to say in your defence,' she concluded tightly. 'It was most definitely me!'

'Then let me try asking him——'

'You?' she scoffed, sending him a look fit to wither. Jamie was not one of Guy's most favourite people. In fact, it could be said that Jamie was Guy's least favourite person in the whole wide world! 'You must be feeling desperate if you're thinking of tackling the great man yourself,' she derided. 'He's liable to make mincement out of you in thirty seconds flat—*and* you know it.'

'But if you——'

'*No*——!'

'God, Marnie.' Jamie sank heavily into a chair, defeat sending his thin frame hunching over in distress.

Marnie hardened her heart against the pathetic picture he presented, determined not to weaken this time. It was no use, she told herself firmly. Guy was right. It was time Jamie learned to sort out his own messes. In the four years since she and Guy had parted, Jamie had sent her to him on no less than three occasions to beg on his behalf. That last time had brought Guy's well deserved wrath down on her head, and he had warned her then that the next time she came to him with her brother's problems he would expect something back in return. She had understood instantly what he meant. And there was just no way— *no way* she was going to put herself in that position. Not even for her brother.

'I'll lose everything,' Jamie murmured thickly.

'Good,' she said, not believing him for a moment. 'Perhaps once you have lost it you'll learn the importance of protecting what you had!'

'How can you be so mean?' he choked, lifting his wounded face from his uninjured hand to stare wretchedly at her. He just could not believe she was letting him down this time. 'You've become hard, Marnie,' he accused her, sending her the first look of dislike she had ever received from this only blood relative she had in the world. 'This business with Guy has made you hard.'

'Look...' She sighed, softening slightly because Jamie was right, she had become hard—a necessary shell grown around herself for self-protection. But she didn't want to hurt Jamie. She hated seeing anyone hurt. 'I can probably lay my hands on—ten thousand pounds by tomorrow if that's any good to you.'

'A drop in the ocean,' he mumbled ungratefully, and his sister flared all over again.

'Then what do you expect me to do?' she yelled. 'Sell my damned soul for you?' And that was what it would amount to if she went to Guy for money again. He would demand her soul as payment.

Her brother shook his head. 'God, you make me feel like a heel.'

'Well, that's something, I suppose.' She sighed. 'Why can't you think before you jump, Jamie?' On a gesture of exasperation, she dropped down on the sofa beside him. 'I mean,' she went on, her violet gaze impatient as she studied him, 'to drive a valuable car like that out on the road without insurance!'

The disgust in her voice made him flinch. 'I was delivering it,' he muttered defensively. 'I didn't expect a dirty great lorry to drive smack into the side of me!'

'But isn't that what insurance is for?' his sister mocked scathingly. 'To protect you against the unexpected?'

Her brother was a master at rebuilding very rare and very expensive old-model high-performance cars. It was probably his only saving grace—that and managing to catch and marry about the most sweetest creature on this earth. But this affinity he had with anything mechanical was something special. Marnie had seen him painstakingly take apart and put back together again everything from an old baby carriage to a vintage Rolls in his time.

'Guy has a 1955 Jaguar XK140 Drophead similar to the one I smashed up.' Never one to give up easily, Jamie was reminding her of a fact she had already remembered. 'He might, if you asked him, consider selling it to me on a long-term loan.'

Guy had a whole fleet of fast cars. It was one of his *grandes passions*, possessing cars with an awesome power under their bonnets. As an ex-Formula One

racing car driver and world champion himself, his love
of speed had once excited Marnie beyond bearing.
There had been something incredibly stimulating in
dicing with death at one-hundred-plus miles per hour.
Guy had taken her out several times to share that kind
of exciting feeling with him, his dark face vibrant with
life, eyes flashing, mouth stretched into a devilish
smile as he glanced—too often for her peace of
mind—at her wide-eyed and anxious expression as
their speed increased on surge after surge of fierce
growling power. The next best thing to sex, he called
it. And it certainly left them both on a high which
could only be assuaged in one all-consuming way.

'Please, Marnie...' Her brother's voice shook with
desperation. 'You've got to help me out on this one!'

'I can't believe you drove a car of that value out
on the roads without bothering to insure it!' she
snapped out angrily.

Jamie lifted his hands in an empty gesture. 'It wasn't
that I didn't bother, I just—forgot,' he admitted. 'You
know what I'm like, sis, when I get engrossed in
something.' His blue eyes pleaded for understanding.
'I tend to forget everything else!'

'Including your responsibility to the poor fool who
trusted you with his precious car!'

Jamie winced and she let out an impatient sigh. 'The
last time you got yourself in a mess, it was because
you went over budget and omitted to warn your client
that it was going to cost him several thousand more
than you quoted!'

'I don't do half a job!' he haughtily defended that
particular criticism. 'He wanted his car looking like
new, so I rebuilt it to look like new.'

'Then he refused to take delivery of it until you cut down the bill—which you refused to do. Which meant Guy had to step in and sort the mess out—yet again!'

'You know as well as I do that Guy made on the deal in the end,' Jamie derided that accusation. 'The crafty devil bought the damned car from the man at less than it was worth, and put it into his own collection! It cost me fifteen thousand pounds to put that car back together, of which I saw only ten!'

'And two thousand of that I lent to you and never saw again!'

'OK—OK . . .' Jamie sighed, making a weary retreat by getting up from the sofa to lope over to the window where a bright June sun was beginning to ruin what light she had left of the morning to paint by. 'So, I'm a lousy businessman. You don't have to rub it in.'

Marnie looked at him in impatient sympathy. He was quite right. He was a lousy businessman. He was like the proverbial absent-minded professor when he got his head beneath the bonnet of a new challenge. But she'd thought he'd got himself together in the business department over the last year since Clare had taken over that side of things for him.

She frowned at that last thought, wondering why Clare hadn't made sure his insurance was up to date. It wasn't like her sister-in-law to forget something as basic as that.

'If you won't help me, Marnie,' Jamie murmured into the dull silence that was throbbing all around them, 'I don't know what I'm going to do. The guy is threatening nasty reprisals if I don't come up with his money.'

'Oh, Jamie!' she sighed, leaning forward to rub her forehead with a hand.

'But that's not all...'

No? she wondered cynically. Could there *be* more?

'It's Clare,' he said.

'Clare?' Her head shot away from her hand.

'She's—she's pregnant again.'

'What—already?' Instant concern darkened his sister's eyes, her face going pale as she stared at him. 'Isn't it a bit too soon?' she whispered.

'Yes,' he sighed, turning to look at her, then, sighing again, he came back to throw himself down next to her. 'Too damn soon for anyone's peace of mind...'

Marnie swallowed, her anger with her brother evaporating with this new and far more worrying concern. Clare had gone through what could only be described as a woman's worst nightmare, having lost her first baby right on the three-month borderline the experts liked to call safe. Safe. She scorned it bitterly. There was no such thing as safe during a nine-month-long confinement. Fate and Mother Nature saw to that.

The doctors had warned them not to rush straight into trying for another. 'Give your body time to heal,' they'd advised. 'And your hearts time to grieve.'

'How—how far is she?' She could hardly speak for the hard lump which had formed in her throat.

'Two months.' Jamie glanced at her, his thin face strained. 'Marnie... You have to understand now that this has all come at a bad time for me. I can't afford to let Clare know about this.' He dropped his head, giving his sandy hair a frustrated tug. 'She's worried half out of her mind as it is, wondering, frightened...'

She swallowed, nodding, unable to say a single word.

'If you could just find it in yourself to help me out of this one—I swear to you, Marnie,' he promised huskily, 'I swear on the——'

'Don't say it!' she rasped, her hand shaking as it snapped out to grip tightly at his wrist. 'Don't even think it!'

'God, no!' he groaned, shuddering when he realised just what he had been going to say. 'Hell—I don't know what's happening to me,' he choked. 'I can't think straight for worrying about Clare, never mind this mess with the Jag. I——'

'Is this why you weren't insured?' she asked with sudden insight. 'Has Clare stopped doing all the clerical work since she suspected she was pregnant?'

Jamie nodded. 'God,' he went on distractedly, 'it was bad enough me having to walk into the flat with this arm in a sling, and my face in this kind of mess— she almost fainted in fright!' A ragged sigh shot from him. 'I didn't dare tell her she'd forgotten to renew my insurance! She'd have...' His voice trailed off, and they both sat, their hearts thumping heavily in their breasts.

'All right,' Marnie murmured huskily. 'I'll go and see Guy today.'

Jamie's relief was so palpable that it was almost worth it—almost. Jamie had no idea—couldn't know what this was going to cost her.

'Listen, tell Guy I've found a brilliant MG K3 Magnette!' he said urgently, trying his best to make up for putting her in this position. 'Tell—tell him he can have it for his collection when it's finished,' he offered. 'It isn't as good as the one he's already got, and it won't cover the debt I'll owe him, but...' he swallowed, emotion thickening his voice '...I'll pay him back every penny this time, Marnie. That's a promise. And thank you—thank you for doing this for me this one last time.'

'I'm doing it for Clare, not for you.' Why she'd said that Marnie wasn't about to analyse, but the way her brother's face paled she knew the remark had cut—as, perhaps, it had meant to. But at this moment Marnie found she hated every single one of the male race.

'I know that,' he said, getting up. 'I know both you and Guy don't think my neck worth saving.'

'That's not true, and you know it,' Marnie sighed, softening her manner slightly. 'But I do think it's about time you took care of your own affairs properly, Jamie—and by that I mean yourself, and not leaving it all to Clare.'

'I mean to from now on.' He sounded so determined that Marnie was surprised into believing him. 'After all, she's going to have enough on her plate with—everything else.'

He was by the door, eager to leave now he'd got that promise from Marnie. 'Will—will you give me a call as soon as you've spoken to Guy?' It was tentatively said, but insistent all the same, and Marine glanced sharply at him.

'That urgent, huh?' she drawled.

He nodded and flushed. 'The man is riding on my back,' he admitted.

Just as you are riding on mine, Marnie thought as she watched him go. Then took back that thought with a bitter twist to her tensely held mouth. It was unworthy. She loved her brother, and for once the mess he was in was not of his own making but poor Clare's.

Clare... her eyes clouded over as she thought of her pretty little sister-in-law and the minefield of anxieties she must be negotiating right now. And Jamie was right; Clare was not in any fit condition to take any more stress.

Even if it meant Marnie placing herself in the hands of the enemy!

A shiver rippled through her, leaving her cold even though the sun was warm in the room, the unwanted memories managing to crawl through the thick protective casing she wore around herself, sending her blue eyes bleak as the artist in her began to construct his image in front of her.

Guy, she thought achingly, unable to stop the picture from building. A big man, but lean and muscular, with the kind of naturally tanned skin that enhanced his dark good looks. His chocolate-brown eyes always made exciting promises, and that lazy, sexy smile he used to save for her alone could... She gave an inner sigh that stayed just this side of pain. Her dark Italian love, she remembered wistfully. The only man who had ever managed to get her soul to leave her body and soar on an eddying wave of pure exquisite feeling.

Guy was a man of the earth and air, with banked-down fires inside him that would flare and turn the blood to sizzling, spitting flames.

He was the kind of man whose charismatic power over the opposite sex had given him an arrogance few would deny him. His huge ego was well deserved—

along with his colourful reputation. Guy was a man's idea of a man—the kind of man who walked right out of a woman's foolish dreams. And a selfish, cruel and faithless swine! she reminded herself bitterly. He saw what he wanted, and took it with all the fire and passion in his hot Latin nature—just as he had seen and taken her! In his arrogance, he'd made her fall in love with him, then ruthlessly and callously thrown that love right back in her face! She would never forgive him for that. Never.

Four years ago, Guy had hurt her so deeply that she had prayed never to set eyes on him again. But with his usual arrogance he had refused to allow her that one small relief. And, four years on, they now shared a different kind of relationship, one which had them tiptoeing around each other like wary adversaries, using their tongues instead of their bodies to strike sparks off each other. Hostile yet close—oddly close. In the four long years since she and Guy had split up in a blaze of pain and anger, he had not allowed her to cut him out of her life. Guy possessed a tenacity which surprised her somewhat. For a man who was able to get whatever he wished at the simple click of his fingers, it seemed odd to her that he should still want her. She was, after all, one of his few failures in life, and his ego did not usually like being reminded of those.

Now, and for the first time in a long time, she sensed her own vulnerability, and another smile touched her mouth—one full of rueful whimsy this time. Guy had always predicted that Jamie would be the source of her inevitable downfall.

It seemed that his years of patience were about to bear fruit.

She glanced across the mad clutter of her busy studio room to where the telephone sat innocent and inert on the small table by the door, and slowly, carefully she steadied her emotions, settled her features into their normal cool, calm mask, and readied herself for what was to come. For Jamie might be placing her on a plate for Guy, but it did not mean she was going to sit still on it!

With these defiant thoughts to accompany her across the room, Marnie lifted the receiver off its rest and began to dial the never-to-be-forgotten number of *il signor* Guy Frabosa's London home.

CHAPTER TWO

HE WASN'T there.

'Typical,' Marnie muttered as she replaced the receiver, 'just damned typical!' feeling all that careful mental preparation going frustratingly to waste.

Guy might live in London, have his business base there, but the very nature of that business kept him constantly on the move, personally overseeing every aspect of the conglomerate of companies he had inherited from his abdicating father on Guy's own retirement from motor racing. And it took several calls to different numbers suggested to her before she eventually tracked him down, in Edinburgh of all places.

She was put through to a plastic-sounding female voice who seemed about as approachable as a polar bear. 'Mr Frabosa is in conference,' came the uncompromising block to Marie's request to speak to him. 'He does not wish to be disturbed.'

Is that so? mused Marnie, the woman's frigid tone putting a mulish glint into her blue eyes. For the last hour she had been passed from pillar to post in her attempt to contact Guy, and in the end she had only got the Edinburgh information by pulling rank on the frosty-voiced female blocking her request. It wasn't often that Marnie laid claim to her married title, but she felt no qualms about doing so when she thought

the moment warranted it. She had more than earned
the right, after all.

And it seemed the same tactic was required again!
'Just inform him that *Mrs* Frabosa wishes to speak
to him, will you?' she said coldly, and gained the expected result as the woman stammered through a
nervous apology and went off to inform Guy of his
caller.

For the next five minutes, she hung on the line with
only the intermittent crackle of static to tell her she
was still connected while she waited for Guy to come
dutifully to the phone.

He didn't.

Instead she got the plastic voice again, sounding
flustered. 'Mr Frabosa sends his apologies, Mrs
Frabosa, but asks if he could call you back as soon
as he returns to London?'

Marnie's lips tightened. 'When will that be exactly?'
she asked.

'The day after tomorrow, Mrs Frabosa.'

The day after tomorrow. Marnie paused for a
moment to consider her next move. The very fact that
she was calling him must in itself tell Guy that she
needed to speak to him urgently, since it was such a
rare occurrence. It was typical, she irritably supposed, for him to make her wait. He always had liked
to annoy her by stretching her patience to its limits.

Well, two could play at this game, she decided, as
sly calculation joined the sense of mutiny. 'Then tell
him thank you, but it doesn't matter,' she announced, and calmly replaced the receiver.

She knew Guy, she knew him well.

It took just three minutes for him to get back to her. And, just to annoy him, she waited until she had counted six hollow rings before she lifted the receiver and casually chanted her name.

'Sometimes, *cara*, you try my patience just a little too far.'

The deep velvet tones of his voice swimming so smoothly down the line had her closing her eyes and clenching her teeth in an effort to stop herself responding to the sheer beauty of it. Loving or hating this man, he still had the power to move her sexually.

'Hello, Guy. How are you?' Of the people who knew him in England—his adopted country since his father emigrated here some decades ago—most called him Guy with a hard G. Marnie, on the other hand, had always preferred the European pronunciation, and the way the softer-sounding 'ghee' slid so sensually off the tongue. And Guy loved it. He said just hearing her say his name was enough to make his body respond to the promise it seemed to offer. Once upon a time she would say his name just to witness that unhidden burning response. Now she said it to annoy him because he was well aware it held no invitation any more.

'I am well, Marnie,' he politely replied, before going on to wryly mock, 'Right up until I heard you wished to speak to me, that is.'

'Poor darling,' she mourned, quite falsely. 'What a troublesome ex-wife you have.'

'Is that what you're going to be?' he enquired. 'Troublesome?'

'Probably,' she admitted, keeping her voice light. It always paid to be in control around Guy; he was

just too quick to turn the slightest sign of weakness
to his own advantage. And the advantage was going
to be with him all too soon enough. 'It's rather important that I see you today. Can it be arranged?'

'Not unless you can get to Edinburgh,' he told her
bluntly. 'I will be stuck here for at least another two
days.'

Marnie suppressed an impatient sigh. Could Jamie's
problem wait that long? Going by the sense of urgency her brother had brought in with him that
afternoon, the answer was no, it would not wait.

Marnie chewed on her bottom lip, considering
calling his bluff a second time and just severing the
conversation with a light, 'Shame, but no matter,
forget I even called,' kind of reply. It had worked
several times in the past. They might be divorced, but
not with Guy's blessing. He had fought her all the
way, until she had turned totally ruthless and used her
trump card against him. But he made no secret of the
fact that he was quite willing to do almost anything
for her but die at her feet, and usually when she
snapped her fingers he came running.

Then she remembered Clare, and any idea of
playing cat and mouse with Guy on this one slid
quietly and irrevocably from her mind.

'I suppose you have your plane up there with you?'
she said.

'Correct, my love,' he said quite happily. Guy liked
to thwart her when possible. She allowed it to happen
so rarely that he tended to wallow in the few occasions when it did occur. 'Of course,' he went on,
his velvet voice smoothly mocking, 'if the idea of

flying shuttle up here is totally abhorrent to you, then
I think I can put Sunday afternoon aside for you...'

And what about Saturday? she wondered, feeling
the biting discomfort of evil suspicion creep insidi-
ously through her blood. Today was Wednesday. He
said he was stuck up there for two days. That brought
him to Friday. That could only mean one thing in
Guy's book, for he had this—unbroken little rule
about never spending Saturday alone! He most
probably had her with him now! Her suspicious mind
took her on another step. After all, hadn't she personal experience of Guy's passions? One night without
a woman and he wasn't fit to know!

'And I also suppose you are entertaining one of
your *ladies* up there?'

'Am I?' he murmured in a maddeningly unre-
vealing drawl.

'If I make the effort to get to Edinburgh, Guy,' she
went on tightly, 'it will not be to play gooseberry to
your latest fancy piece!'

'Darling,' he drawled, silky-voiced, refusing to be
riled by her frankly aggravating tone, 'if you can take
so much trouble just to share my company, then I will
make sure I am free.'

Which still told her exactly nothing! 'And the poor
fool who is living under the mistaken belief that she
will be enjoying your full attention—what happens to
her?'

'Why?' he countered. 'Are you expecting to stay
with me all night?' He sounded insufferably at ease,
mildly surprised, and horribly mocking. 'If that is the
case, darling, then I most certainly will make sure I
am free.'

Marnie's lips tightened. 'If you're still hankering after that, Guy,' she told him witheringly, 'then I feel sorry for you. I happen to be rather fastidious about the men who share my bed. One cannot be too careful these days.'

'Bitch,' he said. 'Take care, Marnie, that one day I don't decide to prove to you just how weak your aversion to me actually is, because you would never forgive yourself for surrendering to this—now, what was it you once called me?' He was playing the silky snake now, slithering along her nerve-ends with that lethal weapon of a tongue of his. 'A middle-aged has-been putting himself out for voluntary stud? Quaint,' he drawled. 'Very quaint.'

Marnie had the grace to wince at the hard reminder of those particular words. She had flung some terrible things at him four years ago. Unforgivable things, most of them. But she had been hurting so badly at the time, while he had been so calm, so utterly gentle with her that she had simply exploded, wanting to rile his sleeping devil with terrible insults and bitter accusations. She had not succeeded. All she had achieved was to make him walk abruptly away from her. It was either that or hit her, she knew that now. But four years ago his turning his back on her at that moment had hurt almost as much as everything else he had done to her.

'It isn't my fault you crave variety,' she put in waspishly to hide her own discomfort.

'It is that same "craving", as you so sweetly put it,' he countered, 'that made our nights such—exquisite adventures.'

'And I was so endearingly naïve, wasn't I?' Her full bottom lip curled in derision. 'Such a pathetically gullible thing, and so willing to let you walk all over me.'

'Look.' His patience suddenly snapped. 'I really have no more time to give to this kind of verbal battle today. If you called me up just to fill in a few spare moments trying to irritate me, then I think I should inform you that you have managed it. Now,' he said curtly, 'do you come up to Edinburgh or do we sever this conversation before it deteriorates into a real slanging match?'

'I'll check the times of the shuttle and let your secretary know my arrival time,' she muttered, backing down. It would do her cause no good to have put him in one of his black moods before she'd even got to see him. Things were going to be difficult enough as it was.

'I think I should also mention at this juncture that if this has anything to do with that brother of yours then you will be wasting your time taking that shuttle,' he warned.

'I'll see you later,' she said, and heard his sigh of impatience as she quickly replaced the receiver.

Jamie must have been standing by the telephone waiting for her to call, because he answered it on the first ring. 'Clare's resting upstairs,' he explained. 'I didn't want the telephone to disturb her. Have you spoken to Guy?'

'He's in Edinburgh,' she informed him. 'I'm on my way up to see him right now.'

'Thanks for doing this for me, Marnie,' he murmured gruffly. 'I know how much you hate going to him for anything, and believe me, I wouldn't have asked you to do it this time if it weren't for Clare...'

'How is she?' Marnie enquired concernedly.

'Tense,' her brother clipped. 'Over-bright. Pretending she's worrying about nothing, when really she's so afraid of doing the wrong thing that she barely makes a move without giving it careful consideration first.'

'Yes,' murmured Marnie, well aware of all Clare's painful heart-searching. after that first miscarriage. She could understand how a woman must inevitably put the blame upon herself. Common sense and all the doctors in the world might tell you that it was just one of those natural tragedies that happened in life, but no matter how hard you tried you could never quite convince yourself of that. The feelings of guilt still tormented you day and night.

'If we can just get her through this next vital month, then maybe she'll begin to believe it's going to be all right this time...'

'Well, give her my love,' Marnie said. 'And just make sure you don't give her anything else to worry about.'

'I'm not a complete fool, Marnie,' her brother said tightly. 'I do know when I'm standing right on the bottom line.'

Well, that was something, Marnie supposed on an inner sigh. Perhaps—perhaps, she considered hopefully, this double crisis could just be the making of her scatter-brained, preoccupied brother. 'I'll give you a call the moment Guy decides what he's going to do about it all,' she assured him. 'You just take good care of Clare.'

'I intend to,' he said firmly. 'And—thanks again for doing this for me.'

'Don't thank me, Jamie,' Marnie sighed a little wearily. 'Thank Guy—if he agrees to help you out of this one.'

No one knowing only the Marnie Western-Frabosa who was the beautiful but very Bohemian-styled artist usually dressed in a paint smudged T-shirt and faded jeans would recognise her in the elegant creature who came gracefully through the Arrivals gate at Edinburgh Airport late that same afternoon.

To the man whose lazy black eyes followed her progress across the busy concourse she represented everything he desired in a woman. The first time he had ever set eyes on her had been enough to make his jaded senses throb with a need to possess, solely and totally. Five long and eventful years had passed by since then, and he still could not control that dragging clutch at his loins simply gazing at her caused.

Her skin was pure peaches and cream, so perfect, it fascinated. Her hair, long and finely spun, had been twisted in a knot on top of her head today, but the severity of the style could not dim the thousand and one different shades of reds and golds running through it. It shimmered in the overhead lights. Hers was a rich and golden beauty, made more enchanting by the pure oval of her softly featured face. Her eyes were blue—the shade of blue that could blaze purple with passion or icy grey with anger. Her nose was small and straight—with just the slightest tendency to look haughty when she lifted her chin a certain defiant way. And her mouth...he studied her mouth, lifted slightly at the corners at the moment by some rueful thought she was considering—that mouth had to be the most sensually evocative mouth he had ever seen. The fact that he knew it felt and tasted even more exciting than it looked did not ease the slow burn at present taking place low in his gut.

She was wearing purple, a colour that had always suited her. It was nothing but a simple off-the-peg cotton jersey dress, but it did wonderful things for her figure, hugging the curving shape of her body from neck to hip to just above the curve of her slender knees, leaving little work left to the imagination. And long, slender legs he knew from experience did not stop until they reached her waist brought her onwards towards him with an inbuilt sensual grace which put a smouldering glint in his hooded eyes.

Marnie saw the gleam as she made eye-to-eye contact with the darkly handsome and dangerously charismatic Guy Frabosa.

Sired by an Italian father to a French mother, brought up from the age of ten in England, then having spent most of his adult life frequenting most of the major countries in the world, Guy should have considered himself very cosmopolitan, yet he considered himself Italian to the very last drop of blood in his veins. And perhaps he was right to do so, since it was the Italian side of his breeding that burned through him like a warning beacon to any woman receptive to sheer male virility.

Of course, he, in his conceit, did pander to it, using the liquid smoothness of his Italian accent as one of his most effective weapons, refusing stubbornly to allow it to give way to his superb grasp of the English language, so the 'r's rolled off his tongue like purrs, sexy enough to make any woman quiver.

He was tall, powerfully built yet surprisingly lithe with it. A figure to hang fine clothes on, good quality hand-made clothes with a cut to suit the man—exclusive. His Latin black hair had given way to silver at the temples but that only added to his attraction rather than diminished it. For a thirty-nine-year-old man who had lived every single one of those years to its fullest potential, Guy still packed a fair punch in the solar plexus. He was one of those lucky men who improved with the years—like fine wine, he matured instead of ageing. Eyes of a dark, dark brown were generally lazily sensual, but could, if he wanted them to, harden to cold black pebbles which could freeze out the most tenacious foe. His nose was long and thin—not slim, thin, with a tendency to flare at the nostrils. Arrogant, and, like the rock-hard set of his chin, a direct warning to the ruthless streak in his character. Whereas his mouth by contrast was truly sensual, a very expressive tool he used to convey his moods, thin and tight when angry, sardonically twisted when mildly amused, a wide and attractive frame to perfect white teeth when touched into full-blown laughter, and soft, full and passionate when sexually aroused.

Then there was that other mouth, the one he saved for Marnie alone. The one he was wearing right at this moment as he watched her approach him through the mill of commuter bodies.

It was the half-soft, half-twisted, half-smiling mouth that said he didn't really know how to feel about her, and really never had.

That, Marnie thought as she carefully doused down her own inevitable response to this first glimpse of him—that deep and all-consuming inner recognition of her body's perfect master—was and always had been her most powerful weapon over Guy: his inability to decide just where she fitted into his life. He had once thought he'd done it, fitted her neatly into the box marked 'wife', of the forbearing and dutiful kind. Blindly besotted, safely caught and netted—only to find out, when he tried testing the springs of his trap, that he had made the biggest mistake of his life.

She reached him, waited calmly for his dark eyes to make their slow and lazy climb of her body from soft purple suede shoes to the scoop-necked top of her simple dress. Then they lifted to wryly take in the proud tilt to her chin, her mouth, heart-shaped and slightly mocking, along the straight line of her small nose until at last clashing with the full and striking blueness of her eyes.

The muscles around her stomach quivered. Standing this close to him, it was impossible not to respond to the raw beauty of Guy's face.

'Marnie,' he murmured.

'Hello, Guy,' she quietly replied, smiling a little, because even though she hated him she loved him, if it was possible to feel the two emotions at the same time.

He knew it too, which put that look of rueful irony in his eyes as he took another step to close the gap between them. Guy was Italian enough to express a greeting with a kiss on both cheeks, and Marnie had long since given up trying to deter him. So she stood calmly waiting for the embrace with no thought of drawing back.

His hands lifted to gently curve the lightly padded bones at her shoulders, and he leaned forward, brushing his mouth across one softly perfumed cheek then the other. Then, just as she was about to take that vital step back so that she could smile at him with studied indifference, he outmanoeuvred her, holding her firmly in front of him, eyes flashing wickedly just before his mouth came to cover hers in a hot and hungry kiss which took no account of how public he was being, or how blithely he had overstepped the invisible line she had drawn between them four years ago.

It took several long, turbulent seconds for her to realise just what he was doing, but by then it was too late; shock had already sent her arching into the familiar hardness of his body, and her mouth—parting on a gasp of surprise—was suddenly consumed by the feel and taste of him, remembering, and she quivered, the sheer horror of what was happening sending her eyes wide to stare in mute protest into the flashing triumph in his. Then his dark lashes were lowering sensually over his eyes, and he was giving himself up to the sheer pleasure of the kiss, drawing her even closer to him, forcing her to acknowledge the damning evidence of her own response when her breasts swelled and hardened, aroused by the crushing pressure of his chest.

'You have no idea how much I needed that,' he murmured with heavy satisfaction when at last he allowed their mouths to separate.

She jerked angrily away from him, dazed by the unexpected onslaught, and dizzy with the sight and sound and smell of him. She was trembling all over, and guilty heat ran up her cheeks. Guy had not affected her like this for years.

OK, she reasoned with herself as she struggled to pull herself together. So the bitterness she used to feel towards him had slowly faded, but she had never expected this—this swamp of feeling to overtake her! She slid a shaking hand across her mouth in a useless attempt to wipe away the lingering throb of his kiss, glancing up at him through her lashes with dark, angry eyes. 'God, Guy,' she whispered huskily. 'Sometimes you behave like a——'

'I do hope, *cara*,' he interrupted lazily, 'that you are not about to deny your own response to that kiss.' He quirked an eyebrow at her, daring her with the taunting mockery in his gaze to do just that. 'Nor mine to you,' he added silkily. 'For, while you bow your head in that oh, so demure way and make believe you are too *fastidious* to enjoy a kiss from me, you are also glaring in the general direction where your own twin proofs still peak in recognition of their master... You really should wear more concealing undergarments, Marnie, my love, if you do not wish to be so—exposed, as they say.'

'God, I hate you!'

'I know,' he drawled, unrepentant.

'Does it give you some kind of perverted kick to embarrass me this way?'

'Oh, it gives me all kinds of kicks to see you knocked off balance now and then.' The curt remark was accompanied by his abrupt withdrawal from her, leaving her standing alone, trying hard not to sway dizzily. The angry heat in her cheeks told him he had easily won that round. 'Come,' he said, suddenly cool and aloof. 'We have business to discuss. I have a car waiting outside.'

With that, he took her arm in a possessive hold, and, keeping her close to his side, led her towards the airport exit.

'No luggage?' he enquired a few steps further on.

She shook her head. 'I was hoping to catch the last shuttle back to London.'

'Which leaves in about—one hour,' he informed her with dry sarcasm. 'Rather optimistic of you, to believe we can talk and get back here in that time, don't you think?'

'An hour?' She stopped to stare at him in horror. It had never occurred to her to check the times of the London shuttle! She had just automatically assumed they ran day and night—the way the trains did.

'What will you do now?' Guy murmured provokingly. 'Stuck here in this strange city with a man you say you hate!'

'I'll most probably survive,' she threw back tartly, 'since the man in question can't possibly hurt me more than he has already!'

His mouth tightened, but he said nothing, pulling her along beside him as he strode through the exit doors. The waiting car was long and dark and

chauffeur-driven. Guy politely saw her seated before
sliding in beside her, and almost before the door had
closed them in they were moving smoothly away
from the kerb.

CHAPTER THREE

'I'M GOING to have to find somewhere to stay over-night,' Marnie sighed, still irritated because she had been so stupid as to not check the times of the return shuttle back to London. A couple of hours of Guy's company was all she ever allowed herself at one swallow. The mere idea of spending a whole evening in his proximity was enough to make her voice sound pettish as she added, 'And I'm hungry; I missed my lunch today and you——' '

'Do be quiet, Marnie,' Guy cut in, sending her a look of such flat derision that her cheeks actually flushed at it. 'You know as well as I do that I will have made any necessary arrangements. I am nothing if not competent, Marnie—nothing if not that...'

She glared at him balefully, hating him with her eyes for his ever-present sarcasm. Oh, yes, she agreed, Guy was competent, all right. So competent, in fact, that it had taken her almost a year to find out that he was cheating on her with another woman. And she would not have found out then if Jamie hadn't opened his mouth over something he'd thought completely innocent at the time.

Jamie. She shivered suddenly. God, how Guy hated her brother for that bit of indiscretion. He had vowed once never to forgive him. Just as she had vowed never to forgive Guy.

'Cold?' he murmured, noting the small shiver.

'No.' She shook her head. 'Just...' Her lips closed over what she had been going to say, and she turned her face away from him with a small non-committal shrug. She could feel the sharpness of his gaze on her and tensed slightly, waiting for him to prompt her into finishing the sentence. The silence between them grew fraught, shortening her breathing and making her heart beat faster. There was so much bitterness between them, so much dissension, she didn't know whether she could actually go through with this.

'Easy, Marnie...' Guy's hand reached out to cover her own, and it was only as the warm brown fingers closed gently over hers that she realised she was sitting with her hands locked into a white-knuckled clench. 'It cannot be this bad, surely?' he murmured huskily.

Oh, yes, it could, she thought silently. I hate you and you hate Jamie and Jamie hates himself. It couldn't be much worse! 'Guy,' she began tentatively, 'about Jamie...'

'No.' He removed his hand, and at the same time removed the caring expression from his face. And Marnie felt her heart sink as he leaned back and closed his eyes, effectively shutting her out. It was an old habit of his, and one she knew well. If Guy wished to defer a discussion he simply gave you no room to speak. On a soft sigh, she subsided, accepting that it was no use her trying to force the issue. Even if she tried, he would completely ignore her. It was the way of the man, hard, stubborn, despotic to a certain extent. He played at life by his own set of rules and principles and never allowed anyone to dictate to him.

Besides his undeniably fantastic looks, Guy was a brilliant businessman, a wildly exciting athlete and a

dynamic lover. True to his Latin blood, he possessed
charm in abundance, arrogance by the ton, energy
enough to satisfy six women, and money enough to
keep them all in luxury while he did so.

It was that same surfeit of money in the family
which gave him the means to indulge his second most
favourite passion: that for racing cars. It was a passion
that had taken him all over the world to race, living
the kind of life that automatically went along with it,
his striking good looks and innate charm making
sexual conquests so easy for him that by the time he
met her Guy had grown cynical beyond belief about
the opposite sex.

He had just passed his thirty-fourth birthday by
then, and retired from racing on a blaze of glory by
winning his second world championship crown, to take
up the reins of business from his father 'so the old
man can go and tend to his roses,' as Guy so drolly
liked to put it.

Papa Frabosa...a small frown pulled at her smooth
brow. It was ages since she'd seen him. And not because of her break-up with his son, she reminded
herself grimly. No, not even that had been able to
break the loving bond she and Roberto had forged
during her short foray into their lives. But he liked to
keep to his Berkshire home these days, since the small
stroke several months ago, and Marnie had refused
to so much as set foot on the estate since she'd left
Guy. The place resurrected too many painful
memories.

Opening her mouth to ask him about how his father
was, she turned her head to look at him—and im-

mediately forgot all about Roberto Frabosa when she
found herself gazing at Guy's lean, dark profile.

Such a beautiful man, she observed with an ache.
A man with everything going for him. Too much for
her to cope with. That dynamic character of his needed
far more stimulation than an ordinary little artist girl
had been able to offer him. She was at least ten years
too young for him, ten years behind him in experience—a lesson she had learned the hard way, and
had no desire to repeat even though she knew without
a single doubt that if she said to him right now, and
with no prior warning, that she wanted to be his wife
again, Guy would take her back without question. He
loved her in his own way, with passion and with spirit.
But not in the way she needed to be loved—faithfully.
His need to supplement his physical desires with other
women had driven a stake so deeply into her heart
that the wound still bled profusely—four years on.

He didn't know, of course, just how deeply he had
hurt her. He only knew the small amount she had
allowed him to know—and to be fair to him he had
never forgiven himself for hurting her that much. His
sense of remorse and the knowledge that he had no
defence for his behaviour had kept him coming back
to her throughout the years in the bleak hope that she
might one day learn to forgive him and perhaps take
him back. He was a Catholic by religion, and,
although they had not married in the Catholic faith,
and their divorce had been quite legal, Guy had never
accepted it as so. 'One life, one wife' was his motto,
and she was it. Guy had refused to melt out of her
life, and with his usual stubbornness had refused to
let her do the melting. So they'd gone on over the

years, sharing a strange kind of relationship that hovered somewhere between very close friends and bitter adversaries. He lived in hope that one day she might find it in her to forgive him, and she lived in the hope that one day she would force him to accept that she would not—which was why she did all the bitter biting, and he allowed her to get away with it.

A penance, he'd described it once. A penance for his sins, like the four years they had spent apart. He quite readily accepted it all as deserved. 'You'll forgive me one day, Marnie,' he told her once when one of his many seduction scenes had been foiled—by the skin of her chattering teeth! 'I will allow you some more time—but not much more,' he'd warned. 'Because time is slowly running out for both of us. Papa wants to hold his grandson in his arms before he dies, and I mean to see that he does.'

'Then don't look to me to provide it!' she flashed with enough bitter venom to whiten his face. 'You would do better, Guy, finding yourself the kind of wife who doesn't mind sharing you, because this one has no intention of going through that kind of hell again!'

'And I have already vowed to you that it would not happen again!' he said haughtily. Guy always became haughty when on the defensive; he hated it so much. 'That one time was a mistake, one which——'

'One which was more than enough for me!' she'd cut him off before he'd got started—as she always did when he tried to explain. 'Why can't you get it into your thick head that I don't love you any more?' she'd added ruthlessly, yet felt no satisfaction in the way

his expression had closed her out, the flicker of pain
she'd glimpsed in him managing only to hurt her too.

That was all of five months ago, and since then
she'd steered well clear of Guy. But now here she was,
driving with him through the streets of Edinburgh
knowing with a dull sinking feeling inside that this
time he held all the cards, and she had nothing but
her pride—if he allowed her to keep it, that was, which
was no real certainty.

'We have arrived,' his quiet voice broke into her
thoughts, and she turned to glance at the porticoed
entrance to one of the city's most exclusive hotels.

He helped her alight, as always the complete
gentleman in public, his hand lightly cupping her
elbow as they walked inside and led the way to the
waiting lift. Neither of them spoke a single word;
neither of them felt inclined to. It was the calm before
the storm, with both of them conserving their energies
for what they knew was to come.

The lift doors closed then opened again several
seconds later. Guy guided her out on to the quiet
landing and towards a pair of rather imposing white-
painted doors, a key dangling casually from his
fingers.

She shuddered—she couldn't help it—and he
glanced sharply at her, his mouth tightening into a
stubborn line because he knew exactly what she was
thinking, and his fingers tightened on her arm as if
in confirmation of her fear that this time—this time
there would be no compromises, no escape for her.

The suite was more a mini-apartment, with several
doors leading off from a small hallway. Guy pushed
open one of the doors and indicated that she should

precede him into a large and luxuriously furnished sitting-room.

'Nice,' she drawled, impressed.

'Adequate,' dismissed the man who had spent most of his life living out of a suitcase. He possessed a real contempt of hotels now. He much preferred his rambling country home in Berkshire, or his beautiful apartment in London. 'Sit down and I'll mix us both a drink,' he invited.

Moving with the lean grace Marnie always associated with him, Guy went over to the small bar and began opening cupboard doors while she hovered for a moment, wondering on a sudden swell of panic if she should just turn right around and get out of here while she still could.

Then she remembered Jamie's bruised and swollen face, and that linen sling around his broken arm. And she remembered Clare, and the desire to run and save her own skin faded away.

For Clare's peace of mind it was worth it, she told herself as a memory so painful that it clenched at her chest struck her. Stress was a dangerous state of mind—could even kill if left to run wild. She would do almost anything to ensure her sister-in-law never had to experience it.

With a grim setting of her lips, she moved across the room and sat down in one of the soft-cushioned armchairs.

'Here.' Guy handed her a tall glass filled almost to the rim with a clear sparkling liquid. 'Dry martini with lots of soda,' he informed her, going to sit in the other chair while she smiled wryly at the sardonic tone he had used. It had always amused him that she disliked the taste of alcohol in any form. A dry martini well watered down was just about her limit.

The ice cubes clinked against the side of the glass as Guy took a sip at his own gin and tonic. Then, 'OK, Marnie,' he said briskly. 'Let me have it. What's that stupid brother of yours done now that could make you come to me for help?'

'How do you know it's Jamie who needs your help?' she flashed indignantly, annoyed that he wasn't even giving her a chance to work up to mentioning Jamie, and forgetting that she had already given him a clue in the car. 'I could be here on my own behalf, you know, but typical of you: you immediately jump to your own conclusions and——'

'*Are* you here for your own sake?' he cut in smoothly.

'No...' Marnie wriggled uncomfortably where she sat. 'But you could at least give me a chance to explain before you——'

'Then it has to be for Jamie,' he said, ignoring her indignation. 'I warned you, Marnie,' he inserted grimly, ignoring all the rest, 'not to bring your brother's troubles to me again, and I meant it.'

'This time it's different, though,' she told him, her mouth thin and tight because, no matter how sure she was that she was doing the right thing, she didn't have to like it, 'or I wouldn't have involved you at all, but this time it's Clare I'm worried about, and...'

'Clare?' he repeated sharply. His eyes suddenly narrowed and went hard. 'What's he done to her?' he demanded harshly.

'Nothing!' Marnie denied, resenting his condemning tone. 'He worships the ground she walks on and you know it. Of course Jamie hasn't done anything to hurt Clare—how could you even think such a thing?'

'I worshipped the ground you walked on and look how badly I hurt you,' he pointed out.

'No, you didn't,' she denied that deridingly. 'You worshipped my body, and when it wasn't available for you you just went out and found a substitute for it. So don't you dare try putting Jamie into the same selfish mould as you exist in! He *loves* Clare,' she stated tightly, 'loves as in lifelong caring and fidelity—something you've never felt for anyone in your whole life!'

'Finished?' he clipped.

'Yes.' She subsided at the angry glint now glowing in his narrowed eyes.

'Then if Jamie is this—caring of Clare, why have you been forced to come to me to beg help for her?'

'Because...' She sucked in a deep breath, trying to get a grasp on her growling temper. He could always do it. One minute in his company and he could always rile her until she didn't know what she was saying! 'She's pregnant,' she said.

'What—already?' Guy made a sound of grinding impatience. 'I don't call that damned caring of your brother, Marnie,' he muttered angrily. 'I call it downright irresponsible!'

So do I, she thought, but held the words back. Guy didn't need any help in finding faults with her brother. He had an unerring ability to just pluck them out of the air like rabbits from a magician's hat!

'What's the matter with her?' he went on grimly. 'Is she ill—does she need money for medical care?'

Already he was fishing inside jacket pocket for his cheque-book, his glass discarded so he could write out a cheque for whatever amount Marnie wished to demand from him.

And she was tempted—oh, so severely tempted to just let it go at that and name a figure which would probably choke him at the size of it but would not stop him giving it to her because it was for little Clare, whom he'd always had a soft spot for and therefore would do anything for.

But that would not be right—nor fair, she acknowledged heavily. If he was going to help them out, then he had a right to know the truth.

'Wait a mintue,' she said, swallowing because the truth was going to be that much harder to tell now he'd all but convinced himself Clare was in dire need of his financial asistance. 'You haven't heard it all, and I would rather you did before you agreed to anything. Clare is pregnant, but not in any danger of losing this one just yet, though it is the fear that it may happen which made me come to you.'

'Jamie,' he said, sitting back, the cheque-book thrown contemptuously aside.

She nodded, deciding it was time to stop prevaricating. He deserved that after the way he had reacted to the thought of Clare's needing his help. It even warmed her to know that Guy could be so generous to someone he barely knew.

'He's just completed the reconstruction of a 1955 Jaguar XK 140 Drophead,' she began.

'I have one of those!' Guy's mood instantly changed to one of glowing enthusiasm. 'I wonder if he managed to solve the problem with the——?'

'While he was delivering it to the owner yesterday...' she interrupted him a trifle impatiently; it was typical of him to be so easily diverted by the name of a precious car '...a lorry coming in the other direction skidded on a patch of oil and ploughed straight into him. The Jaguar was written off.'

'What—totally?' He was horrifed.

'It went up in flames,' she informed him grimly.

'Bloody stupid—anyone seriously hurt?'

'In general, my brother lives a charmed life,' Marnie sighed. 'No, not seriously,' she confirmed. 'Jamie managed to climb out of the tangled mess just before it caught fire with nothing more than a bruised face and a broken arm for his trouble.'

'That beaufiful car,' Guy murmured in the mournful tone of the true car fanatic. 'Jamie must be sick.'

'You could say that,' Marnie agreed. 'The car wasn't insured.'

That dragged Guy surely back on course. He stared at her in blank amazement, then looked appalled, then just downright disgusted. 'How much?' he snapped.

She told him, he swore loudly and she grimaced, entirely in sympathy with him.

'And I suppose he's hoping that good old Guy will come up with the readies to bail him out.' His tone was scathing to say the least. 'Well, you can just go back and tell him that it's no go this time, Marnie! I have just about had enough of that reckless brother of yours and his stupid——'

'You've missed the point,' she put in quietly, catching his attention before his Italian temperament ran away with him.

'What point?' he demanded.

'Clare,' she reminded him.

'Clare?' Guy looked blank for a moment, then went as pale as a ghost. 'She wasn't in the car with him, was she?' he choked.

'No!' Marnie quickly assured him. 'No—that wasn't the point I was trying to make. But—Guy,' she appealed to him for understanding, 'she's pregnant and she shouldn't be! It was already a big enough shock for her to have Jamie come home with his face all bruised and his arm in a sling—how do you think she's going to react when she finds out she forgot to renew his insurance policy and that they've now got to find upwards of fifty thousand pounds to compensate the owner of the car?'

Silence. Guy was staring at her through hard, angry eyes as he let all of it really sink in, and Marnie sat there staring back with her lovely blue eyes wide in anxious appeal, hoping that just this once—this one last time—he would come up trumps for her and help them out without demanding anything back in return.

'He promises to pay you back—Guy,' she added quickly, when he continued to say nothing, 'he—he said to tell you he's managed to acquire an MG K3 Magnette and you can have that as a down-payment. And he's——'

'A damned fool if he thinks I would accept anything from him!' Guy cut in impatiently. 'And I warned you, Marnie, quite distinctly, the last time you came begging to me on his behalf, that I had done more than enough for the man who wrecked our marriage,' he reminded her forcefully.

'Jamie didn't wreck our marriage,' she said wearily. 'You did that all on your own.'

The dark head shook grimly. 'We would still be together,' stated the man who had always preferred to scatter blame around like raindrops so long as none of it stuck to himself, 'living together—loving together, if your stupid brother hadn't stuck his nose into my affairs.'

' "Affairs" being the operative word,' she derided.

'Damn you, Marnie!' Angrily, he climbed out of his chair, frustration making him run a hand through the thick, sleek blackness of his hair. 'I didn't mean it in that way—and you know it!' He turned to glare down at her, then sucked in a deep, calming breath. 'Your brother was directly responsible for——'

'I don't want to discuss it.' It was her turn to cut him short—as she always did when he attempted to bring up the past. 'It's all just dead news now.'

'Not while I'm still breathing, it is not,' he bit out. 'We still have unfinished business, you and I,' he went on to warn, wagging a long finger at her in a way which was consciously gauged to infuriate her. 'And, until you are prepared to give me a fair hearing, it will remain unfinished. Just remember that as you sit there hating me with your beautiful eyes. For one day I will make you listen, and then it will be you doing the apologising and I taking revenge!'

'Oh, yes.' The scorn in her voice derided him outright. 'As I think I've already said, I don't want to talk about it. I came here today to——'

'Beg for more money for your useless brother,' Guy tartly supplied for her.

'No,' she angrily denied that. 'To beg for Clare!'
She too came to her feet, irritation and frustration in
every line of her slender frame. 'I was as determined
as you are not to bail Jamie out of any more of his
disasters,' she snapped. 'I told him this time and in
no uncertain terms that I would not involve you again!
But—God,' she sighed, lifting her strained eyes to his,
'this is different, Guy, you've got to see that? This
time it isn't just you and me and Jamie we're fighting
about; it involves Clare! Sweet, gentle Clare who has
never wished harm on anyone in her entire life! You
can't turn your back on her, Guy, surely? Not just to
gain your sweet revenge over Jamie?'

He was going to refuse, she could see it in the grim,
hard cut of his tightly held mouth, and panic began
to shimmer inside her. 'Please, Guy.' She lifted a
trembling hand to clutch pleadingly at the bunching
muscles in his upper arm. 'Please . . .' she begged.

He looked long and hard into the deep blue of her
pleading eyes, his own so dark and disturbing that
Marnie's insides began to churn with an old memory
so sweet and aching that she wanted to cry out against
it. Once she had drowned in that look, placed all her
vulnerable love and trust in its meaning what it appeared to tell her.

She watched him glance down to where her hand
clutched at him, his beautiful eyelashes forming a
thick, sweeping arch against his strong cheekbones.
Watched the hardness ease from his mouth as he lifted
his gaze back to her own, and suddenly the silence
between them began to throb with tension—a raw
sexual tension that had no right to show itself at this
vital moment! Marnie moved, her tingling fingers

flexing slightly in an effort to dispel the unwanted
sensation, her tongue flicking in agitation across the
fullness of her suddenly dry lips, her breathing slow
and heavy.

Guy saw it all, every revealing thing she was experiencing at this new kind of physical closeness, and
something unfathomable passed across his face...a
further darkening of those rich brown eyes that had
her holding her breath in dear hope that her plea was
reaching him.

'Please...' she repeated huskily. 'Put your prejudices aside this one last time—for Clare's sake?'

He hesitated visibly—long enough to make hope
flare into her eyes—only to have him dip his dark head
a little closer to her own as he countered softly but
with a ruthlessness that left her in no doubt at all to
his meaning, 'And you, Marnie? Are you prepared to
put your own prejudices aside, for sweet Clare's sake?'

Her thudding heart sank, her body went cold, and
she stood very still, staring into the utterly uncompromising set of his lean, dark features, wondering
why she had actually had the gall to convince herself
that she could win him round this one last time. Guy
had, after all, told her in no uncertain terms not to
come begging to him again unless she was prepared
to pay the price. She had never known him say anything without carrying it through. It was what made
him the man he was today, this stubborn unwill-
ingness of his to compromise over anything—even the
way he conducted his life, she reminded herself grimly.
Married or not, Guy had always refused to answer to
anyone but himself.

Unclipping her hand from his arm, she took a shaky step back from him, then turned away so she wouldn't have to witness the flare of triumph her answer would put in his eyes. 'Yes,' she whispered, 'I'm prepared to do that.'

Oddly, and surprisingly since she had just conceded to him what he had been trying to get her to do for four long years now, instead of thrusting his triumph down her throat, Guy too turned away, going to stand over by the window.

'How prepared?' he persisted, not turning to face her with the final challenge, his back a rigid bulk of taut muscle for her to stare bleakly upon.

'Whatever it takes,' she promised flatly. 'Whatever it is you want in return.'

'You.' He turned his head, his expression as cool and uncompromising as she had ever known it. 'I want you back.'

She had expected it. Had travelled up here knowing exactly what he would demand; so why did she experience the sudden drain of blood from her head, or the blow of pain that knocked all the breath from her body in a way that sent her sinking down on to the sofa? 'Oh, God, Guy,' she whispered threadily, 'I don't think I can!'

If she thought him remote before, then her broken little cry managed to close him up completely, seeming to rake over every nerve-end he possessed before turning him into a cold statue of ungiving rock.

'I did warn you not to involve me in your brother's problems again,' he said harshly. 'I also remember warning you that my—penance for hurting you had almost run its course.' He let out a sharp sigh as he watched her wrap her arms tightly around her trembling body as if she was protecting herself from his very words. 'It is time to break this—foolish deadlock we are both stuck in, Marnie!'

'But I don't belong to you any more!' she cried.

'You have always belonged to me!' he snapped, moving at last to come and stand over her, his anger so palpable that she could actually feel it throbbing out of him. 'All you have done here today is save me the trouble of finding my own way to get you back!'

'By using Jamie?' she jeered. 'Using the weak to aid the strong?'

Guy nodded curtly, taking no offence at the accusation. 'Just as Jamie uses your strength to prop up his own weaknesses, Marnie. It works both ways, my dear.'

'And Clare?' she demanded.

'Clare is your weakness, Marnie,' Guy stated. 'Not mine. Not even Jamie's. I wonder why that is?'

Marnie looked away from the probing thrust of his hard black eyes, not willing—never willing to confess just why she held such a vulnerable spot in her heart for her sister-in-law.

'So, in what capacity am I to become your property this time, Guy?' she enquired bitterly, finally conceding the point that she was indeed entirely in his power. She lifted her gaze to show him an ice-cold contempt that held his own face taut and grim. 'Wife or mistress?' she posed. 'Not that one has any precedence over the other in your life,' she acknowledged cynically, 'but your father will condone nothing less than a legal marriage between us, you must already know that.'

'Then for my father's sake, of course——' he shrugged as if it mattered little to him either way '—we will be man and wife again—not that I have considered us anything less during the last four years,' he added drily.

Marnie's mouth took on a contemptuous line. 'If we're to take into consideration your behaviour over the last four years as well as the one we were actually married, Guy, then the adultery charge can be laid at your feet a dozen times over.' Her eyes leapt to spit accusation at him. 'Or is it two dozen—or four?'

'Bitch!' he growled, reaching down to grasp hold of her. 'That is for me to know and you to wonder about! A wife's place is at her husband's side, warming his bed and keeping his body content! Your desertion of those duties leaves you with no right to question how I quenched my needs, and nor ever will it in the future!'

'I see,' she sneered, 'then what is good for the goose is most definitely good enough for the gander—remember that, Mr God's-Gift-to-Women Frabosa, when you carry on your little affairs. I may be back in your power again, but only for as long as it takes me to prove what a worthless rat you really are!'

'Be careful what you say to me, Marnie!' he warned, the anger vibrating from every pore as he took hold of her shoulders in a rough grip. 'I have taken the bitterness from your vicious tongue for long enough—paid for my crimes a thousand times over, and will pay no longer!'

Flushed and trembling with hurts which went back years, and quivering with a hated, hot searing sense of awareness at his physical closeness, Marnie glared at him with contempt. 'So get thee behind me, woman!' she scorned his arrogance. 'For I am your lord and master!'

'Yes!' he hissed, almost lifting her out of the chair with the hard grasp of his hands. 'That is exactly it! Now stop riling me to anger.' He threw her away from him, to straighten up. 'And accept the inevitable with the kind of grace I know you to possess. It is over, at last and with deep relief on my part. You and I are as one from this moment on and I will hear no more of your malice—understand?'

She understood only too well, sliding from anger to depression with a speed that spoke volumes about her defeat.

He remained standing over her for a long time, staring down at her bent head until her nerves began to fray beneath the tension she was putting on them. Then, with a sigh which came from somewhere deep and dark inside him, he moved away, slamming out of the door without another word.

CHAPTER FOUR

SIGHING, Marnie let her head sink back into the soft-cushioned sofa and closed her eyes.

So, she thought heavily. After four years of relative peace and contentment, she was back with a man who could only make her life hell for a second time. Living with Guy the first time had been no picnic. He possessed too volatile a temperament to make him a comfortable person to be around. And she was just too spirited to be anything but a spark to his fire. The only place they had ever found any mutual accord had been in bed, and even that had proved itself inadequate in the end.

Did he believe that forcing her to come back to him would automatically heal all that had gone before? she wondered cynically. Or was it just that he did not care so long as he had her back where he considered she belonged. He possessed a colossal pride, and she had dented it badly when she walked out on him. Having her back would mend that dent, show him to be the irresistible Guy Frabosa everyone always thought him to be.

He came back into the room, and Marnie stirred herself enough to stand up. 'I need to use the bathroom,' she said coolly.

'Of course.' His dark head dipped, a new stiffness entering the atmosphere now the main battle was over. He opened the sitting-room door again and waited for her to precede him out of it, then indicated another door in the tiny hall. A bedroom, she discovered as she stepped inside. 'There is a bathroom *en suite* through that door opposite.' He informed her. 'While you freshen up, I shall go and order us something to eat.' With another nod he was gone, closing the door behind him on Marnie's wretched sigh of relief.

When she came back to the sitting-room Guy was talking on the telephone, his tone that brisk, clipped, arrogant one he used when issuing orders to his minions; she smiled at it, hoping it was that frosty-voiced woman she had come up against earlier. It gave her a real sense of satisfaction to know that that was one tone of voice Guy had never used with her—thank God, because it sent ice-cold shivers up and down her spine just listening to it.

He hadn't noticed her return, his dark head bowed to study the shiny leather of his hand-made shoes as he leaned against the edge of the huge desk which had always been an essential requisite for any hotel room he stayed in. And she paused on the threshold of the room, the artist in her drawn to follow the long, lean length of him.

He hadn't altered much in the last five years, she noted wryly, sliding her eyes along the full length of his powerful legs encased in their usual expensive silk-wool mix with creases so sharp, they accentuated the flatness of his taut, narrow hips.

She had once painted Guy in many guises. The dynamic racing-car driver decked out in a silver space-suit, his head lost beneath a big crash helmet which left only his eyes, gleaming out from the gap where the protective plastic visor would be flicked into place the moment he climbed behind the wheel. But, while he waited, those eyes would spark and glitter with all the fevered impatience for what he was about to take on. Then there was the mocking painting she'd done of him when he looked like a sloth, lazily stretched out in an armchair wearing nothing more than a loosely tied robe about his naked body, hair ruffled and his square chin roughened by a twelve-hour shadow, attention fixed on the Sunday newspaper like any ordinary mortal man. As studies, they were almost ridiculous in their stark contrast to each other, yet both held a kind of magic that could set a thrill of excitement tingling up and down her spine, because nothing could ever disguise the latent power of the man himself. Not the all-encompassing space-suit or the unkempt sloth—or even this elegantly clad, super-dynamic tycoon she was looking at now, she added as her eyes lifted to take in the muscled beauty of his torso beneath the crisp white shirt he was wearing. In every persona, Guy always managed to exude what was the sheer male essence of the man—that hot, pulsing core of raw sexuality which could still make her body react violently, even while her heart remained coldly unimpressed.

He muttered something, and her eyes flicked up to clash with his, heat crawling up her cheeks because he had caught her staring so blatantly at him. She stiffened slightly, her chin coming up in defiance of the expression he had managed to catch on her face before she blanked it out, but his own eyes mocked her as they stared back, his hand slow in setting the telephone receiver back on its rest.

Damn his sex appeal! she thought as the tension began whipping itself up between them. Damn him for thrusting his sexuality at her! And damn herself for responding to it.

'I—I forgot to fetch my bag,' she said, forcibly dragging her eyes away from him to send them on a slightly hazy search of the luxurious lounge. 'Did you see where I put it when I came in?' She was too busy refusing to let her eyes be drawn back to him to see the sudden narrowing of his eyes. 'I'm sure I dropped it down here,' she murmured, walking over to the sofa to frown down at the place she'd expected the bag to be.

'What do you need it for?' he asked.

'My comb.' Her hand jerked nervously up to her where her hair, newly released from its severe style, hung in thick silk tendrils down her back. 'I'd let it down before I realised I hadn't got my comb.'

'Here.' She glanced at him, expecting to find her bag dangling from his outstretched fingers, but frowned when all he held was his own tortoiseshell comb.

'No, thank you,' she primly refused, and returned to searching for her bag. 'I have my own somewhere if I could lay my hands on my...'

It hit her then, why he was standing there looking so studiedly casual, and she turned back to glare at him. 'You've got it!' she accused, her hands going to rest on her hips in an unconsciously shrewish pose.

He took his time enjoying the highly provocative stance, an aggravating smile playing about his lips as he slid his gaze along the figure-hugging purple dress which did little to hide the sensual curves in her body or the too expressive heave of her full breasts. 'Have you any idea what you look like standing there like that?' he drawled.

'A mess, most likely,' she dismissed the husky tease in his voice. 'My bag, Guy,' she clipped. 'You've moved it and I want it.' A slender hand came out in demand.

Guy glanced at it then back at her face, then, still smiling lazily, he gave a slow shake of his head. 'No,' he said. 'I'm sorry *cara*, but until you are legally tied to me once again, you will need nothing that is in that bag.'

'What's that supposed to mean?' she asked in genuine bewilderment.

'Exactly what it said,' he drawled. 'For the next few days you will be making not a single move without me at your side. Anything you may require will be provided by me, including a comb for your lovely hair.'

'But Guy,' she protested in disbelief, 'that's——'

'Not up for discussion,' he inserted, straightening from the desk to begin walking towards her, his tortoiseshell comb held out once again. 'I do not trust you, Marnie, to keep your part of our bargain,' he informed her bluntly. 'And, since my part has already been attended to while you were out of the room, I feel the need of some assurance that you will not cheat me. Here, take the comb.' He thrust it at her, and Marnie took it simply because he gave her no choice.

'But this is ridiculous!' she choked. 'Guy, I have no intention of cheating you! Stop being so childish and hand over my bag,' she demanded. 'There are other things I need from it beside a damned comb!'

'A lipstick, perhaps? I prefer your mouth exactly as it is, soft and pulsing with its own natural colour.' Arrogantly he reached up to rub the pad of his thumb against her bottom lip, and instantly the blood began to pump into the sensitive flesh, filling it out and bringing a blaze of fury to her eyes as she angrily slapped him away. 'Or maybe you want your neat stack of credit cards,' he continued unperturbed. 'Or the wallet of paper money which would easily get you a ride out of here.'

'But I have no intention of going anywhere!' she cried in exasperation.

'And I have no intention of giving you the chance,' he agreed. 'So drop the outrage,' he ordered coolly. 'You know me well enough to know that I always learn by my mistakes. Disappearing is something you do too well for my peace of mind. So I have taken the necessary precautions to make sure you cannot.'

Wilting on a wave of defeat, she sank down on to the cushioned arm of the sofa and sighed, his last remarks cooling her temper more than anything else could have done. Four years ago he had trusted her to stay put in Berkshire where he had left her, stupidly believing the move from London to his country home was a sensible way of giving her time to get over her understandable aversion to him. She stayed put only long enough to watch him drive away, then, while his father had believed her safely ensconced in her room, she had left, taking nothing with her but the clothes she stood up in and her bag containing enough money to get her as far away from Guy's influence as she could get.

She had ended up in a tiny village in the Fens, where she had succeeded in hiding herself away for six long, wretched months before she'd felt fit to face the world—and Guy again.

No, she conceded heavily, Guy was not a man to make the same mistake twice. There was no way he would give her the opportunity to repeat that particular trick.

A knock at the outer suite door broke the sudden heavy silence throbbing in the air between them. Guy hesitated, looking as if he was going to say something, then sighed and turned away, walking with a smooth animal grace out of the room.

He came back wheeling a dinner-trolley in front of him, his expression hooded as he glanced across to where Marnie still sat, staring blankly at some indefinable spot on the carpet.

'Come and eat,' he said gruffly.

Marnie gave a small shake of her head in an effort to re-focus her thoughts, then came to her feet. 'I want to tidy my hair first,' she said, and left the room before Guy could glimpse the pain her short flight into the past had put into her eyes.

Five minutes later, her hair and her composure restored to something closer to their usual smoothness, she turned her attention for the first time on the room she was standing in, and forced herself to consider what Guy's intentions regarding their sleeping arrangements would be. The room was furnished in classical tones: Wedgwood blue and neutral beige, the big double bed the one piece of furniture which dominated the room.

Signs—unnervingly familiar signs—of Guy's habitation of the room were scattered about. His black silk robe, thrown negligently over a chair. A white shirt he must have discarded for a clean one before coming to meet her at the airport tossed upon the bed. And a stack of small change, thrown negligently on to the bedside table and forgotten about as had always been his way. He held a real contempt of the sound of small change jingling in his pocket and tended to discard it the first chance he could get, so she would save it all up in a big coffee-jar, then carefully count it out and bag it before taking it to her favourite charity, more respectful of money, having never been used to having it, than he would ever be. It had amused him, to watch her hoarding his cast-off money like that, and she had glared defiantly at him. 'You can stand there and laugh,' she'd snapped once. 'But do you realise that you've managed to discard one hundred and ninety-five pounds in small change this month? It's a good job the Salvation Army aren't so picky,' she'd grumbled. 'They're not too proud to have it jingle in their pockets!'

'So, they should be grateful that I dislike it jingling in mine so much,' dismissed a man who refused to be anything but amused at her contempt.

Marnie smiled to herself, going over to sift with an idle finger through the small heap. Five pound coins at a glance, she gauged ruefully. Shame she wasn't around any longer to bag it for the Salvation Army.

But she was around, she remembered on a small shiver. Back in Guy's orbit and destined to stay this time. Her stomach knotted, catching at her breath as she turned to scan the elegant room.

Would he expect her to sleep here with him tonight? Her gaze settled on his dark silk robe, and almost instantly she conjured up a vision of him throwing it there, his body smooth and tight and disturbingly graceful in its nakedness. No pyjamas to be seen. She knew without having to look that she could turn this room upside-down without finding any. Guy never wore anything in bed. 'Except you,' he'd grinned once when she had dared ask the question. 'You are all I need to keep me warm.'

God. Her chest lifted and fell on a thickened heave of air. She just couldn't do it—couldn't! Not just calmly go to bed with him tonight as if nothing untoward had occurred in the last four years!

Shifting jerkily, she sent that damning bed one last pensive glance before she walked out of the room and stood, hovering in the hallway, small teeth pressing down on her trembling bottom lip as she glanced at the other couple of doors which led off from here.

More bedrooms? Her heart thudded with hope, and she stepped over to open the one next to Guy's, almost wilting in relief when she saw it was indeed another bedroom.

Perhaps, she mused thoughtfully as she quietly closed the door again, if she played it very carefully, this would be the room she'd sleep in tonight—alone. She knew Guy, knew his strengths and his weaknesses. With a little clever manipulation on her part, she should be able to swing things to suit herself.

'What are you doing?' His voice made her jump, and swing around to find him standing in the sitting-room doorway.

'Checking out my prision,' she countered. 'Why, have you some objection to my doing that as well?' Her tone was a challenge as well as a defiance to his power over her.

'No, no objection,' he assured, leaning his shoulder against the open door and thrusting his hands into his pockets as he studied her narrowly. 'So, what have you discovered—besides the fact that I have no "little fancy piece" hidden away in one of the other rooms?' he mocked.

The thought having never entered her head, Marnie was instantly on the attack at being reminded of his— habit of travelling nowhere without the necessary woman in tow.

'So, where is she, then?' she demanded. 'Perhaps occupying the suite next door?'

'Wherever she is, she will sleep alone tonight.' His dismissive shrug was both lazy and indifferent, but his eyes held a promise that left Marnie in no doubt why this faceless creature would be alone.

Quelling the urge to tell him that he too was in for a disappointment, she kept balefully silent instead.

He wasn't sure what was going on behind the look, but experience warned him that something was, and he continued to study her narrowly for a few tense seconds before letting out a dry little sigh and levering himself away from the door.

'Dinner's getting cold,' he murmured.

'Is it?' she said. 'Then we'd better go and eat it, hadn't we?' And in a complete turnabout of mood she sent him a bright smile as she walked past him. 'What did you order?' she asked as she went over to the heated serving trolley to begin lifting covers curiously. 'Mmm,' she drooled, 'is that freshwater bream? Oh, you darling, Guy, I haven't eaten freshwater bream in years! Fancy you remembering how much I love it! What's for starters?' she asked eagerly, lifting covers and peering inside with an outward ignorance of the frowning suspicion written on his face. 'Melon. Great!' She sat herself down at the table. 'If there is one thing for which I could never fault you, Guy,' she enthused, 'it was your unerring ability to always know exactly what to order for me.'

With a flick of her freshly combed hair, she sent him a wide, warm smile, wanting to laugh at his comical expression. Guy had always had difficulty following her quickfire changes of mood. He had never been certain of what she was really thinking or feeling at any one time. The fifteen years that separated their ages had their advantages on both sides, and for Marnie it meant she was like a completely new species of woman to a man of his sophistication. It had always puzzled her as to why he should turn his practised eye on someone so young and obviously unsophisticated as herself. In the end she had decided it must be the Italian in him, demanding an untouched woman for his wife, and finding innocent virgins of a more mature and sophisticated age was well nigh an impossibility these days. So once she had decided that her innocence was her only attraction she had gone into emotional hiding, treating him to a clever blend of light-hearted affection and flirtatious mockery that kept him constantly unsure of her.

Marnie had never considered herself a fool. Her mother had died when she was only sixteen, leaving her and Jamie to cope alone in the big bad world outside. But, although Jamie was several years older than Marnie, he had never been a strength for her to rely on, and she had had to learn quickly to fend for herself. Sheer guts and determination had taken her through her final few years at school and on to art college. She had paid her own way by working seven nights a week as a waitress in a wine-bar, learning very early on how to deflect any male interest in her without once feeling the urge to experiment with what they were offering her. She was willing to paint anything and everything that brought her a fee for doing it, and by the time she was in her second college year had already built a reputation for herself as an artist—nothing spectacular, but good enough to have the small commissions coming in on a regular basis. By her twentieth birthday she had had her own small flat, run her own small car—with a lot of nursing from her brother—and had already found it necessary to resign from college so she could meet her growing commitments, her career seeming to create itself out of nothing for her.

No. Nobody's fool but Guy's, she concluded. Falling in love with him had to go down as the biggest piece of folly she had ever committed in her short, busy life! Not that she had ever let him know how completely he had beguiled her. And anyway, she had fought it, fought her feelings all the way through their short, hot, volcanic courtship and right into their equally short, hot and volcanic marriage.

She'd decided that he wanted a virgin for a wife and a woman he had trained to his own personal sexual satisfaction in his bed, which was exactly what he got—and nothing else. While she got—well, what

she deserved, she wryly supposed. A man who gave
her everything from fine clothes and fast cars to long,
hot, passionate nights that left her replete but spent,
having had to fight the urge to tell him just how
wretchedly she loved him.

But that was a long time ago, she concluded as she
glanced up to catch him still watching her narrowly
and smiled a bright, false, capricious smile which
made his own mouth turn down into a scowl. Now,
even the love was dead, choked out of her by his own
uncaring hands, and all that was really left between
them was a bitter enmity mutually felt, and a refusal
on his part to let go of something he considered his
property.

On a mental shrug, she turned her attention to the
dinner-trolley, intending to serve up the melon Guy
had ordered as a first course, but his hand, coming
tightly around her slender wrist, brought her attention sharply back to him. He was glaring at her,
his dark brown eyes brooding and intent.

'I cannot pretend to know what was just going on
behind that false smile of yours, Marnie, but I do
warn you, most sincerely, to take care.'

The warning shivered through her. She might pride
herself on being no one's fool, but neither was Guy.
'All I want to do is eat my dinner,' she said. 'You did
promise me dinner and a bed, didn't you? So let me
eat, then find the bed.'

'My bed,' he agreed with grim satisfaction, letting
go of her wrist and sitting back in his chair, relaxing
because he believed she'd walked herself right into that
trap when really it was she doing the trapping.

'My own bed,' she corrected, placing large spoonfuls of the beautifully prepared melon into two dishes before passing one to him. 'I'll be sleeping alone tonight and every night until we are married again,' she flatly informed him.

'You'll sleep where I tell you to sleep, when I let you sleep,' he countered, just as flatly.

Marnie turned her attention to the melon, taking a small square into her mouth and murmuring at the sweetly delicious taste. 'This is very good,' she announced. 'Try it. It has something added to it that gives it a fantastic tangy flavour.'

He ignored her. 'We have a bargain, Marnie,' he reminded her. 'I dig your brother out of his mess and you——'

'Which reminds me,' she cut in on him. 'I must give Jamie a ring and let him know he can stop worrying. I'd forgotten all about him, poor thing.'

'There is no need for you to speak to Jamie,' Guy interrupted her drifting thoughts, 'because I have already done so.'

'Oh.' She glanced ruefully at him. 'I hope you didn't rip him into shreds—he's frightened enough of you as it is.'

'It seems a pity that his sister does not possess the same healthy instinct,' he muttered.

'If you'd wanted a simpering idiot for a wife, Guy,' she mocked, 'then you would not have looked twice at me.'

'True.' He smiled, relaxing enough at last to begin enjoying his melon. 'It has always been a big regret of mine that I did not take my own advice on that first day we met, and just turn tail and run in the other direction before I did take that—fatal second look.'

His eyes gleamed at her and Marnie grimaced, knowing exactly what he meant. Until he had met her, Guy had been used to women simpering all over him. He had been used to them sending out promises to him with their eyes, using every sexual lure in the book to attract his attention. He could handle all that by either responding or ignoring it depending on his mood. Marnie, by contrast, had never gone out of her way to attract him—and if anything had done everything she could to freeze him out. Guy had done all the running, all the careful luring—until the days and weeks of patient but fruitless persuasion eventually turned him into a quick-tempered and very frustrated man while Marnie, though half out of her mind in love with him, had continued to hold herself aloof, pretending to even be a little amused by his attention.

The bream was all it promised to be, and they managed to finish their meal in a companionable manner, both deliberately keeping the conversation light after that. The new mood suited Marnie. Having planted the seed of doubt about their sleeping arrangements tonight, she was quite happy to let that seed take root before she tackled the problem again. She wasn't worried; she knew she could win this one. Guy was an honourable man in his own way, and it was to that honour she was going to plead.

So it was gone ten o'clock before they both sat back in their seats and away from their empty coffee-cups, and Marnie stretched into a tired yawn which announced that she was more than ready for bed. 'Can

I borrow one of your shirts to sleep in?' she asked, getting to her feet.

Guy rose more slowly, the relaxed mood they'd managed to maintain throughout the meal shot to death. 'You will need no shirt to keep you warm tonight, Marnie,' he informed her smoothly, 'for I will be right beside you to ensure you do not catch a chill.'

Marnie paused in her movement away from the dining-table and took her time turning back to face him with a look of grave contemplation. 'You know, Guy,' she said quietly, 'for all that has gone between us—and some of it I accept has not been particularly nice—I have never once doubted that you respected me deeply as a person.'

The remark took him completely by surprise, sending him erect in a way that said she'd activated his enormous banks of pride. 'Which I do,' he immediately confirmed.

'And before we were married the last time—and no matter how—passionately you desired me, you always managed to demonstrate that respect by drawing back before you became too—carried away.'

He nodded curtly. 'You are referring, no doubt, to the fact that I wished my bride to come to me innocent on our wedding night.'

'Quite,' she agreed, unexpectedly touched by the degree of reverence he'd placed in that statement. 'You do know, don't you, Guy,' she went on, holding his gaze steady with her own, 'that there has been no other man but you in my life?'

His eyes blazed with a pride and a triumph he could not contain. 'I accept that—totally.' His trust in her was unequivocal—another fact which unexpectedly warmed her. 'It—it has always humbled me, Marnie,' he murmured huskily, 'that you can be so pure of heart and body when I know the depth of the passion which runs in your veins. Are you afraid that I may hurt you?' he asked suddenly, completely misunderstanding the point she was trying to make. He came around the table to take her shoulders in a gentle reassuring grip. 'I am very aware of the length of time it has been since we made love with each other, Marnie. And I am hungry for you—quite desperate in fact to feel your body warm and responsive beneath my own again, but my loving will be as gentle as it was the first time I took you as my own. You have nothing to fear from me.'

'No—you've...'

Misunderstood, she had been about to say. But his mouth was drowning out the telling word before it reached her lips, and nothing, nothing in all her careful planning prepared her for the kind of kiss he offered her, though perhaps his words should have done as he began to kiss her with such exquisite sweetness that she felt herself being hurled back across five long years to that moment on their wedding night when Guy had taken her in his arms as his wife.

And Marnie, with that memory filling her mind, responded, her mouth clinging to his while she tried desperately to untangle the past from the present, tried to remember why she was here and who she was with and what he would do to her if she so much as lowered her defences an inch. But the kiss was special, tender, loving, offering promises she'd once yearned for with all her heart. And as he gently urged her closer to the hard-packed, powerful wall of his chest she let herself relax, let her arms creep hungrily around his neck, let her lips part and their tongues meet and the heady, hot tide of desire wash languidly over her.

'Marnie,' he whispered against her clinging mouth. 'Sweet—sweet heaven.'

Then he brought her tumbling back down to a horrified sense of what was actually happening as he bent to lift her into his arms.

'No——!' she cried, twisting away from him before he'd managed to do more than flex his muscles in readiness to lift her.

He staggered slightly at her sudden escape, and Marnie found herself standing, swaying dizzily barely a foot away from him, breathing hectically, her eyes dark and glowing with a crazy mixture of self-aimed fury and deep disturbing sensuality.

'What do you mean, no?' he demanded in husky-voiced bewilderment.

Marnie swallowed, having to fight for breath before she could answer. 'I w-won't be seduced into your bed, Guy,' she whispered.

'And why not?' he demanded arrogantly. 'It was a mutual seduction, Marnie. I was being beautifully seduced also.'

Her cheeks coloured then went pale because she knew he was telling the truth. She had lost all control of herself for a moment there, had been more than matching him kiss for hungry, seductive kiss.

'You're used to it. I'm not.'

He stiffened. 'What is that supposed to mean?' he demanded.

'It means,' she said, outwardly beginning to pull herself back together, although inside she was a quivering, shivering wreck, 'that I expect you to treat me with the respect you've just claimed you always had for me by allowing me to keep my body for my husband alone.'

Silence, as he stared at her with a slow dawning understanding that took the light of passion out of his eyes, to be replaced with a look of hard, cynical appreciation when he realised just how cleverly she had been manipulating him all evening. 'You truly are the most cruel and calculating bitch of my acquaintance,' he then said, quite casually.

Her chin came up, defiance masking the sudden twinge of remorse she experienced inside. 'I can't ever forgive you, Guy,' she told him flatly. 'And although I also can't deny that you—you can make me want you physically, I'll never let you touch my heart again.'

'When did you ever?' he drawled, and turned away from her, but not before she'd glimpsed the look of bitterness in his eyes. 'Go.' He waved a careless hand towards the sitting-room door. 'Go to your cold and lonely bed, Marnie,' he invited. 'Take your high-minded principles and your unforgiving heart with you, since they seem to be the kind of bed partners you prefer. But remember this,' he added as he turned back to face her grimly. 'We have made a bargain tonight. And I expect you to stick to your side of it as fully as I intend to stick to mine. The day we become man and wife again, Marnie,' he ordained, 'will also be the day you will accept me back into your bed, and I will expect both the principles and the unforgiving heart to step aside for me.'

'Then you expect too much,' she said, forcing herself to move towards the sitting-room door.

'And why do I?' he posed silkily. 'I always believed, Marnie, that one first had to care to hurt as badly as you profess to do.'

'I cared,' she said, spinning back to face him. 'Or why else did I marry you?'

His smile was both mocking and self-derisive. 'I thought we both knew the answer to that, my dear. Because I gave you no damned choice.'

CHAPTER FIVE

NO CHOICE. Well, of everything he'd said tonight, Guy
had been most right about that. If she had been given
any choice at all, she would never have let him talk
her into marrying him.

Bullied, Marnie corrected, and smiled bleakly into
the dark silence which shrouded her in her bed. From
the first moment he had ever set eyes on her Guy had
pursued, seduced and bullied her until eventually she
had wilted under the strain of it all and finally let him
marry her.

Sighing, she turned on to her side to gaze sleep-
lessly out on to the clear navy blue sky beyond her
bedroom window.

The first time she'd seen Guy, she had fancifully
believed herself to have stumbled across some noble
throwback from the last century.

He reminded her of the wicked baron portrayed in
so many hot romantic novels. Big, dark and
dangerous, with just enough charm to make the
cynicism etched into his handsome face bearable. And
more than enough sex appeal to make her heart quiver
with a fatal mixture of excitement and alarm.

Of course, she'd known exactly who Jamie worked
for that day she had decided on the spur of the
moment to make a flying visit to her brother, but she
hadn't for one moment expected actually to meet the
man himself. What she knew about Guy Frabosa had

been learned from newspaper and magazine articles—most of them painting a picture of a man who lived and slept with his ego. But they also presented a man who spent most of his busy life jetting around the world keeping the family empire running smoothly, and so she had driven through the tall wrought-iron gates of Oaklands expecting to see nothing more than her oil-smeared brother in his element, working on one of the many high-performance cars in Guy Frabosa's collection which he helped maintain, then leave again, completely untouched by the personality of the man who paid her brother's wages.

Coming upon Oaklands itself, nestling in its own small private valley, had been an artist's delight. And as she'd driven down the gently rolling hillside into the basin of the valley itself and cut across a wide stretch of tarmac roadway towards the elegant cream-painted Georgian mansion house she could see in the distance, it had never occurred to her that she had just driven over Guy Frabosa's own personal racing track, or that it circumvented the whole estate, built by professionals for a professional to practise upon. Her concentration then had been too enthralled by the beauty of the gardens she had been passing through.

I could sit and paint this forever, she recalled thinking as she brought the car to a stop in the circular courtyard in front of the house and climbed out of her battered old Mini to absorb the wonderful air of peace and tranquillity around her. The air smelled fresh and country-clean, weighed down with the heady scent of roses—roses she had not known then were Roberto Frabosa's pride and joy.

It was the distinctive throaty roar of a powerful engine revving that had told her in which direction to go looking for her brother, and she had followed the sound around the side of the house and along a pretty winding path through a narrow wood until she found herself standing on the edge of a courtyard that must once have been the stable-yard, but now housed the workshops and garages for Guy's impresive collection of cars.

And it was there, while she stood beneath the shelter of a spreading chestnut tree, that she had experienced her first shock sighting of the man she had later married...

He was standing like a Michelangelo's David among a clutch of Lowrie figures as his team of mechanics clustered around him, towering over them as he talked, his dark head thrown up at an arrogant angle while his mouth, firm and shockingly sensual, was stretched into a grin which completely belied the arrogance.

They were talking engines, of course, but then Marnie could only appreciate the sheer artistry of the scene—he, Guy, thrown into strong stomach-churning contrast, in his crisp white shirt and immaculate dark trousers, to the murky cluster of oil-stained-overalled men gathered about him.

A king with his minions, she titled the scene, already capturing it in oils in her mind. He spoke quickly but smoothly, the rich timbre of his voice, attractively spiced with an accent, reaching out to her across the cobbled courtyard to keep her held breathless and still.

Her experience of the opposite sex then was poor
to say the least; not finding the time to learn about
them had been the main culprit for her ignorance because she'd never seemed to have enough of it to spare
for the lighter side of living. But even she, wrapped
in the protection of her complete innocence, could
pick up danger signals when they were there.

'Marnie!' It was Jamie who saw her first. And she
just had time to see Guy's dark head turn sharply,
glimpse the sudden narrowing of his dark eyes, note
the tensing stillness of his body, before she dragged
her wide eyes away from him and forced them to rest
on her brother.

Jamie came over to her, so pleased to see her that
he was grinning from ear to ear. 'What are you doing
here?' he demanded in surprise.

She told him, trying desperately not to allow her
attention to wander over to where she knew Guy was
watching them with that same silent stillness he hadn't
even tried to snap out of since their eyes clashed.

'But this is great!' her brother exclaimed. 'Can you
stay long enough to have lunch with me? There's a
pub just down the road from here that puts on a great
ploughman's; we could——'

'Introduce me, Jamie.'

Just like that, she recalled. Introduce me. Make me
known. I want. Give me. Mine. It had all been there
in that one huskily voiced demand.

Not that her brother noticed any of that as he
happily complied, moving a step away from her to
leave her feeling oddly exposed and very vulnerable
to that hot dark stare. 'This is my sister, Marnie,'

Jamie announced. 'Marnie, meet my employer, Mr Frabosa.'

'Guy,' corrected the man himself, letting the true pronunciation of his name slide sensually off his tongue.

He lifted a long, tanned, beautifully constructed hand to her in invitation for her to take it. She did so nervously, trembling a little, a bit bewildered by what was happening to her churning insides, and shaken even more off balance when instead of the polite handshake she had been expecting he lifted her hand to his lips, his eyes refusing to break contact with the dense blueness of hers.

It had taken him just that long to make her fall head over heels in love with him—not that she'd understood what it was then. Because she was unawakened to her own sexuality and quite content to stay that way, that sudden overpowering burst of emotion had frightened her then—it still did now. But then she had been in no way equipped to deal with it, and the fact that he was making no effort to hide how powerfully she attracted him had the adverse effect of sending her scuttling off in the other direction. She snatched her hand away and took a jerky but very necessary step back from him, and he smiled at her in a way that mocked her small rejection.

He invited her to take tea in his home. She refused, reminding him coolly that it was her brother she had come here to see. When Guy then blandly informed her that Jamie would not be free from his duties until the evening and repeated the invitation while she waited for her brother to finish his work, she glanced ruefully at her brother, who was looking bemused at

Guy's announcement, and still refused to allow him to act host in her brother's absence, inventing a fictitious date waiting for her in London which brought Jamie's gaze swinging around to her in open-mouthed amazement, since he was well aware of her lack of interest in the kind of date she was implying. 'I can only stay five minutes at most,' she added hurriedly, wishing she had not given in to the sudden urge to come and see her brother.

Guy stared at her, bringing a guilty flush to her cheeks because the mockery in his gaze said he knew she was lying, and with a bow and a smile that did nothing to ease her anxious desire to get away from him he excused himself and strode off towards the front of the house while Jamie stared after him in frowning confusion.

'I don't understand any of that,' he gasped. 'Guy isn't usually so...'

'Five minutes, Western!' The curt warning had come from the disappearing figure of Guy Frabosa as he rounded the corner of the house.

'I don't understand that, either!' Jamie exclaimed. 'Why were you so cool with him, Marnie?' he demanded, deciding that the blame for it all had to belong to her. 'I thought it was very nice of him to welcome you like that—and you turn all icy on him—you've offended him now!'

'I came to see you, Jamie,' she reminded her brother coolly. 'Not to take tea with a man who is a complete stranger to me.'

He shrugged, still baffled by the whole odd encounter, and walked her back around the house to her car, chatting lightly, but she could tell he was jumpy,

eager to get back to work before Guy decided to come
down on him a second time. And she was more than
ready to get away before his boss disturbed her level
senses a second time. Jamie saw her seated behind the
wheel of her Mini, quizzing her on how it was running,
and smiling when she assured him the little car gave
her no trouble at all, her eyes skipping nervously along
the rows of windows in the house, somehow knowing
that Guy Frabosa was observing her departure from
the shadows somewhere inside.

She turned the key in the ignition, now quite desperate to get away.

Nothing happened. She tried again. Nothing.

After several tries, her brother muttered something
derogatory about stupid women flooding the engine,
and ordered her out so he could get in instead. He
messed, he fiddled, then climbed out and lifted the
bonnet, disappearing beneath it with all the concentration of a born mechanic while Marnie stood,
knowing, without knowing how she knew, that her
car had not let her down without help from
somewhere.

She watched Guy stroll out of the front door with
a fatalistic acceptance that must have shown on her
face, because he sent her a lazy mocking look as he
went to join her brother.

A small smile touched her lips as she lay now in her
bed with only the moon as witness. It was months
later before Guy had actually admitted to doctoring
her car.

'I was not prepared to let you go,' he had told her
with all the lazy arrogance of his nature.

'Did Jamie know it was your doing?' she'd demanded.

'Since it took him five hours to find the fault, I would have to presume that, on finding it, he must have guessed,' Guy had answered blandly. 'He is too good a mechanic not to have realised quite early on that the car had been tampered with. His problem was discovering just what it was I had done to it.'

'Sometimes, Guy, I hate your arrogance.'

'And sometimes, *cara*, you literally drown in it,' he'd growled, pulling her into his arms to prove his point. She had had no control whatsoever of the passion he could arouse in her. And even in the very early days of their relationship, when he was very aware of her inexperience, he had been able to turn her blood to fire with an ease that had both shocked and frightened her.

A fear that had kept her fighting him right through the turbulent weeks which had followed as Guy, true to the stubborn, selfish character he was, set himself out to take what he wanted.

And take he eventually had. Ruthlessly, passionately, unassailingly and with scant regard to whether or not it was what she wanted. Or maybe he did regard it but chose to dismiss it, she allowed. Because even Guy, thick-skinned as he was, had to know that although he had forced her to surrender physically to him he had never really managed to beat down her mental reserves towards him.

Sighing wearily, Marnie gave up trying to stop the memories from coming, and climbed out of bed to go and stand by the moonlit window.

Marriage to Guy had been no less fraught than their turbulent courtship. He'd decided on marriage, he'd informed her then, because he just could not bring himself to take her innocence without the legal right to do so. And she had been so damned weakened by his sensual assaults on her that she'd foolishly agreed.

So married they were, and he took her off to his native Italy where, in a secluded villa overlooking his own private piece of the Med, he taught her all there was to learn about the physical side of love. And he possessed her to such a devastating degree that he only had to look at her to make her want him. True to his nature, he had no inhibitions about the forms their lovemaking could take, and taught her to cast off any she might have wanted to hold on to. Her body became an instrument tuned like one of his precious cars to his own personal specification, and for six dizzy, passionate months they drifted through life in a haze of mutual engrossment where the only cloud cluttering their sensual haven was a distinct absence of any sincere words of love.

Guy seemed only to require the delight of her young and responsive body, while she—well, she just accepted what crumbs of himself he threw at her and kept a vital part of herself hidden away from him in readiness for the time when the novelty would die and he would begin looking about him for pastures new.

And why did she think it would come to that? Because she had seen the way he was around other women. Guy was a born egotist, forever needing to feed that ego through the constant adoration of any woman prepared to offer it to him.

She suspected that he didn't really see her as a living, breathing person with thoughts and feelings of her own but more like a new possession he liked to show off to his friends—like a mascot, kept for his own amusement. It never occurred to him that she wouldn't like his friends, that the constant vying for the centre of attention by both sexes and the suggestive remarks that were thrown about so freely actually shocked and embarrassed her.

Shy by nature, she was always rather quiet and withdrawn in company, and they felt no qualms about teasing her about her quietness, making her feel more uncomfortable in their company, showing her in their cruel, deriding way that she was not and never would be one of them.

On top of that, she had to grin and bear the sight of Guy enjoying the over-amorous advances of one or other of the many women who threw themselves at him. He was that kind of man: handsome, worldly, and full of a charisma that had been earned by the dangerous way he'd achieved his fame. Women adored him, and he took their adoration entirely as his due, and wasn't past encouraging it when the mood took him.

It was witnessing one of the more—obvious displays of adoration one night that decided Marnie that she'd had enough.

The party was being held by one of Guy's old racing cronies, in a big London town-house with several reception-rooms packed to bursting with people enjoying themselves in their brittle, sophisticated way. She had learned early on that there were no holds barred at these functions. Drink yourself silly if you wanted to, make passes at anyone you fancy—which did not count her out just because she was the great Guy Frabosa's wife! And it was even acceptable for some couples to disappear for a significant length of time during the evening, and not always with the person they'd arrived with! It forced her to wonder about the times she couldn't find Guy in the crush these parties always were; to wonder if he too was not averse to sneaking off for a quick tumble with some willing creature.

But that particular night, the crunch came for Marnie when it happened to be Anthea Cole who decided to drape herself around him from the moment they arrived, and not let go since. Anthea was the woman Marnie had usurped from Guy's bed. And to see her of all people hanging all over him, knowing that the other woman was as knowledgeable about Guy's lovemaking as she was herself, just about blew her usual cool as a hard, hot, ugly sting of jealousy ripped through her. Then, to top it all, seeing Guy busy with Anthea, Derek Fowler had the gall to chance his arm with Marnie! She slapped him down, coldly and precisely, leaving him in absolutely no doubt what she thought of him, then walked out of the party, leaving Guy to do as he pleased.

He was furious, of course. When he arrived back at the apartment he came storming into their bedroom where she was emerging from the adjoining bathroom after a long, hot, angry shower, rubbing at her wet hair with a towel.

'What the hell is the matter with you?' he snapped, slamming the door shut so hard that she winced.

'What the bloody hell were you trying to prove, walking out on me in front of my friends?'

'You call them friends?' she scoffed. 'I call them a bunch of ravenous wolves, existing for only one thing in life—sex!' she said in disgust. 'Wherever and however they can get it. And if they are your friends, then for God's sake don't count me as one of them; I don't think I could live with the taint of it!' She spun away from him, the towel rubbing furiously at her long wet hair.

'Someone has offended you,' he said, coming down from his own anger because he thought he could soothe away hers now he knew the reason for it.

'You could say that,' she snapped. '*You've* offended me. You offend me every time you take me to parties like that one we went to tonight.' She turned to view the look of surprise written on his hard, handsome face. 'You then consolidate the offence by just dropping me to go in search of your own pleasures in another woman's arms while expecting me to stand meekly by and await your wonderful return!'

'Anthea,' he said. 'You're angry because you're jealous of Anthea!'

He sounded so damned self-satisfied that Marnie actually did bare her nails and her teeth as she shouted, 'Anthea? What the hell is Anthea except for one in a long long line of Antheas who've been led to believe that you're open to anything they want to offer you? Well, not this woman any more!' Angrily, she threw the towel aside and walked threateningly towards him. 'Because this woman has more self-respect than to sleep with an ageing old stallion who sees his main function in life as putting himself out for stud!'

Oh, she shouldn't have said it. And even now, all these years later, she could still feel the clutch of remorse she'd felt then as she watched his face go pale, and his body jerk as if in reaction to a vicious blow.

And vicious it had been, because she'd known how sensitive Guy was to the difference in their ages. It was perhaps his one and only Achilles' heel, and she'd cruelly pierced it dead in the centre.

Of course, he went all cold and haughty on her. It was perhaps either that or seduce her senseless. She'd deserved both. But it was the haughtiness she got, and with such devastating impact that she could even find it in her to admire him for it now. Though not then—not then when he said coldly, 'Then, of course, you must sleep alone, my dear Marnie. While I, poor ageing stud that I am, will go out and find a less discerning creature to share my humble bed.'

Which he had, she recalled bitterly now. He left the apartment and did not come back for three days—by which time she had gone from remorse to resentment and from there to an angry defiance which had her accepting a commission which took her off to Manchester for a week.

She arrived back tired, miserable and so riddled with guilt for those terrible words she had thrown at him that she was quite prepared to go down on her knees and beg so long as he forgave her for them. It was late, and Guy was already in bed when she let herself quietly into their bedroom. She wasn't sure if he was awake, but she sensed that he was as she crossed to the bathroom and quickly showered before going and climbing into the bed beside him.

He didn't say a word, not a single word, but the way he reached for her was a message in itself, and they made love with a kind of wild desperation that shook them both. But if she had been secretly hoping he would reassure her about those other women then she was disappointed, and a new restraint entered their relationship, the strain that last row had placed between them always hovering in the tense air around them.

Nothing was really the same after that. They went to no more parties. That complaint at least had seemed to get through to him. But Guy treated her with a new kind of respect which verged on indifference, while she threw herself into her work, accepting commissions wherever they were offered which took her away from London for long days on end. And Guy had his own commitments to fulfil, flying off to all corners of the world, so they became more like strangers than husband and wife, meeting briefly in the darkness of their bedroom to slake a hunger that was all the more wretched because it was all they seemed to have.

The strain of it all became too much for Marnie, and a depression began to set in. She came back home after spending a miserable week in Kent to find the apartment empty because Guy was away somewhere in the wilds of Yorkshire. He was away a week, and by the time he came back she was feeling so low that he took one hard look at her pale, unhappy face and gathered her into his arms.

She thought he was after sex, and retaliated accordingly by pushing him angrily away. So he did his usual, and bit out some deriding words at her about what a mess she looked and how he was going out to find someone who knew how to keep her man. He didn't return that night. When he did, he looked as though he had just rolled out of someone's bed to come straight home.

They had another row—one which ended up with him bundling her into his car and taking her to Oaklands. Where he left her—to decide, he said, which was more important to her: her marriage or her work.

It was the first time he had challenged the amount of time she devoted to her work. And she read it clearly for what it was: an ultimatum. He wanted total devotion or nothing, and for the next week she seethed bitterly over the choice, wishing she could just up and leave him and knowing wretchedly that she could not. She loved him too much.

Then something happened to make the decision for her. And suddenly she was in a fever of excitement, racing back to London to see Guy.

She arrived at the apartment in time for dinner, but Guy wasn't there and Mrs Dukes, the housekeeper, said she had hardly seen him since Marnie went away. Casting aside the small sting of alarm she experienced, she set about ringing around in an effort to find him. Calling her brother was just a spur-of-the-moment idea. Guy had recently set Jamie up in his own small garage just outside London, and she knew he liked to call in and show an interest in whatever car Jamie was working on at the time.

'Have you tried Derek Fowler's house?' he suggested. 'There's some kind of big party going on there tonight, so I heard. Perhaps Guy has gone there.

You should keep a tighter rein on that man of yours, Marnie,' he then went on to admonish. 'Guy is too hot a property for you to let run around London as freely as he does. Women just can't keep their hands off him.'

But they will learn, she thought grimly as she set out for the party. From now on, all of them will learn that Guy Frabosa is well and truly taken!

She arrived at Derek Fowler's home to find the party in full swing. She and Derek Fowler had become cold antagonists since she'd slapped him down, so stepping over the threshold into his house took a certain amount of courage. But she was desperate to see Guy, and that was all that was in her mind as she squeezed a way through the crush of people to go in search of him, having no idea just what she was walking into.

It took just ten minutes to find out.

She found Derek Fowler first, flirting lazily with a slinky model type wearing a red silk dress and nothing else, by the look of it.

'Is Guy here?' she asked him coolly.

He turned slightly bloodshot eyes on her, and the lazy smile he had been wearing changed into a taunting leer. 'Well, well, well,' he drawled. 'If it isn't the child bride herself.'

'Is he here?' she repeated coldly, refusing to rise to the bait. Guy hated it when his friends referred to her in that way. He was sensitive enough about their age-difference without having 'cradle-snatcher' thrown at him.

'Upstairs, I think,' he informed her carelessly. 'Second door on the right, sleeping off the old plonko the last time I saw him...' Something else caught his attention then, sending his gaze narrowing over to the stairs, which were just visible through the crush of people spilling out into the hallway. When he looked back at Marnie there was a new vindictive light in his narrowed eyes. 'Why don't you go and wake the prince with a kiss?' he suggested silkily. 'You never know, Marnie, you might even get a nice surprise.'

Not understanding the taunt—and not even trying to—she turned away, struggling back through the crowds towards the hallway and from there up the stairs, sighing with relief at the respite from the noise and the crush of bodies on the floor below.

It was dark inside the room Derek had directed her to. She stepped inside and fumbled blindly for the light switch. 'Guy?' she called out softly. 'Guy, are you awake?'

Light flooded the room, and at the same cataclysmic moment that she heard the muffled murmur of her name Marnie stood frozen by the horror of what she was being forced to recognise as Guy's beautiful body lying naked in a tumble of white bedding, with the lovely Anthea coiled intimately around him—as naked as he.

CHAPTER SIX

'CAN'T you sleep?' a quiet voice enquired behind her. Marnie started violently, spinning around too quickly to mask the pain her memories had laid naked on her face. Guy saw the look, knew its source, and his own expression closed in grim response to it.

He was leaning against the open doorway, dark hair ruffled by restless fingers as if he too had been having a struggle with sleep. And for once he looked his age, harsh lines pulling at his lean features, scoring deep grooves down the sides of his nose and the taut turned-down corners of his mouth.

Older, but still the same potently sexual man who drew the opposite sex to him like bees to honey, she acknowledged bleakly as her eyes made a swift sweep of his tightly muscled body covered only by the short black robe before looking quickly away. He could still stir her senses just by being in the same room, and she hated herself for it—hated herself.

'My shirt looks better on you than it does on me,' he murmured huskily. 'But then, they always did.'

Her body began to tingle in instant response to the lazy way he ran his eyes over the fine silk shirt she had taken from his room before retiring, sending her arms wrapping around her body as the tingle centred itself in the very tips of her sensitive nipples.

'What do you want, Guy?' she demanded stiffly.

'You,' he answered without hesitation. 'But since that is nothing new to either of us,' he added drily, 'and since we both seem unable to sleep tonight, I wondered if you would like to share a pot of tea with me?'

'Tea?' Sheer surprise diverted her away from the provocation in the earlier remark. 'Since when have you been drinking tea?'

Guy had always shown a scathing contempt for the English love of the beverage. He liked coffee, strong and black and sugarless.

'Actually——' an oddly sheepish smile took the harshness out of his features '—I was going to treat myself to a brandy. The suggestion of tea was an afterthought—offered as an incentive for you to join me. Will you?'

Slowly, tentatively almost, his hand came out in front of him. Marnie stared unblinkingly at it for a moment. A long, strong, capable hand, a hand she knew so intimately that it was like an extension of her own self. A hand which seemed to be offering more than just an invitation to join him.

Her glance flicked warily to his face, but found nothing to mistrust written there, just a wry twist of a smile that said he was quite ready for her usual rebuttal.

'Well . . . ?' he murmured softly.

'Yes,' she heard herself say. 'Yes, I'd like that.' Why, she had no idea, except maybe she found suddenly that she didn't want to be alone, and even Guy's company was better than the kind of cold company her black thoughts had been to her.

Easing himself away from the door as she drew near, he let her brush by him before falling into step behind her. The door to his own bedroom stood open, the soft glow from his bedside lamp illuminating the stacks of papers littered about his untidy bed telling their own story.

'You know me, Marnie,' he murmured. 'I need little sleep.'

No, four hours a night was just about his limit, she recalled. As to the rest of the hours of darkness— well, Guy had had his own method of amusing himself, a method that was best not dwelt upon right now.

She curled herself up in the corner of the sofa while he prepared the tea. He wasn't such a chauvinist that he'd ever minded taking on such a menial task. In fact, Marnie could recall several times when he had wandered into her studio in their London apartment with a tea-tray in his hands.

'Drink it,' he had used to command; peer over her shoulder at whatever she was working on, give no opinion whatsoever, brush a light kiss across the exposed nape of her neck, then walk out again, whistling quietly to himself.

They'd been married for several months before it had dawned on her that he only used the tea as an excuse to enter what was essentially her domain. If she turned and smiled at him he used to grin and pull her into his arms for a good long kiss before walking out again. If she ignored him, she used to receive that peck on the neck before he wandered out, whistling. But he never tried to break her concentration.

'Why?' she asked him once.

'You have two great passions in your life, Marnie,' he said. 'One is your work and the other is me. When you are working, your art takes precedence. I am man enough to accept second place on those occasions so long as, once your work is done, I then fill your world.'

It was a shame he had not applied the same philosophy to himself.

'Here.' He offered her a cup and saucer.

'Thank you.' She took it from him, then watched as he took his brandy glass and threw himself down in the chair opposite her, his weariness showing in the long sigh he gave as he stretched himself out, long tanned legs with their liberal covering of crisp dark hair extending beyond the black silk covering of his brief robe.

Marnie swallowed drily, lowering her eyes to the steaming brew in her cup. Looking at him hurt. It always had, even when they'd been supposedly happy. He was that kind of man, painfully, heartbreakingly beautiful.

'How is your father?' she enquired, as a direct snub to the kind of thinking she had been about to indulge in.

'Resigned to using a walking stick, at last.' Guy grimaced. Roberto, like his son, had his fair share of pride. When a slight stroke had left a stiffness down one side of his body, he had not taken kindly to the idea of using a stick to get about. 'He has a different stick for all occasions now,' he added drily. 'Your doing, I suspect.' There was a half-question in his mocking gaze.

Marnie smiled. 'I just happened to mention to him—in passing, you know—how interesting a man of his good looks and charm could look sporting a walking stick.'

'You mean you pandered to his ego.'

'The Italian in him,' she corrected. 'Goodness, but you Latin types place so much importance on your outward appearance,' she complained. 'I don't think there is a race of people more egotistical, arrogant, proud——'

'It was all of those things which attracted you to me once,' Guy mildly pointed out.

She ignored the remark. 'I thought,' she went on consideringly instead, 'that since I have to be in Berkshire myself next week I might call in to see him on my way. I could perhaps beg dinner and a bed for the night, then I can spend the whole evening flattering him a little before I need to be on my way.'

'We shall certainly be going to Oaklands,' Guy murmured slowly, watching her through hooded eyes. 'But, as to anything you have planned in Berkshire, I am afraid you will have to cancel it.'

Marnie uncurled her legs from beneath her, alarm skittering along her spine. 'What do you mean?' she demanded sharply.

Guy yawned lazily. 'Exactly what you think I meant,' he said, getting up to pour himself another drink. 'As from tonight, you became my property again—which means you'll be taking no more commissions which take you away from home.'

'I won't give up my work for you, Guy!' she stated sharply.

'You will do exactly as I say,' he informed her, quite casually, as though the subject did not warrant him raising his voice to it. 'Accept, Marnie—just as my father has had to accept his walking stick—that you are mine again, and in so being your commitments to me will override any others you may have already made.'

'Not my work.' She shook her head adamantly. 'I will not give up my work and—dammit, Guy, but you can't make me!'

'I can,' he assured her, 'and I intend to.'

The sardonic raising of his brows brought her climbing furiously to her feet. 'But y-you let me continue working the last time we were together!' she choked. 'I——'

'Just one of the mistakes I made in our marriage,' he declared. 'One which will be corrected this time around.'

Struggling to maintain a grasp on her sanity, Marnie tried to be reasonable. In all honesty, she had not expected this. Of all the other horrors she had forced herself to think about concerning the situation, this was one she had not even so much as considered!

'But—my work is my life!' she cried. 'You know it is! You can't just——'

'I can do whatever I please,' he cut in with infuriating calm. 'One of the most fundamental errors I made when dealing with you before, Marnie, was——'

'Sleeping around!' she snapped out bitterly.

His curt nod was an acknowledgment of a direct hit, but barely rattled his composure. 'Was allowing you,' he went on regardless of her outburst, 'too much of your own way. I let you roam about the countryside like a gypsy with hardly a complaint. I let you choose which friends I could keep and which I had to discard. I . . .'

'You didn't discard Anthea, I made painful note!'

'I let you, Marnie,' he continued grimly, 'run my life to such an extent that I began to lose my own identity!'

'*You* lost *your* identity?' she scoffed out scornfully. 'What do you think our marriage did for me? I became Guy Frabosa's woman! The silly child-bride who was as naïve as she was blind!'

'But that is just the point,' Guy put in silkily. 'You are no longer a child, Marnie. Remember that, because I don't intend to treat you as one. This time you will be a proper wife to me—a full-time wife! The kind of wife every man who is honest with himself wants in a marriage, which is the old-fashioned, home-loving, child-bearing kind!'

Her face drained of colour, the uncaring arrogance of his words hurting her in a way Guy would never know. 'God, how I hate you!' she whispered, teeth clenched and chattering in the bloodless tension in her face.

'And what a passionate hatred it is,' he derided. 'For if I touched you now, Marnie, while you *hate* so spectacularly, you would go up in flames, and you know it!' With a condemning flick of his black gaze he glanced down her quivering body, missing nothing, not the hectic heave of her breasts or the damning evidence of her nipples pushing hard and tight against the fine white silk covering of his shirt. 'Your body yearns for mine,' he accused condemningly. 'That is why you fight so hard against your own desires, Marnie: because you want me. Want me so badly that it was a relief to you when your brother gave you the opportunity to place yourself at my mercy!'

'That's a lie!' she rasped. 'I despise the very thought of you so much as touching me!'

'Is that so?' he murmured silkily, lifting his hand towards her in a way that had her shrinking shakily back from him.

'No decent woman would ever want you, Guy,' she threw at him contemptuously. 'Not one who has seen with her own eyes how freely you put yourself about!'

'You only saw what you think you saw!' he snapped, angry suddenly because the argument had taken a turn he had much rather it hadn't. 'But that period in our lives is no longer up for discussion,' he then stated grimly. 'I have tried too many times to make you listen while I explained it all to you; now I find I no longer want to. What has gone before today, Marnie, is now dead and gone, and must now be forgotten, because what follows in its wake will begin with a new set of rules which will leave no room for further dissension, on either side.'

Dead, gone, forgotten. Those three words echoed hollowly in her mind, bringing her swooping down from anger into weariness far more successfully than any attempt at subjugation on Guy's part.

'Let me continue working,' she requested. If he would just concede this one point to her, then perhaps, she hoped, she could manage to put the rest aside as he wanted her to do. 'The only thing I'll ask of you, Guy!' she pleaded when she saw the uncompromising set of his jaw. 'The rest I—promise to abide by, so long as I can at least have my work!'

'No compromises this time. I'm sorry.' He sounded it too, his tone rough but firm. 'But your work got in the way of us ever having a chance of making a success of our marriage the first time around. This time it has to be different.'

'And your other women?' she demanded. 'Do they stop also?'

'Do you want them to?' he enquired smoothly.

God. She closed her eyes, swallowing on the bank of bitterness lying like acid in her throat. 'Do what you want,' she sighed, turning towards the door. 'I find I don't give a damn!'

'Then why all this fuss?' he demanded. 'For someone who professes not to care at all, Marnie, you are giving a remarkable show of caring—perhaps too much?'

There was enough truth in that final taunt to sting her into spinning back to face him. 'I will always despise you for forcing me into accepting you back like this! Is that what you want?' she asked. 'A woman— a wife who will resent every moment she has to spend in your arms? Is the price *you're* going to pay for having me back in your life really worth the satisfaction you think you'll feel at managing it?'

'I know it will be,' he said, taking the single stride which brought his body hard up against her own. She took a jerky step back, and found her back pressed hard against the solid wood of the door.

'Let go of me,' she muttered, trying to push his hands away. 'Your touch makes my skin crawl!'

Guy smiled. 'Crawl with what, I wonder?' he murmured, placing his hands on her waist and crushing the fine silk fabric of his shirt against her naked flesh.

She began to tremble, tremble so badly that she could barely breathe. 'No,' she groaned as he began to lower his mouth to hers.

'No?' he taunted. 'Are you very sure of that?'

His mouth landed, splitting her sanity into a million atoms of pure sensation. He began slowly drawing the silk up her body, drawing her deeper and deeper into the kiss as he slowly—agonisingly almost—exposed the bottom half of her body then pressed the thrusting heat of his own against her. Her senses responded instantly, making her squirm in an effort to combat the flood of sensual delight that ran through her.

She felt drenched in her own desire; her mouth opened, parting to allow him to deepen the kiss. His hands reached the undercurve of her breasts, the silk bunched up beneath them, and on a smooth sensual movement he slid his fingers beneath to cup and lift her before knowingly brushing his thumbs across the waiting points of her nipples.

She moaned, moving instinctively against him, her hands dragging tensely up the sides of his lean body to clutch at the bunched muscles of his shoulder-blades. 'Stop it,' she gasped.

He ignored her. Her fingers clenched, then gripped hard, digging into the taut flesh beneath them as she fought the rage of feeling she was suffering inside. 'Why don't you just stop trying to fight me, Marnie?' Guy murmured seductively. 'You know you want to.'

'No——'

'Yes!' he insisted, and parted her lips with the sensual force of his own. It was a kiss like no other. Hungry, passionate, charged with an angry urgency that sent her senses spinning out of control. Hazily, she tried to stop herself responding. But it was too late; their tongues met in a wild tangling that set them both breathing harshly.

His hands moved, but before she had a chance to groan out in protest at losing their electric caress to her breasts they were sliding sensually down her body to cup possessively at her buttocks, and it was only as he thrust his lower body towards her that she realised he had untied his robe, and she stopped breathing altogether as he pushed the throbbing fullness of his manhood between her trembling thighs.

'God in heaven,' he breathed, dragging his mouth from hers so he could bury it in her throat.

Her face was pushed against the thick mat of crisp dark hair on his chest. She tried to pull herself together, sucking in deep gulps of air, but the thundering sound of his heartbeat against her parted mouth seemed to overwhelm everything. They were almost one. Their bodies melded so closely together that she felt drunk and dizzy with the pleasure of it. His fingers were tense and restless, kneading her tender flesh while her own had somehow found their way over his shoulders and were clinging to the muscled tautness of his neck.

He moved against her, just once, shuddered violently and stopped, his breathing so harsh that she realised just how close he was to losing complete control.

'Guy,' she whispered desperately, not really sure what she was pleading for.

'Give me back my promise, Marnie,' he pleaded huskily against her throat. 'I need to be inside you.'

Oh, God. She closed her eyes. This should not be happening. She should not be allowing this to happen! It was lust, she told herself madly. Sheer uncontrollable lust. The last time she had seen him this aroused, it had been in the arms of another woman.

'No——!' From somewhere she found the strength to push him away, sending him staggering backwards in surprise while she turned, trembling badly, to press her face into the door.

'Why not?' he rasped, his voice so raw she barely recognised it. 'You want me! You can no longer go on pretending you do not!'

'And for that I hate myself,' she confessed wretchedly. She spun round, eyes bright with pain and unshed tears. 'Can you even begin to know what it feels like to want a man you've seen with your own eyes beneath the naked body of another woman?'

Guy blanched, his hand coming up between them in abject appeal. 'No! Marnie, it——'

But she reeled away from him, her arms once more hugging herself protectively. 'No,' she choked, cutting him off before he could even begin the explanation she heard hovering on his tongue. 'Nothing—nothing can ever dismiss that vision from my mind, Guy. Nothing, do you understand?'

On a choking sob, she turned and fled from the room, taking that final bitter vision with her.

She could still replay, with vivid accuracy, that dreadful night she had found him in bed with Anthea.

He had not been long behind her in returning to their apartment, but finding her locked behind her studio door and refusing to answer his plea for her to open the door had driven him to kicking it down.

'Will you let me explain?' he had rasped, coming swaying to a halt as the solid wood door with its freshly splintered lock landed with a resounding crash against the wall behind it. 'It was not what you think!'

It was probably the only time she had ever seen him looking anything but immaculate. His clothes, hastily pulled on, hung about him. Shirt half fastened, trousers creased and beltless. Wherever his jacket had been, it had not been on his back. Face white and drawn, eyes wild, and his hair, that head of silky black hair, a crumpled mess—made that way by Anthea's fingers.

The memory of all of that still had the ability to crush her inside. A living nightmare four years on.

Her refusal to so much as look at him, never mind listen to him, had him dragging her against his violently shaking frame. 'Marnie,' he'd pleaded hoarsely. 'You have to listen to me!'

The stench of whisky had been strong, mingling with a cloying perfume that made her gag, his touch so repulsive to her that she had had to wrench herself free and run into the bathroom, where she was violently sick while Guy had stood, leaning heavily against the door-frame, watching her suffer with a look of hell in his eyes.

'I was drunk,' he'd said. 'I had been drinking steadily all day. I arrived at the party already slewed out of my mind. Derek took one look at me and pushed me up the stairs and into that room where he stripped me off and put me to bed. I never knew another thing until Anthea ...'

She had turned on him then, her eyes touched with a kind of madness. The sickness had left her weak and shaky, but the bitterness and pain had been making the adrenalin pump hotly through her blood, and she had launched herself at him, her hand making violent contact with his face, her fingers, unknowingly set into claws, scoring into the taut flesh of his cheek.

He hadn't even flinched. He had just stood there staring at her, grim, white-faced and with tortured eyes, but passive.

She remembered standing there for a wild unaccountable moment watching the blood begin to trickle down his cheek, following its progress with a kind of dazed fascination, not really aware that she had actually inflicted the wound on him.

'I hate you,' she'd whispered then, in a voice so devoid of emotion that he had shuddered. 'You don't know what you've done to me, and I shall never forgive you—never.'

She had turned away, meaning to leave right there and then. But Guy had made the mistake of touching her, begging her again to just listen to him, and she had turned on him again, hitting out at him with her fist, her feet, showering blows on his body while once again he stood rock-solid-still and let her do her worst until, weak with exhaustion, she had collapsed against him, to sob brokenly into his gaping shirt.

Without a single word he had just picked her up in his arms and carried her through to their bedroom,

where he'd laid her down and covered her with the
duvet before turning and walking out of the room.
Leaving her alone to weep.

She had been alone ever since.

CHAPTER SEVEN

'LOOK.' The grim tension simmering between them had not eased in the slightest over the last two miserable days, and Guy was at last sounding utterly fed up as he drove them from the airport into London. 'I am not prepared to argue about it any more! We are going directly to my apartment and that's where you will sleep tonight!'

Marnie's mouth was set in a petulant line, Guy's own expression not much better. The row about where she would sleep tonight had been going on since they'd boarded his private jet in Edinburgh. She was tired, irritable and depressed—the worst of those three things being the tiredness, since she had barely slept a wink during the two nights they had spent in Edinburgh. If she hadn't been lying there tossing and turning restlessly while she battled with her black memories, she had been lying there battling against the damned traitorous way her body wanted to remember how good Guy could make it feel if she would only give in and let him.

'I'm not intending running away, for God's sake,' she sighed wearily.

'No? Well, I am not prepared to trust your word on that. So stop nagging!'

'I only want to get a decent night's sleep in my own bed before I have to face your father tomorrow! God knows,' she complained, eyeing her sadly creased and unhappy dress with distaste, 'I must look a wreck! All I want now is a shower, a change of clothes and my own bed for one last night! I couldn't care less about running away, Guy! I don't think I have the energy left in me to try!' she added drily.

'You had the option to buy fresh clothes in Edinburgh. It was through your own stubbornness that you look a wreck. The rest you can get at the apartment,' he dismissed.

'But I could see to my packing tonight rather than having to do it tomorrow,' she attempted a bit of cajolery.

'No.'

She glared at him. 'Did you bully the girls when you were a little boy, too?' she threw at him tightly.

'I was known for my charm as a child, actually,' he answered with the first hint of a smile for days. 'Only you have ever forced me to resort to bullying tactics.'

'Because I won't let you walk all over me.'

'Because you never know when to give up!' he snapped, then glanced briefly at her and sighed. 'Look, you are tired, I am tired. And—dammit, Marnie, but I can still remember the last time I trusted you to remain where I left you only to find you had disappeared within an hour of my leaving you! And I have no intention of suffering another six months like those again,' he said grimly.

So, he'd suffered: good. So had she. He deserved to. She did not. She felt no pangs of sympathy, no twinges of remorse for worrying him as she had. Her own sorrow had been much harder to shut out. Guy had not held the monopoly on distress.

On her return to London there had been plenty of people more than ready to tell her how much he had suffered during her absence, how Roberto had found it necessary to take back control of the company while his son went demented trying to find her. How Guy had, on drawing a blank with every avenue he tried, turned to the bottle instead and for weeks refused to listen to reason while he drowned his suffering in whisky.

Only when she had felt able to face the world again had she come out of hiding. And she had made Guy aware of her return in the most fitting way possible: with a legal notification that she had filed for divorce.

He had ranted, he had raved, he'd threatened her, and eventually, when he'd come to accept that nothing he could do was going to change her mind, he'd left her alone.

But he had continued to refuse to agree to a divorce. 'I will pay any penance you consider due to you, Marnie, with good grace,' he'd told her grimly. 'But not by taking back the vows I made to you. Those will stay, no matter what you say.'

'I say I will never be your wife again,' she'd told him bluntly. 'Which leaves us both living in a state of limbo if you continue to be stubborn about this.'

'Then limbo it has to be,' he agreed. 'But no divorce. It is an unarguable fact that time eventaully heals all wounds. You will forgive me one day, Marnie. We will stay in limbo until that day arrives.'

And they would have done, if Marnie had not played her final trump card. 'Sign the papers, Guy, or I will change the plea to adultery, citing Anthea, and drag the whole mucky thing through the courts in the most public way I can manage.'

He had signed. They both knew what her threat would do to his father if she carried it out, and Guy had just not been prepared to risk calling her bluff on it...

The car drew to a halt, and Marnie blinked, bringing her own wandering mind to a halt also, finding herself in the once familiar dimness of the basement car park to his private block of luxury apartments.

'Out,' Guy said, snapping open his own seatbelt and climbing lithely out of the low-slung car. Doing the same, Marnie stretched her tension-locked muscles while he moved to the boot and collected his suitcase.

They rode the lift to the penthouse floor in silence, neither apparently prepared to risk another row by making eye-contact, which seemed to be all it took to give the tension buzzing between them cause to vent itself.

Nothing really changes, Marnie thought ruefully to herself as she followed him into the apartment. Everything looked very much as it had done the last time she had been here. Oh, no doubt the walls had enjoyed a fresh lick of paint, she allowed, but other than that it felt a bit like walking through a time warp coming back here.

She shivered delicately.

'You know the layout,' Guy said. 'Take your pick of the guest rooms. I'll just get rid of this case...' He was already striding down the wide caramel and cream hallway towards the master bedroom. 'Be an

angel, Marnie,' he called over his shoulder. 'See what
Mrs Dukes has left in the fridge for dinner, will you?'

'You still have Mrs Dukes?' she asked in surprise.
The prune-faced housekeeper had worked for Guy
long before Marnie arrived on the scene.

He stopped, turning to mock her with a cynical
look. 'Not everyone finds me as objectionable as you
do, you know,' he drawled, and moved on, leaving
her feeling ever so thoroughly put down.

She found a ready cooked chicken *cacciatore* sitting
in the fridge with detailed instructions on how to heat
it placed neatly on top of the dish.

That made Marnie smile, despite her mood. Neither
she nor Guy was much use in the kitchen, and Mrs
Dukes had a habit of leaving precise instructions on
how not to ruin her carefully prepared dishes.

Marnie followed the instructions to the letter,
gaining some childish kind of pleasure in mockingly
checking each command as it came up on the list. Mrs
Dukes was a quiet, aloof kind of woman. Nice, but
not someone Marnie had ever felt she could get close
to. The housekeeper had always considered the kitchen
her domain. And if she and Guy ever had ventured
in here in the dead of night to pillage the fridge, they
had used to do it like two naughty children. Mrs
Dukes' kitchen, they'd used to call it. Mrs Dukes'
cooker. Mrs Dukes' fridge.

A sharp pang of something she had no wish to acknowledge pulled her up short and she walked quickly
out of the room, turning towards the guest bedrooms
in search of the room she would be using tonight.
Only her feet slowed outside another door. The door

to her old studio. A room she had not entered since the night four years ago when she'd flown at Guy.

If the kitchen had been Mrs Dukes' domain, then this, Marnie recalled, had been hers. North-facing, wide-windowed and converted exclusively to suit her needs. Guy had provided her with every conceivable artistic aid she could possibly require.

Slowly, almost unsure that she actually wanted to do it, she turned the handle and stepped quietly inside.

It was empty. Her heart gave a painful dive. The room was bare, completely stripped of everything that had once been so familiar to her. Weak tears beginning to cloud her vision, she moved slowly to the middle of the room.

All gone. Everything. Her easel from where it used to stand by the window, the draughtsman's board from close by where she worked for hours on her sketches before turning her attention to a canvas. The canvases themselves, rows of them which used to lean, face turned inwards to the walls, all gone. Things she had loved too much to sell but had never quite got around to hanging on the walls.

She had painted Guy in this room. He had stood— just there. Her misty gaze went to the spot on the polished floor where he had posed naked for her in that oh, so arrogant way of his. 'Like this?' he'd teased her, turning his impressive body into some disgustingly provoking pose or other. 'Or this perhaps?' taking up another pose which would verge on the indecent while she tried to remain professional and shift him into a more respectable position. 'How am I supposed to stand here calmly dressed like this?' he'd demanded when she'd scolded him.

'You aren't dressed in anything!' she'd laughingly pointed out.

'Neither will you be in a minute,' he'd growled.

Now there was nothing left in the room but the echoes, echoes of something warm and special . . .

'I had the room cleared when it became—obvious that you had no intention of coming back to me,' a deep voice murmured from the doorway, making her spin round to find him standing there with his dark eyes guarded. 'I thought, for a time,' he went on quietly, 'that you might have at least wanted your canvases, but . . .' His shrug said all the rest, leaving a heavy silence behind it.

Marnie blinked away the mists from her eyes. 'W-what did you do with them?'

'Put them into store.' Another shrug. 'They are at Oaklands. Everything.' His gaze drifted around the bare emptiness of the room. 'The lot.'

She just hadn't been able to bear the idea of coming in here again to get anything. Not the tools of her trade or even her precious paintings.

'Still,' Guy went on more briskly, 'you can set up shop again at Oaklands once we've settled in there—so long as you don't take in any outside work, that is. Did you find anything to eat in the kitchen?'

Just like that. The subject of her continuing to work, opened and closed, just like that. Her mouth tightened, any hint of softening in her mood gone. 'A chicken *cacciatore*,' she answered coolly. 'Ready in about fifteen minutes.'

'Good.' He nodded. 'That will give us time to take a quick shower before we eat,' he decided, levering himself away from the door-frame. 'Have you decided which room you want to use?'

'It's all the same to me, since there is nothing here I relate to any more,' she answered bitterly. Then, because she did not feel she had the energy for a return to hostilities, she added flatly, 'I'll use the one next door to yours, if it's all the same to you.'

'But it isn't all the same to me,' he grunted. 'And you know it.' She glared at him and he sighed heavily. 'All right, Marnie. Use what bloody room you want to use. You know Mrs Dukes; she will have left them all prepared ready for unexpected guests.'

'I need a change of clothes,' she reminded him as he turned to leave. 'I suppose there's no chance you have any of my old things hanging around?' she enquired hopefully.

'No,' he muttered. 'If you must know, I had them sent to your favourite charity—at least that should please you, since nothing else around here seems to!'

'You gave all my lovely clothes to the Sally Army?' she choked out disbelievingly.

'What the hell did you expect me to do with them— have them lovingly preserved behind glass just in case you decided on a whim to come and collect them?'

'No, of course not!' she answered stiffly. 'I just thought...' Her voice trailed off. She didn't know what she'd thought—or even if she had so much as wondered about her clothes before this moment. 'It— it doesn't matter.' Dully she dropped the subject.

Guy seemed happy to do that too, because he nodded grimly and said, 'I will get you a pair of my pyjamas and a spare bathrobe. Tomorrow, first thing, we will go and collect your things from your flat, if that makes you feel any better.'

And he disappeared down the hall, his movements sharp with irritation. She followed, passing his door to open the one next to it, feeling as though she'd been dragged through the emotional food-mixer, the way they had to constantly keep sniping at each other.

Oh, God. She sat down wearily on the bed. What was she doing, letting herself become trapped by him again? She knew it could only lead to more heartache. More wretched pain. She was in pain now—the constant nagging pain of forced remembrance. Being with him all the time like this was making her face all those things she had thrust so utterly to the back of her mind.

Good things as well as bad. And she wasn't at all sure which side of the balance-scale was weighing down the heaviest. That frightened her, frightened because it had to mean that her grievances towards Guy were slowly beginning to fade away—just as he had always said they would do.

'Here. I've brought you . . .'

Guy halted a stride inside the room, his words dying as he looked down at her pale, forlorn face.

'Oh, Marnie,' he sighed, his mouth taking on a grim downward turn as he came over to where she sat and threw down the pyjamas and robe before squatting on his haunches in front of her. He took up her hands, long-fingered and so slender-boned that you only had to look at them to know they belonged to someone who possessed special artistic gifts. They were cold and trembling, and Guy sighed again before he lifted them to his lips and gently kissed them. He had discarded his jacket somewhere, and his tie, so the tanned skin at his throat where he had yanked open the top button of his shirt gleamed smoothly in the dying sunlight.

'Can't you simply forgive?' he murmured suddenly. 'Put us both out of our wretched misery and forgive so we can at least try to move forward into a better understanding than all this bitter standing still?'

She looked down into his face—so handsome, so sleekly hewn beneath its smooth, dark skin. His eyes, dark and deep, lacking any hint of mockery or cynicism or even the impatience he had been showing her all day. And his mouth, grim but soft, not tight and hard. Unhappy, like hers. Weary, like hers.

'I'll—try,' she whispered thickly, then sucked in a breath of air that entered her lungs like a shaky sigh, the tears she had been trying to hold back since she entered her old studio minutes ago suddenly bulging in her eyes.

Guy's mouth moved on a grimace of sombre understanding. And he lifted one of his hands to gently stroke her long bright hair away from the single tear trailing down her pale cheek. He made no effort to wipe the tear away, but simply squatted there watching its downward path until it reached the corner of her trembling mouth, when he leaned forward and gently kissed it away.

'I ask for nothing more,' he murmured gruffly. 'Nothing more.'

Marnie made an effort to gather herself, pulling her hands free and sitting up straighter on the bed, effectively putting much needed distance between them, both on a physical and a spiritual plane.

'The chicken will be ruined,' she said, trying for a rueful smile.

'Not if we're quick,' he countered, taking his lead from her and straightening his long body into a standing position. 'A quick shower each, and we'll meet in the kitchen in five minutes.' He turned to walk back to the door—then stopped, turning back to glance around the room.

'This is all right for you?' he asked politely.

Marnie stood up. 'Yes,' she said uninterestedly. 'It's fine.'

'You . . .' He lifted a hand to run it through his hair in a oddly uncertain gesture. 'Would you prefer to use our old room while I use this one?'

The action and his curious tone made her frown. 'No,' she refused. 'That's your room. You'll sleep better in your own bed. Of course I don't want to take it from you.'

'Sleep?' he murmured drily. 'What's that?' The hand moved to the back of his neck, holding it while he grimaced wryly at her. 'I have not had a single moment's sleep since you came back into my life two nights ago,' he admitted. 'I just lie there, listening to every move you make, on the alert in case you decide to make a bolt for it again.'

'I told you I wouldn't,' she reminded him.

'I know.' The hand dropped heavily to his side and clenched into a fist. 'But it makes no difference. What is it that keeps you awake, Marnie?' he then posed softly.

You, she wanted to say. Memories. My own black thoughts. 'I give you my solemn vow, Guy,' she said drily instead, 'that I will not move out of this bed once I am in it—will that help ease your fractious mind?'

'No.' He smiled. 'But I suppose it will have to do. See you in five minutes.' Then he was gone, leaving her feeling ever so slightly—perplexed.

They ate in silence, Marnie with the long sleeves of his pyjama top rolled over several times before she found her hands. He'd grinned at the sight of her when she'd first walked into the kitchen but had said nothing, the small compromise she had allowed seeming to have taken all the tension out of the air. The chicken was not quite ruined, the pasta still edible, just about, and they washed it down with a glass of good Italian white wine.

Not very long after they had finished the meal, Marnie yawned and got up, more than ready for her bed.

She only hoped she could manage to sleep a little tonight. Certainly she was more than tired enough to do so.

And thankfully she did, dropping off to sleep almost as soon as her head hit the pillow, curling herself into a loose ball with the feel of Guy's pyjamas cocooning her in sensual silk. In fact, the feeling was so provocative that she found herself drifting into an erotic dream, where Guy was no longer her enemy and she was welcoming him into her bed and her arms as though he had never left them.

He felt wonderful to the touch, his skin like fine leather beneath her exploring fingertips, her mouth automatically softening as he gently kissed her.

'Mmm,' she sighed out pleasurably.

'Go back to sleep,' he murmured.

Back to sleep——? Her eyes flew open, her heart beginning to race madly when she found herself securely curled into the warm curve of his body.

'What are you doing here?' she gasped, trying to pull away.

He wouldn't let her. 'Don't start, Marnie.' He sighed out wearily. 'I have not come here to seduce you, if that is what you are thinking.'

'Then why are you here?' she demanded, glaring coldly at him as he reluctantly opened his eyes.

'I still couldn't sleep. So I decided the next best option was to join you here. As a therapy, it is working,' he yawned, his eyes closing sleepily. 'I am almost dead to the world already.'

'But—Guy!' she cried, managing to get an arm free and flinging it out to grab hold of his shoulder. It felt like satin beneath her touch, warm and tightly muscled. 'Guy!' she snapped, giving him a shake.

But he was already asleep! She couldn't believe it! Could not believe his utter gall in just calmly climbing into bed with her. She sighed angrily, gave the satin shoulder a mulish slap and sighed again, letting her head fall back on to the pillow because, fast asleep or not, he was still holding on to her, giving her no room to escape.

'If you're kidding me with this stupid game, I'll kill you, Guy Frabosa!' she muttered, watching his relaxed face for any hint that he was just feigning sleep.

His breathing was light and even, his mouth parted slightly and relaxed, eyes closed so the silken brush of his long dark lashes lay in a perfect arch across his high cheekbones.

She studied him closely for long, suspicious minutes, his face bare inches away from her own, waiting for the slightest hint that he was only waiting for her to relax before he pounced. But he hardly moved, his body completely relaxed beneath the soft warm duvet, and as the minutes ticked by her own body became used to having his wound so intimately around it, legs tangled, the comforting feel of his arms folded so possessively around her, her breasts brushing lightly against his chest as she breathed.

The only man ever to hold her like this, she thought sadly. Guy. The man she loved to hate and hated to love.

'Why do you still do this to me?' she whispered to his sleeping face. 'Why does this feel so right?'

She sighed softly, her eyes full of a kind of tender tragedy as she closed the few small inches between them and gently kissed him on the mouth. He did not respond; was too deeply asleep to have even noticed.

Sighing again, she relaxed back on to the pillows, her expression open and vulnerable as she continued to watch him sleep in her arms until slowly her own eyes began to droop, her body growing heavy until it relaxed tiredly into his.

Then she too slept.

The morning wasn't so easy to accept when she awoke to find herself still curled cosily into his warm body. She opened her eyes to find his brown ones watching her lazily.

'This is nice.' Guy obviously felt no qualms about voicing what she was guiltily thinking. 'I did consider waking the Sleeping Beauty with a kiss,' he teased her wryly. 'But I am afraid I feared the reprisals.'

She droped her gaze from his, then wished she hadn't when her gaze fell on to her hand, still lovingly curled around his satin shoulder. Carefully, she removed it, then let it hover, not knowing quite what to do with it now, since the only other places she could rest it involved the warm flesh of the man lying beside her.

'Here.' Reaching out, he took the hand in his own, his fingers closing around hers as he brought them up to his mouth to brush a light kiss against them then folded them beneath the duvet into the narrow gap between their bodies. 'Do you know how peacefully you sleep?' he murmured questioningly. 'You barely move, barely breathe—I used to lie watching you for hours, you know,' he confessed, 'envying you that blissful peace.'

'You're too over-active-minded to sleep with any hope of peace,' she threw back drily, smiling, despite her discomfort with the situation.

'Over-active other parts of me as well, if I recall,' he teased.

Marnie blushed and quickly changed the subject. 'You have more of these,' she noted, freeing her captured hand so she could comb a finger through the silvered hairs at his temple.

'My father was completely grey by his fiftieth birthday,' he informed her, sounding gruffly defensive suddenly.

Marnie glanced into his guarded eyes. 'It wasn't a criticism,' she told him quietly, realising where the defensiveness had come from. 'I like the silver. I always did. It makes you look so distinguished. I like Roberto's hair, too,' she added quickly to defuse any hint of intimacy he might have read into the remark. 'It makes *him* look distinguished.'

Guy just smiled, moving his gaze to her own hair, lying like a rippling red-gold stream out across the pillow behind her. Reaching over her, he picked up a silken tendril and brought it to his face, his eyelids lowering as he inhaled the rose-scented smell of it in a way which made her stomach curl. Guy could always make the simplest gesture seem so exquisitely sensual.

The heavy lids lifted again, catching her expression. 'I . . .' she floundered, not sure what she wanted to say, not sure if there was anything she could say to stop what was actually beginning to happen between them.

His own eyes darkened, his hand moving to her shoulder, and slowly, giving her more than enough time to realise what he intended to do, he gently pushed her on to her back, then came to lean over her.

'Say no, if you want to,' he murmured huskily, then brought his mouth down warmly on to hers.

CHAPTER EIGHT

THE night's stubble on Guy's chin rasped lightly
against Marnie's more sensitive flesh. Their warm
bodies gravitated instinctively towards one another;
her limbs parted to accommodate him, and Guy
obliged by covering her completely, sending a thrill
of pleasure rushing through her as she languidly accepted his weight.

The kiss went on and on, neither deepening nor
receding. No tangled tongues, no desperate surge of
passion to force her to make the unwanted decision
as to whether she let them continue further down the
road to ultimate union.

It was as though they were content to just recapture
a poignant moment from the past when they could
exchange kisses like this, warm, tender, giving kisses
that did not necessarily need to tumble into the heated
fire of sensuality to give satisfaction.

Marnie lifted her hands to his throat, then slid them
to his nape, her fingers burying themselves in the jet-
dark mass of his hair.

Guy let out a short, breathy sigh, and tangled his
own hands in her hair, cupping her head, lifting her
closer to him, his body beginning to move slightly,
just the merest hint of a thrusting rhythm that made
her stomach clench and begin to churn.

She wasn't sure whose mouth parted first, or whose
tongue went in sensual search of the other, but

suddenly their mouths were straining, the kiss becoming heated, their breathing agitated enough to make them both move restlessly against each other. She felt the hardened thrust of his arousal, gasped and arched as it moved pleasurably against her.

'Guy,' she whispered feverishly.

'Ssh,' he said, sliding his moist mouth across her cheek to begin sucking seductively at her earlobe, while his hand slid between their bodies, finger sliding buttons free, parting her top so he could bring his chest back down upon her naked skin.

He sighed tremulously as she responded to the new delight of flesh against flesh, and brought his mouth back to hers, warm and seductive, his hands moving on further down until they were gently kneading her soft flesh as his hips thrust insistently against her own.

Moisture began to spring out all over his skin, musky-scented and so familiar to her that she groaned in pleasure as it assailed her nostrils. Her fingertips dug in as they ran from muscle-packed shoulders down the full length of his long back until they reached his waist, where they slid sideways, making him shudder, his muscles jerking in spasm as she searched out his acutely sensitive groin, cupping the rigid bones in his hips with her palms while her fingers moved incitingly.

And, as if her joining in the sensual foreplay he had begun was like giving leave for him to do his worst to her, Guy gasped something and slid his hand inside her pyjama bottoms so he could push them out of his way.

Marnie felt something buried deep inside her crack, and like a dam with its seams burst open wide all her long-suppressed passions came flooding through, sending her arching towards that knowing hand, and on a husky groan she bit sensually down into his lower lip, making him start, jerk away from her to gaze hotly down into her flushed face. The mayhem going on inside her must have shown in the passionate glitter in her eyes, because Guy muttered something beneath his breath, and tried shakily to calm her.

'I hate what you do to me!' she choked out wretchedly.

'No, you don't,' he denied, stroking a shaking hand across her flaming hair in an odd gesture of sympathy. 'You only wish you did, my darling,' he murmured, and brought his mouth back on to her before she could say another bitter word, burning her with a kiss that banished every other feeling from her but the hungry need to touch and feel.

His caresses grew urgent, more intimate, giving her no opportunity to return to the sanity she had let go of, his mouth sliding down her body to nip, lick and kiss her into a frenzy of desire. Her breathing was out of control, rasping hectically from her lips as he took one of her thrusting breasts into his mouth and sucked hard, until the pain of it became a terrible pleasure.

'You want me,' he said hoarsely, knowing her body better than she even did herself.

'Yes,' she answered, not even sorry to admit it any more.

'How much?' He ran his tongue across the recently abused tip of her breast, its newly heightened sensitivity making her cry out in pleasure.

She didn't answer. Her teeth clenched tightly against her searing breath to stop the words he wanted to hear escaping through.

His hot breath burned her where it brushed, his body, slick with sweat, moving with a slow eroticism against her, arousing her with the sensual experience of a man who knew his own power.

Barely able to breathe as that slow, desperate build-up of feeling began to grow within the centre of her, she could feel herself beginning to float, her limbs tightening, her mind losing itself in the dizzy mists of sexual ecstasy.

'How much?' he demanded again.

Heart, body and soul. He wanted to hear her repeat the husky little love chant he had forced from her every time they made love before. But——

She shook her head. 'No,' she refused again, sane enough to know she could not give him more than she was already giving him. Desperate enough to sob at her own strength to refuse him this one simple but oh, so telling little phrase. 'Never again,' she whispered wretchedly. 'Never again, Guy, never again.'

'The heated throb of your body says you want me,' he muttered. 'It pulses with a need to feel me filling you inside! Your soul cries out for reunion with mine—I can hear it, even now while you lie here beneath me trying to deny its right to belong! I can hear it, Marnie, calling out to mine! And your heart.' He covered her left breast where her heart pumped heavily against his resting hand. 'What does this wildly pulsating heartbeat tell me?'

'It tells you nothing—nothing!' she cried, finding enough strength to push him away from her and rolling dizzily off the bed to stand. 'I wonder sometimes if you're some kind of throwback from the Dark Ages,' she muttered, hugging her trembling body because she had a terrible feeling it was going to shatter if she didn't. 'How dare you expect more from me than you're capable of giving yourself?'

He was lying where she had left him, on his back in all his arrogant nakedness, his expression grimly closed. 'I gave you everything of myself the day we married,' he stated coolly.

Marnie let out a deriding sound, dragging the flaps of her top around her aching breasts and trying to pretend that she didn't give a damn that he had managed to bring her tumbling back to her senses before the whole thing had spun way out of control. 'And Anthea?' she threw at him bitterly. 'What was she supposed to be—a moment's loss of sanity?'

He nodded. 'You could call her that,' he agreed. 'But, as I said to you only the other day, Anthea is a part of the past and is no longer up for discussion. It is over——'

'Gone, forgotten, I know,' she finished for him. 'Well,' she snapped, 'so are the promises from the past. If you want my full commitment to you a second time, then you will have to earn it a second time.' Jerkily she moved across the room to the adjoining bathroom door. 'Now get off my bed, and out of my room,' she told him as she tugged open the door. 'The right to enter either is not yours quite yet!'

Slamming the bathroom door shut behind her and locking it, Marnie then leaned back against the solid safety of the wood and closed her eyes.

She hated him! Hated! she told herself fiercely.

But a lump formed in her aching throat, put there by the guilty knowledge that, even while she did hate, she wanted him with a hunger that was growing stronger with each hour she spent in his company. And if he hadn't pushed his luck too far just now, then she would be still lying beneath him, glorying in the pleasure only Guy could give her.

Emerging half an hour later, Marnie made directly for the sitting-room with the intention of using the telephone extension in there. But she was brought up short for a moment when she found Guy lounging on one of the soft-cushioned sofas reading his daily newspaper.

He didn't look up, and, lifting her chin in outright defiance at the sudden hungry jolt her senses gave her, she marched over to the phone and picked it up.

'What are you doing?' Guy enquired lazily.

'Ringing Jamie,' she told him, holding the receiver to her ear. 'I want to know how Clare is, and if——'

'They're not there,' he said coolly, flipping over a newspaper sheet.

'Not there?' Alarm skittered down her spine. 'Why?' she gasped. 'Is it Clare? Is she——?'

'Of course not!' he sighed. 'So stop letting that wild imagination of yours run away with you. Clare is fine.'

'Then why are you so certain they won't be at the garage?' she demanded. 'It's Saturday. Jamie is open on a Saturday. He——'

'They are not your concern any more,' Guy inserted levelly. 'Leave them to get on with their own lives.'

'Not my concern? Of course they're my concern!' she snapped. 'They're my family!'

'I am the only family you need concern yourself about from now on.'

'No way!' Marnie shook her bright head. 'I've willingly given up everything else for you, Guy. I will not give up my family as well!'

'Willingly?' he quizzed, lifting his dark head from his newspaper to mock her with a look.

'Willingly or unwillingly,' she snapped. 'What difference does it make? I've done it. But Jamie and Clare are all I have left, and I won't let you take them away from me, too!'

'You have me,' he pointed out.

But I don't want you! she wanted to tell him, but held the words back, snapping her lips shut over her clenched teeth as she turned her attention back to the telephone again. No answer; she let it ring and ring, then, in the end, placed the receiver slowly back on its rest and turned to look at Guy.

'What have you done with them, Guy?' she demanded huskily.

'Done?' He glanced at her with amusement spiking his eyes, then away again. 'That is charming,' he scoffed. 'Are you suspecting me of some dastardly crime, Marnie?' he mocked. 'Like spiriting them away to some wretched place and doing them in?'

'Don't be stupid!' she snapped. Then, doubtfully, 'What have you done with them?'

He sighed, his eyes flicking impatiently over the newspaper sheets as if he was intending not to answer. Then he said flatly, 'They are not at the garage because they are at Oaklands. Your brother is working for me again. He and Clare moved into the Lodge House by the West Gate yesterday.'

'Jamie—working back at Oaklands?' Her voice mirrored her shocked disbelief. Her brother had always vowed never to work for anyone but himself again. 'But why? How——?'

'Why?' Guy drawled sardonically. 'Because he is not fit to run his own business. And how? By doing as he was told and transporting himself, his charming wife, his impressive collection of tools—and my MG Magnette—down to Oaklands the day after he talked you into taking the rap for his own sins.'

'My God.' Stunned at how quickly he had turned all their lives inside out, she sank weakly into a nearby chair. 'You mean—you took them over, lock, stock and barrel, just like that?'

'Just like that,' he agreed. 'Let's call it—protecting my investment,' he smiled. 'With your brother and his wife solely reliant on my goodwill to keep food on their plates and a roof over their heads, I should have no problem keeping my feisty wife in order.'

But her mind was too busy working overtime even to care about his provoking sarcasm. There was more to all of this than Guy was actually telling her—or her brother if she was reading her prickling instincts correctly. 'And the garage?' she questioned narrowly. 'What is to become of that?'

'That now belongs to me,' he said. 'And it goes up for sale first thing Monday morning.'

'How much?' she then demanded grimly. 'How much exactly does my brother owe you?'

He ignored the question, seemingly engrossed in an article he was reading. Blue eyes beginning to burn, Marnie got up and stepped over to flick at the wretched newspaper he was so interested in with her hand. 'How much?' she demanded.

Guy took his time bringing his head up to look at her, and when he did there was more than just a mild warning in his eyes. 'None of your damned business,' he enunciated slowly. 'If I was stupid enough to let him tap me for money, then that is my affair, not yours.'

'But——'

'Drop it, Marnie!' he ground out suddenly, thrusting the newspaper aside and surging to his feet. 'Just drop it before I get really angry, which I could very easily do, the way I feel right now. So be warned!'

'No,' she refused, taking hold of his arm as he went to stride away. 'Guy, please tell me just how deeply we are in your debt.'

'Enough to keep you in line, Marnie, never fear,' he derided.

'Oh, God.' White-faced, she sank down on the sofa where Guy had just been sitting. 'I had no idea,' she whispered. 'Jamie never uttered a single word that he'd been borrowing money from you of his own volition.'

His mouth tightened at her obvious distress. 'Look,' he sighed. 'If it makes you feel any better about it, it was Jamie who suggested he come back to Oaklands to work for me. And it was he who offered his garage to me as collateral against the money he owes me. He's learning, Marnie,' he added grimly. 'Learning to take responsibility for his own life at last. Let him be. Let him do it. He has used you and me and what we feel for each other for quite long enough.'

'And Clare?' she whispered thickly. 'Is she to be cast out in the cold also?'

'No one,' Guy said heavily, 'is being cast out! Only made to bear the brunt of their own actions. And if you think about it, Marnie,' he added quietly, 'Clare will be living a mere stone's throw away from you from now on. Surely that makes it easier for you to cosset her, not less? Now,' he said briskly 'let's get over to your flat. I want to be at Oaklands before sundown.'

He drove her to her flat in an atmosphere of grim silence, Marnie's thoughts locked on the shocked discovery that her brother had even dared to approach Guy for money on his own! And Guy, she wondered frowningly. What had driven him to so much as give a penny to a man he liked to blame his broken marriage on?

You know the answer. a little voice said inside her head. He did it because of you.

He had never been inside her flat before. She went off to her bedroom to change into fresh underwear and a short straight apple-green silk skirt which had its own matching loosely cut jacket, and a white silk blouse before turning her attention to her packing.

She could hear Guy moving about in her studio-cum-sitting-room, arrogantly fishing around her private possessions as if he had the right. Her mouth tightened, resentment at his presumptuousness sending her stalking around her bedroom collecting and throwing her clothes into her open suitcases with scant regard to how they were going to look when she unpacked them again.

He was standing viewing her latest painting when she emerged, his dark head tilted to one side in interested study.

'This is good,' he said without turning to look at her. 'Who is it?'

'Amelia Sangster,' she answered shortly. Then couldn't help adding with a smile in her voice, 'And the cat's name is Dickens.'

'Heavy name for such a sweet little cat,' he mocked.

'He doesn't think so.' Marnie walked over to stand beside him. 'He sleeps every night curled up on Amelia's leather-bound volumes of Dickens' full works—— Will I be allowed to deliver this?' she asked shortly. 'Or is poor Amelia to be disappointed like all my other expectant clients?'

Guy turned his head to look down at her, his expression telling her absolutely nothing as he searched her cool face. She had left her hair down this morning, and the waving tresses shimmered around her face and shoulders, lit by the sunlight seeping in through the window.

'Is it finished?' he asked.

'Can't you tell?' she drawled sarcastically, refusing point-blank to admit that the picture was so close to being finished that probably only an expert eye would be able to tell it wasn't. And Guy had never professed to being an art expert.

He ignored the sarcasm. 'Do you want to finish it?'

'Of course!' she snapped, amazed that he should even have to ask such a stupid question.

He just shrugged. 'Then I will have it picked up and delivered to Oaklands,' he said. 'But the rest——' he lifted his right hand up so she could see the big black appointments book he was holding '—will have to stay disappointed.'

'But—that's my appointments book!' she exclaimed. 'What are you doing with it?'

'Holding on to it for future reference,' he drawled.

'Future reference to what?'

'To all those poor people we are going to disappoint,' he answered with maddening calm. 'I will have my secretary write them all a nice letter, letting them down gently.'

'I can do that myself,' she clipped, reaching out to take the book.

He moved it smoothly out of her way. 'No, you won't,' he murmured, returning his attention back to Amelia and her cat. 'I don't trust you, Marnie,' he informed her quite casually, 'to do what is needed to be done. So I will pass the job on to my very reliable secretary.'

'God, I despise you,' she muttered, moving away from him.

He shrugged as if that didn't matter to him either. 'Packed everything you need?' he enquired.

'Yes.' Suddenly she felt like weeping, coming to a standstill in the middle of the cluttered studio and gazing around her like a child about to lose everything that was comfortable and secure in its life.

She'd been happy here—if happiness could be gauged by the gentle waves of peace and contentment she had managed to surround herself with. Like an island, she realised. Living here alone for the last four years had been like living on a tranquil island, after spending a year in the ruthless jungle Guy existed in.

'Then the rest can be delivered along with the painting,' Guy decided. 'Show me where your cases are and let's get going.'

The tears remained clogging the back of her throat as she watched Guy lift her suitcases and carry them to the door. Once there, he turned back to find her standing there, her face white with misery.

'Guy——?' she whispered pleadingly, but what she was pleading for Marnie just did not know.

His face darkened, his expression suddenly fierce as he spun away from her. 'I'll take these down to the car,' he muttered, and walked out, leaving her standing there, feeling about as lost and helpless as she had ever felt in her whole life.

He didn't come back, and Marnie knew why. He was waiting for her to go to him. If he had to come back and drag her out, then it would mean that she was still fighting him for every inch of herself she could keep. If she walked out of the flat of her own accord, then he'd won another small battle. Small, because they both knew she really had no choice.

He was sitting with the car window rolled down, his arm resting on it, his long fingers lying along the thin line of his mouth. He looked darkly handsome and grimly forbidding with his profile turned to her like that, and she felt her heart squeeze on a final clutch of regret at what she was leaving behind.

He didn't turn his head to look at her as she closed the main door to the Victorian town-house her flat was a part of. Or bother to watch her walk to the car and around it to climb into the passenger seat beside him. Neither did he move while she settled herself, locking home her safety-belt, flicking back her hair from her pale face. When she finally went still, he straightened in his seat, reached out to start the engine, pressed a button which sent his window sliding smoothly upwards, then slid the car into gear.

Marnie swallowed, keeping her own eyes staring bleakly frontwards. They moved into the traffic. And, as they left the flat as she had called home for four blessed years, she finally accepted that her life would never be her own again.

Guy owned it now.

Perhaps more solidly than he had done the first time around.

'What now?' she managed to ask once she felt she had her voice under control.

'Now, we begin,' he said, and that was all, the words simple but profound.

CHAPTER NINE

IT WAS a perfect time to be arriving at Oaklands. They entered by the East Gate late afternoon, as the June sun hovered high above the hilltop opposite.

'Guy—stop a moment,'

He glanced questioningly at her, his eyes darkened as he brought the car to a halt and turned to watch the enchantment light her face.

'I always loved this place,' she murmured, unaware of just how much of her inner self she was revealing with that wistfully spoken statement. 'Oh, look, Guy!' she cried, leaning forward in her eagerness. 'The stream is swollen so wide it could almost be a river!'

'The weather has been poor in the hills for this time of year,' he told her, his gaze remaining fixed on her rapt profile. 'There was a time a few weeks ago when we worried it might burst its banks.'

'I can see that the lake is full, too,' she said, gazing down to where the water lapped the rim of the rickety old jetty where Roberto's small rowing-boat bobbed gently up and down.

The house was there. Big and solid and sure. Standing as it had done for two centuries, surviving everything the years had thrown at it through a succession of owners, not all of them kind to its sturdy walls.

'You've made some changes over there,' she noticed, pointing towards the stable block where, just beyond and to the right, her artistic eye for detail had picked out a new addition. A small building that looked like a cottage, built to blend graciously in with its present surroundings. 'A new annexe for your cars?' she supposed, frowning because it seemed a long way from the other buildings where Guy housed his precious collection.

'Something like that,' he answered unrevealingly, then put the car in motion again. 'My father will have already spotted us coming in the gates,' he said. 'If we don't drive down there soon, he will be striding up here to meet us!'

'W-what have you told him?'

Guy glanced at her, and saw she had gone pale, even with the warmth of the sun on her face. 'That we are reconciled,' he said, returning his attention back to the road. 'He is, as you would expect, ecstatic about it.' He sounded a trifle cynical. 'And I would prefer it, Marnie, if he remain that way.'

'Of course!' she cried, hurt that Guy should feel it necessary to warn her like that. 'You know I would never do anything to hurt your father!'

'You hurt him when you left us,' Guy reminded her.

'That was different,' she said uncomfortably. 'Roberto knows I still adore him.'

'I once believed you adored me, too. And look where it got me.'

'It got you what you deserved!' Marnie flashed. 'And I would think your father knows it!'

'You are probably right,' Guy ruefully agreed, slowing to guide the car deftly over the narrow little bridge which spanned the stream. 'Still,' he shrugged, 'he likes to kid himself that I am a son to be proud of. It would be a shame to disillusion him too much.'

'Well, his disillusionment will not come from me,' Marnie stated coolly. 'It never did.'

After crossing the racing track, the driveway took a sharp bend to the left, taking them sailing through the thick cluster of majestic oaks which gave the estate its name, and around to the front of the house which faced south, so it could catch the full day's sun in its face, no matter what time of year it was.

Guy drew the car to a stop then turned to look at her. 'Ready?' he asked.

'Yes.' She nodded, but her insides were trembling as she climbed out of the car.

Guy came to join her, his hand slipping around her waist and firmly drawing her body closer to his side. Marnie stiffened a little, appalled by how violently her senses reacted.

'Relax!' he admonished. 'And turn your face and smile at me! Do it!' he whispered fiercely when she went to refuse. 'My father has just come out of the house and is watching us!'

Having to force it, Marnie turned her bright head, tilted her face and smiled up at him. Their eyes clashed, and held, the air around them suddenly too dense to breathe, when she felt something sting her sharply. She gasped. Guy went tense, his heartbeat quickening. And she felt her own begin to hammer, that strange imaginary sting sending tingling shock-waves outwards to every corner of her body. His irises darkened, spiralling out from rich liquid brown to deep black pits that seemed to be drawing her closer and closer.

'Marnie,' Guy whispered hoarsely.

'No.' She tried to deny what she knew was happening to both of them. But her voice held no strength, and, even as she mouthed the word, her tongue was coming out to run sensually around her parted lips.

She wanted him to kiss her, she realised with a small shock. She not only wanted it, her whole body was crying out for it. Begging for it. Needing it.

His hand moved, flattening against her spine so he could urge her around in front of him. Then she was pressed against the solid length of his body, and Guy was slowly bringing his mouth down to cover her own.

The world began to spin, her senses spiralling with it. The hand at her back urged her closer, bending her into a subtle arch which brought her thighs into quivering contact with his hard arousal. His other hand buried itself in her hair, cupping her head so he could deepen the kiss, and Marnie let her hands drift restlessly over his muscled arms until they fell heavily over his shoulders. Her breasts tightened, the stinging nubs pushing themselves against the warm hardness of his chest. Guy drew in a shaky breath and held on to it, his body beginning to tremble. She felt it just as her own began to do the same. And when he eventually dragged his mouth away from hers they both looked dazed, bewildered, heavy-eyed with need.

'Don't ever deny that we have this!' he rasped out thickly. 'No matter what else we lost, Marnie, we never lost this!'

He made to take her mouth again, but she pulled stiffly out of his arms, suddenly feeling so cold and empty inside that she shivered.

She moved away from him, swallowing in an effort to shift the lump from her throat, and struggling to pull herself together before turning her attention on the watchful Roberto Frabosa.

He looked older than the last time she'd seen him, and so infinitely frail, standing there with his tall, thin body leaning so elegantly on his walking stick, that she found it easy to discover her smile again, warm it, make it the most natural smile she had used in days.

'Papa,' she murmured, and began to move quickly towards him.

His free arm went tightly around her, his face burying itself into her hair for a long emotional moment before he said gruffly, 'This has to be the most beautiful moment of my life, Marnie. The most beautiful.'

He lifted his head, gazing at her with suspiciously moist eyes. 'Thank you,' she said simply.

'And it is all over now?' he demanded, glancing at his son as he came to join them. 'You love each other again?'

Love? Marnie's smile faltered. She didn't think she was capable of loving anyone again.

'The point is, Papa——' Guy's arm came possessively around her waist '—did we ever actually stop?'

'Well, you stopped doing something,' Roberto pointed out, 'or the last four years would not have been what they were!' He shook his silvered head. 'Barren years!' he condemned them impatiently. 'Such wasted, barren years!'

'Papa!' Guy's voice was unusually harsh as he felt Marnie jerk back against his arm as if she'd been shot.

'Take a small piece of advice from your son if you will——' with effort, he strained the harshness out of his voice but still sounded grim '—and resist the temptation to prod unstable substances. They tend to have this irritating tendency to explode in one's face!'

Marnie gasped at the unexpected outburst, and Roberto stared at Guy in sharp surprise. And in the ensuing silence which followed something passed between father and son over the top of Marnie's head that made Roberto go pale before he recovered, to send her a rueful smile.

'I have a cryptic for a son,' he mocked.

'Why did he snap at you like that?'

Marnie and Roberto were sitting alone in his private study, sipping coffee, surrounded by the precious books he spent most of his time poring over these days. Guy had disappeared as soon as good manners allowed, making for his workshops with all the eagerness of a young boy wanting to play with his favourite toys. Away in the distance she could hear the throaty roar of a car engine being revved experimentally, and could see in her mind's eye the circle of grease-covered bodies bent over the car listening with expert ears to the finely tuned sound.

When Guy had bought this private estate, some fifteen years ago now, he had done so with the intention of building his own racing track and workshops in the grounds. He had done all of this without managing to spoil the natural beauty of the surrounding valley, sparing no expense to achieve it, just as he would spare no expense to keep his precious collection in the very peak of its original condition.

He would, during their stay here, take each car out and put it through its paces, listen for faults, test its performance—but most of all enjoy himself—before railing at his mechanic if everything was not exactly as he expected it to be.

According to Roberto, the success of Guy's transition from world-class Grand Prix driver to high-powered businessman was entirely due to his having an outlet for his natural restlessness in his collection of cars.

He was a man of many faces, many moods. Quick to temper, quick to humour, and quick to passion. But for all that she had seen him curse and swear, laugh and tease, burn up with desire and seem to die in release, she had never seen him be anything but lovingly respectful to his father.

Roberto glanced sharply at her. 'You think I did not deserve my roasting?' he quizzed.

'No,' she answered. 'And it just isn't like him to speak to you like that.'

'But there you have just hit the nail unwittingly on its head, my dear,' Roberto said gravely. 'My son is not himself. And has not been for a long time. Four years, in fact.'

Marnie lowered her face, refusing to take him on with that one.

'I am a very proud and loving father, Marnie,' he went on coolly. 'But do not think me blind to his faults, for I am not.'

'Guy has no faults,' she mocked.

Roberto smiled at her joke, but shook his head in a refusal to be diverted. 'And I find myself wondering, you know, why, after all the pain and misery you have put each other through, you are now deciding to try again at a marriage which could not have been as good as it seemed the first time, for it to falter so totally at the first obstacle it came up against.'

But what an obstacle, Marnie thought, then glanced narrowly at Roberto. 'We don't do it for the sake of an old man, if that's what you're thinking,' she said shrewdly.

He nodded slowly. 'But maybe you do it for the sake of your brother?'

Her face stiffened, her body along with it. 'Not for him, either,' she said.

'Then maybe,' Roberto suggested silkily, 'you do it for that sweet angel of a wife your brother brought here with him yesterday?'

'You've seen Clare?' Marnie asked eagerly. 'How did she look? Did she look well? She's pregnant, you know, and she shouldn't be.' Her face clouded, aching concern showing in her blue eyes. 'She lost a baby a couple of months ago and the doctors warned her then that her body needed time to heal; I . . .'

'She is well, Marnie—very well,' Roberto reassured her gently. 'She spent the whole afternoon here with me, while your brother and Guy's team of mechanics moved their things into the lodge. She was happy, excited about the baby. Excited about the move to the country. Excited about the vacation her husband has taken her on for the next few weeks to get them over the—er—critical time.'

Vacation? Marnie's eyes sharpened. What vacation? Jamie couldn't afford to take a——

Guy. She sat back, not sure if she was angry or grateful to him for that piece of thoughtfulness. Then she realised this was yet another thing he had done of his own volition: showing thoughtfulness and caring where none had been requested.

She frowned, trying to work out why on the one hand he could cut her brother into little pieces with his tongue, then on the other do something as beautiful as this.

Because of you, a small voice said. He does it for you. Don't you know he would do anything to ease your troubles? You were worried about Clare's health, so he packed her off on a holiday so she could relax and be cosseted through the next vital month.

Then why am I sitting here, she challenged that voice, being blackmailed by him to do the last thing on this earth I want to do?

Is it? the silent voice asked.

She wriggled uncomfortably.

Roberto watched the changing expressions passing across her open face for a while, then made to get up. 'Come,' he said, using his ever-present stick to help him rise from the chair. 'I want to show you something. And it is best viewed in good light.' A hand wafted imperiously at her when she didn't immediately respond. 'Come, come!' he commanded. 'My son will not thank me for stealing his thunder on this, but I believe the moment is right and not worth wasting. So come.'

Marnie came reluctantly to her feet. 'Roberto, do you think it worth risking Guy's wrath a second time in one day?' she posed dubiously.

'Why, what are you afraid he will do to me?' His dark eyes began to twinkle. 'Beat me with my own walking stick?

'No.' She laughed, shaking her head ruefully. 'But on your own head be it if he tears you off another strip with his tongue!'

He just tucked her hand into the crook of his arm, and with a deft flick of his wrist set his walking stick in front of him and led them out through the French windows which opened on to a winding pathway that led through his many carefully pruned rose-beds.

'Where are we going?' she asked curiously.

'You will see soon enough,' he murmured secretively. 'Ah, but this is good,' he sighed. 'Walking the garden with a beautiful woman on my arm. I had forgotten just how good it can feel!'

'You old charmer,' Marnie teased, and reached over to kiss his leathery cheek.

'Now that,' he drawled, 'was even better!'

She laughed, and so did he, neither aware of how easily the sound of their laughter floated on the still air to where several men stood talking in a huddle.

A head came up, dark and sleek, standing head and shoulders above the rest. He pin-pointed the sound, frowned for a moment, then went back into the huddle, his concentration broken while he puzzled over what was eluding him.

'Oh——!' Marnie cried as they emerged through a small clump of trees into the evening sunlight again. 'How absolutely enchanting!'

In front of them, about a hundred feet away, stood the quaintest, sweetest little cottage she had ever seen. It could have been stolen right out of a child's picture story-book with its cream-washed walls clamouring with red and yellow roses.

'What is it?' she asked excitedly, realising that this must have been the building she'd picked out when she and Guy arrived on the estate. But she was at a complete loss as to why Guy would have constructed such a beautiful thing in this idyllic spot.

Then a sudden thought occurred to her and she turned sharply to her companion. 'Roberto?' she gasped. 'Is this for you? Have you decided to move out of the main house to live here?'

He just shook his head and refused to answer. 'Let us go inside,' he said, his smile enigmatic.

Letting him urge her forward again, Marnie found herself half expecting Little Miss Moffat sitting primly inside.

She could not have been more wrong, and stopped dead in her tracks, her breath suddenly imprisoned in her breast.

Not a cottage at all, her stunned mind was telling her, but a studio, a light and airy one-roomed studio made to look like a cottage from the outside so it could blend so perfectly with its surroundings.

They had come upon the place from the south, and really that sweet fairy-tale frontage was only a façade. The rest of the walls were wall-to-wall glass! Glass from the deep window-ledge that ran around the room from thigh-height onwards. And furnished with purely functional Venetian blinds, rolled away at the moment to let in maximum light, but there to use when necessary.

Her easel stood there—not the one from her London studio with Amelia and her cat resting upon it, but her old easel, the one from Guy's apartment, and her old draughtsman's board, with a sheet of white sketching paper lying on its top.

On unsteady legs, she walked over to it and looked down. It was the same sketch she had been doing four years ago when her life had fallen apart. She ran her fingertips over the sharp lines of an abstract she had been working on, its image just a blurred memory now, the clean symmetrical lines pulling chords in her creative mind, but not the burning inspiration which had urged her to begin it then.

'Why?' she whispered to the old man watching her in silence from the open door.

He didn't answer straight away, and when eventually she turned to look at him there were tears shining in her blue eyes.

'Why?' she repeated.

'He had everything moved from London to here after this had been completed. It helped him, I think.' His gaze flicked grimly around the sunny room before settling back on Marnie's shock-white face. 'As a kind of therapy, during a time when he was . . .' He paused and grimaced. 'Your continued absence from Oaklands has given it all a maturity. So I suppose this makes it perfect for seeing for the first time.' There was a hint of bitterness in his voice then, and Marnie averted her face, knowing it was probably meant for her.

So, Guy had created this heavenly place for her. The tears grew hotter, burning her eyes as she let them wander over all the other achingly familiar things placed neatly about the room, her emotions in a state of numbing confusion. Shock, surprise, pleasure,

pain. And, raking under all of that, suspicion of his
motives.

Was this her ivory tower, then? she wondered. The
place Guy had always wanted to hide her right away?

'My wife—mine!' He could have been standing
right beside her as those fiercely possessive words shot
right out of the past to grate fiercely on her senses.
He had said them the day they were married, when
he took her in his arms for the first time as his wife.

'My son is not guilty of the terrible crime you believe of him, Marnie,' Roberto dropped into the
throbbing silence.

She tensed up. 'You don't know what you're talking
about,' she dismissed coldly.

Roberto shook his silver head, leaning with the aid
of both hands on his elegant walking stick. 'I may be
old, my dear,' he murmured drily, 'but I am not senile.
And nor am I so surrendered to my infirmity that I
am incapable of finding out for myself those things
I wish to know.'

Like father, like son, she recognised bitterly. Of
course Roberto would have left no stone unturned in
his determination to discover why his son's marriage
fell apart so dramatically. When Roberto had retired
from business, he had done so because he was weary
of the constant race for power, not because he was
no longer capable of winning the race.

'And,' he went on grimly, 'there were plenty of
people present at the fated party willing to relay events
as they saw them—not good people,' he conceded to
her bitter look. 'But knowledgeable people, none
the less.'

'Then you know the truth,' she clipped, and turned
away to stare unseeing out of the window, her hair
like living flame around her pale face where the sun
caught it. 'I would have spared you that, Roberto,'
she added bleakly.

'As I said,' he agreed, 'they were not good people.
They did not consider an old man's feelings in their
eagerness to please his curiosity. But,' he went on, 'on
knowing the truth *you* believe, Marnie, my dear, I
then have to ask myself why you are allowing yourself
to become tied to a man who could so callously use
you in that way? Which is why I brought you here,'
he added before she could answer. 'I see a recipe for
disaster broiling up between you and my son for a
second time, and I cannot—will not allow it to
happen!'

'Roberto!' she sighed, turning impatiently. 'You
can't——'

'My son, Marnie, is using your brother and the
delicate condition of his wife to coerce you into
marrying him again.' He held up a silencing hand
when she went to gainsay it. 'It is no use denying it,'
he stated. 'I saw the truth written in your eyes when
I quizzed you earlier in my study. You only confirmed
my initial suspicions. But, on doing so, I knew I had
to act. For, just as I cannot allow Guy to do that to
you, nor can I allow you to go on believing a lie
cleverly staged for your benefit by wicked and bored
people who believe fun can only be gained at the expense of someone else's happiness!'

'But that's all crazy!' she cried, pulling herself
together because she suddenly realised that Roberto
meant business here. She could see it in the hard flash

of his eyes—hints of the ruthless man he used to be before he bestowed all his power on to his son. 'Guy and I are marrying because we find we still love each other!' she insisted, and wondered why the lie did not feel like a lie. 'The past is over! We've come to terms with it and decided to put it all aside! That's all, Roberto!'

'With a four-year-old lie festering between you?' he challenged harshly. 'May I sit down?'

'Oh, goodness! Of course!' Instantly she was all concern when she realised just how long he had been standing on that bad leg. She darted across the room and pulled out a chair for him, then went to help him into it.

'Ah, that's better,' he sighed, then gave his weakened leg an impatient slap. 'You have no idea how much I hate this incapacity!' he complained. 'It makes me want to hit something!'

'You just did,' she said, grinning teasingly at him. 'Your poor leg.'

Roberto grimaced, then smiled himself, and thankfully some of the tension between them faded away— but only for a moment. Roberto caught her wrist as Marnie went to move away again, his grip urgent.

'I brought you here, Marnie, in the hope that seeing this beautiful place my son created for you would soften your heart enough to let you listen to the story I want to tell you. Will you?' He gave the wrist a pleading shake. 'Will you at least listen to what I have to say?'

'Oh, Roberto.' Sighing, she twisted her wrist free. 'Why can't you just leave well alone?'

'Because it just is not good enough!' he grunted. 'Not now. Not when you and Guy are embarking on yet another road to disaster! The truth must come out, Marnie. And the truth is that Guy was so drunk that night you caught him with that woman, he had no idea she was there!'

'My God, Roberto, will you stop it?' she cried, the pain that vision resurrected almost making her sway.

'They saw you enter the party,' he pushed on regardless. 'Fowler and Anthea Cole. They set you up for that tasty little bedroom scene. Fowler hated you because you turned him down when he tried to proposition you. And Anthea hated you because you took her lover away from her! They wanted to see you bleed!'

And they did! Marnie thought as she reeled away from Roberto's fiercely sincere gaze. 'That's enough!' she whispered painfully. 'You are making Guy out to be a blind and gullible fool by saying all of this. And really I don't think he would appreciate it!'

'Too true,' a coldly sardonic voice drawled.

CHAPTER TEN

MARNIE swung round sharply to find Guy standing in the open doorway, the sheer strength of his anger filling the whole aperture.

Roberto muttered something. Then after that there was complete silence, the tension so thick you could almost taste it as Guy flicked his angry gaze from one to the other of them several times before finally settling on Marnie's paste-white features.

'Please leave us, Father,' he said, stepping away from the door in a pointed way which had Roberto struggling to his feet and limping towards it.

But he halted when he drew level with his son. 'She has a right to know the truth!' he insisted harshly. 'What you are both doing to each other is wrong! And the truth must come out!'

'I asked you not to interfere in this,' Guy said tightly. 'I did think I had your trust!'

'You have, son, you have,' Roberto sighed wearily. 'What I find sad, though, is that I do not have yours.'

Guy relented a little at his father's crestfallen expression, reaching out a hand to squeeze the old gentleman's shoulder. 'Leave us,' he urged quietly. 'Please.'

'The truth, Guy,' Roberto insisted grimly. 'The only way forward for both of you is through the truth.'

Guy just nodded. And Roberto limped out of the door, leaving them alone and facing each other across the sun-filled room.

Marnie turned her back to Guy, unable to continue looking at him while her mind was running frantically over everything Roberto had said to her. She didn't want to believe him. In fact, she could see what a clever little let-out a story like that could be for someone caught in the situation Guy had been caught in. Yet Guy himself had never tried to excuse his behaviour by feeding her the same story. Or had he? she thought suddenly, her mind filtering back to a scene on the same night she had caught him with Anthea. A scene when she was wild with pain and the bitter humiliation of one who had discovered the very worst about her own husband. When she had flown at him with her nails, and Guy, white-faced and trying desperately to hold her still in front of him, had said something very similar to her. And drunk, she remembered. He had still been half drunk when he had turned up at the apartment that night, could hardly hold himself up straight when he'd lurched into the room.

She heard the quiet closing of the door behind her, then Guy's footsteps sounding on the tiled floor as he crossed the room. Her nerves began to buzz, and she stiffened slightly, not sure what was going to happen next.

She saw, from the corner of her eye, him go to the wide white porcelain sink in one corner and turn on the taps. It was then she realised that he must have come straight from the workshop, because, although he was still wearing the clothes he had travelled down in, he had rid himself of the dark jumper and had rolled back the cuffs of his shirtsleeves to his elbows.

His back was to her, and she turned slightly to watch him take up the bottle of liquid cleaner she used to clean the paint from her fingers, and squeeze some into the palm of his grease-covered hands.

'Well,' he said after a moment, 'what do you think of this place?' He didn't turn, his attention fixed firmly on removing the grease from his long blunt-ended fingers.

'Why?' she asked. 'Why did you build it?'

'As a place you could be happy.' He shrugged, rubbing his hands under the running tap to wash away the dirt. 'I thought,' he went on, reaching for the roll of paper towel and tearing off several squares, 'I thought that if I could create a place beautiful enough for you—somewhere here at Oaklands where you could paint, away from the rest of what goes on here, somewhere you could call entirely your own and even pretend it was miles from anywhere if you wanted to feel that isolated—then maybe you would lose that restless urge you have always possessed to be taking off somewhere alone.'

'An artist's life by necessity is a wandering one, Guy,' she pointed out. 'We need time and space to work to our best potential.'

'Well, here I give you both,' he murmured simply.

'No.' Marnie shook her head. 'You will give me the time and the space to work. You always gave me those things before. But this time you want to take away my right to find inspiration where it takes me. You want to imprison me here!'

'Ah!' He threw away the paper towel, smiling ruefully as he walked over to stand beside her. 'Your precious commissions,' he realised. 'But did you not tell me once, Marnie, that you could paint this valley for a hundred years and never go short of fresh inspiration? Well, now I give you that opportunity.' He waved an expressive hand. 'Paint—paint to your heart's content. The valley awaits your gifted touch.'

'While you do what exactly?' she snapped. 'Go back to London? Coming down here to visit your *contented* wife only when the whim takes you?'

'Do you want me to be here more than the odd weekend?' he challenged.

She didn't answer—found she hadn't got one. Not one she would admit to, anyway. 'Roberto is right,' she murmured after a while. 'We have to both be crazy to be considering returning to that kind of sham again.'

'There was no sham,' he denied, 'just two married people who somehow lost their way. Whether or not we make a better job of our marriage on this second chance will depend entirely on the way we work at it.'

'And working at it, in your book, means me staying tucked away here at Oaklands while you carry on as you've always done in London.'

'I have a business to run.'

'So have I,' she countered, though it had not been quite the point she had been trying to make, her mind still fixed on Anthea as it was.

'Had, Marnie, had,' he corrected. 'Now that you have me to give you everything your heart desires, you no longer need to paint to earn a living, but only to paint because it is what you truly want to paint.'

'On condition I stay within the boundaries of the Oaklands walls, of course.'

'Did I ever make that stipulation?' he challenged. 'I only said you would not be going away for days on end and leaving me as you used to do the last time.'

'And how many days and weeks are you going to spend up in London?' she asked drily.

'None, if you are not with me,' he answered, mocking the surprised look on her face. 'From now on, Marnie, we do everything together. Live together, sleep together, laugh, cry and even fight together, since we seem to like sparring so much.'

A gibe at the way they were sparring now, she supposed. She took in a deep breath and decided to change the subject. 'Roberto tells me you've sent Jamie and Clare off on holiday.'

'He has been busy, hasn't he?' Guy murmured drily. 'Any other little—surprises of mine he has stolen the thunder of?'

She frowned, her thoughts turning back to Roberto's disturbing words. Could there be any truth in them? Could Guy really have been just an innocent victim of his friends' idea of a practical joke?

She took in a deep breath and let it out again on a long, discontented sigh. 'How much of what your father was saying to me did you overhear?' she murmured huskily.

'Most of it.'

'W-was he telling the truth?'

He didn't answer straight away, his attention seemingly fixed on the view beyond the window, then he said quietly, 'You already know the truth. I was unfaithful to you and you caught me out.'

'So, he was lying to me?'

'No,' Guy answered slowly. 'It would not be fair to say he lied exactly—just told it as he prefers to believe it to be.'

'That we were set up,' she nodded. 'That you were an innocent victim of a nasty practical joke and I the blind, gullible fool for believing what my eyes were telling me.'

'Why all this sudden curiosity to know,' he asked, 'when over the last four years you have point-blank refused to so much as think about that damned night?'

'Because—because...' Oh, God. She pushed a hand up to cover her eyes, eyes which were seeing things, things she had refused to attach any importance to before.

Things like the sharp glance Derek Fowler had sent over her shoulder, and the malicious smile on his face when he'd looked back at her. Things like Anthea's equally malicious smile when she had lifted her face out of Guy's throat, her naked limbs wrapped around him; Guy's muffled groan and the blank dazed look in his eyes when he had managed to drag them open, a look that had turned to confusion, then horror, then utter disgust before he'd hoarsely murmured her own name.

Slowly, her face pale with tension, she looked up at him. 'If I ask you now, to explain what happened then, will you tell me?'

'And are you asking?'

Am I? A wave of panic fluttered through her, put there because she had an awful suspicion that, if she said yes, Guy was going to rock the very foundations her life had stood upon over the last four years.

'Yes,' she whispered, dragging her eyes away from him. 'Yes, I am asking.'

There was a moment's silence, while Guy stood beside her with his hands thrust into his trouser pockets. She could sense the indecision in him, the grim reluctance to rake over it all again. Then he sighed, and shifted his posiition, turning to rest his hips on the low window-ledge so he could look directly into her face.

'If I explain what really happened that night,' he said quietly, 'will you in turn explain to me what made you chase up to London looking for me so urgently?'

Marnie lowered her eyes, refusing to answer. 'Your father says we were set up by your friends,' she repeated instead. 'He insists she was there with you without your knowledge. That you were drunk. But you didn't drink!' She sighed, shaking her bright head because her battle with what was the truth and what was lies was beginning to make her head whirl. 'Not in excess, anyway,' she added. She glanced frowningly at him. 'Were you drunk?'

A strange smile touched his lips. 'Out of my mind with it,' he admitted, then grimaced, dropping his gaze and folding his arms across his broad chest to stare grimly at his feet. 'I had been drinking steadily all day. Concerned about you, about the direction our marriage was taking...' He looked up, his expression sombre. 'Marnie—our marriage was falling apart at the seams long before the night of that party. We cannot—either of us—blame one isolated incident for its collapse.'

'I know.' Her voice sounded thick. 'But it was the final straw, Guy. One that maybe could have been avoided if...'

'If what?' he asked. 'If I had not taken myself off to Derek's house? If you had not come rushing up to London to find me? If Jamie had not suggested Derek's place to you as a good place to find me? If Anthea had not been such a vindictive little bitch that she was prepared to crucify both of us just to get her revenge on me for replacing her with you?'

'So we *were* set up?'

'Yes.' He sighed heavily. 'I arrived at the party so drunk I could hardly stand...'

'I put him to bed to sleep off the old plonko...' Marnie closed her eyes, quivering on a wave of sickness as she heard Derek Fowler's jeering words echo down the years. Then he had glanced over his shoulder at something or someone on the stairs and that calculating gleam had entered his eyes...

'I did not know a damned thing about anything until I heard you calling to me,' Guy was saying flatly. 'I opened my eyes to see you standing there looking like death. I remember thinking—through the haze of whisky, of course,' he inserted acidly, 'what the hell has happened to make her look like that?' He huffed out a grim laugh, shaking his dark head. 'Then that bitch moved, and I realised she was there, and—well——' he shrugged '—you know the rest.'

Her hand leapt up to cover her trembling mouth, that scene, no matter how false it had been, still having the power to fill her with nausea. 'Oh, God, Guy,' she whispered, not even thinking of questioning his honesty. For some reason she knew it to be the truth.

Four years on, and four years too late, she knew that this was the full destructive truth. 'I'm so sorry...'

'For believing what you were expected to believe?' He lifted his hands emptily in front of him.

'But I should have listened to you, Guy!' she choked out, feeling wretched in her own guilt. 'I could have at least given you the chance to explain!'

'Explain what?' he asked. 'That what you saw with your own eyes was an illusion?' He shook his dark head. 'I tell you this, Marnie—if the roles had been reversed between you and me, I would not have listened. I would not have believed.'

'Is that supposed to make me feel better?' she demanded shrilly. 'To know that for the last four years I've been punishing you for something you didn't even do!'

'I was not aware that we were discussing this with the aim of making you feel better,' he mocked drily. 'I thought we were supposed to be simply sharing the truth!'

'A truth you should have made me listen to long ago!' she cried. 'A truth you *would* have made me listen to if it had been at all important to you that I hear it!'

'Are you trying to imply that I did not care?' he demanded incredulously. 'After the way I have let you wipe your feet on my feelings for the last four years, are you actually daring to——?'

'God, no,' she sighed, accepting that his burst of anger was well deserved. She had been at it again— no sooner believing him to be the innocent party in a game that had ripped her world apart than she was accusing him of another unjustified sin.

In fact, she realised starkly, it seemed that it was Guy who should be doing the accusing, and she who should be begging forgiveness.

Forgiveness for a lot of things. Some of them that he—thankfully—knew nothing about! And never would, she vowed grimly. Never.

So? she wondered dully, seeing no use in a marriage between them now. Not unless Guy was planning to take revenge on her for the four years. She glanced at him sitting there in profile to her, deep in his own private brooding.

He always did brood magnificently, she noted when her heart picked up a few beats as she studied him. But then, she wryly extended on that thought, he tended to do everything magnificently. Shout, laugh, run, dance, sing, drive his fast cars—make love!

The sun was gleaming on the top of his head, adding depth to the sleek blue-blackness of his hair. His skin—born to have the sun caress it, glowing rich and sexy.

He was a man of wildly exciting contrasts. Far, far too much for her to deal with five years ago. Did she have any hope of dealing with him any better now? She didn't think so. Guy was one of those rare people who belonged exclusively to himself. What bit he did give out of himself was maybe enough for other women, but not for her. Wasn't that the main reason why she had fought against his power when they had first met—because she had wanted more from him than she'd known he would ever want to give?

'Why did you ever marry me at all, Guy?' she asked impulsively. 'I mean, it was obvious to everyone, including all your friends, that I was way out of my

depth with you. So what made you marry someone
like me?'

'Because I could not help myself, I suppose.' He
grimaced. 'It was either marry you or lock you away
so no other man could get you. I wanted your innocence, Marnie,' he taunted cruelly. 'All of it. Every
last exquisite bit of it. So I flattered you with my lethal
charm, and impressed you with my dynamic sex
appeal!'

'Stop it,' she snapped, frowning because she suspected his mockery was aimed entirely at himself.

'Seduced and bullied you,' he continued regardless, 'then waited for the magic I had so carefully
woven around you to wear off, and that delightful
hero-worship you repaid me with to——'

'I never did hero-worship you!' she exclaimed, appalled by the very idea.

'Did you not?' He lifted a challenging brow at her.
'Then why did you marry me, Marnie?' he threw back
silkily.

She looked away, refusing to answer. What was the
use? She should have told him she loved him five years
ago when their marriage still had a chance. It was too
late now—much, much too late.

'No answer?' He laughed softly. 'So instead give
me an answer to the question I asked you earlier, if
you will. Why did you come chasing up to London
that fated night?' He waited for some time in the
deadly silence which followed, then laughed softly
again. 'No answer yet again,' he mocked. 'It seems
to me, Marnie, that all the secrets between us have
not yet been fully aired. Still,' he dismissed, coming
to his feet, 'we have time for all of that. Plenty of

time now to learn about each other—perhaps better than we managed the first time we married.'

'You can't seriously still be considering marrying me after what's come out today!' she cried, staring at him in horror.

'But Marnie,' he drawled sardonically, 'you seem to forget. I knew it all before today.'

'And now I know!' she cried. 'Guy—I wronged you! It has to change things!'

'What has changed other than that you now know I am gullible enough to allow myself to become so drunk I did not know what I was doing—or who I was doing it with? Does knowing I was in no fit state to know what was going on condone that kind of behaviour?' he demanded. 'Is it OK to find me in bed with another woman so long as you can blame it on the evil drink?'

'No,' she whispered. 'But——' That wasn't how it happened, she was going to say, but he cut her short.

'Then I am guilty as always charged,' he snapped. 'And that is all that needs to be said on the subject.' He turned away. 'Come on,' he said flatly. 'Dinner will be ready soon and I haven't even shown you to your room.'

'But Guy!' she appealed in exasperation. 'We can't just——'

'Enough!' He turned suddenly, and in one lurching stride was back in front of her. The flash of blazing anger burning in his eyes was the only warning she got before he grabbed her and pulled her hard against him.

What followed was a forceful and angry method of silencing her. By the time he let her go again she was trembling so badly she could barely stand up.

'That is all that matters now, Marnie,' he said harshly. 'You still want me physically. And God knows I still want you! So, we remarry in two days' time——'

'Two days?' she choked. 'But——'

'No buts,' he inserted. 'We made a bargain. I have stuck to my part in it and you will stick to yours. And you will do it,' he warned threateningly, 'with a smile on your face that will convince my father that nothing on this earth can part us a second time!' He reached for her chin, holding it between finger and thumb with just enough pressure to let her know he could hurt her if he wished to. 'Got that?'

Licking her throbbing lips, she nodded uncertainly.

'Right,' he said. 'Then let's go.' He turned his back on her, walking arrogantly to the door and throwing it open. She followed him wearily, wondering what the hell she was following him into.

They were married as decreed, two days later, by the local registrar, followed by having their union blessed by a Catholic priest whose liberal thinking—plus a generous donation to his church roof fund—allowed him to forget the fact that they had once been married and divorced.

'A life sentence this time, Marnie,' Guy murmured with grim satisfaction as they drove back to the house. 'Do you think you can stand it?'

He was being sarcastic because he was well aware that she had only just controlled the urge to run and keep on running before her actual 'sentencing' became official.

Whatever Guy had told his father when they had locked themselves away in Roberto's study the other night she had no idea, but he had clearly allayed his father's fears, because Roberto had looked as pleased as punch ever since! Aided and abetted by Guy, of course, who missed no opportunity to force Marnie into confirming their undying love for each other in front of the old man.

Roberto kissed her on both cheeks then formally welcomed her back into the family. 'Not,' he adjoined, 'that we ever considered you anything else. Now what you both need is half a dozen pairs of tiny feet running about the place,' he grinned. 'That is the surest way of giving neither of you any time to think of falling out again!'

She felt herself go pale. The only thing stopping her from losing her balance on suddenly shaky legs was Guy's arm fixed like a vice around her waist.

'When we are ready, Papa, and not before,' he threw back lightly. 'So take that twinkle of anticipation out of your eyes for now.'

'I'm going to the studio,' she informed Guy tensely as soon as his father disappeared into his study.

'Running away again?' he mocked.

'Where to?' she snapped back. 'You know as well as I do that there is nowhere left for me to run to. You've closed down all escape routes,' she reminded him. 'So even my brother isn't mine any more.'

'You have me,' he said quietly. 'Think about it, Marnie. When have you not had me to run to since the day we met?'

'The day I lost——' She had her lips snapped shut just in time, eyes closing out the sudden anguish in her eyes. 'Do you really mind if I go to the studio for an hour or two?' she pleaded anxiously.

'Why?' he murmured a trifle cynically. 'Will it make a difference if I say I do mind?'

'Of course it will make a difference!' She sighed, unable to hold back the note of frustration in her voice. 'But...'

'You are riddled with bridal nerves,' he suggested, so poker-faced she could have hit him.

'Please, Guy!' she was driven to plead with him. If it wasn't bad enough that he was wearing the most exquisite black suit, made of pure silk, that did the most disturbing things to his muscle-packed frame, then he had to taunt her with the lazy mockery of his liquid brown eyes, offering promises with them that turned her insides to jelly. 'Let me go! Just while I get used to——'

'Being married again,' he inserted for her. And, as if tuned in to what was really bothering her, he let his own eyes run slowly over the simple cream silk suit dress she was wearing beneath its matching bolero jacket. A dress with a heart-shaped boned bodice that stayed up of its own volition and showed more than enough of her shadowed cleavage. She had taken her hair away from her face with two creamy combs, then left it to tumble in a riot of loose curls down her back. He took it all in: the dress, the cleavage, the hairstyle and the anxious face it flattered so nicely; then he let his eyes come firmly on to hers.

'I'm sorry, Marnie,' he said quietly. 'But today is special, and I insist we spend it together.'

So by the time the 'day' grew to its inevitable con-
clusion Marnie was so uptight about what came next
that even a long soak in a hot bath could not ease the
tension from her aching body.

It took Guy to do that. With his usual devastating
force.

He was standing in the shadows of the deep bay
window when she eventually came out of the adjoining bathroom. The curtains had not yet been
drawn, and Guy seemed engrossed in whatever he
could see beyond the bedroom window. A bedroom
lit by the muted glow from one small light bulb hidden
beneath the pale gold shade of the bedside lamp. A
bedroom they had shared before.

A bedroom they were about to share again.

Her stomach knotted, that awful tension centering
itself in one vulnerable spot.

So this was it, she told herself nervously. Pay-up
time.

Did she have it in her to just give herself to him as
though the wedding-ring now gleaming on her finger
automatically made it right?

He looked oddly remote standing there so deeply
lost in his own thoughts that he wasn't even aware of
her presence. A big, lean man dressed in nothing more
than his usual black silk robe. A man whose natural
dark colouring seemed to reflect the mood surrounding him tonight, more so while he stood as deep
in the shadows as he did.

She chewed down uncertainly on her bottom lip,
not quite knowing what she should do next.

Either climb in the bed and think of England, Marnie, she mocked herself acidly, or show a little grace in defeat and go and stand beside him.

She chose the latter, but it took all the courage she had left in her to force her bare feet to walk silently across the thick wool carpet until she reached his side.

'It—it's a beautiful night,' she observed, then could have bitten off her tongue for coming out with such a silly opening remark as that.

Her face muscles clenched, waiting for him to make some mockingly sarcastic remark in return. But he didn't. Didn't say anything for a while, and the tension in her increased, making her tremble a little, wishing herself a million miles away. Wishing she'd had the sense to run and keep on running the moment Jamie had walked into her flat with his latest problem.

'They forecast rain for later,' Guy answered suddenly, making her jump. Her reaction brought his hooded gaze on her. 'You look beautiful,' he murmured, a dry twist of a smile spoiling the compliment. 'Quite the perfect sacrifice, in fact.'

Unexpected tears began to fill her eyes so she had to avert her face until she had blinked them firmly away, finding this role reversal from being the wronged to the wrongdoer very difficult to cope with. And his sarcasm only managed to make her feel more tense, more miserable.

She could feel his eyes still on her, and the familiar tingling sensation started seeping its way throughout her system, beginning in that ball of tension in her stomach then slowly spreading out until it had encompassed every part of her, from the very roots of her softly falling hair to the tips of her fingers and toes.

Then suddenly he reached for her, his two hands spanning her waist to lift her off the ground before settling her back on her feet directly in front of him.

She glanced up, startled and wary, but Guy's attention was on her hair, his fingers coming up to thread absently through the long, loose tresses, then down to her shoulders where only the flimsy bootlace straps of her pale pink nightgown stopped the fine silk from slithering to her feet. He ran light fingertips over her skin, and down her arms, raising goosebumps where he touched.

'Do you think,' he murmured in a deep quiet voice that revealed an odd touch of bleakness, 'that as the years go by the gap in our ages will narrow?' He took up her hands and held them loosely in his own, studying them with his dark lashes lowered over his eyes. 'You look very young tonight, Marnie,' he added huskily. 'As young as the first time we stood together on a night like this. Do I, by contrast, look as old to you?'

Old? she thought, almost smiling at the idea. Guy was not and never would be 'old'. She had never understood this one small chink in an otherwise impregnable armour of self-confidence.

Her blue eyes drifted across the lean, sleek lines of his face with the detailed intensity of a trained artist. Guy was the most beautiful man she had ever seen. There wasn't a single thing about his physical appearance she would want to change.

How could someone like him seem to need reassurance from someone like her? She didn't understand it—never had before.

'No,' she answered him at last. That was all. Just that one simple word that to her said it all—and sent some unknown emotions flashing across his face.

He lifted his eyes and let them clash with hers; dark and burning, telling her without words what he was thinking, feeling—wanting. She shuddered, not sure she could answer the look, and had to look down and away.

'If I never made you feel loved in my arms before, Marnie,' he muttered thickly, 'then I promise you that tonight you will feel it right through to your very soul!'

He caught her mouth, not harshly, as his tone had been, but with a kiss so achingly gentle that she found herself responding almost without realising it.

He still held her hands, and he lifted them around his neck. The action arched her body closer to his, and he spanned her slender waist, holding her close while slowly—oh, so slowly—deepening the kiss into something beyond sweetness.

Her lips parted easily, her tongue waiting to tangle sensually with his. He breathed deeply on a sigh. So did she, and it seemed to herald an end to the final threads of inner resistance she had been trying to cling on to. She wanted this. Why should she pretend otherwise when this was what she had been pining for for days now—since that wild scene at his apartment the morning after they'd arrived there?

And perhaps even before that, a small voice suggested. Perhaps you've been pining for this for years.

Her hands moved to find the collar of his robe, fingers creeping beneath it, sliding against his warm skin and urging the robe away from his shoulders at the same time. She revelled in the heated silk of his smooth shoulders, in the muscled tension in his upper arms, the robe sliding slowly away until she had exposed the full beauty of his hair-covered chest.

Guy gave a shudder of pleasure as she dragged her mouth from his to capture a male nipple instead, sucking on it, biting at it in a way that made his chest expand on a pleasurable gasp, and her fingers moved to untie the robe, setting his whole body free, giving her access to his lean waist, his tight buttocks and long hair-roughened thighs.

Her nightgown rippled down her body to land in a silken pool of pink ice at her feet. His hands were on her body, stroking with slow feather-light caresses that tempted each nerve-end to come to the surface of her skin so her pleasure was heightened, making her groan and arch and sway with his touch.

'Marnie...' he murmured when she ran her fingers along his highly sensitive groin, catching her roving hand tightly in his own. 'Don't,' he whispered. 'My control is not that good.'

She found his mouth again, swamping out the need for words with a kiss that was so sensual, it fired his blood. And he arched her slender body so it bent like a supple wand against the pulsing rock of his.

And they began to move across the dimly lit room in a kind of primeval love dance that brought them to the bed. When he had eased her down on the pale peach cover he took great care to smooth her long hair out behind her, his expression intent, as though he was acting out some private fantasy of his own.

Marnie lay very still, watching him through dark unguarded eyes. When he caught her gaze he smiled, a soft kind of smile that was so infinitely gentle that it touched something achingly beautiful inside her, and she smiled back, reaching up to pull him down on her.

He went, covering her naked body with his own as though understanding her need at that moment to feel again his total mastery over her in the full weight of his body pressing down on hers.

Their mouths joined and remained joined, even as their caresses became more heated, more intimate. Need began to build like a coiled spring inside both of them, building and building until on a sob she spread her legs and wound them invitingly around him.

It was all the prompting he needed. He entered her on a single swift, sure thrust, then lay heavily against her, his heart, like her own, thundering out of control, mouths still locked while he battled to maintain some control over himself.

She had closed around him like a silken sheath, taking in and holding the pulsing force of him deep, deep inside her.

Then, 'Love me,' she whispered breathlessly.

'I've always loved you, Marnie,' he murmured thickly back. 'How could you ever believe otherwise?'

'No!' she whimpered, shaking her head because she didn't want to hear those words, didn't want to have to think about them, dissect them, understand the devastating import of what they meant.

'Oh, yes, angel,' he sighed out caressingly. 'Yes.'

He moved then, and suddenly words didn't matter. Their bodies were so in tune that they climbed together in a rhapsody of deep, slow body movements, and when the climax did come it hit her with a sudden racing of the pulses, and that wonderful high tensile floating of the senses held her hovering for endless moments of incredible beauty before she was released, pulling Guy with her into the storm awaiting them, ripples becoming waves, and waves a riptide of pure sensation that carried them on and on before finally, inevitably letting them swim lazily into quieter waters.

They lay spent for a long time before either of them felt willing to move. And then only Guy seemed to find the strength to do it, sliding away from her then reaching to flip back the covers before lifting her gently beneath them and joining her there.

He took her back into his arms, and Marnie lay wrapped in the wonderful afterglow of a beautiful experience, her mind still drifting somewhere high above the clouds, limbs heavy, body replete, senses content to settle back into a languid calm while she listened to the comforting throb of his heartbeat beneath her cheek.

Guy moved again, scooping up the thick curtain of her hair and giving it one gentle twist around his fist— as he always used to do—just before he set it on the pillow behind her.

Then he settled his cheek lightly on top of her head, brushed his lips against her hair and said quietly, 'Tell me about the child we made and lost, Marnie,' and succeeded in exploding her contented world into a million broken pieces.

CHAPTER ELEVEN

MARNIE came awake the next morning to find herself alone. And only the imprint on the pillow beside her said that Guy had ever been there.

But he had been, she remembered dully. Carefully, steadily—ruthlessly stripping her of every last layer of protection she had grown around herself over the years until all that was left was the raw and tortured woman he found beneath.

So, now he knew everything. She had told him the lot, dumping it all on his lap with a bitter malice which showed how thoroughly he had deranged her with his cruel shock-tactics.

And if she had locked it all away inside her because it was the only way to deal with the pain of it all, then the opening up of that terrible door had inflicted double the pain, double the anger and double the guilt for what she saw as her own unforgivable selfishness in running away as she had, giving no thought to the fragile life growing inside her.

To be fair to Guy, when it had all come pouring out, he had held on to her tightly, refusing to let go even when she fought him like a wildcat in an effort to break free.

Oh, he had held her close, given her his strength and his comfort throughout the whole ordeal. But he had not been satisfied until he had wrenched every last detail from her.

'You should have told me all this a long time ago!' he had censured angrily when her sobs had threatened to tear her apart inside. 'Look how it hurts for its four years' festering. See what you do to yourself now.'

'How did you find out?' she asked when she had enough control over herself to wonder at his uncanny knowledge. She had told no one about her poor baby. No one. Not even Clare, when she'd gone through a similar tragedy.

'Let's just leave it that I did know,' he said grimly. 'For now it is all out in the open, Marnie, it should be let go. God knows, we've both suffered enough over it—more than enough.'

For some reason, the dull throb in his voice set her crying all over again. He drew her closer, and it was in his arms that she fell asleep—only to wake up to find him gone.

And she didn't dare wonder what that had to mean.

It was then she heard it—the distinctive growl of a powerful engine revving in the distance. She climbed out of bed and, grabbing the loose end of the sheet, wrapped it around her naked body and moved over to the window to wait, knowing that the sound meant that Guy was already down at the track and preparing to take out one of his cars.

It must have rained in the night, she noticed. The air had a fresh, damp smell about it, the lawns below her sparkling in the weak morning sun. She could see the stream babbling more fiercely down towards the lake. And over to the west, just beyond the valley itself, she could see more clouds gathering, thick and dark, promising yet more rain soon.

But the sun still shone on Oaklands, and Roberto's roses seemed happy enough to lift their heads and open their petals, so maybe the storm was not coming this way——

She heard it then, the sudden change in motor noise, followed quickly by a throaty roar which said Guy had put the car in gear and was speeding smoothly out of the pit lane.

She had often stood here like this waiting for him to go flashing by in some sleek growling monster at awe-inspiring speed. And she closed her eyes now, so she could watch with her mind's eye him shoot out of the pit lane on to the track itself, each small cut in engine sound denoting a split-second change in gear.

He was already in top gear by the time he hit the track, accelerating away down the main straight on a roar which set her pulses racing along with it. In a second or two he would reach the first sharp curve which sent the track into a tricky S-bend. She heard the distinctive sound as he changed down, the throaty noise as he throttled back followed by the frightening surge of power that said he was out of the bend and accelerating towards the bridge which would take him over the stream then on around the lake until he hit the straight directly in front of the house, coming into her view just as he cleared the water.

Her breath caught in anticipation, eyes wide with a mixture of excitement and fear, for when he hit the length of road in front of her it meant he would have whichever car it was he had decided to take out travelling at its maximum speed.

But it was only when she saw the flash of blue and white as he came into view that she realised he wasn't driving one of the beautiful museum pieces, but the Frabosa Formula One.

The updated and daunting car was similar to the one he had won his world championships in, but had since moved on a pace in its development to become one of the best cars on the circuit this decade. Guy had decided to include this one in his collection as a testimony to his own success.

And it was the car she hated the most, for its gruesome power, for its flimsy build, and for its total lack of respect for anything human. And because Guy only ever drove that awful car when he was in the blackest of moods.

But what had her heart thudding heavily in her breast as she watched him fly past was the knowledge that he was driving that thing because of what she had told him last night. She was sure of it, just as she was suddenly sickeningly sure that he had taken the blame for their lost child entirely on himself.

With her eyes tightly closed, and lips drawn tight across her teeth, her ears took up her whole concentration, listening for and interpreting each minute sound the engine made for signs of malfunction. Or, worse—any bad timing on the driver's part. You didn't spend twelve months of your life around men like Guy without learning quickly the sounds which mattered.

He should be changing gear—now!

He did. Marnie wilted gratefully. The timing was that crucial. For, after the straight in front of the house, he had to negotiate the chicane, a cleverly constructed piece of engineering which also took him back across the stream again, through a series of tricky bends then back towards the main section in front of the pits.

. She followed each sound all the way around, knowing to within a metre just where the car should be.

By the time he hit the pits straight he would really be opening up the throttle, his tyres warmed and ready to respond to his lightest command. It would be the second or maybe the third circuit before he was really flying. And then the crew would be out with their stop-watches, clocking his track time, just as they would do in a real race.

Trembling, she spun away from the window and made for the dressing-room, dragging on a pair of jeans and a sweatshirt without bothering with underwear, determined to be back at the window by the time he came past again.

She just made it, breathing fast. He roared past at full throttle, a mere blur on her vision. And she closed her eyes on a silent prayer that he would judge the first bend correctly.

He did. She held her breath. The chicane next. Through—tyres prostesting when he must have touched one of the concrete kerbs on a slight error of judgement.

Don't do it again! she scolded him silently as he began negotiating the series of bends. Then the smooth roar as he reached full speed past the pits. She waited for him to reach the S-bend, hating his need to test himself in such a way. Hating even more his reason for doing it.

Marnie watched him go by her a third time, and knew with a sinking heart that he had to be driving

that car with the turbo charger full on, because she
had never seen it go so fast! She almost dropped to
the floor with relief when he got safely around the
next bend, then the chicane—it was like having her
own personal scaled-down model running around her
head, she could be that accurate on where he was at
any moment.

The straight in front of the pits again, and the roar
as he boosted the turbo, the sound seeming to fill the
whole valley. Then the S-bend——

She waited breathlessly for the familiar protest from
the engine as he throttled back sharply—and certainly
the change-down did occur, but the immediate uplift
of power never followed it. Instead there was the
tooth-grating sound of squealing brakes and screaming
tyres followed all too quickly by nothing.

Absolute silence.

For a full five seconds Marnie didn't move a muscle,
the echo of those screaming tyres consuming her every
sense, while she used those few precious seconds to
accept what had happened.

Then she was running, barefoot, out of the
bedroom, along the landing and down the stairs. Hair
streaming out behind her, face pure white, she ran
across the hall, past Roberto without stopping, even
though some sane portion of her mind told her that
he too must have heard the crash and understood its
frightening possibilities. But she was too wrapped up
in her own terror to stop, running out of the door and
around the side of the house, racing across neatly
shorn lawns, slipping on the wet grass as she went,
knowing exactly where she was making for, exactly
at what spot Guy had spun the car.

She saw the plume of thick black smoke curling up into the sky just as she reached the thick hedge which separated the track from the house, and she stopped, taking this next horror with a choking whimper before she was off and running again, forcing herself through the hedge without a care to the scratches it issued to her arms and face. Careless of everything but the one thought that was going around and around in her head.

Guy was dead, and she had not told him she loved him.

She saw the emergency van at the scene as she rounded a curve in the track. The red van was parked at an angle, its doors all swinging open. The blue and white car was not far away, lost to a blaze of fire and smoke while the men fought to contain the flames. White clouds of foam were emitting from their hand-held extinguishers, fluffy particles of the stuff floating in the air all around them.

Dismay took her legs from under her, sending her tumbling to the ground, her choked cry of horror splitting the air around her. Then she struggled up again, pushing her hair out of her face, terrified of going on yet drawn by some morbid desire to see, witness the worst for herself.

It was as she neared the emergency van that she saw him. He was standing by one of the open doors, his left hand holding his right shoulder, his attention fixed on the tangled mess which was all that was left of the car.

For some reason, seeing him just standing there as large as life, silver flame-proofed suit hardly marked, protective helmet still firmly on his head, Marnie lost

touch with reality, and on a surge of white hot fury
she launched herself at him.

'You crazy, stupid man!' she yelled, the grinding
force of her voice bringing his head sharply around
to see her running furiously towards him.

'Marnie...' He put out his left hand in a calming
gesture. 'It's all right. I am not——'

But she wasn't listening. Rage consumed her. And
on a cry that came out like an animal howl she threw
herself at him, hitting out with her fists, tears pouring
down her cheeks, eyes almost blind with shock and
anger.

Guy tried to field her blows by catching her fists,
but she was too quick and he was still feeling dazed
from the crash. And she caught him on his right
shoulder, making him wince, and draw back
instinctively.

Then someone was catching her from behind. And
a different voice tried bringing the tirade to a halt.
'Mrs Frabosa!' it said sternly. 'The man is injured;
you can't——'

'Let go of her,' Guy rasped. Marnie was sobbing
by now, great big racking sobs that by far outstripped
the ones she had sobbed the night before. 'Let go of
her, Tom.'

'But she——'

'Let go.'

The man set her free and stood back, but ready,
despite what his employer said, to catch her if she
made another attack on Guy.

But she had already hit herself out, the anger replaced with a deep inner ache that sent her crumbling
to her knees on the wet ground in front of them.

She looked pathetic, jeans scuffed, bare feet all muddied, hair a tangled mess around her face and shoulders, and hands shaking so violently that she had to clutch them together on her lap to keep them still.

Guy muttered something beneath his breath, trying to unclip the strap holding his helmet in place.

'Dammit, Tom!' he rasped. 'Do this for me, will you?'

He stood impatiently while Tom struggled with the strap, both men more concerned with the state Marnie had got herself into than the car or Guy's injuries now.

'Shock,' Tom muttered. 'She must have thought——'

'I know exactly what she thought,' Guy cut in grimly.

The helmet came off, followed by the white flame-proof snood he always wore beneath. 'Get back to the car,' he said to Tom, thrusting both items at him, then dropped down on his knees in front of Marnie, shielding her from the sympathetic glances she was receiving from the rest of the team, but not attempting to touch her while he waited once again for her to cry herself out.

After a while, he sighed heavily and glanced at the burned-out remains of the car, steaming passively now. The first spot of rain hit his cheek, and even as he went to wipe it away the deluge came, drenching them all in seconds.

'If the fire is out, then get back to the house and let my father know I am OK,' he told the crew.

They went quickly, glad to get out of the rain but curious as to why Guy was just kneeling there in front of his wife, doing nothing in the way of either trying to comfort her or protecting them both from the deluge.

They drove away in the red van. Guy watched them go, his eyes grim and bleak. Then he turned his attention back to Marnie, and, still without attempting to touch her, began to talk, quietly, levelly, with little to no emotion sounding in his tone, and she went silent as she knelt there in front of him, listening, with her heart locked in her aching throat.

'You know,' he began, 'the first time I saw you, here in the yard behind the house, I thought to myself, My God, this is it. The one I have been waiting for for so many years! I wanted to grab hold of you there and then and never let you go. But even as I stood there just drinking you in I could also see that you were about the most innocent creature I had ever laid eyes on. I knew, also, that it would be wrong of me to follow my greedy instincts, though. I was too old for you—oh, not only in years,' he sighed out heavily, 'but in experience. In life! I had done too much, seen too much, and, God help me, *been* too much to be even daring to consider contaminating you with it all. And you possessed special self-protective instincts, too. Instincts that warned you to have nothing to do with a cynical old devil like me. You disapproved of me, Marnie, from the moment our eyes clashed.'

'I didn't disapprove of you,' she denied, the rain pouring on to the top of her bowed head and running down the long pelt of her hair.

Even with her face averted, she knew he smiled. 'You did, Marnie,' he insisted. 'Disapproved of everything about me. My so-called friends. My arrogance. My rather notorious reputation—even my practised methods of seduction! The only glimmer of hope you ever allowed me then was the fact that you could not stop yourself responding to me despite the disapproval! And it was that—need you developed for my physical touch that I exploited ruthlessly to get you to marry me,' he admitted, 'then spent the next year trying to live up to the illusion I had created that it was just your body I coveted. When all the time, Marnie——' his hand came up to lightly touch her cheek '—what I coveted deeply was your love.'

'Oh, Guy,' Marnie sighed. 'How can such an intelligent man be so stupid?'

'Stupid just about says it,' he agreed. 'I knew you were pregnant with our child, Marnie,' he told her, swallowing down on the sudden lump which had formed in his throat. Unable to look at her, he glanced over the track to where the house stood shrouded by the pounding rain. 'Even before you came looking for me that night, I knew.'

'But you couldn't have!' she cried. 'I didn't even know myself!'

'But I did not know that.' He faced her grimly. 'I came back from my business trip to find you standing there looking so wan and frail that it just—hit me— and I knew you were pregnant.' He shrugged helplessly. 'It was logical to assume that you must know also. But you never said a word about it to me, and you looked so unhappy, as if a child between us was the last thing on earth you wanted, and I was hurt, enough to want to hurt you in return, so I threw some nasty little remark at you about the mess you looked, and turned round and walked out again!'

'And didn't come back again that night,' she inserted painfully.

'I sat in my car, in the basement car park,' he confessed, smiling bleakly at her look of surprise. 'Sat there all night just thinking, feeling rotten for speaking to you like that, and seething with my own hurt because you could not bring yourself to even tell me we had made a child! I came back into the apartment the next morning——'

'Looking as if you'd just crawled out of someone's bed to come straight home.'

He nodded, his expression rueful. 'I know exactly how I must have looked to you,' he acknowledged. 'So we started rowing again, and, in the end—through sheer desperation more than anything else because you were actually voicing the idea of leaving me by then— I packed you off down here. Told you brutally to choose between me and your precious work. Smiled and waved arrogantly at you and drove away. Back to London and to blessed relief in a whisky bottle.'

'Not expecting me to come chasing up to London when I eventually realised I was pregnant, wanting only to share the news with you.'

'But instead you found me with another woman.' He lifted his pained eyes to hers. 'That was the night I came to realise just how much you loved me,' he said roughly. 'And just how much I had lost.'

'But Guy,' Marnie frowned, 'if you never knew before how much I loved you, then how——?'

'You were destroyed, Marnie,' he said. 'I destroyed you that night you found me in bed with Anthea. And it does not matter whether I was innocent or not, or whether I was too drunk to know anything about it or not. The simple fact of the matter was that I had been so busy hiding my own love from you that I had not even noticed you were loving me too! And when you flew at me when I got home that night you did not do it in anger, but with all the pain and anguish of one who saw their hopes and dreams lying dead and bloodied at their feet. Only a heart bleeds like that, Marnie. I know because my own heart bled along with yours.'

'Oh, Guy,' Marnie whispered unhappily. 'Of course it matters! There's a whole world of difference between seeing your husband in bed with another woman because it's where he prefers to be, and seeing your husband in bed with another woman because his awful friends thought it a great way of having some fun with his stupid young wife while he was too drunk to do anything about it!'

'But how did I explain that to you?' he challenged her logic. 'How does a man who has taken great care to make you believe that he only wants you for your delicious body—and was even guilty of threatening to take another woman to his bed when the one he wanted was making herself unavailable to him—how does a man like that defend himself in that kind of damning situation? How could you allow yourself to believe other than what you saw? I had no leg to stand on,' he sighed, 'and I knew, as I watched your love for me turn to hatred in front of my very eyes, that I deserved every last thing I was going to get from you. Though, God, Marnie,' he ground out, 'those six months you disappeared out of sight will always go down as the worst time of my life!

'Then you came back,' he went on hoarsely. 'And the moment I saw your slender figure and that awful lifeless expression in your eyes I knew that the child was gone. And that I was to blame.' He cleared his thickened throat. 'I knew then that I was way beyond forgiveness.'

'So all along,' Marnie concluded, 'when you've talked of penances, you've meant because you blamed yourself because I lost our baby, and not because of Anthea and what I believed you had done.'

He nodded grimly. 'If I had loved you better, Marnie, then——'

'I had a fall, Guy!' she inserted shrilly. 'Neither you nor I could be to blame for that! I fell. I told you last night. I stumbled and fell down some steps. A tragic accident. No one's fault.'

'My fault,' he insisted. 'You are not a careless creature, Marnie. If I had taken better care of you, loved you so openly that you could never have doubted me in any situation you caught me in, then you would not have run away from me. And you would not have become so wrapped up in your misery as to allow yourself to fall!'

'So,' she said, 'because you decided to take the whole guilt of it on to yourself, you then decided the best thing you could do for both of us was jump into that—rotten car and drive it at speeds guaranteed to kill!'

'No.' Reaching out, he took hold of her, dragging her into his arms. 'Never,' he denied. 'I have no intention of ever leaving you again. Be clear on that. But you know my black devils, Marnie. When they drive me I have to answer to them. And behind the wheel of a car I am as cool as a cucumber, clear-headed and clear-eyed. A tyre blew, that's why I spun off the track,' he explained. 'It had nothing to do with my bad driving, or the speed I was travelling at. Or even my trying my best to die for love of you!' he mocked. 'It was just the simple result of a faulty tyre. Nothing else.'

She looked dubiously over at the wrecked car. 'But you could have killed yourself.'

'Impossible,' he said with more his usual arrogance. 'I am too good a driver. Even at speeds of one hundred and fifty miles an hour these cars can be controlled on three wheels. They are built for safety, no matter how flimsy they look.'

'They set on fire at the drop of a hat, too,' she pointed out.

'Which is why I wear all this protective gear, so I can still climb out relatively unscathed.'

It was only then that they both seemed to become aware of the rain pouring relentlessly down on their heads. Of the puddle they were kneeling in. Of their dripping heads and muddy clothes, and their cold, wet faces.

'You look a mess,' Marnie observed frankly. 'And you've hurt yourself—here.' She touched a wet fingertip to his cheek where a bruise was already beginning to swell.

'And you have scratches all over your arms and face.' Guy returned the tender gesture by touching his fingers to the thin red scratch-marks on her cheeks. 'How did they happen?'

'Coming to rescue you,' she told him, blue eyes twinkling ruefully. 'I had to fight my way through a hedge and it fought back—kiss it better?' she murmured huskily.

Guy looked deeply into her love-darkened eyes, then slowly placed a kiss on each red mark. 'Anywhere else?' he enquired as he drew away.

'Oh, all over, I think,' she sighed, the feather-like feel of his mouth leaving her skin tingling with pleasure. 'What about you?' she then asked in sudden concern. 'Did you hurt yourself anywhere else other than that bruise on your eye?'

'Oh, all over, I think,' he mimicked hopefully.

'Seriously?' she demanded.

'Seriously,' he mocked. 'I bashed my shoulder a bit when the car lurched off the track, then received some other more—er—delicate injuries when a wild woman came at me from nowhere and began beating me up!'

'Oh.' She pouted, remembering her mad attack. 'I was angry with you.'

'I did notice,' he drawled.

'Well,' she defended herself, 'I expected to find you dead, at least! And there you were standing there looking as fit as a blooming fiddle!'

'Is there something worse than death?' he enquired curiously.

'Yes,' Marnie answered, her expression suddenly very serious. 'A lifetime of never knowing how much I love you, Guy.'

'Come here,' he muttered, pulling her against him and wrapping her tightly in his arms. 'You are all I have ever wanted in my life from the moment you entered it, Marnie.'

'Then let's go home, Guy,' she whispered. 'I want to hold you close in that big warm bed I woke up feeling so alone in this morning.'

'Bed?' His mood brightened, his manner with it. 'That has to be a better option than a puddle any day,' he agreed, pulling her to her feet as he got up himself. 'A long hot bath sounds good, too,' he added leeringly.

'A bath for two?' Marnie suggested, tucking her arm around his waist while he hugged her by her shoulders. She lifted her wet face up to him and let her eyes twinkle with promises.

Guy growled something and began to run, dashing with her through the rain towards the house.

'I could paint you looking like this, all wet and sexily tousled,' Marnie told him a few minutes later when they were safely locked behind their bedroom door.

'Not today, you couldn't,' Guy said firmly. 'Today I have other of your—talents to call upon. Mainly making this man you married happy.'

'Be happy, Guy,' she said softly and reached up on tiptoe to brush his lips with hers.

'I will be,' he said, pulling her close again, 'so long as you never leave me again.'

'Never,' she promised. 'You're stuck with me for life.'

FULLY INVOLVED

To Jill, Captain Gardner
and the crew at engine four
for their invaluable assistance

CHAPTER ONE

"CAPTAIN SIMPSON? Regina Lindsay reporting for duty." She checked her gold watch nervously and noted with satisfaction that there were still two minutes to go until the new shift took over. After all her planning, she couldn't afford to make any mistakes now.

The smell of frying bacon from the interior of the station reached her nostrils, making her feel slightly nauseated. She hadn't slept well, anticipating this moment, and couldn't eat breakfast. Her emotions were tying her in knots.

The darkly attractive man seated at the desk put down the copy of *Fire Command* he'd been reading and lifted his head. He was wearing his luxuriant black hair shorter than she remembered. In his days as a newspaper foreign correspondent, he rarely found the time to get it cut. She'd always liked his hair longer because it had a tendency to curl, reminding her of a gypsy's.

Slowly his grey eyes took in the regulation black trousers and grey shirt she wore, then shot her a cold, dispassionate glance. Not by a twitch of the tiny scar at the corner of his mouth did he let her know that her presence affected him.

"Gina. I'm not even going to try to guess why you've shown up here—let alone outfitted like that. I'm on duty for the next twenty-four hours. If this has something to do with alimony payments, call your attorney. He's still in the phone book. Presuming you plan to be in town that long."

He reached for his magazine again, but she noted with satisfaction that his gaze fell on the hurry-ups propped next to her shoes, and his dark brows furrowed in displeasure. She had his attention at last! The standard-issue black boots, trousers, helmet and yellow coat stood ready beside her. As if in slow motion his stormy eyes played over her face and figure once more, fastening on her slender waist where she'd attached her walkie-talkie.

At this point he rose to his full six feet two inches, looking leaner and fitter than she'd ever seen him. In full dress uniform he was heartbreakingly handsome. "If this is some kind of joke, I'm not amused."

She cleared her throat. "You asked for a replacement while Whittaker is on a leave of absence. I'm swinging in from Engine House Number Three. Call Captain Carrera if you want."

He scowled. "Captain Carrera is a pushover for a pretty face. What's going on, Gina?" he asked in a wintry tone. "Where did you get that turnout gear?"

"In San Francisco, when I graduated and started to work." She pulled her badge out of her shirt pocket and put it on top of the magazine. He stared at the official insignia of the Salt Lake City Fire Department as if he'd never seen it before. His hand closed over the badge.

"Your approach is very novel, Gina, but enough's enough. I'm warning you—"

"Hey, Grady! I'm in!" One of the fire fighters poked his head inside the door, took one look at Gina and grinned. "Oops! Sorry, Captain. Just wanted you to know I'm here." Gina couldn't look at Grady as the fire fighter walked through the engine house calling, "Eighty-six! Eighty-six!" It was the code that meant a woman was on the premises. Everyone would be on his best behaviour.

"Captain?" A man who seemed close to fifty knocked on the door and then came in without asking. "I'm going to fuel the truck unless you have other work assigned for me right now."

"Go ahead," Grady muttered.

"Ma'am." The older fire fighter nodded politely to Gina before leaving them alone once more. Following his exit four other men came into Grady's office on the pretext of checking in, but Gina was well aware of the real reason, and she had an idea that Grady was, too. Her gilt-blonde hair drew attention wherever she went. In an effort to minimise her attractiveness, she wore it in a ponytail while on duty, but she had no way of hiding her unusual violet eyes with their dark lashes. As Grady had once told her, no other woman he'd ever met possessed her unique colouring—then he'd whispered that she was some kind of miracle as he pulled her into his arms. But she knew those memories had no place here today.

"All right, now that you've gained the attention of the entire department," he said, pointedly eyeing the last man out of the door before flicking her a hostile glance, "I'm afraid you'll have to leave."

Gina stood her ground but Grady would never know what it cost her to remain upright when her legs felt like buckling. "You requested a replacement because you're a person short. I'm the one who's been sent."

His eyes narrowed to silvery slits. "If you're a fire fighter, I'm Mary Poppins!"

Warmth suffused her cheeks. "Call headquarters. They'll verify my status as a paramedic, as well."

"I don't have time to listen to this," he bit out. "Goodbye, Gina. Whatever it is you want can be accomplished through the mail. I believe I've made myself clear. The door is be—"

"Ladder one respond to concession fire in Liberty Park area." The dispatcher's voice over the gong accomplished what nothing else could have. A fire fighter's sole function was to respond to the alarm once it sounded. Grady left her standing there as if she didn't exist and ran to the truck. Already she could hear the revving of the engine and shouts from the men. And she could feel the familiar surge of adrenalin that filled every fire fighter's veins once a call came. It was as natural as breathing for her to want to respond, but she'd been assigned to engine one. So therefore she had no choice but to go inside and settle in until the gong sounded for their rescue unit.

The truck left the station, its siren wailing, within twenty seconds of the time the alarm had come in. Anything under a minute was good, Gina mused, feeling inordinately proud of the work Grady did. So many times in their short-lived marriage, he'd tried to explain this pride and sense of exhilaration to her, but she hadn't understood. In all honesty, she hadn't wanted to. Out of fear that he might get killed, she'd accused him of trying to be a macho man who got his kicks from playing with fire.

How wrong she'd been. How little she'd understood what motivated him. Not until she'd been through the rigorous training herself had she begun to comprehend his love of fire fighting. It gave him a natural high that not even his work as a correspondent, covering explosive situations in the Middle East and Central America, had offered. That high was contagious and had finally infected her. But how to make *him* see that?

She reached down for her turnout gear, aware that seeing Grady for the first time since the divorce had shaken her badly. She'd rehearsed the moment a thousand times in her mind, imagining—fearing—it would go exactly as it did. But his indifference to her physical presence managed to twist the knife a little deeper, dissolving her hopes that somewhere inside him he still cared.

If he'd been told ahead of time that she worked for the fire department and was being sent to his station, he'd have been on the phone to the battalion chief to protest. She wouldn't have been able to get near him.

This way, she had the slight advantage of cornering him in his own territory. She knew enough about her ex-husband to realise he detested making his private business public. He wouldn't be able to get rid of her in front of the others without creating an embarrassing scene.

So when he came back and found her in residence, he'd have to live with the fact until they could be completely alone. A shiver crept along her spine at the thought of that confrontation, but too much was at stake for her to back down now.

As a friend had once innocently said when Gina admitted she was still in love with Grady, "Then stop moaning about it. Go after him! Fight fire with fire!" Gina had done exactly that. And she'd come face-to-face with a man whose eyes were as dead to her as the ashes of last winter's grate fire.

Someone's tuneless whistle broke in on her thoughts. One of the men she'd seen a few minutes ago came into the office on a lope, but he stopped short when he noticed her gear. His light blue eyes smiled. "Hi. I'm Lieutenant Corby. You must be Ron Whittaker's replacement."

"That's right. I'm Gina Lindsay." She shook his outstretched hand with difficulty because of the helmet and boots she carried, and they both laughed. The sandy-haired man didn't seem to take himself too seriously. Gina liked that.

"Since the captain's not here, I'll show you around. For a minute there, we all thought you were his latest conquest." Relieving her of the boots, he grinned in a mischievous manner that exuded confidence.

Gina fought to keep the smile pasted on her face. "The captain has a reputation, does he?" she asked as she followed him into the large room behind the office that served as a living-room-cum-lounge.

"Only after hours. He's a stickler for the rules. Fortunately for me, I'm not. You married?"

"You're straightforward, I'll grant you that, Lieutenant, so I'll return the favour. I'm not married but I made an ironclad rule when I became a fire fighter— no mingling with the crew except on a professional basis." In fact, she hadn't accepted a date since her return to Salt Lake and generally preferred the company of Susan Orr, a fire fighter from engine five.

"Not ever?" His mock expression of pain made her laugh again, and this in turn brought two other men out of the kitchen, carrying mugs of coffee.

"Howard? Ed? Meet Gina. She's the swing-in for Whittaker."

The men said hello and eyed her speculatively, but not with the same glimmer of male admiration they'd displayed earlier when they thought she was a visitor. She'd come to expect this reaction from her male co-workers. Only in recent years had women intruded on their all-male fraternity.

Gina tried hard to blend into the background and not call attention to herself. Most of the fire fighters she knew were becoming accustomed to females in the department, but a few still had trouble accepting women in the traditionally male role. She could understand their feelings. She was a woman, and that made a difference in their eyes. It always would. The only thing to do was try to get along, and for the most part Gina had succeeded. But it took time to ease in and become a part of the family.

"You can bunk in that bed next to the wall," the lieutenant continued, setting her boots down beside it. He gave her a quick tour of the kitchen, bathroom and dorm. "We've all eaten breakfast, but there's plenty left if you're hungry."

"Thanks. I might take you up on that after I settle in."

"Grab it while you can. We get busy around here. Working under the captain, you'll learn stuff that wasn't in the textbooks. Here. Let me put your coat and helmet out by the truck, and call me Bob when the captain's not around. Okay?"

"Okay." Once again, she relinquished her things to him without the argument that she could do it herself. Some men couldn't break the habit of treating her like a woman instead of simply a co-worker. She didn't mind at all.

Once alone, she surveyed her kingdom. Eight beds and eight individual lockers took up most of the dorm's space. She straightened her hurry-ups and threw her small overnight bag on the bed, pulling out a pair of overalls before she went into the bathroom to dress. She expected to be uncomfortably warm; the weatherman predicted ninety-eight degrees by mid-afternoon, a typical July day. However, she liked the dry heat of Utah after the dampness of the Coast.

Gina forced herself to eat a light breakfast, but any second she expected to hear the truck returning to the station and the sound of Grady's deep voice issuing orders. She decided to do without coffee because she didn't need a stimulant. The dispatcher's voice coming periodically over the radio kept her adrenalin flowing at a fairly steady pace. That, combined with the fact that she'd be working with Grady, had her heart pumping overtime as it was.

"We're going to play tennis before it gets too hot," Bob called out from the next room. "You ready?"

"I'll be right there." She finished putting her dishes in the cupboard and ran out of the kitchen. Howard and Ed were already on board the engine. Bob held the door open for her, but to her dismay she could hear the ladder truck already entering the bay.

"Ms Lindsay. If I could have a word with you," Grady ordered as he jumped off the rig that had backed into the station. He tossed his helmet on the peg and walked over to her, his eyes a smouldering black. He was her superior, so Gina had no choice but to obey. She removed her booted foot from the step.

"Next time," Bob promised. The other men waved and the engine roared off.

Gina followed Grady to his office with trepidation, while the other men headed for the kitchen. She sensed Grady had now had time for the shock to wear off. Inside the office, he turned around and leaned against the door, arms folded. His silence, ominous and unforgiving, made her feel uneasy, and she sought refuge in one of the chairs facing his desk.

"I hoped you'd be gone when we came back, but I suppose it was too much to ask for. You've got exactly one minute to tell me what this is all about." She heard the underlying threat in his tone.

"I'm not the person you should be asking since I have no validity in your eyes," she answered calmly. "Call anybody at number three. I've been working there for two months, and before that, in Carmel and San Francisco. Yesterday Captain Carrera told me my orders were to report here this morning."

A nasty smile pulled at the corner of his mouth. "Are you honestly trying to tell me that the woman I divorced because of irreconcilable differences to do with my job—among other things—is now a fully certified fire fighter?"

"Yes." Her chin lifted a fraction.

"Forgive me, but my imagination simply won't stretch that far."

Gina got to her feet, needing to choose her words carefully. "Grady, I don't blame you for being incredulous, but a lot has happened in the past three years."

A dark brow quirked disdainfully. "You're asking too much if you expect me to believe you've become an entirely different person in that period of time. The word *fire* used to scare the life out of you."

"That's true," she said forcefully, "until I sought professional help."

"That's an interesting revelation, considering the fact that you point-blank refused to get help all the time we were married." The cords stood out in his bronzed neck. "I begged you to talk to someone. I'd have done anything if I'd thought it would do any good, but you weren't interested."

"You're wrong, Grady. I was too *frightened*." She wiped her moist palms against her hips in an unconscious gesture of frustration and uncertainty. "Don't you see? If I couldn't be helped, then it would have been worse than ever! I was afraid of the answer."

His mouth thinned to a white line. "But *after* our divorce you suddenly found the courage. That pretty well says it all, doesn't it, Gina?"

"Engine one respond to medical assist at 1495 Washington Boulevard."

Grady unexpectedly reached out and grasped her wrist. "Let's find out what kind of fire fighter you've become...with paramedic training to boot! And when we get back you can further enlighten me as to why you've returned to the scene of the crime. I'm not through with you, Gina. Not by a long shot!"

He perforce had to let go of her arm as they entered the lounge. "Winn? You'll ride engine for now. I'm going on this assist." He rapped out the order as they hurried to the ladder truck. Gina could still feel the imprint of Grady's hand on her wrist by the time they arrived at their destination on the west side of town.

Grady rarely lost control in any situation, and the ferocity of his grip told her she'd hit a nerve, one that ran deep.

Rico drove the truck. Next to him sat Frank, then Gina. Grady got in last and shut the door. She was almost sick with excitement at being this close to him after all these years. His body remained rigid. No one in the department would ever have guessed how intimate she and their revered captain had once been. He showed no feelings for her now except a residue of bitterness that her presence had suddenly evoked.

Still, she was where she'd wanted desperately to be. There'd been times during the past few years when she'd wondered if she'd ever realise her dream of being with Grady again.

As they pulled up to a white frame bungalow Grady made the assignments. "Gina will be patient man, Rico, you stay with the rig. Frank, you and I will supply back-up. Let's go."

Gina followed Grady off the truck and strode quickly to the front porch, where a middle-aged woman stood waiting just inside the screen door. She held up her left hand, and Gina could see that her ring finger was swollen to twice its size, constricted by her wedding rings.

"Thank heavens you came," she blurted out, white with pain. "I didn't know what to do. Once in a while I break out in hives, but this sneaked up on me. I can't get my rings off and I'm afraid I'll lose my finger."

"We're here in plenty of time to prevent that from happening," Gina assured her. "Let's go into the kitchen. The table is a perfect place for you to lie down while we get those rings off. I'll just grab a pillow off your couch, and Frank will go out to the truck to get the cutter. What's your name?" As Gina conversed with the woman, Grady stood a few feet away scrutinising her every move.

"Mary Fernandez." The woman sighed as she climbed up on the table with Gina's help and lay flat on her back.

"Well, Mary Fernandez," Gina said, smiling, "we'll have you comfortable within a half-hour. What have you taken for the pain?"

"Aspirin."

"Good. That will help."

"Is it bad?" the woman asked anxiously.

"Swelling often seems worse than it really is. What I don't like to do is cut into your rings. They're beautiful."

"I think so," Mary said. "My husband's away on business. He won't believe this."

"Well, now you'll have something exciting to tell him," Gina soothed, taking the cutter from Frank. "It will hurt for a while because I have to get the underside of the saw around the band. I'm going to cut through in three places. If you want to scream, I won't mind."

"I had five children and never screamed." She chuckled, but Gina could see the way the woman was biting her lip.

As incident commander, Grady had to write a report, and he made notes, asking a few questions while Gina continued to saw carefully through the gold bands. Twenty minutes later, the swollen red finger was free of the constriction.

"Ah..." The woman moaned her relief, and her eyes filled with tears. "You're an angel from heaven and you look like one, too. Thank you."

"You're welcome." Gina assisted the woman to her feet and handed her the pieces of her wedding bands. "These can be made to look like new again."

The older woman smiled. "It doesn't matter. My finger's more important."

"Indeed it is. Do you know what causes your hives?"

"No, but I'm going to call a doctor and find out so nothing like this ever happens again."

"Well, you take care of yourself, Mary. Call us again if you're ever in trouble."

"I will," she murmured, walking them to the door. "What's your name? I want to write a letter to the department to let them know how grateful I am for what you did."

"Just call us station one. Goodbye, Mary." Gina shook hands with the woman before going outside to the truck. By now a medium-sized crowd had gathered around. This time, Gina was last to climb on to the rig.

"How many times have you done that manoeuvre?" Frank wanted to know as they drove into the mainstream of traffic.

"That was my first."

"You could have fooled me. You have a real nice way about you, Gina. Welcome aboard."

"Thanks. Actually, the woman was wonderful. That had to hurt!"

"Rico, pull over at the next supermarket. We'll grab a bite of lunch." Grady's suggestion effectively changed the topic of conversation.

"Will do, Captain. Who wants to go in on barbecued spare ribs?"

"I do." Gina and Frank both spoke at the same time. Under normal circumstances, Gina had a healthy appetite but was fortunate to have a metabolism that kept her nicely rounded figure on the slender side. When she worked a particularly busy and demanding shift, she ate what the men did. Fire fighting devoured calories.

"How about you, Captain?" Rico inquired.

"I don't know. I'll wait till I get in there."

Rico parked in an alley and they all went inside the store. They'd just made their purchases when another call came through on their walkie-talkies. By the time they reached the scene of a car that was on fire, it had burned itself out. Grady made a preliminary report, and then they headed back to the station, eating their food on the way.

Since the bathroom wasn't in use when they returned, Gina slipped inside to wash, thinking she'd relax on her bunk for a while and read the latest issue of *Firework*. But when she walked into the dorm, her cot wasn't there. Puzzled, she went over to the locker, but all her belongings had disappeared.

"I took the liberty of moving your bed and gear to my office, in case you were wondering."

Gina whirled around. "Why would you do that?"

"Because there's no way you're sleeping with seven men," Grady said in an authoritative voice that brooked no argument. They were still alone in the dorm.

"I've never asked for special privileges and I don't intend to start now. It's bad for morale, and I don't want to be singled out."

"In this station, you do it my way, Gina."

"At number three the four of us slept in the same room."

His grey eyes glittered dangerously. "Perhaps now that you've left, they'll be able to get some sleep."

"There are five women in the department and—"

"Half of my crew is married." His face wore a shuttered expression. "I won't allow you to create any undue stress among the wives by sleeping in the same room with their husbands."

"Do you think I'd intentionally try to cause trouble?" Her chest heaved with indignation.

"It follows you, Gina."

"When we were married I don't recall making a fuss because you slept in the same room with female fire fighters."

His mouth twisted in a mockery of a smile. "You have a short memory. When we were married, there were no women in the department. It made life a whole lot easier."

His tone made her wonder if he was one of those men who didn't approve of female fire fighters on principle, but this was not the time to get into that particular discussion. "The crew will know something's wrong."

He paused on his way out the door. "Don't lose any sleep over it. By your next shift, you'll be back at engine three," he stated with familiar arrogance.

"You can't do that, Grady!" she retorted without thinking. She'd only been on duty seven hours and already he wanted her as far away from him as possible.

"Can't I!" He fixed her with a glacial stare. "Just watch me!"

"I didn't mean it that way." She took a deep breath. "I understand Whittaker will be out several more weeks."

"How typical of you, Gina. Now you're certified, you think you're the only paramedic in the department."

She bit her lip in an effort not to rise to the bait. "I don't want to be switched back before the allotted time because it won't look good on my record," she lied. Under no circumstances could she tell Grady the real reason.

"Don't worry." He grimaced and looked at his watch. "Seventeen more hours—after that you're home free. Captain Carrera will understand when I tell him I've found someone else with more years in the department to fill in."

"So you won't give me a chance!" She fought to keep her voice steady.

A nerve twitched alongside his strong jaw. "I'm giving you the same chance you gave *us*, Gina. And now you have approximately five minutes before you're to report to the lounge. We're going to discuss a variety of prefire plans, and we'd all be fascinated by a contribution from you.''

Her delicate brows furrowed. "What do you mean?''

''You trained in San Francisco. Maybe there's something you can teach us," he muttered sarcastically.

''Grady...'' Her eyes pleaded for a little understanding.

''Captain Simpson to you, *Ms Lindsay*.'' He passed a couple of the men on his way out of the dorm. Gina could hear their voices pitched low, then suddenly something Grady said made them burst out laughing. It shouldn't have hurt, but it did...

CHAPTER TWO

WITH ONLY A FEW MINUTES to go until the next shift reported for duty, Gina got up and dressed, made her bed and slipped out of the front door of the station carrying her turnout gear.

She hurried to the private car park out the back and put her things in the Honda, not wanting to be cornered by Grady. Her first twenty-four hours at station one had been enlightening. Fortunately, both the engine and the ladder were kept busy throughout the night, preventing Grady from catching her alone. From time to time, she'd sensed his gaze on her, eyes narrowed in anger, but she didn't acknowledge him unless directly addressed.

A car passed her in the driveway as she pulled out into the street. She expelled a sigh, relieved that she'd managed to escape him, but she knew it was only a temporary respite. Still, she couldn't face him right now. Too many emotions and memories were tearing her apart. She needed a little distance to regain her perspective before he forced a confrontation—and knowing Grady, there would be one....

Traffic was fairly heavy with people anxious to get to work. While she waited through the third red light at the same intersection, she happened to glance in the rear-view mirror. The black Audi several cars behind her wasn't familiar, but she recognised the man at the wheel. Her heart did a funny kick. Was it coincidence or was Grady following her?

Three quarters of the way home to her apartment on the East bench, he still pursued her. Evidently he wanted to get their talk out of the way as soon as possible. A thrill of fear darted through her. His anger had been growing since she'd reported for duty the morning before. Right now she imagined that one wrong word from her might rip away that civilised veneer to reveal the bitter, uncompromising man who'd divorced her.

When she drove into the carport of the duplex she rented, Grady was out of his car and opening her door before she could pull the key from the ignition. "You still drive too fast, Gina."

"Apparently not fast enough," she muttered, sliding out of the driver's seat.

"Something told me I wouldn't find you at home if I came by later." He accompanied her to the front door and stood there, patiently waiting for her to unlock it. She was dismayed to find that her hand trembled. This was *Grady* about to enter her house. She'd imagined it so many times—but not when they'd both just come off duty, dead tired and still wearing their uniforms. Now was not the time for the kind of talk Grady had in mind.

"Come in." She finally found her voice, wondering too late what he would think about her gallery of photographs, covering two entire walls. Many of the pictures were of him, some taken on their honeymoon in Egypt, others in Carmel during a visit to her parents. But he walked into her small living-room without looking around him, his attention focused solely on her. He gave nothing away. His study of her face was almost clinical.

Unable to help herself, Gina stared at him. The first thing she noticed was that he needed a shave. His beard was as black as his curly hair. It gave him a slightly dissipated air that added to his masculine appeal. Without her intending them to, her eyes roamed over the familiar lines and angles of his features and settled on his mouth, a mouth that could curve with a sensuality so beguiling she'd forget everything else.

Three years hadn't changed him, not really. It was more in the way he responded to the people around him that he betrayed a new hardness and cynicism. But maybe it was just with her that he exhibited this dark side. She wondered if the laughing, loving Grady she adored had gone for good—and worse, if she'd been the person to rob him of that *joie de vivre*.

The tempestuous battles leading up to their divorce had killed all the love he'd felt for her. In three years he hadn't once tried to contact her by phone or letter. Like flash fire, their love had burned hot, out of control, sweeping them along in a euphoric blaze. Then suddenly it blew itself out, and she wakened to a nightmare.

"Would you like something to eat or drink?"

"Gina—" he bit out, quickly losing patience with her as he lodged against the arm of the couch. She sat down on the matching sofa across from him. His eyes were a startling grey, impaling her like lasers. "What's going on? What are you doing back in Salt Lake? I'd like an honest answer."

Gina settled back against the cushions and crossed her legs, trying to assume a nonchalance she didn't feel. He wanted honesty but she didn't dare give him that. Not once in twenty-four hours had he shown the least sign that he still had any feelings for her.

All this time she'd held the hope that seeing her again would trigger some kind of positive reaction, however small, however ambivalent.

"I used to live here, Grady."

"More to the point, you died here," he came back in a harsh tone of voice. "The person you were, the marriage we had . . . all dead."

She swallowed hard. "It felt that way at the time—until I sought counselling and started examining the reasons for my so-called phobia."

"Which were?"

"We married without really knowing anything about each other. There I was, teaching English in Beirut, then suddenly I met you and within six weeks we were husband and wife. Our married life in the Middle East was like one long, extended honeymoon with no home base and—"

"And dangerous," he inserted icily. "Certainly as life-threatening as any work I do now, but I don't recall your giving it a thought. If I remember correctly, you were more than eager to be my bride."

Gina averted her eyes. "Grady—" her voice trembled "—you told me that the newspaper you worked for had offered you an editor's job and that you intended to take it so we could start a family. I thought that was why we made our home in Salt Lake. You told me you craved a little domesticity. But after sitting at that desk for a few weeks, you dropped a bomb on me. Without discussing any of it, you resigned and told me you were going to go back to your old job of fire fighting." She got to her feet and began pacing. "I didn't even know you'd been a fire fighter. I thought you'd always been a newspaperman."

"I believe we covered this ground three years ago, Gina."

"And I'm trying to explain to you that I was too young and immature at the time to understand your needs. You were right when you accused me of being spoiled, incapable of giving support or comfort to my husband. It wasn't just my fears of your job. I've never told you this before but I was jealous of your friendship with the crew. I felt as if you loved the fire fighters more than you loved me."

Something flickered in the recesses of his eyes, but he let her go on talking. For the first time she felt that maybe he was listening.

"Don't you see? I wanted to fulfil you in every way, but when you started fire fighting again I thought you must have fallen out of love with me, that I no longer brought you the kind of happiness you needed. As a result, I felt totally inadequate. The psychologist explained that I used the fear of fire to mask my *real* fear of losing you. Perhaps that doesn't make sense to you, but it opened my eyes."

"Go on."

She took a deep breath. "Further along in therapy, I was challenged to explore my fear of fire. The psychologist suggested I observe a fire fighter training session. You see, long after we divorced I was plagued by nightmares, all having to do with fire."

He rubbed the back of his bronzed neck as she spoke. The fact that he didn't interrupt told her he was absorbed in what she had to say.

"Well, I went to a few training sessions and watched and learned. Incredibly, my nightmares went away and I actually found myself wanting to be a participant. The psychologist was right after all. I didn't have a fear of fire. Eventually, one of the trainers suggested I take the examination to see if I could qualify for the school. This didn't happen overnight, of course, but in time I took it and passed, and went on from there."

Grady stared at her for timeless minutes without saying anything. She couldn't imagine what he was thinking.

"Do you remember telling me what it was like to fight and the indescribable feeling you got from helping people?" Her violet eyes beseeched his understanding. "I couldn't relate to that at all. It just made me feel more isolated from you than ever, but—"

"But another miracle occurred and now you understand me completely," he mocked.

"Not completely," she answered, struggling to keep her voice calm, "but I can honestly say I share your love of fire fighting."

His face closed up. "So why didn't you stay in California?"

If only she dared tell Grady what was in her heart, but the very remoteness of his expression prevented her from blurting out her love for him. "I—I suppose deep down I wanted to show you that I had overcome my fear. I knew you'd never believe me unless you actually saw me on the job."

"You're right about that," he said thickly.

"Grady," she began, her voice almost a whisper. "I discovered something else in my counselling sessions. You and I parted with a great deal of bitterness, for which I take most of the blame." She watched his dark brows draw together. "I hoped that if I came back to Salt Lake we could meet as friends and bury past hurts."

He got to his feet, holding himself rigid. "That's asking the impossible, Gina."

She bit her lip and nodded. "Then I'll just have to accept that. I realise our marriage failed mostly because of me. I had this idea that if you heard me say it, it might help to heal some of the wounds. Despite everything, I've always wanted your happiness. And I've always hoped you didn't blame yourself for problems that weren't your fault. You're a fire fighter's fire fighter. I was a naïve little fool to expect you to quit and find something safe and sane to do for the rest of your life. Perhaps a part of me wants your forgiveness.''

His eyes were shuttered. "Forgiveness doesn't come into it, Gina. I was insensitive to your fears and needs, too." She had the impression he was about to say something else and then changed his mind. "I'm glad you got the counselling you needed, but I'm sorry you made the move to Salt Lake to prove something that wasn't necessary. I followed you here because I was afraid you'd come to Utah with the mistaken notion that we could pick up where we left off three years ago.''

She felt like dying. "No. We're both different people now. Firehouse gossip says you have interests elsewhere.''

Grady's intent gaze swept over her. "You've grown up, Gina, and it's all to the good. But it doesn't change the way I feel about your working at station one."

She thrust out her chin. "I figured that was why you followed me home. Well, where do I report for duty tomorrow, or should I call headquarters?"

He didn't say anything for a minute. In the past she'd fought him on everything. Right now he was probably in shock that she was being so amenable. "There will be talk if I switch you to another station before Whittaker comes back, particularly as there were no complaints about your performance. Far be it from me to give you a black mark on your record after one shift because of personal considerations. You can stay on, Gina, until Whittaker reports back, which should be two weeks at the most. But in the meantime, I suggest you bid another couple of stations if you intend to live in Salt Lake."

Two weeks at the most to accomplish the impossible! "I'll take your advice. Thank you, Grady," she whispered, suppressing her joy that he hadn't seen fit to send her out of his domain just yet.

For some reason, Grady didn't seem to like this new side of her, or at least, he didn't seem to know how to respond to her level-headed behaviour. "When you report in the morning, you'll be treated exactly like everyone else."

"Of course."

"Stay away from Frank. He already thinks he's in love with you. He's got a sweet wife at home."

She blinked. "Anything else?"

"Corby's been telling everybody that you don't date fire fighters, but he's going to be the first one to make you break your rule. Don't do it, Gina. It can ruin lives."

They stared at each other across the expanse. "I never have and I never will. Is that good enough for you?"

"You're the one I'm worried about. To be a professional means never to mix business with pleasure. To be a woman in this profession makes it that much more difficult."

Gina smiled. "Do I take it you don't approve of female fire fighters?"

He started walking toward the front door. "Did I say that?" he shot back.

"I'm not sure. I don't remember you expressing your opinion one way or the other when we were married."

"The issue never came up." He gave her an enigmatic look.

"Now that it has, would you tell me your honest feelings?" She'd heard every opinion under the sun, but Grady's was the only one that mattered to her.

He appeared to consider her question for a minute. "If a woman can do her job well, it makes no difference to me."

"But—?" Gina added, sensing a certain hesitancy on his part.

He rubbed the back of his neck thoughtfully. "But I still prefer to retain the image of a woman as I see her. Soft, curvaceous, warm, sweet-smelling...

"I'm afraid a woman in turn-out gear with a mask and Nomex hood loses something in the translation. Particularly when her ears are singed, her knees burned beyond recognition and her face blackened with third-degree burns that never heal properly."

Gina was inordinately pleased with his answer. She cocked her head to the side. "It's a cosmetic thing with you, then."

"I suppose. However, you proved today that you could do the job. So admirably, in fact, that both crews want to hear more from you the next time we discuss prefire procedures. Your comment about always wearing your mask to the scene of a car fire made an impact. In the crew's words, you're all right. High praise indeed after only one shift. Does that answer your question?'' He sounded bored with the whole discussion.

''Yes, but I have one more. Have you told any-one—does anyone know about—''

''About us?'' he interjected sternly. ''No, Gina, and I see no reason for it to ever become public knowl-edge.''

She lowered her eyes. ''No. Of course not.'' Her bottom lip quivered and she bit it. ''What shall I call you at the station? Captain or Grady? The men call you both, depending on circumstances.''

He reached for the front doorknob. ''Do whatever moves you, Gina.''

She drew closer, smiling inside. She wondered what he'd do if she ever called him ''darling'' or ''sweet-heart,'' the way she used to. Neither of them would be able to live it down in front of the crew, but right now she was tempted. ''Well, I'll see you in the morning.''

Grady's pewter eyes played over her features once more before he nodded. Then he was out the door.

She started to shut it but left it open a crack so she could watch him as he strode quickly towards his car and drove away. She hungered for the sight of him and wondered how she would make it through the next twenty hours until she could be with him again.

He'd never know how close she'd come to walking over and putting her arms around him. No matter what their problems, they'd never had trouble com-municating physically. As soon as they were within touching distance, the cares of the world would van-ish. Grady was a passionate lover, always tender and seemingly insatiable. She'd never been intimate with a man until Grady came into her life. After three years, she still couldn't imagine being with anyone else. He'd ruined her for other men; if it was too late for her and Grady now, she had the strong conviction she'd remain single for the rest of her life.

Tears spilled down her cheeks. She missed him terribly. He was the most wonderful thing ever to come into her life, but she'd been too insecure to handle the fact that he lived another life apart from her—a dangerous one.

That was why, at thirty-three, he had an enviable collection of medals for heroism, according to Captain Carrera, and a reputation throughout the city that few men could equal.

Only the most aggressive fire fighters would bid for the kind of action he and others like him faced every time they reported for duty. That reality had paralysed Gina with fear throughout their marriage. Now she quietly preened at all the praise heaped on her ex-husband.

If she hadn't had to keep her former relationship with Grady a secret, she could have entertained the guys with several hair-raising accounts of his daring in Beirut and Nicaragua during his war correspondent days. They'd never hear about it otherwise, because Grady was so modest—always had been. He couldn't see that what he did was in any way out of the ordinary.

To Gina, her husband had been bigger than life. But she'd loved Grady with a possessive love and lost him.

If he'd only give them another chance, she longed to show him how different their marriage could be. There had to be a way to reach him, and she'd find it no matter how long that took!

Naturally Grady would have been with other women since their divorce, but so far no other woman had captivated him to the point that he'd proposed marriage. As far as Gina was concerned, her ex-husband was fair game and she would break any rule to win him back. With luck, Whittaker wouldn't return as quickly as Grady envisaged, giving her more time to rekindle his interest. Then maybe he'd learn to like the woman she'd become—enough to want to see her off duty.

Happier than she'd been in three years, Gina cleaned her apartment from top to bottom, showered, then took a long nap. Later in the day she went to dinner and a movie with her friend, Sue.

They'd met when a fellow fire fighter was injured and taken to the burn unit at University Hospital. During their all-night vigil they'd hit it off famously. When they had free days at the same time, they often watched videos and ordered pizza. Susan was down on policemen at the moment, having dated one who'd turned out to be married.

She and Susan had quite a lot in common, personally and professionally, and it amazed Gina now to think that during the months she lived in Salt Lake with Grady she'd never once gone down to the station house or met any of his crew. She hadn't made any new friends, particularly avoiding people connected with Grady's line of work. Her life had been far too insular, always waiting for Grady to come home. She hadn't wanted anyone else if she couldn't have him. He must have felt so trapped, she mused sadly.

When Gina reported for work the next morning, she could hardly contain her excitement, because she and Grady would be spending the next twenty-four hours under the same roof. Her eyes searched for him hungrily as she let herself in the front door of the station, dressed in overalls. He and the others had already started their routine jobs of checking out the apparatus. Everything had to work, from the siren to the lights. All the breathing equipment had to be in perfect condition.

"Good morning," she called out. The men turned in her direction to greet her. She was conscious of their staring, but it was Grady's grey eyes she sought. To make sure he never forgot that she was a warm, sweet-smelling, curvaceous woman, she'd left her hair long and brushed it until it gleamed a silvery gold. Behind her ears she'd applied a new, expensive perfume Grady wouldn't recognise, but she wore little make-up except lipstick. She returned everyone's smiles, noting that Grady was the only one who merely glanced at her and nodded while he continued to inspect the pump gauges.

"What's my assignment for this morning, Captain?"

"You can start with the windows in the station."

"All right." She headed for the kitchen to fill a pan with hot water and vinegar. No fire fighter loved doing the station's housekeeping duties, but washing w͏ dows was definitely the most abhorrent and demeaning assignment of all. Bathrooms rated higher.

Gina settled down to her task with a vengeance. Grady knew exactly what he was doing—and he wasn't playing fair. He said he'd treat her like the others, but that obviously wasn't the case. There were enough windows in the place to keep her busy and isolated all day, which was exactly his intention. He purposely didn't assign any of the men to help with the job because he didn't want her fraternising with one individual. She knew Grady was determined to keep her as far away from him as possible, without letting the crew suspect his intentions. And his word was law.

When the gong sounded for engine one to respond to a medical assist because of a family fight, Gina had to leave her window-washing unfinished and hurry out to the truck. Grady had warned them that the Fourth of July holiday would bring a lot of calls. Unfortunately Grady rode ladder, which meant she'd see him only in passing. But even in that assumption she was wrong. After they'd assisted at the stabbing, their engine went immediately to a vacant car park where some children had started a fire while trying to light their "snakes."

The few times the engine returned to the station, the ladder truck was out. By eight that evening, the engine had responded to over twenty calls. Gina grabbed a bite to eat and quickly put the window-washing equipment away before another call came through. She'd have to finish the job on her next shift.

Around eleven, they were called to a house fire on the lower avenues. Grady's ladder was already in position when they pulled up to the scene. Gina gathered from Bob's conversation with the batallion chief over the walkie-talkie that the roof had caught fire from an illegal bottle rocket.

The sounds of fireworks and cherry bombs, the popping of firecrackers and the shrill whistling of noisemakers filled the hot night air. Everyone in Salt Lake seemed to be outside, which made driving to the scene much more difficult and gave Howard nightmares that he might run over someone's child suddenly darting into the street.

Smoke was pouring out of the upstairs window and attic area of the huge old house. The enormous pine trees surrounding it could easily catch fire, something they all feared. Grady was up on the roof with the chain-saw to ventilate. She could see his tall body silhouetted against the orange-red glow of the flames. The fire was becoming fully involved, which meant that every part of the structure was burning. Grady and his back-up man would have to relinquish their position soon.

Gina was nozzle-handler and Ed lead-off man. She entered the house with the empty hose; it was easier to manipulate without any water in it. She dashed up the old staircase to the second floor, then sent Ed back to tell the pump man to turn on the water. Another engine had been called to assist, and several hoses were going at once. It didn't take long to contain the fire.

Outside, while they were putting the hoses away a little while later, Gina glanced at the ladder truck but couldn't see Grady. She excused herself for a minute and hurried over to Frank. "Where's the captain?"

His perpetual grin was missing. "They hauled him to Holy Cross Hospital."

It felt as though a giant hand had squeezed her insides. "What happened?"

"I don't know. I was at the other end of the roof when it collapsed."

That was all Gina needed to hear. *Dear God,* she murmured to herself as she hurried back to the engine. "Howard, the captain's been injured."

"Yeah, I heard," he said when they'd all climbed inside. "We'll go by the hospital on the way back to the station and check up on him." No one spoke as they drove away from the scene. The bond between fire fighters was as strong as any blood ties could ever be, and she knew how the crew members felt about Grady.

All Gina could think about was that at least he hadn't been trapped inside the attic or wasn't still missing. Grady had often reminded them that no two fires were alike. The element of surprise lurking at every crisis made their work challenging and often dangerous. Gina tried to mask her feelings and let the others lead as they entered the emergency room.

To her surprise and everlasting gratitude, Grady was sitting on the end of the hospital bed being treated for smoke inhalation. As far as she could see nothing else was wrong.

The sight of four grubby, foul-smelling fire fighters drew everyone's attention, including Grady's. "Get out of here, you guys." He sounded strong and completely like himself. Gina sent up a silent prayer.

"We're going." Bob grinned and punched him in the shoulder. One way or another, all the men managed to give a physical manifestation of their affection and relief by a nudge or some other gesture. Gina kept her distance.

"I'll ride ladder if you'll finish washing my windows when we get back to the station." She spoke boldly with a smile that lit up her violet eyes. "I'd rather be treated for what you've got than these dishpan hands."

The guys hooted and hollered with laughter. Grady's steady gaze met hers. "No, thanks. I'm on to a good thing and I know it. Those windows haven't been that squeaky clean since the place was built." A half smile lifted the corner of his mouth and her heart turned over. It was the first genuine, spontaneous smile he'd given her. If only he knew how she'd been waiting for that much of a response. Even if it had taken this crisis to make him forget for a little while the enmity between them, she was thankful. "I'll see you guys later," he muttered.

"Your captain won't be coming to work for at least forty-eight hours," the attending physician broke in. "It's home and total bed rest." Grady grimaced as the oxygen mask was put over his face again, but Gina rejoiced that the doctor had taken charge.

The ride to the station was entirely different from the earlier journey to the hospital. The men jabbered back and forth, releasing the nervous tension that had gripped them when they'd thought something might be seriously wrong with Grady. Gina felt positively euphoric and suggested they drop by the Pagoda for Chinese take-away—an idea applauded by everyone.

The station house was quiet after their last run. The men took their turns in the shower and when they'd finished, Gina took hers. Her thoughts ran constantly to Grady. He'd need some nursing when he got back to his home. Was there a woman in his life, someone close enough to be there when he really needed help?

That question went around in her head all night. The hours dragged on endlessly. Except for one interruption—a call to put out a brush fire in the foothills—she should have had a good sleep by the time the shift ended at eight o'clock. Nothing could have been further from the truth. And judging from the looks on the faces of the crew, they, too, were concerned about Grady. When a couple of them said they were going to run by the captain's place before going home, she volunteered to go with them, adding that she knew a wonderful hot toddy recipe that soothed sore throats. They grinned at the idea of sampling her brew themselves, and as it turned out, all eight of them decided to visit their revered captain en masse. Gina could have hugged them. This way, she could see for herself that Grady was being looked after, and he couldn't possibly object to her presence—at least, not outwardly.

CHAPTER THREE

GRADY STILL LIVED in the condo Gina had shared with him during their brief marriage. Situated on a steep hill on the avenues high above Lindsay Gardens, its four floors of wood and glass looked out over the Salt Lake Valley in every direction. The stupendous view still had the power to take Gina's breath instantly, reviving a host of memories too painful to examine.

Winn did the phoning to gain them access, and one by one they filed up two flights of the spiral staircases to the third level, which Grady used as a living-room. Everything looked so exactly the same, Gina could scarcely believe it was three years since she'd stepped into this room with its café au lait and dark chocolate-brown accents. The fabulous Armenian rug they'd picked up on their travels still graced the parquet floor.

Standing in the corridor, she could see Grady lying on the brown leather couch in his familiar striped robe—one she'd worn as often as he after a passion-filled night of lovemaking. From this vantage point she couldn't tell his condition, but at least he was talking to the men. Needing to help, she went into the kitchen to make the drink of hot tea with touches of sugar, lemon and rum. She'd stopped at a store for the ingredients on the way, but had to rely on Grady's stock of spirits for the rum. Fortunately he had a quarter of a bottle on the shelf. She used it liberally then put it back, hoping no one would walk in on her in the process. The crew would become suspicious, to say the least, if they saw their newest rookie making herself at home in a strange kitchen, acting as if she belonged there.

She rummaged in the cupboard for a large mug. It didn't surprise her that the kitchen was immaculate. Grady had always kept a cleaner house than most women, with everything neatly in its place. She found a blue mug and poured the steaming liquid into it before hurrying upstairs, passing some of the crew on the way.

"I made enough for all of you," she called over her shoulder and walked toward Grady, now sitting up, propped against the cushions. The pupils of his eyes dilated in surprise at her approach. Apparently he hadn't known she'd come in with the others. She handed him the mug, taking care not to brush his fingers. "Try this, Captain. It's a proved remedy for what ails you."

He stared at her over the rim of the mug before taking a sip. "On whose authority?" At this point some of the others came up from the kitchen with drinks in their hands, ready to propose a toast to the captain's health.

"Mine. A couple of us were treated for smoke inhalation a few months ago. My buddy made this for me, and it really helped."

"It's not half-bad." Frank gave his seal of approval. The others took tentative tastes and echoed his opinion, then began drinking enthusiastically. Gina wondered if she was the only one who noticed the stillness that came over Grady after her explanation. He lifted the mug to his lips, but his unsmiling eyes didn't leave her face, almost as if the unexpected news had suddenly made him realise the dangers she'd been exposing herself to all this time. Was it her imagination, or did she detect a brief flash of anxiety in those grey eyes?

"You're not having any?" he asked after draining his mug. Everyone else was laughing and joking around, seemingly unaware of the tension between them.

Her mouth curved upwards. "This stuff is potent. I have to be able to drive home."

"That's no problem. I'll see you get home safely," Bob piped up, bringing a roar of laughter from the crew.

"Don't you believe it," Howard whispered in her ear conspiratorially.

"Come on, guys," Bob bellowed. "Give me a break, will ya?"

Grady's mouth was pinched to a pencil-thin line, and Gina couldn't tell if it was the conversation or discomfort caused by his condition that produced the reaction. Either way, Gina didn't want their visit to add to his stress, and she began gathering mugs, including Grady's, to take back to the kitchen.

"Want some help?" Bob asked to the accompaniment of more laughter. He didn't know when to quit, she thought in annoyance.

She shook her head. "Don't you think one set of dishpan hands is enough, Lieutenant? You wouldn't want to ruin that macho image at this stage, would you?" This provoked more laughter, allowing her to escape Grady's unswerving stare and Bob's sudden frown.

She cleaned up the kitchen after preparing Grady a breakfast of eggs and toast. When Ed made an appearance with his mug she asked him to take Grady the plate of food. "Make sure he eats it, Ed. I've got to get going."

"Sure," he said, obviously surprised that she was leaving. But he didn't say anything else as she hurried from the kitchen and down the stairs to the front door.

A wall of heat enveloped her the moment she left Grady's air-conditioned condo to walk to her car. Salt Lake was experiencing an intense heatwave with no signs of letting up. Swimming in the pool at Susan's apartment building seemed an appealing prospect as Gina got into her car and drove home. This was her long weekend off, and already she could tell that she'd better fill it with activities or she'd go crazy thinking about Grady all alone in the condo. Or worse, with one of his girlfriends dropping by to keep him company. The pictures that filled her mind made her forget what she was doing, and it took a siren directly behind her to bring her back to awareness.

She glanced in her rear-view mirror to see a police car signaling her to pull over. With a groan, she moved to the side of the boulevard above the cemetery and waited. A female officer approached the car and greeted Gina with a wry smile. Then the officer issued her a speeding ticket, her first since returning to Salt Lake. When she was free to go, she headed for Susan's apartment. They could both complain about the police—anything to take her mind off Grady.

As it turned out, Gina didn't get back to her own apartment until late that night, when she fell into a deep sleep almost before her head touched the pillow. She slept around the clock and awakened late in the morning to the sound of her mother's voice. The answering machine was still on. A twinge of guilt soon had Gina dialling her mother's number in Carmel. She hadn't written or phoned in more than three weeks, and she knew her mother worried.

They had a fairly long chat but by tacit agreement didn't discuss Grady. Her mother didn't approve of Gina's plan to insinuate herself into his life again. She'd argued from the beginning that Grady had married her under false pretences, and as far as she was concerned their marriage had been doomed at the outset because he hadn't revealed his love for fire fighting to Gina. Gina's father kept quiet on the subject, but she knew his opinion was the same as her mother's. They both hated her work.

The conversation ended after they made tentative plans for Gina to fly to California for the Labor Day weekend—one of the few holidays she didn't have to work.

Before she took a shower, Gina played back the tape to see if she had any other messages. It annoyed her to hear Bob Corby's voice asking her to go out with him. He'd left his home number so she could call him back with her answer.

She felt the best thing to do was ignore the message, and the next time he approached her in person, reiterate her rules. In time, he had to get the point! She'd told Grady she didn't date the men she worked with, and she meant it. What Grady didn't know was that no man she'd ever met measured up to *him*—so there was no temptation, not even with the undeniably attractive Lieutenant Corby.

It took all Gina's self-control not to call Grady or go by the condo to see if he was all right. When her next shift began, she arrived fifteen minutes early, only to discover that Grady wouldn't be in for a while. He had to be seen by a doctor before he could report for duty. Her spirits plummeted as she began housekeeping duties along with the others. She purposely avoided Bob, who followed her with his eyes. He was fast becoming a nuisance, but it wasn't until the gong sounded that she realised how angry he felt with her for not returning his call or even acknowledging it.

"Frank?" he shot out, issuing orders as the second in command. "Ms Lindsay will replace you on ladder this run."

Gina didn't know who was more surprised, she or
Frank. The poor man looked as if Bob had just
slapped him in the face. Clearly he wasn't happy about
the sudden switch of assignment, but Gina understood. Bob had decided to set her up for failure. His
ego couldn't stand being dented.

Handling ladders was difficult work, even for
someone of Frank's brawn. Bob wanted her to look
inadequate, unequal to the job.

Rico drove them out of the truck bay to the downtown area. It was noon, the worst possible time of day,
with the heavy traffic impeding their progress. Bob got
on his walkie-talkie with the battalion chief. They were
discussing methods to proceed when Gina spotted
smoke pouring out of a fourth-storey window of the
Duncan office building.

Engine two was first in, but the alarm had sounded
for more help. This was it for Gina. If she made a
mistake at the fire ground now, the other men would
know it and possibly suffer as a result. She'd never be
assigned to Ladder Number One again, and Grady
would make sure she was relocated to the station that
made the lowest number of runs. News of her failure
would spread throughout the department. And this
was exactly what Bob wanted to happen.

"Gina, you'll work with Winn, Rico with me. Let's
go!"

Whether he'd set her up or not, right then Gina had
a fire to fight. For the time being she forgot their personal battle and ran to the back of the truck. "I'll get

the poles,'' she called out to Winn, who nodded and started pulling the ladder off the truck.

The trick with this kind of ladder was to attach the poles to the ladder on the ground and through leverage, hoist the ladder against the building. More than one person was needed to accomplish the manoeuvre. Gina had done it in training more times than she wanted to think about, but she'd hardly ever had to put it into practice during a real call.

Out of the corner of her eye she saw another ladder pull up to the fire ground. Already a couple of men from the engine truck had gone into the building with the hoses.

"Ready?" Winn shouted. Gina gave the sign and together they placed the ladder in an alley that gave access to the building and set it against the wall. Next she worked the rope that raised the extension so they could reach the fourth floor. She couldn't believe it but they managed the whole procedure without problems. Winn flashed her a quick smile that showed his relief. Normally it would have been Frank helping with the equipment, and she knew Winn had been holding his breath.

Gina grabbed her pack, then put the mask over her face before starting up the ladder. Her job was to hunt for any unconscious or injured people trapped in the building. She had no idea how involved the fire had become, but smoke continued to pour out of the fourth-floor windows and the atmosphere grew darker the higher she climbed.

Her turn-out gear felt like a lead weight as she approached the top of the ladder to climb in one of the window frames, the glass blown out by the fire. She could only hope most of the people had left their offices to go to lunch before the outbreak.

The number two ladder truck working farther down the alley was having a tough time opening up the side of the building to ventilate. The smoke was really heavy now. Gina's intuition told her the hoses had probably extinguished most of the fire and what she was seeing was a lot of smoke from burned electrical insulation.

Finally she reached the window and wriggled in on her stomach. She started crawling around, going into one room and then another. It seemed like an eternity that she and Winn, who wasn't far behind, had been going around in circles. Except for the shout of a fire fighter and the sound of the hoses, she thought everyone else must have cleared the building. It was then that she heard a low moan. The adrenalin surged through her.

Gina veered left and her gloved hand suddenly felt a body huddled up against the remains of a file cabinet. With the smoke as thick as mud Gina had no way of knowing it it was a woman or a man. But the body was definitely too heavy to lift.

Squatting, she grabbed the body under the arms and began to drag it, convinced the person was taller than her own five foot six.

The ventilation must have started working, because the smoke was now being drawn away from her.

Gina inched along in the opposite direction, pulling the deadweight slowly down a watery, debris-filled corridor. She'd performed this manoeuvre hundreds of times in practice drills, but this was only her third live rescue. The instructors had told the class that there was no way to simulate the real thing, because practice drills didn't drain you emotionally and psychologically in quite the same way. They knew what they were talking about.

She encountered a nozzle-handler when she rounded a corner leading to a stairwell. Somewhere along the way she and Winn had become separated, so she was thankful when the man signalled to someone farther down the stairs on the hose to come and assist. The smoke had cleared sufficiently for her to see that she'd been dragging a man almost as big as Frank and completely unconscious. She and the other fire fighter managed to get the man down three flights of stairs and outside to the street.

Gina immediately pulled off her mask and put it on him. She flipped it on bypass to give the man air. He eventually started to come to as an ambulance crew took over and carted him away to a hospital. Clutching the mask she made her way back to the truck looking for Winn, but Rico said he hadn't come out yet.

With a sick feeling in the pit of her stomach, Gina hurried into the building again and raced up the stairs as fast as her turn-out boots would allow. Dodging hoses, she replaced her mask and hurried along the floating wreckage, calling out for Winn. They worked on the buddy system. She wouldn't leave the building until she found him!

Panicking because she didn't get a response when she shouted, Gina moved quickly to the area where she'd entered through the window. A dozen different things could have gone wrong, and Winn could be anywhere, hurt or unconscious. She turned one corner on a run and careered into another fire fighter, the collision almost knocking the wind out of her. Her mask fell off. "Winn?" she cried out as the man holding her steady whisked off his own mask. "Grady!"

There was an indescribable look on his blackened face. She must have imagined he said, "Thank God," in a reverent whisper, because in the next instant he was giving her an order. "Go out to the truck, Gina."

"But I have to find Winn!"

"He's out on the ladder lifting someone to the ground right now. Do as I say!"

"But—"

"Don't argue with me," he thundered. "You've caused enough trouble already. Winn said you were up that ladder before he could stop you. You little fool. It wasn't intended that you enter the building on this run."

"But Lieutenant Corby—"

He muttered an epithet beneath his breath, and his hands tightened on her arms before releasing them. "I'll deal with Corby later," he said in a fierce voice, as he handed Gina her mask.

She sucked in her breath. "Yes, sir, Captain, sir!" Anyone overhearing them would automatically assume she was being chastised on the spot by her superior. With cheeks blazing red beneath the grime and soot, she left Grady to his job of filling in the incident report and went back downstairs. She scanned the fire ground for Lieutenant Corby and saw him standing by engine one. Apparently Grady was now in command of ladder one. Joining the others in the process of cleaning up, she walked over to help Winn, who was bringing down the extension. A man with a video camera sporting the Channel Eight logo intercepted her.

"I'd like to interview you for a minute, if I could?"

"Ask him." Gina nodded toward Winn. "He lifted a victim from the fourth floor down a fifty-five-foot extension ladder without being able to see an inch in front of him."

The cameraman scratched his head. "But somebody said a wo—"

"You'll have to clear the area." Grady's voice broke in. "My crew has a lot of clean-up work to do. You could get hurt."

Gina looked at Grady standing there in full turn-out gear with his hands on his hips and couldn't imagine anyone defying him. To her relief, he seemed fully recovered and ready for action. The cameraman backed off and went elsewhere for a story while Gina helped Winn with the ladder.

The crew worked in silence. Back at the station when everyone relaxed, the men loved to chat, but on the job Gina noticed that most of them didn't talk. They simply went about their work in a methodical, orderly manner, unlike a lot of women she'd met, who needed to dissect and discuss every step of the way. Gina enjoyed the difference.

She avoided looking at Grady, and grew more uneasy after they all climbed into the truck and headed back to the station. She purposely scooted in next to Rico and practised her high school Spanish with him in an effort to expend some of her excess energy. Rico had an entertaining personality and kept things light. That prevented her from thinking about the inevitable moment when Grady would tell her she'd been assigned somewhere else for her next shift. She could feel the vibrations coming from him even though Winn sat between them.

Much to her relief, another call sent them out to contain a fire near the airport. It was after ten at night before both the engine and the ladder finally pulled into the station. Everyone was ravenous and stormed the kitchen.

Gina decided this was the best time to take her shower. Her real motive was to stay out of Grady's way. So far her plan to go nice and easy had backfired. She hadn't counted on the torrent of emotions his nearness evoked, and it appeared that her entry into his world had upset him so much he couldn't wait to be rid of her.

Turning off the taps, Gina reached for a towel and stepped from the shower just as the bathroom door opened.

"Grady!" she cried out in shock, hurriedly wrapping the towel around her body. But she hadn't been quick enough to escape the intimate appraisal of his eyes. "I—I thought the door was locked. I *know* I locked it!"

His gaze travelled once more over her silvery-gold hair still wet from a shampoo and came to rest on the little pulse that pounded mercilessly in the scented hollow of her throat. He closed the door, sealing them off from the others.

"How many times has this happened before?" His eyes were mere slits but she saw a telltale flush on his cheeks.

"This is the first. I swear it," she replied. He didn't say anything, though he made no move to leave. "I thought I'd shower while everyone ate. I always pick a time when I think it's safe, but for some reason the lock didn't engage. I don't know why." Her voice trailed off because she had the impression he wasn't listening.

"This could cost you your badge."

"It was an accident, Grady." Her skin flamed with the heat of embarrassment and anger.

"If I didn't know we'd had trouble with this lock before, I'd think you were being deliberately provocative."

Her jaw clenched. "You know me better than that!"

"I thought I did," he ground out, sounding breathless. "If any other man had walked in here tonight and had seen what I saw—" He broke off. Gina looked away. "While you're at station one, you'll refrain from showering or bathing on the premises, and that's an order."

She hitched the towel a little higher and glanced over at him. "I know what you must think but—"

"You haven't the slightest idea," he fired back. Gina's violet eyes played over his face. It had an unnatural pallor and his eyelids drooped. He shouldn't have come back to work this soon. He hadn't fully recovered from his earlier ordeal, she realised now. Compassion for the man she loved made her want to hold out her arms and enfold him. Instead, she averted her eyes.

"If you'll excuse me, I'll get dressed and go to bed," she muttered.

"Before I go I want your promise about not showering."

"You have it." She swallowed hard. "Grady? You don't look well," she said impulsively. "Why didn't you stay home for a few more days?"

He drew in his breath and reached for the doorknob. "It's a good thing I didn't, wouldn't you say? Corby's panting for an opportunity just like this."

"You've made your point, Grady."

"I haven't even started," he growled and left the bathroom. She heard the lock click as he closed the door behind him.

For a moment, the bathroom seemed to tilt and Gina gripped the edge of the sink with both hands. She didn't blame Grady. The coincidence of his walking in just then, of the lock slipping at that very moment, was almost too improbable to believe.

She bit her lip in an effort to stem the tears. Of all the stupid things to have happened, this was the worst. Grady was an extremely private person. This kind of situation could only offend him—the last thing she wanted to do.

The gong sounded for engine one and she threw on her clothes, only to be waylaid by Grady as she opened the door. Apparently he wasn't taking any chances on that lock. "Frank's filling in on this assist," he said coldly. "I want you to go to bed, and I suggest you go there now!"

It was on the tip of her tongue to take issue with his orders, but the angry look in his eye made her reconsider. Without a word, she walked through the station to his dimly lit office and lay down on the bunk, her heart pounding hard. As soon as the engine had left the bay, Grady appeared in the room. He shut the door, and for what seemed like an eternity he stood there, not saying anything.

She couldn't stand the silence any longer. "Am I being punished—sent to my room?"

"Gang fights are no place for a woman, and I wouldn't care if you held ten black belts in karate. One jab of a stiletto in a vulnerable spot could mean a permanent disability."

Gina sat up, tucking her legs beneath her. "You told me at my apartment that you were going to treat me exactly like the others."

"I intended to until you broke all the rules."

She tossed her head. "The Grady I used to know knew how to forgive—particularly an unavoidable accident."

Even in the half-light, she could feel the menace in his expression. "Apparently the job has brought out a dark side in both of us."

"That's not true, Grady." Her voice trembled. "I'm sorry for what happened earlier. Can't we let it go at that?"

"Once again, you're asking the impossible, Gina."

"Oh, for heaven's sake, Grady. We used to be married. It isn't as if you haven't seen me in the shower before. Naturally I'm thankful it was you who happened to walk in on me. If it had been anyone else, I would have died of embarrassment."

She heard a noise come out of him that sounded like ripping silk. "I thought you did a fairly convincing imitation of embarrassment when I walked in. As many times as you've blushed in my arms, I've never seen you look quite that . . . disturbed before."

Gina sank back on the mattress and turned her head away from him. "I don't want to think about it any more."

"So help me, I don't want to think about it, either," he whispered. Abruptly he paced several steps and when he spoke again, his voice was brisk. "You'll ride ladder the rest of the shift."

"Yes, sir."

"Gina?"

"What else have I done wrong?" she asked, sighing wearily.

"Confine your hair to a ponytail while you're on duty. Don't flaunt your beauty in front of the men. Corby lost it this morning when you arrived for work. He's angry because you rebuffed him in front of everyone at the condo. That's why he assigned you to ladder."

"I know." She heaved another sigh. "He phoned me at the apartment, but I didn't return his call and I guess that added fuel to the fire."

"To your credit, the crew is recommending you for a medal for that rescue today, which will only make Corby more determined to get even with you. Be careful, Gina."

"What more can I do? I've told him point-blank I don't date fire fighters."

"Just being who you are is problem enough," he murmured enigmatically. "Stay out of his way until Whittaker gets back."

She raised herself up on one elbow. "You're making me out to be some kind of femme fatale." She laughed nervously.

"Come off it, Gina. You've always been a knock-out, and you know it. If anything, the turn-out gear emphasises your femininity. There's nothing you can do about the way nature made you, but for the good of the station, try not to draw undue attention to yourself."

"Maybe I should get my hair cut."

"Unfortunately that wouldn't change a thing."

The fact that he still found her attractive should have thrilled her, but his voice sounded ragged and she couldn't stop worrying about his physical condition. "You're tired, Grady. Why not lie down and rest?"

"Is that an invitation, Gina?" he mocked in that hateful manner.

"Would you like it to be?" she taunted, after a long silence.

He swore softly, then wheeled from the room. His abrupt departure pleased her. The idea that Grady wasn't as much in control as he'd led her to believe brought a satisfied smile to her lips. There'd been no need for him to follow her back to his office. He'd instigated this last conversation as if he hadn't been able to help himself.

She turned onto her stomach and hugged the pillow. It was the first sign that maybe, just maybe, she was getting under his skin. In fact, she'd begun to think that lasting this long at station one was a miracle in itself.

CHAPTER FOUR

TENNIS AND SWIMMING were Gina's favourite ways of keeping in shape, but some of those activities had to be curtailed during the next week to make time for singing rehearsals. She would be taking part in the entertainment at the annual Fire Fighters' Ball.

Nancy Byington, a fire fighter from station five, had been made cochair of the ball, and she was out to revolutionise what had always been an event sponsored by the men and their wives. Nancy's reputation as a pioneer in forging the way for more female fire fighters preceded her. When Gina received a call from Nancy asking for help, she was delighted to oblige, particularly as the ball was being held at the soon-to-close Hotel Olympus.

Besides being in charge of the intermission activities, Nancy planned to emcee the dance and to force people to mingle and get to know one another. Her plan to remove a few barriers was met with enthusiasm by other veterans in the department. Preball publicity infiltrated all the stations, urging everyone to attend, with or without a partner. This was one event in which all personnel were expected to participate.

The foyer of the famous old hotel had been transformed into a palace garden. Three-tiered topiary trees strung with thousands of tiny white lights, interspersed with baskets of roses and petunias, created a magical mood, enhanced by the magnificent crystal chandelier shimmering above the marble dance floor below. Nancy jokingly told Gina and the others taking part in the entertainment that they wanted to bring down the house, but "please *not* the chandelier."

On one side of the raised platform where the intermission activities would be performed were the buffet tables. Enough room had been left on the other side to accommodate the orchestra. The tables bordering the dance floor had been reserved for VIPs within the various departments, as well as visiting dignitaries in state and local government.

As the time approached for intermission, Gina looked down from her vantage point on the mezzanine floor. The group was highly animated, encouraged, no doubt, by Nancy's guidance. So far, they'd done a conga line, a Virginia reel, break dancing for the more daring, a waltz for all people more than fifty and a foxtrot for everyone between forty and fifty. The list of innovative ways to get everyone involved went on and on. And all the while, Gina's eyes had been searching for Grady. So far she hadn't seen him. Maybe he'd decided not to come, and stayed on at the station with the skeleton crew.

"Can't you find him?" Susan asked in a low voice. She was the only person in the department who knew about Grady.

"Not yet."

"Will I do?"

Gina turned around and began to laugh, and the sound caught the attention of the other two female fire fighters. The four of them were dressed like male fire fighters, in turn-out coats and trousers several sizes too large to accommodate their evening gowns. In gloves, air masks and helmets pulled down to disguise their hair, no one would know they were women. They stood tall in their huge boots, since they were wearing high heels. So far, no one had any idea who they were.

With a great deal of difficulty, they moved down the staircase and walked out onto the platform when Nancy gave the signal. A ripple of laughter started among the audience and began to build as they approached the microphone. Gina could hear several boisterous asides telling them to go back to the station.

Her heart started to run away with her as she quickly scanned the audience now seated at tables to watch the floor show. Several hundred salaried fire fighters and volunteers, with their partners, were assembled, wearing dinner jackets and evening gowns. It was when she looked beneath the overhang where she'd been standing before the show that she saw Grady with a good-looking brunette sparkling up at him. As Grady was one of the VIPs, he sat at a table near the buffet and dance floor, so close she could detect his slightly bored smile. He looked devastatingly handsome, but not nearly as animated as his date. A duty affair like this was not his favourite activity, and she had an idea he'd only come for appearance's sake. How Gina longed to wipe that world-weary expression from his face. Frank sat at Grady's table with a petite redhead. A few tables away she saw Howard and Ed with their wives. No matter how hard Nancy tried to force people to mix, the men tended to stick together.

"Since you guys gate-crashed this party, you're going to have to sing for your supper," Nancy began her introduction as the lights dimmed and the spotlight came on to blind the performers. "What do you say, audience?"

A huge cheer went up from the crowd.

"All right, Firebrands. Take it away!"

Someone behind the scenes started the tape recorder and the women danced and mimed their way through "Smoke Gets in Your Eyes," "Ring of Fire" and "Heat Wave".

The choice of songs was a huge success. When the singers finished, the men in the audience got to their feet and clapped for three minutes. A fire fighter planted in the crowd shouted, "We want to hear what they really sound like!" This brought on a chorus of shouts and joking.

"So you want the real thing, do you?" Nancy's voice rang out.

"Yes!" the audience responded.

"All right. But remember! You asked for it!" When Nancy turned to the women, it was their cue to disrobe. Synchronising their actions, they removed their helmets, masks and gloves, undid their turn-out coats

and trousers, kicked off their boots and wriggled out
of everything to step forward dressed in crimson chiffon, calf-length evening gowns. "The Firebrands,"
Nancy said, motioning them closer to the microphone.

The clapping and whistling started. The men were
on their feet once more. No one had guessed who'd
been hidden beneath the turn-out gear. The quick-change-artist routine was an unqualified success, and
it took time for everyone to quieten down.

"I'm going to ask each of the women to step forward as I say her name and identify her station,"
Nancy continued. "Believe it or not, these ladies are
some of the intrepid fire fighters protecting our city.
Station seven's representative is Karen Slogowski,
station five's is Susan Orr, station four, Mavis Carr
and, last but not least, from our famous station one,
representing Grady's bunch—Gina Lindsay."

Pandemonium broke out with more cheering and
clapping. Finally it subsided as the group began singing to a recorded background music tape of the Beach
Boys' hit, "Kokomo". Gina's voice supplied first alto,
and for a bunch of amateurs, she felt they performed
rather well. The song was a favourite and the long applause at the end of the number reflected the crowd's
approval.

"All right, folks. You've heard from the Firebrands. Now we're going to have them bring back the
dancing by starting out with Ladies' Choice. Now,
confidentially," Nancy told the audience, "our performers haven't rehearsed this part of the pro-

gramme. In fact, they have no idea what's going to happen next.''

A hush fell over Gina and the others. Susan's eyebrows quirked while Gina held her breath, wondering what Nancy was about to pull. She wasn't the emcee for nothing!

''You know,'' Nancy continued, ''these ladies take a lot of orders from their superiors day in and day out. I think it would be kind of nice to turn the tables for a change. Where are the captains of these personifications of courage and pulchritude? Come on—stand up! That's an order! Let's have the lights on.''

While pandemonium reigned once more, Gina felt faint and flashed a distress signal at Susan, who winked conspiratorially. Gina suspected Susan was behind this, but could do absolutely nothing about it as the glittering chandelier illuminated the room.

''Ladies, go find your captains and let the dancing begin! And all you wives and sweethearts out there, once these four have taken a twirl around the dance floor, it's your turn to pick a new partner and *mingle*!'' When Nancy finished her spiel, Sue whispered to Gina that this was her chance.

Flushed with a feverish excitement, Gina made her way slowly across the gleaming marble floor toward Grady. On the periphery, she could see the other women approaching their captains, who stood up amid continued cheering and joking, awaiting their fate. The orchestra had started to play a bossa nova number that lighted a fire in her blood. What was meant to be simply good fun had turned into something else, at least for Gina. The realisation that within seconds she'd be in Grady's strong arms caused a tremor to rock her body.

Grady's eyes ignited to a quicksilver colour as she drew closer. His unsmiling gaze roamed over her face and hair, then fell lower to the curves swathed in crimson chiffon, and lower still to her jewelled high-heeled sandals sparkling like the diamond earrings she wore—the ones he'd given her for a wedding present.

She'd brushed her hair till it gleamed white-gold and curved under her chin from a centre parting. She wore a peach lip gloss and a touch of lavender eye shadow that matched the deeper violet irises. Not even on her wedding night had she wanted to look as beautiful for Grady as she did now. Her cheeks needed no blusher. Hectic colour made her skin hot, and she had difficulty breathing as she finally stopped in front of him.

Other people were at the table, but it seemed to her that a nimbus surrounded Grady, blotting out everyone else. He stood tall and straight, like a prince—magnificent in black with a pearly-grey cummerbund, which matched his crystalline eyes. His indecently long black lashes gave them their particular incandescent quality. For a brief moment his expression sent out a message of sensual awareness that Gina felt to the depths of her being.

"Captain Simpson? May I have this dance?"

His half smile was a slash of white in his bronzed face. "What would you do if I said no?" he asked, his voice mocking, and her heart began to knock in her breast. Nervously, she moistened her glistening lips.

"Then I guess I'd have to ask your second in command."

She'd said it teasingly, but a dull flush suddenly tinged his cheeks as he gathered her in his arms and swung her out on to the dance floor.

During their marriage, their bodies had been so perfectly attuned, that even now Gina's hand slid automatically towards his neck. Then, when she remembered where they were, she quickly moved it to his broad shoulder, in a clumsy, betraying motion. His chest heaved as if he, too, had momentarily gone back in time. In Cairo they'd danced the nights away during their brief honeymoon. Right now, it seemed the most natural thing in the world for Gina to melt against him and make a kind of slow-motion love to him as they danced.... But of course they couldn't do that in sight of hundreds of people—including his date for the evening.

As if by tacit agreement, Grady circled her around the floor at a discreet distance, while other couples started to join in. Gina happened to be wearing Grady's favourite French perfume, and that, combined with the male tang of his body and the hint of musk he wore, intoxicated her. Her eyes were level with his chin where she saw a little telltale nerve throbbing madly near the tiny scar at the corner of his mouth. Whatever his feelings were for her at this point, her nearness disturbed him. She'd been married to him too long not to know the signs. This response of his was something to cherish.

"It's sinful how beautiful you are," he grated, and her eyes flashed upwards, in confusion—and hope. For an unguarded moment his eyes blazed with the old hunger that made her knees go weak.

"I could tell you the same thing," she whispered in a husky voice, not realising she was caressing the palm of his hand with her thumb until she heard his quick intake of breath and felt the pressure of his hand forcing her to stop the teasing motion. "I'm sorry."

He didn't pretend to misunderstand her. "It comes as naturally to you as breathing, doesn't it, Gina?"

The censure in his tone caused her to stiffen and she almost missed her step. "What do you mean?"

"You're a born temptress. The first time I saw you, you flashed those incredible violet eyes at me and I fell a thousand feet without knowing what in the hell had hit me."

She swallowed hard. "I—I felt the same way. You were bigger than life."

"For a little while, we tasted paradise," he murmured with a tinge of sadness in his deep voice, "but apparently it wasn't meant to be a steady diet." He cocked his dark head to the side. "Is that what your floor show was all about? A trip down memory lane?" His smile was more cynical than anything else and didn't reach his eyes. "If so, you succeeded admirably."

His words made her spirits plummet sharply. He might have been in love with her once, but no longer. Searing pain almost immobilised her as she understood what he was telling her—it was too late....

"This whole thing may have looked contrived, but Nancy spoke the truth. Dancing with our captains was her idea. She's determined to promote better relations between the men and the women. She had no way of knowing how...abhorrent it would be to you."

There was a long pause, then, "Never abhorrent, Gina. You're the stuff men's dreams are made of, didn't you know?"

But not your dreams, she agonised inwardly. "I think we've danced long enough to satisfy protocol. Your date will be waiting."

Grady stopped dancing even though the orchestra still played. A strange tension emanated from him. "Where's your date? I'll deliver you back to him."

Ever the gentleman...but his offer had the effect of plunging a dagger in her heart. She would have loved to produce such a person for him, but she'd come alone and would go home alone. She found she couldn't lie to him. "Those of us performing didn't have dates. We need to be on hand to clean up after everything's over. Have a nice evening, Captain Simpson," she whispered, unable to look up at him. If she hadn't known better, she would have thought he let go of her arms reluctantly as she slipped away and moved across the crowded floor toward the buffet. At the moment she desperately needed a cold glass of punch.

Once again Nancy's voice sounded through the mike, announcing that the next dance was for people without partners. Gina grimaced at the irony and swallowed the rest of her punch.

"Do I dare ask for a dance?" The familiar voice came from directly behind her.

"Lieutenant Corby," Gina finally acknowledged him, surprising an unexpected look of contrition shining out of his light blue eyes.

"I did a dumb thing the other day, assigning you to ladder, and I'd like to apologise."

Gina folded her arms. "I'm certified to ride ladder, Bob. No apologies are necessary."

"I know." He nodded, and there was a moment's uncharacteristic hesitation. "It's my reasons for doing it that I'd like to explain."

Gina took a deep breath. "Did the captain ask you to?"

He looked affronted. "We exchanged a few words, but this apology is my own idea." Something in his tone forced Gina to believe him. "I don't usually have trouble getting a woman to go out with me." He scratched his ear. "I know that sounds conceited, but it's true."

"I can believe it," she interjected good-naturedly.

He stared at her for a moment. "It ticked me off that I couldn't get to first base with you. In fact, I'm still having a hard time seeing you as one of the crew."

"You and all the others." She smiled.

He shook his head. "No...some of the guys are further along than I am. I guess I just don't want to fight fires with a woman. There are a lot of other things I'd rather do with her." He grinned.

"I admire your honesty. I suppose if a man started coming to my all-female sewing club, I'd feel uncomfortable about it myself."

His brows quirked. "That's not the best analogy I've ever heard."

Gina laughed. "I know, but I can't think of a better one. Women fire fighters are unprecedented—"

"Particularly ones who look like you," he broke in. "I thought Captain Simpson was immune, judging by the way he's treated you at the station, but after tonight, I can see he's as vulnerable as the rest of us."

"He was ordered to dance with me," she retorted to cover the sudden fluttering of her pulse.

His lips twitched. "Would it take an order to get you out on that dance floor now? I purposely didn't bring a date because I hoped you'd take pity on me." His hands lifted in a gesture of comical despair. "I promise this won't obligate you to anything else."

"Sure, why not?" she answered and allowed him to guide her onto the floor.

"Do you samba?" The orchestra was doing a whole series of Latin dance numbers. Gina nodded. "All right, then."

Bob Corby turned out to be an accomplished dancer, challenging Gina's ability to keep up with him. The first dance was over so soon that he begged for another. Soon Gina forgot to count. She hadn't had this good a time in ages. She'd have the rest of the night—the rest of her life—to torture herself with thoughts of Grady and all she'd lost.

She purposely kept her attention on Bob so she wouldn't be tempted to stare at Grady. But when he suddenly gripped Bob's shoulder during their last dance, Gina was forced to meet grey eyes as dark as storm clouds. Why he should look that angry she had no idea. Dancing with Bob didn't constitute high treason, nor did it mean she'd accept a date with him. She'd already made that promise to Grady, so she couldn't understand what kind of feelings could produce such hostile emotion.

"Captain?" Bob turned to him with the same happy smile he'd been wearing as they danced. "Are you trying to cut in on me?" Gina could hear the crackle of the walkie-talkie.

Something flickered in the recesses of Grady's eyes. "We're all needed back at the station. A tyre warehouse was set on fire by arsonists. They're calling for additional units. Did you both bring cars?" They nodded.

Even as he spoke, she could see various crews walking away from the tables. It was amazing the ball had gone as long as it had without interruption.

"Gina?" He used her first name, which was a shock. "You'll ride back to the station with me. Someone can help you collect your car later." Gina felt too surprised to respond.

"I'll meet you there, Captain." Bob was all business now and took off at a run.

Gina wondered what had happened to Grady's date, but experienced a sudden, unholy surge of joy that he wouldn't be spending the rest of the night in the other

"I'm worried about problems with my crew, Gina. When a crack forms in the foundation, the whole place can come crashing down if you're not careful. We were all getting along fine—"

"Until I came to replace Whittaker." She finished the words for him. "It's no longer a mystery why you wanted this little tête-à-tête. Is this your polite way of getting me to bow out gracefully? Am I supposed to do the noble thing?"

Grady literally stood on his brakes as the car pulled into the parking area behind the station. He jerked his head around and glared at her. "Do you know a better way? Corby has seven years' seniority over you."

"And would bring a nasty lawsuit against you if you had him switched to another station for no good reason," she shot back bitterly. "But of course no one would expect me to bring a suit against him for sexual harassment, because women don't belong in the department to start with." Her eyes flashed purple in the dim interior. "Nancy's right. This department still lives in the dark ages!" On that note she got out of the car and slammed the door before she could hear Grady's response.

"Gina?" he called after her, slamming his own door. He ran to catch up with her. "I'm not through with you." He reached out and grabbed her arm, closing his hand over soft, warm flesh.

She whirled around, causing the chiffon to swing lovingly around her long, shapely legs. "Is that an order, Captain?" The blood was pounding in her

tion and make a friend of him, but no longer. Unfortunately, he was her superior on the engine, which meant spending the rest of the shift in his company.

Other units were already battling the blaze when Gina's engine pulled up to the fire ground. Bob ordered Gina to lead in with the hose and start spraying the exterior of the warehouse to reduce the temperatures for the men on ladders. Ed worked with her, anticipating her movements as they carried the unwieldy hose across the crowded pavement surrounding the building.

Black smoke billowed from the roof, filling the air with hot fumes that burned her lungs. The place was a roaring inferno, singeing her brows and lashes as she trained the powerful spray on the wall of flame threatening the man above her on the ladder. At times she could scarcely see a foot in front of her.

When she heard a shout coming from somewhere overhead, she lifted her face instinctively. And that was the moment something glanced off her helmet, knocking her into oblivion.

"SHE'S COMING AROUND. Other than a gigantic headache, I think she's going to be okay."

Gina was cognisant of several things at once. Cool fresh air was being forced into her starving lungs and she could hear voices around her, one of them Grady's.

She pushed the mask away from her face and opened her eyes to discover she was inside an ambulance. She immediately focused on Grady's blackened face, but what impressed her most was the look of pain in his eyes.

"Don't move, Gina. Just lie still and take it easy."

She couldn't understand why he was there. "What happened? I heard a noise and suddenly everything went black."

He closed his eyes tightly for a minute, apparently held in the grip of some intense emotion. "A man from ladder three was overcome and his hose slipped," Grady started to explain. "His back-up man braced to keep the hose from snaking, but you were standing in its path." His voice shook. "We can thank God it was only the hose and not the nozzle that sent you flying."

She sighed. A full hose running under pressure could break bones, or worse. "Sorry to leave you a man short, Captain." She gave Grady a wan smile.

"Gina…" he whispered in an agonised voice. She'd never heard Grady sound like that before and warmth surged through her heart, quickening her entire body. She no longer felt any pain. Somewhere deep inside him he still had feelings. Feelings for her. The knowledge caused her eyes to fill with tears. She blinked them away.

"You shouldn't be here, Captain. I'm fine. How's the other guy?"

His eyes played over her features for a long moment before he spoke, as if he was having trouble getting his emotions under control. His vulnerability was a revelation to Gina. Did he have any idea how hard he was squeezing her hand?

"I don't know," he finally answered in a thick voice. "We'll find out when we get to Emergency."

"I heard the attendant tell you I was going to be okay."

"You are." His relief was undisguised. "But I want an X ray to find out if you've suffered a concussion."

Gina moved her head tentatively. It was sore at the crown. "I don't feel sick to my stomach. I think that's a pretty good indication it's not serious. Are my pupils still dilated?"

An epithet escaped his taut lips. "You know too much for your own good."

Her smile was impish. "Does that annoy you?"

Her question seemed to catch him off guard. "Do you want the truth?"

"Nothing but."

"I prefer to think of you the way you were a few hours ago, but I'll confess that you're a good fire fighter, with more courage than I've seen in a number of men."

"That's high praise indeed coming from the illustrious Captain Grady."

With that remark his expression sobered. "Whatever the prognosis once we get to the hospital, you're exempted from duty for a while."

Her eyes searched his for reasons. "Why?"

"To give you a chance to fully recover—and to cool an explosive situation with Corby."

Gina ran a shaky hand through her hair. Grady still held on to the other, and it seemed completely natural. "What he did back at the station was inexcusable."

He sucked in his breath. "In all fairness to him, what he did he couldn't help. You're pretty well irresistible to the male of the species, Gina."

"Loyal to your male crew to the bitter end, aren't you, Grady."

"Realistic," he retorted solemnly. "All eyes were on you at the hotel. They couldn't help but be anywhere else. Men are the weaker sex, didn't you know that? Your smile can twist a man into knots and have him begging for more. Corby's no different from any other man in that regard."

"And he's the best fire fighter in the city next to you."

His dark brows furrowed. "He's *one* of the best."

But if it were a choice between her and Lieutenant Corby, Gina knew in her heart which one of them Grady would choose. There was no contest. Suddenly all the fight seemed to go out of her.

"Gina?" He sounded alarmed when he heard the small moan that escaped her lips. "Are you feeling ill?"

"I think I'm tired." Which was the truth, but more than that, she knew she'd lost the battle and the war. Grady couldn't have spelled it out any more plainly, and their conversation had the effect of numbing her.

"I shouldn't have allowed you to talk so long," he muttered.

"I'm glad you did. It's put everything into perspective." Her eyelids fluttered closed but not before she glimpsed the puzzled frown on his face, the uncertainty. It was a rare sight and one that would haunt her over the next few days.

CHAPTER FIVE

THE X RAY REVEALED a minor concussion, and Gina
was ordered to bed for a few days. Sue and Nancy
both came by the apartment several times to visit and
help out. The guys at the station sent Gina a get-well
card. All the signatures were there, including Grady's.

Bob called, leaving a message on the answering
machine. He didn't press for a date. All he wanted was
to wish her well; he also confessed that everyone
missed her around station one.

On her fourth day, she felt pretty much back to
normal, except for an occasional headache. Anxious
to be back on the job, she called the station and asked
for Grady. If he didn't want her returning to his station, then she needed his permission to call headquarters and get reassigned. Someone she didn't know
answered and said Captain Grady was off duty on his
long weekend. Frustrated, Gina phoned Grady's
condo. She didn't have to look up his number; he'd
kept their old one. To her chagrin, he didn't answer
and hadn't switched on his answering machine—if he
even owned an answering machine. She didn't know.

ations; others showed the two of them together. If he found it odd that she still held on to them, he didn't say anything and she didn't explain.

He cast her a level glance over his shoulder. The mocking smile that tugged the corners of his mouth made her feel a need to hide behind her robe.

"Would you like some lemonade?" she asked hastily.

"Only if you don't go to a lot of trouble."

"It's already made."

He drew one bronzed hand through his dark hair. "You look too good for someone recovering from a concussion."

"I feel good. I still have a headache but it's slowly letting up." She hurried into the kitchen and poured them each a glass of lemonade. When she turned around, he was blocking the doorway, and his tall, lean frame seemed to dwarf her compact, tidy kitchen. There was something different about Grady—an intangible quality that stole the ground out from under her. All his pent-up anger seemed to be missing.

"I received the card. Tell everyone thank you." She handed him a glass, which he took and immediately drained then held out for a refill. The action reminded her so much of the old days that she broke into a full-bodied smile, which miraculously he reciprocated.

"The card was Frank's contribution. I think he's gone into mourning that you're not around."

"He's not the only one." She poured the last drop of lemonade from the pitcher into Grady's glass and handed it back. "I'm not used to this much inactivity and I'm going a little stir-crazy."

His devastating smile faded to be replaced by a more serious expression. "That's what I came over to talk to you about—and, of course, to see if you were feeling better."

She tucked a loose strand of hair behind her ear with unconscious allure. "As you can see, I'm fine and eager to get back to work."

He stared hard at her as he finished his second drink. "How would you like to take a drive up into the mountains for the rest of the day? It'll give you a break from this enforced idleness. And we'll have a chance to discuss your future with the department."

His last statement sounded ominous, but the joy she experienced at his invitation superseded all other thoughts. She had to fight to control her reactions. She hadn't seen Grady this mellow since long before the divorce and didn't want to do anything to disturb this momentary truce. "I—I'd love to get out of this heat. Do you mind if I take a quick shower first?"

For the merest fraction of a second, their eyes met in shared remembrance of the countless times he'd joined her there as a prelude to something else equally consuming and intimate. When she realised where her thoughts had wandered, she looked away. Grady shifted his weight as if he, too, had to make a determined effort to keep those memories in the past.

"Take all the time you need. I'll wait for you in the car."

She nodded. "I'll hurry."

Less than ten minutes later, she joined Grady. She'd dressed carefully, choosing white linen shorts and a lavender-blue crocheted top that fitted at the waist and had puffed sleeves. A white silk scarf kept the hair out of her eyes as the Audi's open sunroof let in an exhilarating breeze.

Gina had little inclination to talk and apparently Grady felt the same way. When they entered Parley's Canyon for the steep climb to the summit, she was flooded by a bittersweet sense of *déjà vu*. They'd traveled this section of highway so many times in the past, on their way to picnics in the mountains. The tantalising scent of his musk after-shave blended with the refreshing aroma of pine, and it took her back to those exquisite early days when they could hardly bear to be apart, even for an hour or two.

"I don't know about you but I'm hungry," he said as he took the turn-off for Midway, their favourite spot.

"So am I. Are you in the mood for hamburgers or pizza?"

"Actually, I had a picnic in mind. It's packed in the trunk."

Gina's eyes widened in amazement. "I haven't been on a picnic s—in a long time," she amended, struggling to keep her composure. Like a revelation, it came to her that he'd planned this outing. She couldn't help but wonder where he was taking them and could hardly breathe from excitement.

The back side of Timpanogos Mountain with its snow-crested peaks dominated the Swiss-like countryside. Gina felt a piercingly sweet ache of such longing, she was afraid to look at Grady. This was one time she couldn't disguise her emotions.

He was strangely silent as he drove through the tiny hamlet of Midway, past the post office. When he suddenly turned the corner and stopped in front of her favourite red and white gingerbread house—a type of architecture for which Midway was famous—she didn't understand. The little house with its pointed roof and lacy white scrollwork peered out from four giant blue spruce trees, like some enchanted cottage in the Black Forest. The lawn was a velvety spring green, and the white fence looked freshly painted.

Gina turned to Grady. "Are we going to have our picnic *here*?" she asked incredulously.

His smile was mysterious. "Every time we went past this house, you told me you wanted to have a picnic under those trees. Today I'm granting you your wish."

Her cry of joy could not be restrained. "Did you arrange this with the owners?"

"I did," he affirmed, as he levered himself out of the car. Gina jumped from her side and gazed all around at the magnificent view of the mountains surrounding them. She thought she might die of happiness to have Grady all to herself in this paradise. Her ecstatic glance darted to him.

"Let me help." She reached in the trunk for the blanket while he lifted out the basket of food, then she followed him through the little gate to a nest of spruce needles beneath the largest tree. Gina spread out the blanket and they sat down, revelling in the cool shade.

"Are the people away? How did you manage it?"
She threw him one question after another as he began
to fill her plate with chicken and potato salad. She, in
turn, opened a bottle of sparkling white wine he'd
provided and poured it into paper cups, sneaking a
taste.

Grady sat cross-legged, munching on a drumstick.
"I own it, Gina," he said matter-of-factly. Her mo-
tions abrupt, she put down the wine bottle, her violet
eyes searching his for what seemed a timeless moment. "About six months after our divorce became
final, my estate agent called me and told me it had finally come on the market. I told him to start the paperwork immediately."

Tears came to her eyes unbidden. This little house
had been their dream—their fantasy. To think that all
this time, he'd been the owner, had taken care of it,
lived in it, *without her*.

The wine no longer tasted sweet.

Grady blinked when he saw that she wasn't eating.
He wiped the edge of his mouth with a napkin.
"What's wrong, Gina? Are you feeling ill?"

"No." She shook her head and looked down. "I'm
just surprised the people would sell it. You'd think a
family would want to keep it for generations to come."

"The man who owned it died without leaving any
heirs."

"You must have been thrilled," she said, studying
her nails.

Grady looked pensive. "It's just a house, Gina. A place I come to relax and write—when I can find the time."

She hugged her arms to her chest. "The place looks immaculate."

"I have a caretaker who does odd jobs and house-sits when I'm not here. So far, the arrangement has worked out well."

As far as Gina could tell, Grady's bachelor life-style suited him perfectly. He had no need for permanent entanglements, no romantic notions to complicate his well-ordered existence. Had he brought her up here to demonstrate just how smoothly he'd made the transition from bondage to freedom? She hadn't suspected he had a deliberately cruel side.

"Would you like to come inside and have a look around? I bought it furnished because I haven't had the time to take on a redecorating project."

"Of course I'd like to see it." She rose to her feet and accompanied Grady up the walk to the front porch with its old-fashioned swing. The interior of the house had the makings of a turn-of-the-century museum, from a grandfather clock to a cane-backed rocking chair by the hearth. With a few improvements, it could be a veritable showplace.

Grady had turned the parlour into a den. While he sorted through a pile of manuscripts, Gina went upstairs to survey the two quaint bedrooms. Each window had a view of the mountains. The house was as adorable inside as it was out. And Grady owned it!

Gina felt as if someone had played a cruel trick on her. She'd been allowed a glimpse of paradise before it was gone from sight forever. "Does the reality live up to the fantasy?" Gina hadn't heard him come up the stairs and frantically brushed away the tears with the back of her hand.

"I think you already know the answer to that question." Her voice shook. "Can I ask you one?"

"Fire away."

"Why did you bring me here?"

She could feel the warmth of his body and knew he couldn't be standing more than a few inches away.

"I wanted to talk to you in a favourable ambience—away from everyone else—where we could communicate for once, instead of hurling abuse at each other."

She bowed her head, acknowledging his reasons. For so long their marriage had been little more than a battleground. She had to reach far back to remember times like this. "You didn't need to go to such elaborate lengths to soften me, Grady. I know I'm a complication you can't wait to be rid of." She took a deep breath. "I called you this morning to tell you I'm willing to take the next available posting, if that's what you want. It's not necessary for me to be at station one. Whether you believe me or not, I find no joy in coming between you and your men. Grady's bunch is legendary, you know."

She expected anything but the dark silence that followed her statement.

"I told you in the ambulance that you do good work, Gina," he finally said. "Another station will be lucky to get you, and I mean that sincerely. I'll make it clear on the transfer that the reason for the change is due to Whittaker's return. He'll be back a week from Monday. Your time at the station has only been cut by four days as it is. We can get by with three men on the engine crew for that short a time."

She rubbed her arms as if she were cold. "Then I'll call headquarters in the morning."

"I understand station six needs a paramedic. It's a quieter station, not so many runs. You'd be happy there."

Heat filled her cheeks as she whirled around. "I prefer heavier action, Grady. The more runs, the better."

He frowned, the lines marring his handsome face. "The risk of danger takes a quantum leap in a station like number one. You're still recovering from a concussion. You'd be a fool to go back for more of the same," he said, his voice strained now as the tension began to build.

Her jaw stiffened. "I remember telling you the same thing when we were married."

He gave a short, angry laugh. "I'm a man, Gina. Don't try making comparisons."

"So we're back to that again. For your information, *I* was out there doing my job when a *man* lost his hose and I got the brunt of it."

"Do you think I'll ever forget that?" He suddenly grasped her upper arms in firm hands and shook her.

"The sight of your beautiful body knocked ten feet through the air before crashing against solid concrete? Or the blood in your hair when only an hour before it shimmered like gossamer? How about those stunning eyes closed to me, possibly forever? How about your luscious mouth blistered beyond recognition by heat so intense, a dozen men went to Emergency suffering exhaustion?" His chest heaved. "Do you honestly believe I'll be able to put that picture out of my mind?"

"Grady—" Her voice came out on a gasp. She placed her palms against the warmth of his chest, too shocked by his emotional outpouring to think coherently. His heart galloped beneath her hand.

"Touch me," he begged, covering her hands with his own to slide them around his neck. "Kiss me, Gina. I've needed to feel you like this for too long," he confessed, his voice ragged, breathless. Gina couldn't believe any of this was happening and lifted tremulous eyes to her ex-husband. The eyes staring back were hot coals of desire, blazing for her. "If anything, I want you more now than when we were married."

His dark head lowered, blotting out what little light there was in the bedroom. With a low moan, Gina surrendered her mouth to his, giving herself up wholly to the one man she loved—loved beyond comprehension. The hunger for him grew, even as it was being appeased. She felt that her bloodstream was full of shooting stars as he deepened their kiss, practically swallowing her alive. She had no idea how long they tried to devour each other.

Grady couldn't seem to get enough of her. His magic hands slid into her silky hair, cupping her head to give him easier access to her eyes and mouth.

Her lips chased after his, allowing him no respite as they both clung, delirious with wanting. Like water bursting over a dam, they were caught in a force beyond their control.

"I've dreamed of this so many times," she whispered feverishly, pressing hot kisses against his neck, drowning in the feel and scent of him.

He crushed her voluptuous warmth against him. "I never believed the reality could surpass the dreaming. I'm not going to lie to you, Gina. I want you. So much, it's agony."

"I know. I feel the pain clear to the palms of my hands. I've been in this condition longer than you can imagine."

He groaned at her admission and picked her up in his arms. "Can't you see you were made to be loved? Your skin and hair, everything about you was created to entice me! I can't function any longer without lying in your arms again. Only you can put out the fire that's burning within me, Gina. Help me," he cried out.

His voice shook with raw need. Gina was no more immune to his pleadings than she was to his caresses. How many nights for years had her body been racked with a longing that only his loving could assuage? She wrapped her arms tightly around his neck as he carried her the short distance to the bed, burying her face in his black hair, glorying in the right to be loving him like this again.

"Promise me you'll always stay this way, Gina. I couldn't bear to think of you maimed or disfigured for no good reason. You're so beautiful it hurts," he whispered against her mouth as he placed her gently on the bed and moved to join her. "I'll fix it with Captain Blaylock at station six. It'll minimise the dangers tremendously. I couldn't do my job the way I'm supposed to if I constantly thought I had to worry about you."

A gentle finger traced the fine-boned oval of her face before his lips followed the same path. "This exquisite face, this body, was meant for *me*." On that note he covered her mouth with smothering force to begin his lovemaking in earnest.

At first Gina was too entrapped by her own needs to think coherently. It might have been an hour instead of three years since they'd last made love; it was as if they'd never been apart. But slowly the realisation dawned that they were no longer married and that Grady was assuming she'd abide by his conditions. She needed clarification on one crucial issue before Grady became her whole world once again.

She caught his face in her hands, but when she saw the degree of entrancement that held him, she almost couldn't ask the question.

"What?" he murmured, reading her expression with uncanny perception, kissing her bottom lip with a tenderness that was almost her undoing.

She swallowed hard. "Let's agree to worry about each other on the job. But you weren't really serious about what station I should bid or your ability to perform your own job, were you?"

Instantly a stillness settled over Grady. She watched the glaze of desire diminish until it was no longer there. Suddenly he looked older again, harder. A shudder racked her body, because she'd been the one to extinguish the light.

"I'm deadly serious, Gina," he finally answered, but she knew that already. Slowly he removed her hands from his face and slid off the bed, rubbing the back of his neck in a distracted manner that revealed his turmoil.

She got to her knees. "We're not married any more, Grady. I have to live the life I've made for myself. Isn't that what you told me when I tried to dictate yours?"

His face was ashen. "So now the shoe's on the other foot," he said in a haunted whisper.

"No. That isn't the way it has to be," she cried out in despair. "Haven't we learned anything from past mistakes? I found out how wrong it was to try to make you into something you're not. We fought day and night because of it. Now I'm begging for your understanding. Why is this so different?"

Grady's intelligent face was a study in pain. "It just is."

"So now I'm going to have to bear the burden of guilt because the work I do affects *your* performance?" Her tightly controlled voice cracked before she could finish the sentence.

"Your coming back to Salt Lake has knocked my world sideways, Gina!"

She buried her face in her hands, wondering how to reach him. "In other words I should have stayed in California."

"It was a hell I could have endured," he muttered bleakly. He moved over to the window to stare out at the mountains. "Now it wouldn't matter where you went. You'd be in the thick of the action. Your chances of ending up a casualty are only outnumbered by the chances of ending up a quadriplegic. Or enduring a series of skin grafts and marrow transplants—for starters."

In a daze, Gina slithered off the bed. "We could both be killed in a car accident on the way home today. I learned in therapy that this kind of thinking is a useless expenditure of energy."

"If you're hinting that I need to visit a shrink, then you're way off base."

His words affected her like a slap in the face. "I wouldn't presume to make a suggestion like that. Only a wife has that prerogative."

He spun around. "Meaning that since I'm no longer your husband, I have no right to demand anything of you!" he lashed out. "You're right, Gina. We're both free to pursue our lives and our careers without interference from the other. As long as you're not at my station and you're out of my sight, you're at liberty to skydive if you want to."

"As it happens, I don't." She tried to inject a note of levity into the conversation. "Look, Grady. You said you brought me here hoping the atmosphere was conducive to some real communication. Isn't it possible for us to coexist in the same city without turning everything into a shouting match? We're bound to run into each other occasionally. I don't want to cower every time I see you coming." Her hands lifted in a pleading gesture. "On the strength of the love we once had for each other, can't we pretend to be civil and rational about this?"

His hands tightened into fists and the blood drained from his face. "You just don't understand, do you, Gina? And there's no way I can explain. I wish—"

Gina's head lifted, as she waited for him to finish. When he turned away from her without saying anything, she spoke for him. "I used to say that word like a litany when you went back to fighting fires. In my heart, I'd repeat over and over—I wish we lived somewhere else... I wish we'd never come home from the Middle East... I wish I could send you off to fight fires every day with a kiss and a sack lunch ... I wish I had your baby..."

Her last statement hovered in the air like a live wire, sending out sparks. A flash of pain came and went in his grey eyes so fast, Gina wasn't sure she'd seen it.

"We can thank providence that's one mistake we didn't make," he said in thick tones.

Gina couldn't take any more and hurried out of the room and down the narrow staircase. They'd trespassed on quicksand at the mention of a baby. She fought the tears but it was a losing battle. To fill this adorable cottage with Grady's children had been her greatest secret longing. She closed her eyes in pain. So many dreams gone.

Cleaning up the remains of their picnic gave her something to do. Grady came down the front porch steps as she folded the blanket. His face was devoid of animation. She couldn't remember who had said that nothing was deader than a marriage that had ended, but the thought sprang to Gina's mind as she gazed at her ex-husband's face. Every time she thought she was making a little progress with Grady, the gulf seemed to widen even more. Yet, ironically, they were more physically compatible than ever. But physical desire alone couldn't compensate for everything else that was wrong. It might bring gratification for periods of time, but in the long run, giving in to their longings would only destroy them both. And Gina knew that any kind of relationship with Grady other than marriage would never satisfy her.

Grady put the picnic things in the trunk while she climbed into the passenger seat. "As long as we've come this far, I'd like to drive past Bridal Veil Falls on our way home," he said equably once he was in front of the steering wheel. "Any objections, or are you in a hurry to get back?" He spoke as calmly and matter-of-factly as if the scene in the upstairs bedroom had never taken place.

She took her cue from him. "I'd like that. My air conditioner at the apartment isn't working that well. I don't want to go back until absolutely necessary."

Grady nodded and started the engine. "Here." He handed her the scarf that she'd somehow lost on the bed and forgotten about. She thanked him and put it on, along with a pair of sunglasses, hoping to detach herself. But nothing could erase the sexual tension radiating between them. A fire had been started in the bedroom and only one fire fighter could put it out, she thought with a glimmer of ironic amusement. Then she sighed. It had been bad enough to work beside him day after day, but since he'd touched her, since she'd experienced the ecstasy of being in his arms again; this was agony in a new dimension.

Beneath his cool, implacable exterior, she wondered if he was suffering one tenth of her frustrations. Worse, she feared that he might slake his longings with that brunette he'd brought to the ball. Gina couldn't stand the thought of someone else being the recipient of his lovemaking. Not now...

She rested her head on the back of the seat and closed her eyes. It took every bit of self-control she possessed not to slide over and wrap her arms around his shoulders. She needed his kiss so badly....

He turned on the radio and fiddled with the tuner until he located a station playing soft rock. She found it merely distracting until the Beach Boys started to sing "Kokomo". Grady flipped to another station before she could ask him, and that one motion betrayed that his nerves were as taut as hers after all.

When they arrived at the turn-off for Provo Canyon and the falls, he suddenly turned left towards Salt Lake. She started to say something, but he silenced her. "I've changed my mind. Is that okay with you?" he practically growled at her. Even if it hadn't been okay, she wouldn't have dared argue with him in this mood. The atmosphere was explosive.

They arrived at her apartment an hour later. She got out of his car the minute he pulled to a stop in the driveway. She couldn't tolerate being in his company another minute.

To her amazement he got out of the car and followed her to the door. "I might as well take a look at your air-conditioning unit before I go."

"Th-that's all right, Grady. I've told my landlord about it. He'll be over in the morning to fix it."

He stroked his chin where the beginnings of a beard had started to show. "So . . . I'll leave it to you then to call headquarters and start bidding another station."

She nodded. "Thank you for the picnic. It was delicious."

He scowled. "It was a disaster and we both know it. No more games, Gina."

Her chin lifted. "I was thanking you for the food and the beautiful drive." Her voice quivered slightly.

In a totally unexpected move, he pulled off her sunglasses and stared at her face for a long moment. She didn't understand and her expression must have reflected it. "I'm taking one last, hard look at you, Gina. It's possible that the next time we happen to see each other, your face and body might be changed beyond all recognition."

He thrust the sunglasses into her hand and strode off towards the car. She could still hear the screech of tires a block away as she entered the apartment and collapsed on the couch, her body shaken by deep, racking sobs. The tears weren't just for what they'd lost. She also wept for Grady, because he'd just discovered what it was like to be afraid for someone else. It was the most isolated, lonely, horrifying feeling in the world.

CHAPTER SIX

SUSAN REACHED across the table and stabbed the rest
of Gina's burrito with her fork. "May I?" she asked
after the fact, swallowing the last of their Mexican-
food lunch.

"Be my guest." Gina chuckled and finished off her
Coke. Normally she had a healthy appetite, but since
her trip to Midway with Grady she'd been too upset to
eat much of anything.

"I take it you're not thrilled about being assigned
to station six," Susan said gently. "I'm sorry things
are so bad between you and Grady. But maybe it's
better not to be around him all the time under the circumstances."

"At first I thought so, too. But it's been almost
three weeks since I last saw him. We haven't even
bumped into each other at a fire. I spend the majority
of my time going on building inspections. Nothing
ever goes on at number six. Would you believe I'm
actually hooked on *Days of Our Lives*?"

Susan burst into good-natured laughter, which was
so contagious Gina finally joined in. "What other
stations did you bid?"

"Two and three."

"There'll be an opening at one of them pretty soon," she offered supportively. "If you don't mind my changing the subject, let's talk about our trip to Las Vegas. I told Nancy you and I would be rooming together. She and Karen want to be together, which leaves Mavis as the odd woman out."

"She can room with us. We'll request a triple. I like Mavis. She's a born comedian."

"So do I. Then it's settled." Susan smoothed her brown bangs away from her eyes. "I can hardly wait for the weekend. I've got fifty dollars' worth of nickels to play on the slot machines."

Chuckling, Gina shook her head. "You fool! Don't you know it's all rigged?"

"I don't care. A slot machine is kind of like a mountain. You climb it because it's there."

Gina grinned. "You're right. Just make sure you stick to nickels. Frankly, I think Las Vegas is the last place they should hold the union convention. We're all underpaid as it is."

"Too true." Sue cocked her pert head to the side. "Don't you like Las Vegas?"

"I think it's awful. In fact, I avoid it whenever possible."

"But Grady might be there...."

Gina averted her eyes. "If he does show up, he'll stay away from me. You don't know Grady when he digs in his heels."

Susan was silent a moment, her expression pensive. "For what it's worth, hang in there, Gina. I watched the two of you dancing at the ball." Her warm brown eyes softened. "If a man ever looked at me like that I think I'd die. He may try to act indifferent, but believe me, he was giving off the vibes."

"The situation has deteriorated since the dance," she murmured. "If you don't mind, I'd rather not talk about him." She cleared her throat. "What's happened with Ron?"

"I have no idea. Since I found out he has a wife, I've bowed out of the picture. He keeps leaving messages and I keep not returning them," she said in a bleak tone of voice. She eyed Gina soulfully. "We're a real pair, you know that?"

A sigh escaped Gina's lips. "Why don't we go play some tennis and burn these calories off?"

"Good idea. Let's go."

The heat was too intense for them to play more than one game, so they opted to swim and succeeded in wearing themselves out to the point that Gina fell asleep as soon as her head touched the pillow later that night.

She had only one more shift to go before the trip. Mavis called her at the station and offered to drive everyone to Nevada in her van. Her husband and children would have to get along with the Volkswagen for two days. The arrangement suited Gina just fine. She was sick of her own company. With Mavis entertaining them along the way, the time would pass quickly. For at least the weekend, Gina resolved to ward off all thoughts of Grady.

Fire fighters from around the country poured in to the hotels within walking distance of the convention centre. The union planned to deal with issues ranging from employee benefits to the latest safety features in turn-out gear. This year a session had been added to address the challenges facing female fire fighters.

Since there were too many workshops for one person to attend, Nancy divided up their group so the entire convention was covered and asked them to take notes. They could exchange information afterwards. However, all of them planned to attend the women's session.

Gina enjoyed that session the most. It gave her an opportunity to meet women from every part of the country. The one point that emerged loud and clear was that it would take another generation before women were accepted as an integral part of the system. The guest speaker—a feisty Puerto Rican from the Bronx—brought the house down with her closing remark. "The old guard will have to die off first," she said, "but we'll handle it in the meantime. Right?"

The crowd went crazy, but Gina noticed that a few of the men in attendance were clearly not pleased. The very issue the women had been discussing was brought home a dozen times throughout the day. Loud comments and snickers, rude asides, came from corners of the room at every session Gina attended. Only a small number of men were responsible, but they managed to cast a pall over the activities.

After being propositioned for the third time just walking from one session to the next, Gina had had it and decided to go up to the room to wait for the others.

A couple of men were loitering by the elevator. They threw her furtive glances, then smiled. Angry at this point, Gina needed a release for the adrenalin flowing through her system and dashed up the stairs to the tenth floor.

"Is it my imagination, or are we getting unduly harassed out there?" she burst out the minute she entered their suite.

"I figured something like this might happen," Mavis said. "In fact, my captain warned me about it."

Sue didn't look too happy, either. "Nancy just phoned and said the same thing was happening to her and Karen. It's a put-up job. She thinks we ought to just stay in our rooms for the rest of the night and have dinner delivered."

"I agree," Gina said, nodding. "There's no way I'm willing to face that again."

They heard a knock on the door, and Sue, who was closest, answered it. Gina recognised the man as one of the two down by the elevators. "Is this where the party is?" he asked in a distinctly Southern drawl.

"Not unless you're into karate!" Mavis yelled out as Sue slammed the door in his face.

"I'm calling security," Gina announced, but before she could pick up the receiver, the phone rang. Her eyes darted to Sue. "What do you think?"

Mavis made a face. "It could be my husband."

"I hope it is," Gina said angrily. "Ask him to report the problem."

Mavis nodded and gingerly picked up the receiver. She put the phone to her ear, then held it out in front of her for anyone who cared to listen before putting it back on the hook. "Well, ladies. Shades of the Salem witch hunt."

"It's disgusting," Gina muttered. She tried to call the front desk but the line was busy. After five minutes of unsuccessfully trying to reach someone, her anger started to turn into resignation. She looked at the others and saw the same expression on their faces.

"I'd like to leave Las Vegas. The sooner the better," Sue stated unequivocally. Gina tried the phone again, even as Sue spoke. It was still busy.

There was another knock at the door. By tacit agreement no one moved. Gina kept phoning. The knock grew more persistent. "Gina? Are you in there?" a male voice demanded anxiously.

Gina's eyes locked with Sue's as the receiver slipped out of her hand. "Grady." Her heart in her throat, she flew across the room and opened the door. By the greatest strength of will she kept herself from leaping into his arms.

His penetrating gaze swept over her in one all-encompassing motion. "Are you all right? The troublemakers have been rounded up and dealt with. I tried to get through to your room but the line was busy."

Gina swallowed hard. "I was trying to phone security."

If he noted her pallor, he didn't say anything.

"It's good to see you, Captain Simpson," Mavis greeted him with a broad smile. Sue's eyes communicated a private signal to Gina before she joined Mavis in saying hello to Grady. Her glance clearly said "I told you so."

Grady was at his most charming, dressed informally in a cream sport shirt and dark grey trousers. "Ladies, I'm afraid that sort of element will always be present at a function like this. Don't let it put you off. The night's still young." His dazzling smile took Gina's breath.

"Good," Sue piped up. "I'm ready to go hit the slot machines. Come on, Mavis. You can help me lose all my gambling money."

"I'm real good at doing that. Show me the way." They were out of the room so fast Gina didn't have a chance to say anything. She couldn't. After three weeks' separation, it was heaven just to look at Grady.

A slow heat invaded her body as his eyes took in the raw silk dress she wore, its colour the exact shade of her violet eyes. "Did anyone approach you, Gina?"

"Yes," she answered in a breathy voice.

His eyes narrowed perceptibly. "Could you identify him?"

"You mean all three?"

She heard him say something unintelligible under his breath. "The hotel security officers are holding them downstairs. If you're able to make a positive identification, you can lay formal charges against them."

She rubbed her temples. "Much as I hate the whole idea, I'll do it. No women in any line of work should have to put up with that."

"I agree. Word will spread and—let's hope—prevent this from happening again next year. A couple of other women are also willing to co-operate. Would you like me to go down with you?"

"Please." Her eyes implored him.

"Then why don't we get it over with right now?"

Gina nodded gratefully and went downstairs with Grady. The whole process took only a couple of minutes. There was strength in numbers, and the other women showed no hesitation in picking out the men responsible for casting a blight on the conference. One positive outcome of the incident manifested itself in the tremendous sense of bonding Gina felt with the other women, and men, determined to stamp out this kind of behaviour.

"Do you have plans for the evening?" He'd accompanied her to the door of her suite. She almost fainted at the question. The last time they were together he'd walked away from her in anger.

"No. You know how I feel about Las Vegas. I'd rather go back to Salt Lake tonight. The only reason I came was because Nancy said it would be a good experience and she's been at this a lot longer than I have."

His dark brows quirked. "And was it a good experience, apart from the obvious?"

She gave him a full, unguarded smile. "Yes. It did my heart good to see so many female fire fighters all assembled. The speaker in our section said there are more than forty women assigned in New York City alone. That's impressive, and it makes me more certain than ever that there's room for everyone if we're given half a chance.''

His lips quirked. "That was quite a speech. You almost convince me.''

She inhaled a deep breath. "To quote you, I'd be a liar if I said anything else. I used to love teaching, but nothing compares with that moment when the gong sounds and the adrenalin spurts through your veins. You don't know what you're going to find till you get there, but you know somebody needs help. Instead of standing idly by listening to the sirens go down the street, you're able to respond. Qualified to respond. No wonder you quit your job at the newspaper.''

They looked into each other's eyes for a long, silent moment. She couldn't read his enigmatic expression. But it was his next statement that really shook her. "I have to get back to Salt Lake tonight. You're welcome to ride with me. I'm leaving now.''

She couldn't believe he'd made such an offer, not when every time they were together ended in pain and bitterness. She knew what she *should* do, but where Grady was concerned, she was willing to undergo anything to be with him. Even if they fought every step of the way. Grady left a void in her life nothing or no one could fill.

"Just give me long enough to gather my things and write a note to the girls.''

He nodded his head, though his solemn expression made her wonder if he regretted the offer already. "I'll go down for the car and meet you in the breezeway.''

She put a hand on his arm. "Thank you, Grady, and I don't just mean for the lift home."

A distinct frown marred his handsome features. "I guess it would do no good at this stage to point out to you that a female fire fighter faces drawbacks a man never encounters."

"You mean you've never been propositioned?" she asked with a sparkle in her eyes, trying to keep the conversation light. Already he'd introduced a sensitive subject, and he seemed determined to press on it, like repeatedly probing a sore tooth with your tongue.

A smile broke out, dazzling her with its brilliance. "Touché," he murmured mysteriously, removing her hand.

Her eyes narrowed. "I seem to remember a certain black-eyed belly dancer in Istanbul lying in wait for you on several occasions."

"Were you jealous?" he quipped playfully.

"I hated her."

Grady burst out laughing, the deep, rich kind of laughter that took her back to those heavenly days when they'd first fallen in love. "Believe me, sweetheart, she hated you much more."

The endearment was a slip of the tongue but it had the power to rob her of breath. And it caused Grady to revert to his inscrutable self. "I'll meet you downstairs in ten minutes."

Her hands literally shook as she hurriedly packed and dashed off a note to Sue and Mavis. She left a twenty-dollar bill on top of the note to pay her share of the petrol. With a large family, she knew Mavis didn't have extra money to squander. Although she couldn't hope to fool Sue, she indicated in the note that the incident had upset her and Captain Simpson was willing to drive her home because he had to leave early for business reasons, anyway.

Grady stood by the Audi and put her things in the trunk before helping her into the car. "We'll grab a hamburger on the way out of town."

Suddenly a hamburger sounded divine. If they took the time to go to dinner at a restaurant, they wouldn't get served for an hour. And she couldn't wait to get away from people.

The stark beauty of the desert held Gina entranced for a long time. They rode in companionable silence until they reached St. George, where Grady filled the tank with gas.

Traces of fatigue fanned out from his eyes. Gina handed him a Coke and bought one for herself while he paid the attendant. "Would you trust me to drive your car for a while? You look like you could use a nap."

After a moment of uncharacteristic hesitation, he finally shook his head. "We usually end up with a speeding ticket when you drive. I'm not in the mood to be pulled over tonight."

Gina had the grace to blush, and Grady, ever alert, noticed.

"How many tickets have you had since you came to Utah? The truth now."

"Only one." The day she'd gone to see him . . .

He finished off his Coke and threw the can in the wastebasket. "That's one too many."

On that succinct note they got back into the car and drove on. Ironically, it was Gina who fell asleep en route and awoke a while later to discover that Grady had pulled off the freeway on to a side road at the exit leading to her apartment building.

"What's the matter?" she whispered, still disoriented from sleep. She raised her head from the window, rubbing her stiff neck. "Is something wrong with the car?"

"No."

That one word delivered in a still-familiar husky timbre set her pulses racing and she woke up fully. "Are you too tired to drive any farther?" she asked in a quiet voice, unconsciously running her palm up and down her silk-clad thigh.

"No."

A strange tension filled the car and she was acutely aware of his whipcord-lean body inches from her own. The ache that never truly left her throbbed to life, and she didn't know where to look or what to say.

"I want to make love to you tonight, Gina."

A moan escaped her throat. "Here?" She almost choked getting the question out. Was she dreaming?

"If this weren't such a public place, I'd say yes. I brought you back to Salt Lake tonight for that very reason. I want to take you home with me. If your answer is no, then I'll drive you to your apartment."

She couldn't believe any of it. "Grady—" She turned her head to stare at him. "I—I don't understand."

He was half lounging against the door, with one hand resting on the steering wheel. It was dark inside the car and she could scarcely make out his features. "What could you possibly not understand?" he asked wryly. "It's a simple yes or no."

Her mouth had gone so dry she couldn't swallow. "Nothing's simple where our relationship is concerned."

"We don't have a relationship."

Her cheeks burned crimson. "Then there's a name for what you're asking," she whispered.

He stifled an epithet and sat up. "I asked you for an answer, not a cross-examination."

She folded her arms across her stomach. "The answer is no."

He started the engine immediately. "That's all I need to hear." He drove back onto the freeway, and within a minute they were pulling up the driveway of her building.

"Grady—" her voice shook with emotion "—I don't know you like this."

He left the motor running and stared straight ahead. "Surely you don't put me in the same category with the other men in your life?"

It was on the tip of her tongue to tell him there were no other men in her life, but she didn't want to give him that satisfaction. The fact that he expected her to sleep with him—because *he* suddenly wanted to—hurt her deeply. Maybe she'd have flung herself at him if he'd asked her that question in the beginning, but by now too much had happened and she wanted more than a night of passion with him. She wanted all his nights for the rest of their lives. "If you mean that having been married to me once gives you special privileges, then you're mistaken. If we were dating again, it might be different, but we're not. As you said, we haven't got a relationship."

She heard the mocking tone of his laughter. "So if I were to begin courting you again, you just might condescend to offer me the pleasure of your delectable body?"

"If you started dating me again, I'd know why. The answer would still be no."

"Can you actually conceive of my ever asking you for a date? Because if you can, your imagination is more creative than mine."

She grasped the door handle. "You offered me a ride home from Las Vegas, for which I'm thankful. Let's leave it at that. What you want can be had anytime, anywhere, with anyone."

She got out of the car, slammed the door and walked around to the boot, then realised it needed a key to open. Grady suddenly appeared. The moonlight revealed that the sarcastic smile was gone from his face, replaced by an expressionless mask. He handed her the bag and shut the trunk.

"Just so we understand each other, Gina. Tonight I wanted that total communion of body and soul we always managed to achieve in bed together, despite our problems. I thought you wanted it, too. Forgive me if it sounded as if I was insulting you. I'll never ask you again.''

Quickly Gina turned her head away. If he'd said *that* to her in *those* words, she couldn't possibly have refused him. Just when she thought she understood him, he changed everything around, making her feel the guilty party. It should have thrilled her that Grady could admit he still craved the intense, passionate bond they'd shared. But that wasn't enough. They probably wouldn't be able to stop at one night. In the end she'd be his mistress. From wife to mistress. It defied logic!

''It isn't possible to achieve a total communion when so much else is wrong, Grady. We found that out while we were married. You're choosing to ignore that part.''

His gaze slanted toward her in the remote manner she'd grown to fear during their marriage. ''You've changed, Gina. I've been looking for some vestige of the woman I married, but she's not there.''

Gina blinked. ''You divorced that woman, Grady.''

His deep sigh seemed to reverberate beneath her heated skin. ''A paradox within a paradox,'' he muttered cryptically, then reached into his trouser pocket. ''I had rather elaborate plans for returning these to you tonight, but under the circumstances I'll just give them back now.''

Gina couldn't imagine what he was talking about until he took her hand and dropped her diamond earrings into the palm. The moonlight turned them into a thousand little prisms. The significance of what he said hit her so hard she stood there like a statue. Grady had wanted to recreate their wedding night. Had he been planning this since her accident, the night of the ball?

"Did you even know they were missing?" he asked in a dull voice.

She put them carefully in her purse. "I assumed they were still in my turn-out coat."

His smile was one of self-mockery. "A fitting place for them."

She couldn't let Grady think she was that callous. "I decided my turnout coat was the best hiding place for something so valuable. For your information, I bought a new turnout coat to wear at station six. My old one is hanging in my bedroom closet. I had no idea you'd removed the earrings at the hospital, and since I've had no occasion to wear them, I had no reason to be—" She stopped and took a deep breath. "Why am I bothering to explain? You think the worst, no matter what I say or do."

"Am I that bad, Gina?" The teasing gruffness of his tone startled her, but it also told her Grady was satisfied with her explanation. Those earrings were sacred to her—and perhaps to him.

"You're much worse, actually. I have trouble understanding how you inspire such fierce loyalty among your crew."

He rubbed his lower lip with the pad of his thumb. "Then you should be grateful to have Captain Blaylock giving you orders."

"What orders? Rescuing kittens from trees, or dispensing plastic leaf-bags?"

His smile was complacent. "Look on the bright side. You've still got all your body parts in all the right places."

Gina ran a nervous hand through her hair. "If I don't get transferred soon, I'll be going somewhere else to look for work."

"Where?" He fired the question abruptly.

"I'm going to California for the Labor Day weekend. If there's an opening at my old station in San Francisco, I'll take it."

There was a slight pause. "What's the attraction, apart from the fact that your parents live there?"

"I've always loved to swim, as you know. My station covered the harbour, boat fires, oil rigs, that sort of thing. I got into quite a bit of underwater rescue work, which beats watching soap operas in the afternoon."

He drew himself up, and she could see his muscles tauten. "What's this about, Gina? A little moral blackmail so I'll find a place for you at station one?"

"I thought you were beyond blackmail of any kind, Grady. This may come as a surprise, but working at station one is not my aim in life. I'm planning for my future and I've been checking out all the possibilities here and in Northern California. Since none of the busy stations have openings here, and since it doesn't look as if there'll be any in the near or distant future—for political reasons or otherwise—I don't have any choice but to go back."

She expected Grady to hurl some retort, but he remained unexpectedly silent.

"To be honest, it's not as hard to make it as a female fire fighter in California," she went on. "There are more of us down there and we're more accepted. I'm afraid Salt Lake is man's last bastion. You're in your element, Grady Simpson."

"You've changed almost beyond recognition, Gina."

"Then I have you to thank. To think if I hadn't met you, I'd probably be—"

"Dead! Blown up by a terrorist bomb. The American school where you taught has been a target many times in the past few years. The fact that you didn't leave Beirut when the government was urging all Americans to go should have warned me that you have an unhealthy sense of adventure."

Gina was incredulous. "Do you mean to tell me that all the time I was worried about you getting killed behind enemy lines, you were worried about *me*?"

"I felt that anxiety in the pit of my stomach from the moment we met." His voice rang with the truth.

"I can't believe it. You never said anything. I never knew."

"I never intended you to know. A man doesn't like to admit that kind of fear, not even to himself. All I knew was that I wanted you for my wife and dreamed about you becoming the mother of my children. I couldn't get you out of the Middle East fast enough."

She drew closer. "If you hadn't met me, would you still be over there?"

"In all probability, I'd still be a war correspondent somewhere on the globe."

Gina was aghast. "Did you love it so much?"

"I only loved one thing more," he whispered.

"Grady." She shook her head in a daze. "Why didn't you tell me any of this? When you found out you couldn't tolerate that desk job, why didn't you say something? I'd have gone anywhere with you."

He absently rubbed the back of his neck. "I wanted us to have roots, Gina. A real home, not some hotel room for two weeks at a time with five minutes' notice to evacuate. Fire fighting gave me the adventure I craved, and a home base as well. The best part was that I had my wife to come home to after a twenty-four-hour shift. She smelled like flowers, was beautiful beyond description and held me in her arms at night. I knew that when I was away from her, she wouldn't be kidnapped or blown up or shot." Or knocked unconscious by a runaway fire hose...

Gina sagged against the fender of the car, unable to take it all in. He'd given up so much for her, only to be alone now. "Grady—after our divorce, why didn't you go back to the newspaper?"

"That only appealed while I was a headstrong bachelor without responsibilities. When you work in a war zone, you live on the edge. For me, that time has passed, Gina. Now you couldn't lure me away from the department. When I came back to Salt Lake, I came home, literally."

There was too much to absorb. Gina needed some time to herself to sort everything through. Grady had just revealed a side of himself she hadn't known about. He was more vulnerable than she'd ever imagined. His fears were as real as hers had been. Their lives were like a jigsaw puzzle with a piece askew. And every time you tried to fit it back in place, another piece was moved out of position until you couldn't remember how to put it all back together again. "I wish you'd told me all this three years ago."

His mouth thinned. "All the talk in the world wouldn't have affected the outcome." The air hung heavy with his parting comment, made all the more devastating because it was the truth. "See you around, Gina."

She let herself in the front door, then fell limp against it. *See you around, Gina*. To hear that from him after all they'd shared and lived through. It wasn't fair. She should never have come back to Salt Lake. Doing that had only plunged them deeper into pain. It was best for her to go back to California. Right now she couldn't relate to the Gina who'd reported to Captain Simpson one beautiful summer morning full of bright hope and expectations....

CHAPTER SEVEN

"Ms LINDSAY. The phone's for you."

"Thanks, Captain." Gina took the receiver from Captain Blaylock, a man the same age as her father with the same loving disposition and warm, caring spirit. "This is Gina Lindsay."

"Gina—thank heaven I reached you before you went off duty. Remember Jay, that fire fighter from engine seven I met in Las Vegas? He took me to breakfast?"

"Remember?" Gina said, laughing. "He's all you've talked about for the past two weeks!"

"Well," Sue drawled, "he finally swung a shift that gave him today off. He wants to spend the whole day with me. And if everything goes the way I hope it does, we'll end up at my place for dinner."

"That's wonderful." Gina was really thrilled for her.

"And he has a friend. Another fire fighter you once swung shift with, Stephen Panos. Remember him?"

"Yes. He could pass for a younger Omar Sharif."

"You noticed!"

"I noticed. He's nice."

"Well, he noticed you, but he's never been able to work up the courage to ask you out, because your blasted rules precede you."

"You know why I've had to stick to them, Sue. I haven't wanted to give Grady a reason not to trust me."

"Look, I don't mean to sound cruel, but does it really matter any more what he thinks? You haven't seen or heard from him since he drove you home from Las Vegas. You admitted to me that it's really, truly over this time. So break your rules and come out with us today. Please. How long has it been since you went out on a real date, Gina?"

"A date?" she repeated.

The captain smiled, forcing Gina to turn her back on him. She sighed. "A long time, since before I came back to Salt Lake."

"*That* long?" Susan gasped. "You're way past due, my friend. We're going to play a little tennis, swim, get acquainted. That's all. What do you say?"

"Well..."

"Do it," the captain barked without lifting his head from his stack of paperwork. "That's an order."

Gina laughed. "Sue? Did you hear? Captain Blaylock just ordered me to go with you. How about that?"

"Tell him he'll receive a medal for co-operation in the line of duty. Gina—do you mean it? You'll come?"

She took a deep breath. "Why not? I probably won't be working in Salt Lake much longer anyway."

The captain's head came up. "What's that?" He frowned. She really had his attention now and could have kicked herself for what she'd said.

"Nothing, Captain."

"I didn't like the sound of that. You and I need to have a talk before you go on vacation."

"Gina, the guys will be by for me in a few minutes, then we'll come for you. You can leave your car there, can't you?" Sue's voice dragged Gina back to their conversation.

"Sure. That's fine. But remember that I've been on duty twenty-four hours. And I look it."

"That's the beauty of keeping it in the family. We all look awful. Who cares? They appreciate us on the inside."

Gina started to chuckle. "Wouldn't it be nice if that were true?"

"It's going to make Stephen's day, Gina. You might even enjoy yourself. Thanks for being a good friend. See you in a little while." Gina mumbled her good-byes and hung up the phone with trepidation.

The captain looked at her for a full minute, waiting for an explanation. "It's obvious you're not happy here, so we need to discuss the problem," he finally said. "Go have fun today, but remember that you and I will have a talk." He sounded just like her father and was every bit as kind. Best of all, the captain was one man who didn't have a problem with female fire fighters. What a difference that feeling of acceptance made.

"Thanks, Captain. I promise we will."

In the bathroom she changed into Jamaica shorts and a T-shirt. With a little effort, she soon felt halfway presentable. It seemed so strange to be getting ready for a date. She wondered if she'd ever overcome the pangs of guilt, the sense of being disloyal to Grady by going out with another man.

The new shift arrived as Gina was walking out the door to put her things in the car and lock up. They exchanged greetings and kidded around until Sue arrived in Jay's car. Stephen got out of the back and ambled slowly toward Gina.

"What do you know?" he said, giving her a wide smile. "Everyone said it couldn't be done, but here you are in the flesh, Ms Lindsay. Unless Sue's putting me on, she says you're willing to spend an entire day with me. Is that true?"

Gina always thought of Stephen as the strong, silent type, but he had absolutely no trouble communicating and was even more attractive than she remembered. "Only if it's what you want, Mr. Panos."

He eyed her appreciatively. "I've been wanting a date with you since your first day on the rig. I'm not even going to ask why the fates have suddenly decided to deliver you into my hands."

"We can thank Sue, I believe." She smiled back.

"Oh, I do." He nodded his head slowly. "I don't know about you, but I have the feeling this could be the start of a memorable relationship. Shall we go?"

In some ways Stephen reminded her a little of Bob Corby. He was confident and at ease with women but didn't have Bob's arrogance. Gina liked that about Stephen and realised that, if she weren't so deeply in love with Grady, Stephen could be a man she'd be interested in.

Sue introduced Jay to Gina, and plans were made to go to breakfast. Over waffles and sausage they mapped out their day, which they filled to the brim with tennis, swimming, videos and some napping in between activities—inevitable, since they'd all been up for twenty-four hours before that.

It was almost ten o'clock by the time they called an end to their relaxing, fun-filled day. Stephen borrowed Jay's car long enough to drive Gina back to the station for her own car. He seemed reluctant to let her go.

"I'm off duty the day after tomorrow. Will you spend it with me? My folks have a cabin on Bear Lake. We could water-ski."

Gina rubbed her eyes with the palms of her hands. "If I weren't going out of town, I'd love to."

"Where are you going? For how long?"

"I'm going to spend Labor Day with my folks in Carmel, then go on to San Francisco. I'll be gone about a week."

"A week, huh?" He frowned. "I guess I can last that long. Barely," he amended.

"You're very nice, Stephen. I've enjoyed this day a lot. I'll call you when I get back. All right?" She couldn't believe she was saying that to him. Maybe she was just using him because she was in so much pain over Grady. If that was true, then it wouldn't be fair to Stephen, but she wasn't in a position to have a perspective on her emotions right now. Stephen had been divorced for five years, and, unlike her, didn't seem to have any obsessions about the past. At least, not outwardly.

"I wish this weren't our first date, Gina. I'd like to kiss you goodnight." Stephen was always direct. In that respect, at least, he reminded her of Grady.

She flashed him a smile. "Didn't someone once say that getting there was half the fun?"

He had an attractive chuckle. "Whoever said it was right, but I can assure you I'm going to get there, Ms Lindsay."

"Is that a warning?"

"It's a promise." His black eyes sparkled.

He started to get out of the car but she put a detaining hand on his arm. "Don't bother. My car's right next to us. Goodnight."

"Goodnight," he said reluctantly, gently squeezing her arm. She got out of the car and shut the door, then threw him a cheerful wave. He tooted the horn a couple of times and drove away while she started to unlock her car.

"I thought he'd never leave," someone muttered behind her. Gina whirled around in stunned surprise.

"Grady?" she cried out as her heart began to thud unmercifully. "How long have you been standing there?"

In the moonlight, his eyes glittered silver. "Long enough to feel sorry for the poor devil. He could hardly keep his hands off you."

"It's not nice to spy on people." She said the first thing that came into her mind, too disturbed to think coherently.

"Your protracted goodnight was done in plain view of anyone who happened to be in the car park. The fact that I've spent two hours here waiting for you has nothing to do with it."

"Two hours? What could be that important? I'm tired, Grady, and it's been a long day."

"I'll just bet it has," he bit out fiercely.

She opened her car door. "Why don't you say what's on your mind so I can go home?" All day she'd actually managed to subdue the inevitable thoughts of Grady and she'd had a pleasant time for once. Now, within seconds, he'd reduced her to a trembling mass of nerves and desires.

"I'll follow you. What I've got to say is going to take awhile."

"No, Grady." She swung around, the light catching the purple sparks in her eyes. "We've said it all. Over and over again. I can't take it any more."

"And you think I can?" he lashed out, sounding breathless. "You've got your choice. We can talk here where someone from the station is sure to see us, or we leave and go someplace private. Preferably the condo. It's a lot closer than your apartment."

In truth, the condo *was* closer. And she had her car; she could leave whenever she wanted. She couldn't imagine what he wanted to talk to her about, but judging by his anger, it wouldn't be pleasant. "I'll follow you," she agreed at last.

He couldn't be jealous of her date with Stephen. That would imply that he still cared for her, which he didn't. Maybe he intended to upbraid her for breaking her promise not to get involved with a fire fighter. The questions plagued her until she wanted to scream. But what terrified her most of all was this tremendous power Grady had over her. All he had to do was beckon and she came running. He was her obsession and the longer she allowed the situation to continue, the less chance she'd have of ever carving out a little happiness for herself. Her plan to win him back had blown up in her face, just as her mother had predicted.

In a few minutes she'd parked her car and was following him up the stairs as he took them two at a time to the living-room of the condo. She unwillingly admired the fit of his Levi's. He had a magnificent body and he moved with fluid grace. Every motion, even the way he ate his food, intrigued her.

"Can I offer you a drink? Some wine?" Suddenly he'd turned into the urbane host and it confused her.

"No, thank you," she murmured, sitting down on the small love seat opposite the leather couch. "Please say what you have to say, Grady. I'm exhausted."

His eyes played over her suntanned face as he stood in front of her with his hands on his hips. "I can tell. Under the circumstances it might be better if we made you more comfortable." Lightning fast, he swooped down and picked her up in his arms. Her cry of surprise was smothered by the mouth that closed over hers, demanding a response. He carried her to the couch and sat down with Gina still in his arms, lying across his lap.

He hadn't given her time to think. She only knew that this was Grady holding her, kissing her as if he were trying to summon the very breath from her body. The terrible thing was that Gina gave him what he wanted, because it was what she wanted, too.

"Grady—love me. Please love me," she begged, burying her face in his black curls, curving her body against him. His strong legs wrapped around hers and ignited something deep inside that made her body go molten.

His hands entwined in the silk of her hair and he held her fast. That incredible translucence was there in his eyes. "I want to do much more than that, Gina," he said thickly. "I want to marry you."

Silence fell over the room, and the only sound Gina could hear was the pounding of her heart.

She traced the outline of his sensuous mouth with her finger, as if bewitched. Her eyes were twin fires of purple gazing up at him. "Do you have any idea how long I've been waiting to hear you say that? Grady—" She grasped his face between her hands and searched hungrily for his mouth, giving him her answer.

Suddenly Grady crushed her to him and buried his face in her neck, holding her so tight there was no space between them. "Sweetheart," he whispered with the old tenderness and the trace of tears in his voice. Gina was already in tears and they fell between her dark lashes, wetting them both.

"If I die tonight, it will be from too much happiness," she confessed.

"Don't die on me now." His body shuddered as his mouth found hers and feasted on it till Gina felt drugged with desire. "I have plans for us," he whispered at last, brushing his lips against her eyes and nose.

"So do I."

He caught her hand to his mouth and kissed the palm before putting it against his heart. "Can you feel that?" His mouth curved in that half smile that always sent her into shock with its male beauty. She nodded in a daze. "It beats for *you*, Gina."

A new radiance illuminated her face. "I came back here—to Salt Lake—for you, Grady. You're the most precious thing in my life."

"Thank God you did." His eyes blazed with a silver fire. "I was a fool to ever let you go." His voice shook with urgency and with a self-recrimination that wounded her.

Gina's eyes searched his. "We had a lot to work out, Grady. But we've found each other again. Our marriage will be much stronger than it was before."

His face sobered. "I came to California so many times you never knew about. I even watched you riding horseback along the beach one day, but I could never bring myself to let you know I was there."

"What?" Gina's heart leaped in her breast. "I thought you'd forgotten all about me. Never a phone call or a letter. I've never known such pain."

"Gina..." He buried his face in the silken profusion of her hair. "What have we done to each other? These past three years have been an eternity. I've been surviving, but you wouldn't call it living. I don't think I could describe how it felt to see you standing there at the desk. You were the most beautiful sight I ever saw in my life."

"Then you're the greatest actor alive, my love." His head lifted at that. "I was literally sick to my stomach, I was so frightened by what you'd say or do." Her eyes glistened. "I couldn't bear to think it was really over between us. I had to find out."

"I told you once how courageous you are. I'm in awe of it, Gina," he confessed, his voice softened by an unfamiliar humbleness. "I don't deserve a second chance, but because of you I've got it and I'm not going to do anything that will ever hurt you again. At least, not knowingly."

Gina stared long and hard at him. "I love you, Grady."

He swallowed visibly. "I love you. Will you accept the house in Midway as a belated wedding present? I bought it hoping that one day, by some miracle, you'd live in it with me. I never gave up on us, Gina. I just didn't know how to reach out to you. Every way I turned there was a stumbling block."

"Grady..." She played with the black tendrils curling over his bronzed forehead. "Let's not dwell on the past any more. The time's too short. Can we have a baby right away? It's all I can think about since we drove to Midway."

"Why do you think I drove you there, if not to torture you with the idea? If you couldn't be the mother of my children, then I didn't want anyone else. But first—" he tousled her hair with his hand and kissed her mouth firmly "—I'm planning to fly down to California with you. I want to formally ask for your hand in marriage. I couldn't do that the first time around since we were out of the country."

She grasped one of his hands between hers. "Mother told me I was crazy to try and win you back. She couldn't see that going to Salt Lake would accomplish anything but more pain. It's going to be a shock for Mom and Dad when you come home with me."

"A good one, I hope."

"They love you, Grady. They'll be ecstatic. It's the fire fighting they hate."

"Somebody has to do it."

"I know." She laughed playfully. "But they're more resigned to the idea than they used to be."

"Would you like to be married in California?"

"No, my home is here with you," she said firmly. "I'd like to be married in a church, with all our friends from the various stations joining us."

Grady groaned. "I'm not sure any of my crew will be speaking to me when they find out you were really my ex-wife. I even have it in my heart to feel sorry for Corby—despite the fact that I could have strangled him with my bare hands the night of the ball. He can thank providence you stuck to your rules."

Gina looked sheepish. "Except for Stephen Panos."

His eyes glittered possessively. "How many times have you been out with him, Gina?"

"Today was the first."

His chest heaved as he played with a strand of her hair. "I figured as much. Otherwise he wouldn't have let you go so easily."

Stephen was going to be shocked when he heard the news. She'd given him no clue that anyone else was in the picture. "I'll have to tell him soon." She slanted a provocative glance at him. "What about that brunette? From what I saw, you're going to have a slightly harder time of it."

"Don't worry about that," he murmured against her mouth.

"It's worse than I thought," she shot back.

"I love it when you act jealous. But I'll tell you a secret. Among my many sins throughout our marriage, infidelity was never one."

Gina's heart raced. "And after the divorce?"

Grady tousled her silken hair. "After a time I dated my fair share of women, but compared to you, Gina, there's simply no contest." His eyes narrowed and he caught her face between his hands. "Has there been a man in your life?"

She gazed at him tenderly. "Yes. There was one."

He blinked and she saw a brief flash of pain in his eyes. "You don't have to tell me. I don't think I want to know."

"Darling." She lowered her mouth to his. "It was you. Some women can only love one man. It's the way I'm made."

Grady let out a long, sustained breath and the beautiful smile that broke out on his face made him look ten years younger. "Gina—" He began to shake his head, and suddenly she was crushed in his arms once more. "You've made me the happiest man alive." Gina clung to him for fear he was an illusion and might disappear at any moment. "Let's get married over the holiday. As soon as possible."

She nodded, rubbing her cheek lovingly against the slight rasp of his. "We can get our blood tests in the morning."

"Do you want to live here at the condo, or shall we find a place closer to Midway, so we can get there sooner on our days off?"

"We'll never find a better view of the valley than the one we have right here. Let's stay here for the time being. Maybe when our third baby is on the way we can look for a bigger place."

"It looks as if I'm going to have to keep you busy in that bed if we're going to produce all those children," he whispered against her ear, biting the lobe gently.

"That's the part I'm looking forward to." Her voice was suddenly choked with tears. "I've missed you so terribly, Grady."

"I can't even talk about it," he admitted. "Let's go upstairs. I'll show you what it's been like for me."

Gina's answer was to nestle closer as he picked her up in his arms and started for the spiral staircase leading to the master bedroom. He paused on the way up to drink deeply from her mouth.

"Grady," she whispered, raising passion-glazed eyes to him. "Do you think you could throw some weight around at headquarters so that our schedules are the same? We're going to need all those days off together if we're going to have that big family."

His smile was mysterious. "Sweetheart, you don't need to keep up the pretence any longer. Tomorrow you'll hand in your resignation. You're going to be my wife again. That's all that's important." He continued on up the stairs and strode into the bedroom, carrying her over to the window so they could look at the view together.

"What pretence are you talking about?" She kissed the side of his neck. "What resignation?"

Grady gently lowered her until her feet touched the floor. He pressed her against him and put his hands on her shoulders. "Gina, you've proved to me that you've overcome your fears. You're the most amazing woman I've ever known. But there's only going to be one fire fighter in this family. I want you home, safe and sound, loving me and our children. I don't know another woman who would have gone to the lengths you did to fight for her marriage, but the fight is over, sweetheart. You've won. Thank God nothing serious ever happened to you before we found our way back to each other. Now, no more talk. I'm going to love you all night long. I need to love you." His voice shook with naked emotion.

The blood drained from Gina's face and she felt light-headed. When he started to draw her towards the bed she resisted. She felt as if a steel vice trapped her, constricting her breath. The plunge from heaven to hell was swift.

Grady's brow furrowed in concern and genuine surprise. "What is it? Your skin's gone so pale."

"Hold me, Grady," she cried out. "Hold me and listen."

He clutched her to him and for a few seconds, she rested in the strength of his arms. "What's wrong, Gina? Are you ill?" He sounded anxious.

"Yes. I'm ill." She tried to swallow. She didn't know how to say what needed to be said. "How do I tell you this without the pain starting all over again?"

He didn't have to say a word, but she felt some intangible energy leave his body. He didn't stop holding her, but the oneness had stopped flowing between them, leaving her bereft once more.

"I don't want to resign, Grady. I love my work. I— I thought you understood. I thought you'd come to terms with it. And all this time you thought it was a pretence." He started to pull away from her, but she held on to him fiercely and wouldn't let him go. "Listen. Please."

"No!" he cried out, shaking his head. Now his skin looked like parchment. "Don't tell me this now. I can't take it." She'd only seen tears in his eyes on one other occasion—the day he'd told her he couldn't go on, that he was divorcing her. With almost superhuman strength he broke free of her arms and took a step backward, as if he were dazed. "I *refuse* to believe you love the job enough to let it come between us, Gina. You *couldn't* love it. It's the most dangerous job in the world! It's dirty and hard and exhausting and often terrifying. It's no place for my wife!'' His face had a pinched look.

''Why isn't it?'' Gina's chest heaved. ''Am I exempt from the more unpleasant aspects of life?''

''Come off it, Gina. *The more unpleasant aspects of life,*'' he yelled. ''Have you ever seen the charred remains of a buddy when you couldn't get to him in time? *Have you?*'' The tension that gripped him made the cords stand out in his neck. ''Well, I *have!*'' he answered without waiting for a response. ''I've seen five men vaporise in a fireball and I couldn't do a damn thing about it. I'm still haunted by those memories. It could happen to you, any time, any day of the week.''

''Of course there are risks, Grady. *You* take them every time you go on duty. But think of the good we do, the service. There's no other feeling like it. I hoped we could always be together, work together. I thought you'd changed and wanted that, too.''

''Then you were wrong.''

She closed her eyes in pain. ''I love you, Grady. I'll always love you, but I guess this really is goodbye.''

''Don't ever come near me again.'' Eyes of flint pierced through her as he delivered his ultimatum.

That moment would stand out in Gina's mind and heart as the blackest of her life. She never remembered her flight from the bedroom or her drive back to the apartment.

compelling Cindy Simpson's name on the phone. Let's start with him."

Gina tried to find words, but nothing would come out, and in her humiliation, self-tears rolled down her cheeks, she needed something to break them

CHAPTER EIGHT

"CAPTAIN BLAYLOCK?" Gina poked her head into one of the offices at headquarters, gratified to find the captain alone. Sunglasses hid her puffy eyes.

"Good. You're here. Come on in, Gina. I know you're getting ready to go on vacation, but I thought we'd better have things out before you go away." Gina nodded and entered the room, finding a seat opposite the desk. She felt like death and hadn't slept all night. Like a person in shock, she'd sat on the couch staring into the darkness. Captain Blaylock's phone call was the only thing to rouse her from a near-catatonic state.

He sat back in the swivel chair and touched the tips of his fingers together, eyeing her curiously. "I raised five daughters," he started off without preamble, "which qualifies me to read between the lines. You're a fine fire fighter and getting better all the time. But you have a big problem in your personal life." Gina averted her head, not so much surprised by his frank speaking as by his astute observation. "Nothing you tell me will ever go beyond this room, but I want to know what's going on. In time, this problem will start to affect your job and then we're all in trouble. I heard you mention Grady Simpson's name on the phone. Let's start with him."

Gina tried to find words but nothing would come out, and to her humiliation, giant tears rolled down her cheeks. She took off the glasses to brush them away. The captain sat forward.

"I've known Grady a long time and they don't come any better, but if I don't miss my guess, something's going on between the two of you."

The captain saw too much, Gina mused brokenheartedly, but she still couldn't talk as she attempted to stifle the sobs.

"I checked with Captain Carrera this morning and he had no complaints about your work, professionally or otherwise, which leads me to believe the trouble started when you went to station one. Are you in love with Simpson?"

Gina's gasp resounded in the room and the captain nodded. "I thought as much after watching the two of you at the Fire Fighters' Ball. My wife made the comment that she'd never seen two people who looked so much in love and I agreed with her." He paused. "Have you quarrelled? Is that what this is all about? Because if it is, you need to straighten things out for both your sakes and the good of the department. Gina? You're a lot like my daughter Kathy. You're proud and you try to stay cool, but inside you're mush." Gina's strangled laugh broke the tension. "Forget I'm your superior and just talk to me as a friend."

"You should have been a psychiatrist." She sniffed hard. "In order for you to understand, I'll have to tell everything and I'd hate to keep you that long when it's your day off."

"Why do you think I'm here?" He chuckled. "I'll be retiring in October and to be honest, I'm dreading it. I've been at this job forty-five years. It's all I know. There's nothing else I'd rather do than try to be of help."

Gina could tell he meant it. "You're one in a million, Captain."

He smiled kindly. "Well, if that's true then you know you have nothing to fear from me."

"I know," she said, nodding. "Well…it all started in Beirut," she began, as if that explained everything.

His eyes crinkled. "As in Lebanon?"

"Yes," she replied, running an unsteady hand through her hair. "That's where Grady and I first met and fell in love." Having said that, Gina felt as if the barriers had come down, and she bared her soul. Except for the intimate details of their life, the captain knew everything by the time she was through speaking. She'd even told him about her plan to look for work in California.

He stared at her for a long time, just as her father always did when he was mulling over an important decision. "What was it John Paul Jones said when all looked hopeless? *I have not yet begun to fight!*'" Gina blinked in absolute amazement. "Where's your courage, my girl? Are you going to run away when the going gets rough? Where's the fighter who crawled around in all that smoke to rescue a two-hundred-pound man without batting an eye?''

Gina clasped her hands together. ''You don't know Grady. His fears are much worse now than mine were in the beginning.''

His brows lifted. ''And then again, maybe they also hide something else. Have you thought of that?''

Their eyes met. ''Like what, Captain?''

He shook his head. ''I don't know. But maybe you ought to think about that while you're visiting your folks. Then come home and show what you're made of. No one knows what the future holds, Gina, but if you don't come back, you'll never find out.''

The captain had given her a lot to think about. ''I appreciate your advice. Your daughters are lucky. I wish all the men in the department were like you. You're not threatened by women.''

His bark of laughter resounded in the room. ''You didn't know me in the days Nancy Byington came to the department. I was her first captain out of school and we lasted exactly one shift together.''

''What?'' Gina cried out incredulously.

''That's right. I didn't believe in women doing men's work. We'd never had a female on the force before. I thought it was a big joke. But that was before my Betsy went into engineering and Kathy into medicine. They managed to turn their old dad's thinking around in a big hurry. Give Grady some time. You're young, both of you. Anything can happen. But if it doesn't—'' he lifted a finger ''—you'll have the

satisfaction of knowing that you gave it all you had.
That way, you can go on.''

Unable to stay seated any longer, Gina covered the
distance in half a dozen quick steps to give him a hug.
''You're wonderful, Captain.''

''That's what I like to hear.'' He laughed jovially,
patting her hands. ''Now go on down to Carmel and
have a good time.''

''I will.'' She squeezed his shoulder in gratitude,
then started for the door, feeling strangely at peace.
She wouldn't have thought it possible when he summoned her that morning.

''And Gina?''

''Yes?'' She whirled around in the open doorway.

''We may not see as much action at number six as
you did at station one, but in order to be the best fire
fighter there is, you need to experience it all. You'll
learn things with us that you need to know, things you
won't learn anywhere else.''

How did he get so wise? ''I already have, sir. I don't
know how you've put up with me. I'll see you next
Tuesday morning.''

A broad smile broke out on his face. ''I knew you
were a fighter!''

The idea that Grady's fear masked something else
stayed in Gina's mind constantly all the time she was
in California. The reunion with her parents shed no
new light, even after a lot of discussion, but she returned to Salt Lake after four days of pampering, determined to stick things out for the time being, to see
where it all led. Captain Blaylock was right about one

thing. If she didn't give Grady more time, she would always have a question, and it could mar any future happiness, period! Grady expected her to remain in California. She wondered what his reaction would be when he found out she'd decided to return to station six. He'd told her never to come near him again, but if they both happened to be fighting the same fire, he'd be forced to acknowledge her presence, if only to himself. Right now, this was her only hope of reaching Grady, and she clutched at it like a drowning man gasping for air. It could be one hour or six weeks before an alarm went off that brought the two of them together, but she was beginning to learn the value of patience—thanks to Captain Blaylock.

Station six was located in a residential area on the northwest side of Salt Lake. Most of the runs involved heart attack victims or incinerator fires, accidents that happened in and around the home. Gina ignored the dispatcher's voice when the first alarm went out signaling a fire in City Creek Canyon, about three miles away. But strong winds hitting the valley were hampering rescue efforts and more units were called out.

"Let's go," the captain shouted, and Gina jumped into her boots and turn-out gear before boarding the rig with Ted and Marty. Captain Blaylock called the battalion chief for more instructions as they crested Capitol Hill, where they could see flames licking up the steep gully. A string of expensive condominiums on top were threatened, and a call had gone out to drop chemicals from the air.

Gina's gaze took in the engines and ladder trucks already assembled, knowing that Grady might be among them, and her heart started to knock in her breast. It was three weeks since her return from Carmel, and she ached for the sight of him.

"Ted? You heard the chief. Drive down to Second Avenue and we'll swing up A Street. Gina, you and Marty go in with the hose and keep that garage watered down till more units arrive."

"Right, Captain," Gina murmured along with the others. When they arrived on the scene moments later, the end condominium was in the greatest danger of going up in flames. Other units were attacking the fire in the gully below.

The captain pulled the plug—attached the hose to the hydrant—with the efficiency of long experience as Gina glanced around and caught sight of a boy of eleven or twelve, standing next to his parents and sobbing his heart out. At least she assumed they were his parents, judging by the way they all held on to each other.

"We'll try to save your place," Gina shouted, reaching for the hose. "Is your car in there?" she asked the father.

"Yes." His voice shook with emotion.

"Any gas cans?"

"One. But there's also my son's new puppy—he crawled under the car and won't come out."

Gina could remember her first puppy and she darted compassionate eyes at the boy. "What's his name?"

"Chester," he said on a half sob. "He's howling in there."

"We'll try to get him out. Ready, Marty?" she called over her shoulder. Marty gave the thumbs-up signal, and they began to pour water on the garage.

"Captain?" Gina asked as he approached to survey the situation. "We've got an animal in there, sir. I'd like permission to go in and get him. I can slide under the car more easily than anyone."

Captain Blaylock nodded his head. "I'll give you two minutes. That's it. If you haven't found the animal in that time, get out of there."

He took over her position on hose. Gina ran to the truck and put on her air mask, then hurried towards the garage.

Flames were licking around it and on the roof, but all Gina could see was the boy's heartbroken expression. She lifted the electric door manually. As soon as she did, she could hear the puppy's hysterical yelping and feel the intense build-up of heat. Gina groaned to herself when she considered inching her way under the gleaming red Porsche 911. Why didn't they own a Wagoneer instead?

She crouched on the cement and started calling to Chester. The puppy yelped a little harder when it heard her voice. "Come here, boy. Come on." She lay flat on her back and wriggled partially underneath the car. Her mask prevented her from going any farther, and she needed another couple of inches to grab the dog. Taking a deep breath, she removed her mask and glove and felt all around. Gratified when the dog's warm tongue started to lick at her fingers, she urged him on. "Come on. That's it," she crooned to him, and finally caught hold of an ear. He had to be a basset hound. She could hear the captain shouting to her.

"I don't like this any better than you do," she muttered, pulling the puppy out by the ear. He howled his head off, but she finally managed to get her arm around his wriggling body. He began to lick her face as she grabbed her mask and glove and dashed out of the garage, needing air before her lungs burst.

By now three hoses were trained on the garage and condo, containing the blaze. Gina's eyes searched out the boy, and she walked over to him, passing a group of other fire fighters.

"Chester!" The boy screamed with joy and hugged the puppy to him. His eyes were like stars as they looked up at Gina. "Thanks." That was all he said, but it was enough.

"You don't know how much this means...." The mother started to cry, leaning against her husband, who was talking to the captain.

"I think I do." Gina smiled as she watched the boy kissing his dog, murmuring baby talk to it.

"Our family dog died last month and we didn't think Max would ever get over it, but Jerry brought this puppy home the other night and it was love at first sight. If anything had happened to this one, I just don't know." She shook her head. "You've saved our house, too, and the car. We'll never be able to thank you enough. It's a good thing you're a woman," she added. "My husband was going to try and get down under the car, but he's too big and bulky."

"Did you hear that, Captain?" Gina winked, observing the clean-up operation out of the corner of her eye. But whatever the captain said in response faded away as her gaze connected with Grady's. He was standing patiently next to the boy, Max, listening to him and petting the puppy. *Where had he come from?*

"She's the one!" The boy pointed to Gina. "My dad couldn't get under the car, but *she* did." He ran over to her. "Do you want to hold Chester? He wants to thank you."

"I'd love to." Gina took the wriggling puppy in her arms, and he immediately proceeded to wet the front of her turn-out coat. Gina started to laugh and couldn't stop.

Grady moved closer, his lips twitching. "It looks like you'll have to get your old turn-out coat out of mothballs."

"Will you come to my school?" Max asked excitedly, unaware of any undercurrents. Gina tried hard to concentrate on the boy, which was almost impossible with Grady standing only a foot away. She couldn't have described the expression on his face, but he didn't resemble that other man who'd told her to leave and never come near him again. Her heart gave a kick. At least in front of his crew and the public, he'd decided to be civil to her and she could be thankful for that much positive reaction.

"You didn't answer his question," Grady prodded.

"Oh!" She looked away and tried to gather her wits. "You want me to come and give a talk?" She handed the dog back to him.

"Some of the kids get their parents to come if they have neat jobs. My mom works in a dumb office. I wish she rode a fire engine like you. Will you come?"

"Sure. Call station six and I'll see what can be arranged. I can do it on my day off."

"Cool!" A big grin spread on his face. "Hey, Mom! Dad!" He ran off to tell them, leaving Gina alone with Grady for a moment. There was activity all around them, but for some reason, Grady didn't seem to be in any hurry to get back to his crew. She should have been helping Marty with the hoses but she couldn't move. Again that tension streamed between the two of them, holding her fast.

"What are you doing back in Salt Lake, Gina? Wasn't there an opening in California?" Now that no one was around, the polite veneer had disappeared.

She tipped back her helmet so she could look at him squarely. "Captain Blaylock pointed out to me that I could learn a lot from working at station six, so I didn't go to San Francisco. I'm going to stay in Salt Lake."

He cursed beneath his breath, but for one brief moment a haunted look lurked in his eyes before he recovered from the shock. "I hope you don't mean permanently."

"As permanent as one can be about anything, barring unforeseen circumstances." She stood her ground.

"I thought station six was too tame for you." He sounded angry.

"I was wrong."

His face darkened and his voice was dangerously quiet now. "What are you playing at, Gina?"

"Rescuing puppies from burning garages."

Another epithet escaped. "And underneath a car with a full tank of gas just ready to explode!"

"You know that's not true, Grady. That tank wasn't close to igniting. The—"

He cut her off rudely. "You know where you should be, don't you? You should be that woman standing there with a son of your own, dammit!"

She started to shake. "It would help if there were a *man* standing next to me, first!"

"I don't believe what I'm hearing." His hands tightened into fists.

"Believe it."

"We're ready to roll," Marty called to her.

"Tell him to go to blazes," Grady muttered. "I'm not through talking to you."

"I shouldn't have to remind you of all people that I'm still on duty, Captain." She'd never seen him lose control in front of anyone before, and the fact that he had was exhilarating to Gina.

"I'm warning you, Gina. Just stay out of my way."

Her chin lifted. "I'm trying to, but you won't let me, Captain, sir."

His eyes had gone black with anger. "So help me, Gina—"

She didn't stay to hear the rest. Everyone was on the rig waiting. Captain Blaylock eyed her flushed cheeks with interest as she climbed on board, and he gave her his secret smile. Nothing escaped the captain's notice. But if he thought Gina had some progress to report about her situation with Grady, he was mistaken. Grady was furious about her decision to stay in Salt Lake. Beyond that, she couldn't read his mind or his heart.

There was a message from Stephen Panos on her answering machine when she got home the next morning. She'd been putting him off since she came back from vacation. Although she liked him, she knew she could never feel more than that, and she had no desire to hurt him. Yet if she continued to put him off, she could easily end up living her life alone, something her parents harped on over and over again.

She finally called him back around three and he asked her to double with Sue and Jay for the fire fighters' annual Lagoon celebration. Besides the Lagoon Amusement Park attractions, there were going to be games and competitions among the crews, with a big barbecue in the evening and a dance to follow. She decided to accept the invitation. It wasn't an intimate dinner, after all. If she could keep things friendly and light, Stephen wouldn't be able to read any more into the relationship than was there. And if her real underlying motive for going with Stephen was to make Grady jealous, then she wasn't admitting to it.

Gina loved Indian summer in Salt Lake; September was her favourite month of the year. The days were hot and the nights cool. She dressed in a navy and white sailor top and white shorts for the outing and caught her hair into two ponytails. Stephen said teasingly that she looked sixteen, but the male appreciation in his eyes told her he wasn't complaining.

Sue and Jay had already fallen in love and seemed oblivious to most of what went on around them. Gina watched them with envy. Their relationship appeared uncomplicated and secure. Jay had no hang-ups about Sue's work. Again Gina was reminded of Captain Blaylock's statement that something else could be behind Grady's fears, but her frustration grew because she had no contact with him. She'd seen him twice since the episode with the puppy—once at headquarters when they passed each other in the hallway, and then at the downtown mall while she was doing some shopping. He walked by her both times without acknowledging her presence. That had never happened before, not even when they were both at their angriest during the divorce.

As each day drew to a close, Gina felt less and less confident that there could ever be a future with Grady. Maybe she was a fool to keep on hoping and longing for a sign, she thought. Then, at Lagoon, she saw him feeding candy floss to the same brunette he'd taken to the dance, and she felt another bit of hope die out. Gina and Stephen had strolled along the path towards the picnic area where the competitions were being held, when she spotted Grady's curly black head among the crowd. In white aviator pants and shirt, contrasting with his bronzed skin, he made every other man around him pale into insignificance.

This time Gina paused to satisfy her curiosity about the woman who held his attention. She was Grady's age, sophisticated and attractive in a dark, almost Spanish way. Gina felt something snap inside her as the woman stood on tiptoe and kissed Grady's mouth after giving him back some candy floss. In excruciating pain, Gina looked away but not quickly enough. Grady's startling grey eyes penetrated hers for an instant, their look triumphant.

Embarrassed to have been caught staring so openly, Gina turned to Stephen and suggested they sign up for the three-legged race. Jealousy tore at her insides; Grady knew how to get to her. The outing had lost its appeal and Gina wanted to go home. But because she couldn't, she assumed an artificial gaiety, trying desperately to put Grady out of her mind for the rest of the afternoon and evening. She encouraged Stephen to enter all the events with her. Two hours later, they were exhausted.

"How about a swim before the barbecue?" Stephen suggested. "Let's just lie back in the cool water and relax. How does that sound?"

"Heavenly."

"Good. I'm a little tired of crowds and I'd like to get you all to myself, even if it means underwater."

Gina chuckled nervously, recognising certain signs. Apparently Grady had no difficulty enjoying a physical relationship with a woman even if his heart wasn't involved, but Gina couldn't give physical affection without love.

Under her clothes she wore a one-piece white bathing suit, so it took only seconds to remove her shorts and top and dive into the deep end of the Olympic-size pool. Stephen wasn't far behind. There weren't very many people in the water at this hour. Most of the guests had started eating over at the picnic tables.

They swam for a while, then Stephen grabbed hold of Gina's ankles and forced her to tread water. "I've got a terrific idea. Why don't I go get us a couple of plates of food and bring them back here? We can dance by the side of the pool and avoid the crush."

Gina had second thoughts but didn't express them. She took advantage of the time he was gone to get dressed in her top and shorts. Stephen looked slightly surprised when he returned with the food, but Gina barely registered his reaction because Grady was directly behind him, with the dark-haired woman clutching his arm. Apparently Grady had also decided to escape the crowds—at least that was what she thought at first, until he found a poolside table close enough to her and Stephen to be able to hear them talking. Gina suspected that Grady had intentionally set out to ruin her evening. He didn't want Gina, but he didn't want her paying attention to anyone else, either. Still, the niggling thought that maybe he was worried about her interest in Stephen gave her a whole new set of possibilities to consider.

He'd told her to stay away from him, yet he seemed to go to great lengths to make his presence known whenever they were in the same place together. Was he trying to force her out of his life by flaunting the other woman? Grady knew how deeply Gina loved him, and his amorous attentions to his date seemed calculated to make Gina miserable.

After a few minutes of trying to ignore Grady, Gina couldn't take any more and suggested to Stephen that they head back to Salt Lake. He readily agreed, probably because he hadn't managed to spend any time alone with her, after all.

"Stephen," she began as he pulled into her driveway, "I haven't been the greatest company in the world today. I could make up a million reasons, but the truth is, I'm still in love with someone else and until I can do something about it one way or the other, it isn't fair to go on seeing you. You're too nice, and I like you too much."

Stephen tapped the steering wheel with the heel of one hand. "I figured as much. Who's the lucky man?"

"It doesn't really matter, does it?"

"It might. Don't be angry if I wormed something out of Sue, Gina. She told me you'd once been married. If you're still in mourning, I'll wait until that period has passed. There's a difference between being in love and grieving, you know. I can speak with some authority on the subject."

"I know, Sue told me," Gina answered gently. "I'll be honest with you. I've never stopped loving my husband and I'm hoping that one day we'll get back together. It may not be possible, but I refuse to give up.''

Stephen fastened his dark eyes on her. ''Have you let him know you want him back? Does he realise you haven't given up?''

His questions surprised her. ''We still have something to resolve. It may be insurmountable.''

Stephen nodded and then got out of the car, coming around to her side to accompany her to the apartment. ''You know where to find me if you ever decide things won't work out with him. I'm not going anywhere.'' He kissed her forehead and walked away.

Why couldn't she fall in love with someone as nice and uncomplicated as Stephen? Gina asked herself. Someone mellow and steady. Maybe she was crazy to go on loving Grady when nothing could come of it.

Her nerves were wearing thin, yet she had no one to blame but herself. Grady would marry her in an instant if she'd give up fire fighting, but what would she do with those empty hours while he was out on the job? Teaching could never hold her now. If they had a baby, naturally she'd stay home with the child as long as possible and then resume part-time work with the department, but what if they didn't have a baby right away? During their five months of marriage she hadn't become pregnant. She and Grady would be right back where they started, but this time he'd be leaving her at home to go and do the work they both loved.

Gina knew herself too well. The boredom and the sense of loss would cause a fissure that would grow into another break, perhaps more devastating the second time around. To remarry only to separate again— she couldn't tolerate that. If she could just make Grady understand.

As she started getting ready for bed, an idea came to her. It was the only potential solution she could think of, thanks to what Stephen had said in passing about letting Grady know she wanted a reconciliation.

After a long debate with herself, Gina summoned the courage to phone Grady. Maybe he wasn't home, or maybe his girlfriend was there with him. Gina didn't know, but she had to talk to him while she still felt brave enough. He'd warned her to stay away, but a phone call maintained a distance between them. He could hang up on her, but something stronger than fear of rejection compelled her to try to reach him.

He answered on the fifth ring and sounded as if she'd wakened him from sleep. "Grady?"

The silence lasted so long, she thought he'd simply put the receiver on the side table and left it there so he could go back to sleep without fear of being disturbed by her again.

"What is it, Gina?" he finally asked in a flat voice.

"A—are you alone?"

He cursed violently and she quailed at his anger. "That's none of your business."

Her hand gripped the cord tightly. "I only meant that I wanted to talk to you for a little while, and if this is a bad time, I'll try to call you later."

"I'm on duty in six hours. Since no time is a good time for whatever it is you want, say what you have to say and get it over with!"

"I shouldn't have called. You're obviously not in any frame of mind to listen."

"Don't you dare hang up now!" he warned. "Let's get this over with once and for all. You have my undivided attention. What is it?"

She gulped, wondering where she'd found the temerity to approach him in the first place. "Grady— I've been thinking about us since the other night."

"There is no 'us', Gina," he said on such a bitter note she could have wept.

"Maybe there could be if you'd just listen for a minute."

A small silence ensued. "When you hand in your resignation to the fire department, then we'll talk. Not before."

"What if I make a permanent home at station six? What if I don't bid any other stations or do any swing shifts to busier stations? Could you live with that?" she asked with her heart in her throat. It was a compromise, but one that would allow her to do the work she loved and live with the man she loved.

"No, Gina. So don't ask."

His flat-out refusal to consider any options made her indignant. "But why? I thought it was the amount of action and the danger you objected to. If I'm willing to work at the quietest station in the city, why can't you accept that?"

"Because I want you home. Period."

Gina frowned. There was a world of emotion in his voice. She felt she was getting closer to the real problem. Her intuition told her something wasn't right here. On a sudden burst of inspiration, she asked, "Grady...does this have something to do with the fact that your mother wasn't home for you as a child?"

"Don't start psychoanalysing me. Goodbye, Gina." With a simple click of the phone, their conversation was terminated. Gina sat on the bed in a daze. Her thoughts were flying.

Grady's parents had worked at the Salt Lake *Tribune* when he was a boy. But later on there had been a divorce, and his mother had gone to live on the East Coast, where she remarried. She still lived there, and as far as Gina knew, Grady had little to do with her. As for Grady's father, he'd remained with the newspaper until he died of a heart attack. Gina had never met either one of them.

Though Grady had told her everything about his life as a war correspondent, he'd been reticent about telling her the details of his family life. She knew it caused him pain, so she never pried.

Haunted by the little bit she knew, Gina tried to imagine what it would be like to have both parents working all the time, at emotionally draining, all-consuming jobs. Then, during the sensitive adolescent years, to have to deal with a divorce... Apparently he'd chosen to stay with his father when his mother left.

Was Grady afraid their children would suffer if Gina was a working mother?

Captain Blaylock suggested there might be something behind Grady's irrational fear of Gina's getting injured. She was beginning to think he was right. Grady didn't care that she'd been willing to compromise and stay on at station six. To quote Grady, *he wanted her home. Period.*

Another thought occurred to her as she recalled how jealous and excluded she had felt when Grady spent so much time with the fire fighters. In those early days, she'd hated that other family. Was it possible that Grady felt excluded now that Gina had another life at the station?

She tried to think back to when they'd first got married. Had resigning from the school where she'd been teaching been her own idea or Grady's? Their whirlwind courtship had blotted out all other considerations, but she was quite sure Grady had asked her to leave so she would be free to travel with him. It made sense at the time; otherwise they couldn't have been together every possible minute. Besides, Grady had admitted his fear of her being injured if she stayed in Beirut.

Her mind spinning with unanswered questions, Gina flopped on her stomach and stared into the darkness. Somehow, some way, she had to force Grady to open up. Only he held the key to the riddle. Until she got to the bottom of this, there would never be a future with Grady. Never.

CHAPTER NINE

A WEEK WENT BY but Gina didn't see or hear from Grady. She was almost out of her mind with pain and made up projects to do at the station when they weren't out on calls. On one of her days off she made an appearance at the school attended by Max, the boy who owned the puppy Gina had rescued. Usually, she enjoyed visits with schoolchildren; they forced her to put aside her anxieties for a while. But watching these lively, carefree boys and girls only seemed to deepen her longing for a child of her own, and she returned to the apartment even more depressed than she'd been before. The phone was ringing as she walked through the front door, and she could hear Captain Blaylock's voice on the machine, asking her to call station six as soon as possible.

This was their day off, so she knew it had to be important for him to be at work. She dialled his number immediately. He didn't waste time talking but simply asked if she was free to help with an emergency. She rejoiced at the opportunity—anything to keep busy so she wouldn't think about Grady.

"Captain?" Gina entered the station in her coveralls and hurried right into his office. He was conferring with the captain of the other shift. They both looked up when she walked in.

"Sit down, Gina. Captain Michaels and I called you because we need your expertise. There's been a bad accident involving a truck and car—they've both gone into the Jordan River. We don't know any details but people are trapped underwater. A call has gone out requesting scuba divers."

"I'm on my way, Captain."

"Good. I'm coming with you." They all boarded the engine and headed west toward the river. "A rescue unit with special scuba gear is headed for the scene of the accident right now," Captain Blaylock explained.

It was a fairly warm September afternoon. At least, the weather was co-operating, Gina thought. Rescues at night required lighting and everything became even more complicated and difficult.

The crew listened to the battalion chief's directives as they roared down the driveway. Police had already cordoned off the accident site. Approaching the area where the vehicles had gone over the edge into the water, they could see the truck's skid marks. A little farther on, Gina saw the big semi lying in the river, three-fourths of it submerged on the driver's side. The other car was about ten yards downstream and totally submerged. The river wasn't swift, but if the people had been knocked unconscious at impact, the danger of drowning was just as great.

She saw a ladder truck farther down the road and knew it was Grady's: Station one would have been the first to respond. Heart pounding, Gina jumped down from the rig and ran the hundred yards to the rescue unit, where she would change into a wet suit and tanks. Gina had learned to scuba dive when she was a girl in California. It was second nature to her, and never had she been more thankful for those hours of training than now, when so many lives were at stake.

The battalion chief was waiting for her as she approached the jump-off point. ''There were no witnesses when the accident happened so we don't know how many people are down there. Captain Simpson's already in the water with one of his crew, but they need help.''

Gina nodded and did a somersault over the edge, carrying an extra set of tanks. Once she had her bearings, she gave a kick and headed for the truck, swimming around to the front where she could see Bob Corby extricating the driver without any problem. He was already giving the man air from his tank and motioned for her to go help Grady farther downstream. She nodded and shoved off once more, employing her strongest kick to cover the distance as quickly as possible.

The car was jammed against some boulders. It was a white Buick four-door, and as far as she could tell, the windows were closed. If the driver had been running the air-conditioning, there could still be enough air inside the car to keep the person—or persons— alive.

As she rounded the side she saw Grady using an underwater torch to get the door open. In the driver's seat was a young man and strapped next to him in a car seat, a baby. They appeared to be dead, but Gina knew you couldn't be sure until you took vital signs.

Grady was too intent on his work to realise who she was. When he could see that help had arrived, he pointed to the door and she immediately rested her tanks on a boulder and started to pull on the handle, lodging her right foot against the body for leverage.

At first the door wouldn't budge, but after a few more pulls it gave way. Grady went in first and unfastened the young man's seat belt while Gina grabbed the extra tank. She put the mouthpiece into the man's mouth as Grady pulled him out. As soon as the opening was clear, Gina dived into the car and put her mouthpiece into the baby's mouth while she unstrapped the car seat.

Then, tucking the baby under her left arm, she carefully backed out the same way she'd come in and started swimming toward the surface with her precious bundle. It had taken longer than she'd expected to go through the manoeuvre. Her lungs were screaming for air by the time she surfaced.

An ambulance attendant stood ready to take the baby from her, and Captain Blaylock put out his hands for her to grasp as she climbed up the riverbank and collapsed on the dirt for a minute, drinking in fresh air. When she felt recovered, she put on the mask and mouthpiece and dived once more to recover the torch equipment and check for more victims. There could have been another child or even an adult on the floor of the back seat. The impact of a car accident could sometimes cause amazing situations.

Gina entered the interior of the car, but to her relief there were no more bodies or any sign of a pet. As she backed out, she felt a hand on her thigh. Grady had come back, presumably to get the equipment he'd brought down with him.

As she manoeuvred her way around, their eyes met. He motioned at the dashboard of the car and pointed to the keys. Since they were nearest her, she pulled them out of the ignition. Grady took them from her and swam to the rear of the car. Gina followed and helped him to raise the lid once he'd inserted the key in the lock. All they found were a couple of suitcases and a camera, to her relief.

Grady pulled everything out of the trunk while Gina reached for the torch equipment, and then together they kicked towards the surface. Gina felt a rapport so strong and binding with Grady that she didn't want to leave the water. This was the first time they'd actually worked side by side as a team. It was an exhilarating experience, something she'd been waiting for since she began her training.

"Nice work," the battalion commander saluted as Gina was helped from the water, Grady not far behind.

"Did anyone survive?" Gina asked as she whipped off her mask and removed her scuba gear.

"All three are breathing on their own, Ms Lindsay. I understand you were called in for this rescue on your day off. I'm recommending you for a medal. Your second with the Salt Lake Fire Department. We're happy to have you with us.''

"Thank you," Gina beamed, shaking his hand.

"Grady..." he extended his hand "...you and Bob Corby did excellent work, too. Congratulations. The three of you did the cleanest, fastest work I've ever seen in a situation like this. I'm recommending medals for you."

Gina looked over her shoulder to see Grady's reaction. To her shock, he only nodded at the battalion chief and spared her a brief, impersonal glance before walking away towards the truck.

The blood drained from her face at his abrupt departure. Here she'd been feeling this incredible harmony and oneness with him, had hardly been able to restrain herself from throwing her arms around him and shouting for joy because they'd saved lives together. And all Grady felt like doing was walking away.

A pain too deep for tears weighed her down as she walked over to the rescue unit and changed back into her overalls. Clean-up procedures were starting, and a tow truck had arrived by the time the engine pulled away from the scene and headed back to the station.

"That was beautiful, Gina," Captain Blaylock said, patting her hand. The others joined in with complimentary remarks. "I'm proud of you. That young father and his baby were on their way home from the airport for a reunion with his wife. Now it can be a happy one. This is what it's all about, eh, Gina?''

She couldn't speak, so she patted his arm instead. Right now she was fighting tears for herself, for Grady, for the plunge from happiness to despair. If Grady couldn't respond after a moment like this, she felt as if she'd come to the end of a very long journey.

It was dusk before Gina left station six, but instead of going home, she turned towards the mountains. She needed to get away and really think. This was her long weekend off and it didn't matter how long she was gone or if she even told anybody where she went.

When she reached Heber City, she pulled into the Wagon Wheel Café for dinner. No one served better veal cutlets than the Wagon Wheel. The rescue had depleted her energies, and she ate everything she was served, including a piece of homemade rhubarb pie.

Full at last, Gina checked in at her favourite motel down the street, then took a walk through the centre of town, savouring the crisp mountain air.

She'd come to a crossroads in her life. She could not go on working in Salt Lake. This had been Grady's territory first. She was the intruder, and Grady couldn't have made it more apparent. Even if he cared, which she seriously doubted now, he was deeply disturbed by something that he couldn't share with her, couldn't talk about. That left Gina no choice but to walk out of his life for good.

At a little past ten Gina went back to the motel to go to bed. Only a few miles away sat the little ginger-bread house. For all she knew, Grady was there now. All she had to do was get into her car and drive there to find out. But it would profit her nothing and might result in an even more devastating conflict.

She tossed and turned most of the night, then sat at the table of her room and wrote out her resignation on the motel stationery. She had an obligation to give the department two weeks' notice. At nine, she left for Salt Lake.

After going to headquarters to leave her resignation for Captain Blaylock, she stopped by Sue's place but her friend wasn't home. Despondent, Gina went back to her apartment and put in a call to the movers to make arrangements for her return to California in two weeks. She requested some boxes, which were dropped off the next day so she could begin the arduous task of packing. Sue called her that night and they went out to dinner. Gina's friend was disappointed when she heard the news, but thought it the wisest course of action. At least that way, Gina could get on with her life. Gina promised to come back at Thanksgiving for Sue and Jay's wedding.

"I received your resignation, Gina," the captain said as soon as Gina reported for duty on the following Tuesday. "I'm sorry things didn't work out for you and Grady."

"Me, too." She heaved a sigh. "But he refuses to talk about what's really wrong. I've tried everything."

"Not everything, Gina. You could do what he wants and quit fire fighting if he means that much to you."

"I know. But without knowing *why* he wants me to quit working altogether, I'm as much in the dark as ever. Captain, you're right about Grady. There's more bothering him than just my job. I think it has to do with family problems, something that happened in his past, but he's never been able to open up to me about it. Without total honesty, we can't have a future together."

"You're right. So it appears I'm going to lose one of the best fire fighters I've ever had at station six. But until that time comes, there's work to be done. Because it's such nice weather this morning, several of the stations have decided to go do practice drills out by the airport. Let's check out the rig and go on over."

Practice drills were killers, especially when you were wearing full turn-out gear. Gina immediately spotted Mavis plugging a hydrant.

"Let's show these guys how it's done," Mavis whispered as Gina unrolled hose alongside her.

"Why not?" Gina chuckled. Mavis was like a breath of fresh air right now. A little friendly competition with the men would help keep her mind off Grady. But in that regard she was mistaken. The next time she looked up, there was Grady talking to some of the drill instructors. Apparently his crew had decided to join in.

"Hey, Gina!" The guys from station one all waved and shouted to her. She watched them take their place in the lines and had to admit Grady's bunch was an impressive group. She waved back and kept on working with Mavis. A little later the drill instructor announced that everyone would have to climb a ladder to the third-storey window of the vacant building and bring down a live victim in a fireman's lift. *"A live victim?"* Gina muttered to Mavis in shock.

Mavis had the light of battle in her hazel eyes. "I guess they're trying to show us up, Gina, girl. They'll be sorry!"

These were timed drills and every move and procedure was noted and marked. Mavis winked at Gina and off they went. Gina positioned her hands and feet as she'd learned in countless practice sessions, then started up the ladder. On the other drills, she'd beaten almost everyone's time; she wanted to come out first in this one, too. Maybe it was because Grady was here that she felt this sudden excess energy. Whatever the reason, she scurried up the steps as if her feet had wings. Her victim would be lying on the floor inside the window and she'd have to hoist him over her shoulder and then bring him down the ladder.

In a real fire, Gina would have to determine the weight of the victim before deciding which approach to take, but in practice drills, a dummy was usually provided. Evidently not this time!

She spotted her victim lying face down on the floor as she swung her leg inside the building. First she had to take off his turn-out coat and heavy boots to lighten the load.

"Grady!" she cried out in shock as she turned him over. "What's going on?"

"I'm supposed to be unconscious," he replied in a no-nonsense voice. But his eyes were smiling, something she hadn't seen for so long she almost forgot what she was doing. "You're losing precious seconds. Undress me," he whispered in a voice she hadn't heard since that night at the condo. With shaking hands she knelt down and began to unfasten his turn-out coat.

"This isn't fair, Grady. I was supposed to be provided with a victim I could manage," she said quietly, easing his arm out of one sleeve with difficulty because she was getting no co-operation from Grady.

"Don't tell me that now, Gina. A fire fighter needs to have confidence that his buddy can get him out of trouble in any situation."

"If this were a real fire, I'd try to get you out even if I died in the process, but a practice drill is something else again."

His eyes narrowed provocatively. "Everyone's going to be watching you, Gina. If you can't bring me down now, I think you can imagine what the guys are going to say."

Her face went beet-red. "If I crumple from the weight, we'll both end up in the hospital."

His sudden smile mocked her. "I thought you were the woman willing to take any risks. If I'm game, what's the problem?"

"There's no problem," she whispered, but inside her anxiety had reached its peak. "You'll have to co-operate, Grady, or else this will be terribly dangerous."

"Of course. What do you want me to do?" He appeared to be enjoying himself as she pulled off the other sleeve and turned towards his feet to undo the

boots. "I'd like those to stay on, if you don't mind."
He moved his feet away.

"But they weigh too much. Besides, you're supposed to be unconscious—so you can't talk back."

"You'll have to do it my way, Gina, or we won't do
it at all," he said in a tone that brooked no argument.

She bowed her head as a shudder racked her body.
"I'm afraid you'll get hurt, Grady."

"Is that all that's holding you back? Come on,
Gina. Where's your sense of adventure?"

His goading drove her to action and she rolled him
on his side. Next, she crouched in front of him and
placed his arms over her left shoulder, then raised
herself on to her left knee with her right foot flat on
the floor. She counted to three and started to stand up,
clutching him around the thighs, but suddenly she was
pushed to the floor, flat on her back. Grady's body
covered hers from head to foot. Even through the
thick padding of her turn-out coat, she could feel the
pounding of their hearts.

"You did that on purpose," she cried out, furious
with him and far too aware of their closeness.

"That's right." She felt his warm breath against her
mouth and she forgot where they were or what they
were supposed to be doing. "Never underestimate
your victim. He might become uncontrollable, like
this." In a lightning move, Grady's mouth descended
on hers, and she almost lost consciousness under its
driving force. He didn't allow her a breath. He pinned
her hands to the floor on either side of her head, and
she twisted and turned to elude him.

"Someone will see us!" she cried frantically.

His low chuckle sent chills through her quivering body. "No, they won't. I arranged it so you'd be last up the ladder." Again, his lips covered hers with smothering force and he slowly and expertly began drawing a response from her.

Gina couldn't believe this was happening, that Grady was actually making love to her on the floor of an abandoned building at the fire department's practice site. "Grady," she begged when he gave her a moment's respite, "why are you doing this now?"

His answer was to kiss her again, over and over till she wasn't aware of her surroundings.

"You know what, Gina? You ask too many questions, but this is one I'll answer." He finally lifted his head and stared down at her intently. "I'm going away on a leave of absence, and I'm not at all certain that I'm coming back to Utah. I wanted to see you before I left and this seemed as good a time as any."

"What?" she raised her head from the floor, but he held her down with the pressure of his hands on her shoulders. "Grady—where are you going? Why?" Her eyes searched his for answers but they remained a blank gray.

"You're a fine fire fighter, Gina. After our dive in the river the other day, I realised just how fine. You'll go a long way in the department, because you've made a reputation for yourself already. You can have a secure future here." His hand caressed her chin. "I'm proud of you, Gina, and I happen to know that if I'd co-operated, you would have lifted me down that ladder today. I have no doubts.''

Gina's body was racked with fresh pain. ''There's no need for you to leave, Grady. I handed in my resignation the other day. I'm moving back to California on the tenth. I should never have come here in the first place. It's disrupted your whole life.'' Hot tears trickled out of the corners of her eyes. ''Please don't go away on my account.''

''I'm not,'' he murmured, sounding very faraway. ''I'm going for me. Whether you stay here or move to California is immaterial at this point.''

She sensed the finality of his words, and there was nothing more to say. Gina got to her feet and reached for her helmet while Grady shrugged into his turn-out coat. He faced her with a look of incredible tenderness shining out of his eyes. ''For old times' sake, I'm going to carry you over the threshold. It won't be exactly the same as in Beirut, but if we don't get back down that ladder, someone's going to come looking for us.''

He gave her an almost wistful smile, then softly kissed her lips before hoisting her over his shoulder like so much fluff. With his usual economy of movement, he stepped over the ledge to the cheers of everyone below. His arms held her securely around the thighs and her head bobbed as he descended the ladder. He wasn't even out of breath when they reached the ground.

Gina had to put on the performance of her life, smiling as everyone started in with the comments and the ribbing about who was rescuing whom. Grady still held her in his arms.

"I'm afraid I played a little joke on Ms Lindsay," he explained to anyone listening, "but she took it like a man." The guys laughed and joked with Grady, who stood grinning among his crew.

As he lowered her to the ground their eyes met for a brief moment. His said goodbye. She turned away abruptly, needing to escape before she fell apart.

"Gina? Wait up," Mavis called out. "What happened up there?" She hurried to catch up with Gina, who was walking quickly towards the engine.

"I'll call you later and tell you all about it," Gina shouted over her shoulder. Mavis didn't pursue the issue. She eyed Gina thoughtfully for a moment before walking over to her engine.

"Can we go back to the station, Captain?" Gina asked quietly.

Blaylock gave her a shrewd look and nodded. "Sure. We're just waiting for Marty. Are you okay, Gina?"

She couldn't answer him.

CHAPTER TEN

UNBEKNOWN TO GINA, Captain Blaylock had planned a surprise dinner in honour of her last night with the station. Someone had gone out to Bountiful to bring her favourite Chinese food from the Mandarin, while the others had decorated the lounge with crepe paper streamers. A huge chocolate cake with chocolate icing stood in the center of the table. An enormous package was propped on the floor.

Captain Carrera and some of the crew from station three, as well as Frank and Bob from one, joined in the festivities. Gina could hardly believe her eyes when she returned from a run to find everyone assembled and all the goodies waiting on the table.

It was growing dark outside by the time they'd eaten. Gina finally unwrapped her gift, anxious to see what on earth was inside something so huge. A beautiful black and white stuffed Dalmatian dog appeared as she pulled the paper away. The fireman's mascot. And that wasn't all. An exquisite gold locket hung around its neck on a gold chain. Engraved on the back were the words *You're the best. Stations one, three and six.*

Gina promptly made a fool of herself and wept, but her tears turned to laughter as those present "roasted" her, leaving out nothing embarrassing, including Grady's lift down the ladder.

At the mention of Grady, she sobered. Neither Bob nor Frank had any idea where their captain had gone. They didn't seem the least bit happy about it. Bob was acting captain in Grady's place. Now that Whittaker was back, he'd taken over engine, and they'd swung in a new guy to cover ladder while Grady was gone.

Grady had told them the same thing he'd told Gina—that he didn't know if he was coming back.

Everyone in the group speculated on the reasons for Grady's sudden departure. Everyone except Captain Blaylock and Gina. She couldn't help but wonder if he'd gone overseas to see about working as a foreign correspondent again. It was the only thing that made sense. Captain Blaylock kept his ideas to himself, but he gazed at her with compassion several times throughout the dinner.

The gong sounded, effectively ending the festivities. "Ladder one, respond to assist at fire in progress at Hotel Olympus."

"Hotel Olympus!" everyone muttered at once. There'd been talk of reprisals since the building was closed down permanently, shortly after the fire fighters' ball. Some of them had jokingly commented that they wouldn't be surprised if an arsonist set it ablaze to get even. Many businesses in downtown Salt Lake were worried that the closure of the hotel would adversely affect their incomes. Maybe the joking wasn't so farfetched after all.

Frank and Bob got up from the table and each gave Gina a hug, telling her she'd better come back to Salt

Lake to visit soon. Then they hurried out of the station.

In another few seconds the gong sounded again. More stations were called in to assist, including engine six.

"That's us. Let's go." Leaving everything exactly as it was, Gina hurried out to the bay with the others, jumped into her boots and put on her turn-out coat and helmet.

Gina found it incredible that the hotel was billowing black smoke as they pulled up to the fire ground a few minutes later. Every available unit in the city and county had been called in. Not long ago, she'd danced in Grady's arms in this exquisite foyer. Now everything—not just her dreams—was going up in smoke.

"We've got a fire that's fully involved," she heard the battalion chief saying to the captain over the walkie-talkie. The place swarmed with fire fighters.

The captain began giving orders. "Marty, you're nozzle-handler and Gina is lead-off man."

They jumped down from the rig and started pulling the hose forward through the main entrance to the hotel. From what Gina could gather over the radio, an arsonist had started the fire on the mezzanine floor, where the most beautiful and famous rooms of the hotel were located. If it had been on the upper floors the fire wouldn't have been so devastating.

She felt thankful there were no people in the hotel, but it was a showplace and one of the main tourist attractions of the city. There wasn't another hotel like it west of the Mississippi. Gina could have wept to see the intricate cornices and mouldings melting in the blaze.

More than a dozen hoses were going at once. When Marty was in place, Gina ran back outside to tell Joe to start the pump.

It was when she re-entered the building and started across the marble floor towards Marty that she heard a bloodcurdling scream. *"Gina! Run for cover! Run, Gina!"*

It was Grady! She was so stunned to hear his voice above the chaos of sirens and hoses, she thought she must be dreaming. But some instinct propelled her to obey his anguished cry. She began to run back towards the entrance when she heard the tremendous crash behind her. Instantly waves of shattered crystal sprayed out in all directions. The air was filled with shards of the once magnificent chandelier.

Gina lost her footing and was swept forward through the entry as if she were riding the surf. Without her mask and gloves, she'd have been cut to pieces.

A couple of ambulance crews ran past her to search for victims beneath the twisted, glittering wreckage. "Marty!" she screamed, picking herself up, intent on going in to find him. Captain Blaylock held her fast.

"Easy, Gina. Come on out to the rig. We'll know in a minute how he is."

"Grady's here," she said, sobbing, "and he shouted to me."

"I know." The captain nodded, ushering Gina onto the engine. "He's up on the mezzanine with the ladder. He must have seen the chandelier going."

"H-he saved my life."

"That he did. Now you sit here, Gina, and that's an order. I'm going inside for a minute."

"I'm coming with you. I've got to know about Marty."

She didn't have long to wait. Just as the captain reluctantly agreed to let Gina go in with him, Marty was carted out on a stretcher.

Gina ran over to him and cried even more when Marty gave her a weak smile. "I'm all right, Gina. Just some glass in my leg. Whoever called out to you saved my life, too. I just started running like hell."

"Thank God!" She bent over and kissed his forehead before the ambulance crew took over. As they carried him out to the ambulance, Marty held out a gloved hand.

"Will you call Carol? Let her down easy," Marty pleaded with Gina. "She's terrified something bad will happen to me. You know how to talk to her."

"I'll call her right now." She turned to the driver. "What hospital are you taking him to?"

"L.D.S."

"Captain Blaylock? Could you ask for a police officer to take me back to the station so I can call Marty's wife?"

"That won't be necessary." Gina heard a familiar male voice directly behind her. "I'll drive you."

Gina spun around and stared up at Grady. His blackened face was the most beautiful sight she'd ever seen. "Captain Simpson? Whether I have your permission or not, I'm going to kiss you for saving both of our lives." Gina flung her arms around his neck and pressed her mouth to his, standing on tiptoe to do it.

Miraculously Grady's arms came around her and he lifted her off the ground.

So many emotions were bursting inside Gina, she didn't stop to think who might be watching. This was Grady, warm and vital and alive in her arms, kissing her back, tasting of smoke and soot. Tasting divine...

"You came back!" she murmured against his mouth.

"That's right," he whispered. "I flew in from the East Coast a few hours ago. I came to look for you. When I heard about the fire, I drove on over here, knowing I'd find you."

Her body shook with delayed reaction. "If you hadn't come—"

"Don't think about it." He crushed her in his arms, kissing the very life out of her.

Captain Blaylock began clearing his throat. "I think maybe you two better carry on some place else, or you'll find yourselves on the front page of the morning newspaper."

Slowly Grady broke their kiss and let her down gently. "Come on, Gina. Let's get out of here. We need to call Carol and then I want to talk to you."

"Do I have your permiss—"

"You have it," Captain Blaylock broke in with a huge smile.

Grady held Gina's elbow as he ushered her through the maze of hoses and equipment to his car, which was parked next to the ladder. He opened the trunk. "Let's get rid of these." He took off his turn-out coat while she took off hers, and they tossed them inside. He helped her into the car, then went around to the driver's side.

Instead of going west, Grady turned north to Second Avenue. "This isn't the way to the station," she said, puzzled.

"I'm taking you home, Gina."

She watched him, studying his unique profile, the way he handled the car as they drove through the avenues to the condo. Her heart was hammering so loudly she was positive he could hear every beat.

By tacit agreement they went upstairs to the lounge and immediately phoned Marty's wife. Grady was all charm and diplomacy on the phone, before he passed it to Gina. Then it was her turn to reassure Carol, who broke down sobbing and said she'd leave for the hospital immediately. Gina told her that she and Grady would come by later.

"Next order of business," Grady stated as Gina replaced the receiver. "Come with me." He took her hand and led her up the stairs to the master bath. "I'm going to take a bath downstairs while you shower up here. Don't be too long."

His manner was mysterious but Gina didn't mind. She didn't want to say or do anything to alter Grady's mood. Maybe this time they could really talk.

"I'll hurry. I promise."

He seemed reluctant to leave her, but finally strode out of the bathroom.

Taking a deep breath, Gina undressed and got into the shower, reveling in the hot water. She washed her hair with Grady's shampoo, loving the smell because it reminded her of him. When she stepped out of the stall a few minutes later, she reached for his striped, toweling robe that hung on the hook behind the door. A sense of *déjà vu* assailed her.

She wrapped her hair in a towel and left the bathroom. Grady stood in the living room in a clean pair of shorts and T-shirt pouring them each a drink.

"Have a little wine," he suggested, passing her a glass. With only one lamp on, his handsome face was shadowed, yet she caught the slightest tinge of a flush on his cheeks. If she hadn't known better, she'd have said he was nervous, and never in their entire married life had she seen him nervous.

His black curls were still damp from the shower and fell in tendrils over his forehead and around his neck. To Gina, he was the most beautiful man she'd ever known, and never more so than right now, with his gray eyes playing over her face as if he couldn't get enough of her. He tugged on the towel to bring her white-gold hair cascading to her shoulders. Putting down his wineglass, he took the towel in his hands and began drying the strands as if he'd been given a precious task.

Gina felt his touch and it sent shivers of ecstasy through her body. "Grady—" She spoke before it became impossible to do so. "I have a thousand questions to ask, but before I do, I have something to tell you." His hands stopped caressing her hair, but he didn't remove them.

"Until tonight, I felt that if you couldn't tell me the real reason why you didn't want me to work—whether at fire fighting or anything else—then I couldn't accept that and couldn't imagine our marriage succeeding. But now—'' her voice broke ''—I don't care any more. If you want me to stay home and wait for you every day, hold you in my arms every night, smell like flowers for you—if that will make you happy, then that's what I want, too. I love you, Grady. Let me be your wife again, and I promise I'll make you the happiest man alive. But please give me another chance to be the kind of mate I should have been in the first place. You're all that's important to me.''

His hands slid around her from behind and he kissed the tender nape of her neck. ''Gina...'' The emotion in that one word caused her to tremble. ''I don't deserve you or the sacrifices you've made for me. Come here, sweetheart.''

He drew her to the couch, then gently urged her to sit. He remained standing. ''I want to tell you everything. It's something I should have done before we were married, but even I didn't know how deeply I'd been affected until it was too late for us.'' His voice sounded haunted.

''My mother and father were both news reporters working for the same paper. You know that. But what you don't know is that my mother got involved with another reporter on the staff and they had an affair.'' Gina held herself rigid as the revelations unfolded. ''I was caught between my parents. Apparently it was an ugly and bitter divorce. Mother went back East with the man and married him. My father retained custody of me and raised me. I was nine when she left. It was an impressionable, sensitive age, and all I heard from the time she left was that you couldn't trust a woman, let alone a working woman, especially a career woman.''

"Until the day my father died, he warned me to find myself a docile little woman, a homebody, and settle down. Let her know who's boss, he told me. Keep her home, keep her pregnant." Grady sighed. "I know it must all sound outrageous to you, but that was the kind of man my father was. He thought my mother would quit her job on the paper when they got married. He was making plenty of money and couldn't understand why she felt the need to work. They argued incessantly.

"After the divorce, my mother came to Salt Lake quite often to visit me, but as I got older, I felt estranged from her and I'm afraid I viewed her through my father's eyes. I'm the reason we stopped having any communication."

Gina felt sick. She'd had no idea.

"Then I met you," he said thickly. "You were the embodiment of all that is sweet and gentle and beautiful. I wanted to be your hero. I wanted to be the kind of husband that my father had envisaged."

"Oh, Grady—" Gina hid her face in her hands.

There was a long pause.

"Gina . . . I didn't know how much of my father's bias had rubbed off on me until you insisted on staying on with the department. But it was more than the fear of you getting hurt. I've realised that somewhere deep in my psyche I was afraid you'd fall in love with one of the guys and run off and leave me. That I'd turn out like my father, bitter and alone."

Gina couldn't stand any more. She jumped up from the couch and threw her arms around him. "Are you still afraid, Grady?" she whispered against his cheek.

"Maybe. That's why I went to see my mother."

Gina closed her eyes tightly. So that was where he'd gone.

"She painted a rather different picture from the one my father had drawn, but what came out of her talk was that my father was too authoritarian for her to live with any longer. She felt caught in a trap. They had no happiness, Gina. That's why she left, and her feelings of guilt over the adultery were so terrible, she didn't fight my father for custody."

Gina drew him closer. "So you found out she really did love you very much."

"Yes." He nodded into her neck. "I'm afraid my father did a lot of damage to her, as well as to me. Now I can see reasons for the way things happened in our lives. That's why I came back."

He lifted his head and grasped Gina by the shoulders. "I know there are no guarantees in this life, but I want you for my wife, Gina. Not the way my father envisaged. I want you to be happy, too. You need your freedom. Talking to Mother made me realise that. You can't put your wife in a box the way my father wanted. It doesn't work like that—but what did he know? It wasn't all his fault. He was raised by Victorian standards and didn't have a clue about a woman's needs. Gina—I'm trying to understand—"

"Are you asking me to marry you, Grady Simpson?" Her violet eyes shimmered as they gazed up at him.

"You know I am, Regina Lindsay. But only on conditions we can both accept. Fair enough?"

"Grady..." she whispered achingly, loving him too much.

"I happen to know Captain Blaylock is retiring in a few weeks. Could you live with me being captain of station six and you as one of the crew?"

"Grady!" she shrieked with joy.

"I've done nothing but think for the past week. Barring unforeseen dangers, we should be able to live a long, healthy life at six. And when the children come, you can decide the number of hours you want. Do you think you could be happy?"

The earnestness of his pleading was Gina's undoing. "I've already told you that just being your wife is all that matters."

He shook his head. "No—that isn't all that matters. I adore you for being willing to sacrifice, but I don't want our life to be like that. I want us to both be fulfilled. If I move to six, I'll have more time to write free-lance. I still have that urge in my blood."

She gave him her most beguiling smile. "Who knows? Maybe you'll write a bestselling novel about a married couple's life with the fire department. We can retire in luxury."

His smile faded to be replaced by a look of such tenderness, it almost overwhelmed her. "Gina... my mother wants to meet you."

"I want to meet her. I'm thrilled with the idea that you have family. I wanted to get to know her ages ago, but you never offered and I hated to pry."

"Gina, I swear. No more secrets. From here on, we talk over everything, no matter how painful. Agreed?"

"Agreed, my darling." She nestled against him.

His hands played with her hair. "Do you have any idea how utterly desirable you are, standing there in my robe with your hair smelling like sunshine?"

She cocked her head to the side and ran her hands over his broad chest. "I think I'd have a better idea if you showed me."

The devastating smile that always took her breath flashed for her now. "Oh, I'm going to show you all right, but we're not married yet."

"Well, you're the captain." She kissed the end of his nose and moved out of his arms. "Whatever you say goes." She started to laugh at the horrified expression on his face and ran for the stairs.

"You'll pay for that, my lovely," he warned, chasing her up the steps, but he was too late. She'd shut the door and locked it.

"Gina?" He pounded on the door. "Let me in."

"No. I always obey my captain's orders."

"I'm not your captain, I'm your husband," he shouted.

"Not yet, you aren't. Right now you're my fiancé."

"Gina—"

"I want a *white* wedding."

"Don't do this to me," he begged in a hoarse voice.

"And I want you in full dress uniform."

"We'll talk about it when you open the door."

"Absolutely no one looks better than you do in uniform, Grady."

"Well, I'm happy you feel that way, sweetheart. Now open the door."

"What will you do if I open it?"

"That, my love, is for me to know and you to find out."

"I'm frightened, Grady."

There was silence. "Of what? Me?"

"I haven't been married for a long time. What if I'm a big disappointment to you?"

"In what way?"

"What if you decide you like that brunette better than you like me?"

"I thought you'd overcome your jealous tendencies?"

"Well, I haven't."

"What if I told you I've been faithful to you since our divorce?"

The lock clicked and the door opened a crack. Grady helped a little with the palm of his hand. Gina's gaze locked with his. "Is that the truth?"

"Do you even have to ask, Gina? My fate was sealed the first moment I saw you. Come to me, sweetheart. We have so much to make up for."

Gina ran into his arms and gloried in her right to be there. "Someone once told me that if I wanted you back, I'd have to fight fire with fire."

Grady's eyes smouldered. "I'd like to meet that someone and say thank-you, because from now on we're going to be fully involved. Some fires are like that, sweetheart. They're meant to burn forever."

MILLS & BOON

By Request

Bestselling romances brought back to you by popular demand

Two complete novels in one volume
by bestselling author

Roberta Leigh

Two-Timing Man

◆

Bachelor at Heart

Available: March 1996   Price: £4.50

Happy Mother's Day

Don't miss this year's exciting Mother's Day Gift Pack—4 new
heartwarming romances featuring three babies and a wedding!

The Right Kind of Girl	Betty Neels
The Baby Caper	Emma Goldrick
Part-Time Father	Sharon Kendrick
The Male Animal	Suzanne Carey

This special Gift Pack of four romances is priced at just £5.99

(normal retail price £7.96)

 Available: February 1996   *Price:* £5.99

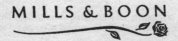

MILLS & BOON

MILLS & BOON

PENNINGTON

Everyone's favourite town—delightful people, prosperity and picturesque charm.

We know you'll love reading about this charming English town in Catherine George's latest Pennington novel:

Earthbound Angel

After her husband's death Imogen was lonely in her cottage in the country. When Gabriel came to do her gardening he seemed to provide the answer. But could she risk an affair? After all, Gabriel was her employee and, surely younger than herself...

Available: March 1996

MILLS & BOON

Today's Woman

Mills & Boon brings you a new series of seven
fantastic romances by some of your favourite
authors. One for every day of the week in fact
and each featuring a truly wonderful woman
who's story fits the lines of the old rhyme
'Monday's child is...'

Look out for Patricia Wilson's *Coming Home*
in March '96.

Wednesday's child Sophie seems to have the
cares of the world on her shoulders but will
handsome widower Matthew Trevelyan and his
young son Phillip help her find a happy ever
after?

Temptation

THREE GROOMS:
Case, Carter and Mike

TWO WORDS:
"We Don't!"

*ONE
MINI-SERIES:*

GROOMS ON THE RUN

Starting in March 1996, Mills & Boon Temptation brings you this exciting new mini-series.

Each book (and there'll be one a month for three months) features a sexy hero who's ready to say "I do!" but ends up saying, "I don't!"

Look out for these special Temptations:

In March, I WON'T! by Gina Wilkins
In April, JILT TRIP by Heather MacAllister
In May, NOT THIS GUY! by Glenda Sanders

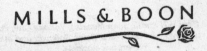

MILLS & BOON